Divine Retribution

Catalyst Trilogy Book Two

TIMOTHY DIAMOND

Divine Retribution
Author: Timothy Diamond

National Library of Australia Cataloguing-in-Publication entry

Creator: Diamond, Timothy author.

Title: Divine Retribution / Timothy Diamond.

ISBN: 9780994263124 (paperback)

Series: Diamond, Timothy. Catalyst Trilogy ; bk. 2.

Subjects: Vietnam War, 1961-1975--Fiction.
              Special forces (Military science)--Fiction.
              Espionage--Fiction..

Dewey Number: A823.4
Published with the assistance of www.loveofbooks.com.au

"Catalyst"
By Timothy Diamond

"Catalyst":

/'katalist/n – 1. A chemical agent that causes catalysis

2. A substance (e g an enzyme) that changes especially increases, the rate of a chemical reaction, but itself remains chemically unchanged.

3. Somebody or something whose action inspires further and usually more important events.

As defined by: The Longman Pocket English Dictionary

First published 1986

Third Impression 1987

ABOUT THE AUTHOR

"Timothy Diamond" is a pseudonym for my real name.

I grew up in the provincial town of Rockhampton in Central Queensland, and the exploits of my hero, "Tom Davis," are loosely based on actual events in my own life. (Hence the pseudonym)

My story is original and exciting; it contains elements of young love, teenage rebellion, family conflict, corruption, war time experiences, and espionage, a book that could rival the works of Clive Cussler and Ken Follett.

The Catalyst Trilogy is my first full length work of fiction. However, between 1988 and 1994, I wrote multiple articles and reports on recreational diving that were published in *Scuba Diver Magazine* and the *Gold Coast Bulletin*. I also wrote the feature article 'The Round Trip' for *Yachting Australia* magazine in 2009.

The first book in the "Catalyst" trilogy, "Playing with Fire" was written and published in 2014, and is selling well. After taking a break, I started writing this second book of the trilogy, "Divine Retribution", and completed it in April 2015. After it was completed, I started work on the final book of the trilogy, "Last Man Standing" which I completed in October.

ACKNOWLEDGEMENTS

To Diane, without your insistence, patience, putting up with my all night sessions, first draft editing, and cover design, and even waiting for household chores to be done, this book could not have been written. Thank you, I love you.

Ralf B: for 30 odd years, you gained snippets that hinted at some of the things I had been involved in, you suggested that I write a book, well now it's all out there; I hope you enjoy the full story in the right sequence. To change Spock's dialogue a little, "you have been, and always will be, my 'best' friend".

Diana Mason: for keeping an eye on my health, and helping me function.

Julie McGregor, my Publisher: for her patience, and all the help.

GLOSSARY OF
TERMS & ABBREVIATIONS

Military or 24 hour time is used in this book, expressed in hundreds. 3pm+12hrs would be 1500 hundred. Each time zone is given a designation in the phonetic alphabet GMT is expressed as Zulu time.

Distance is measured in both old imperial measure, and also metric. Even though we changed to the metric system in 1964, some people and places still use the imperial system.

2IC – Second in Command

64 set - Long distance radio (500 mts)

ADF – Australian Defence Forces

AO - area of operations

ASAP – As Soon As Possible

ASAP -As Soon As Possible

ASIS – Australian Secret Intelligence Service (the more militarized spy agency, much more competent that its civillian counterpart)

ASIO – Australian Secret Intelligence Organization (considered a joke in some circles, particularly the military)

CIA – Central Intelligence Agency

Click – Kilometre

CnC – Commander in Chief

CO – Commanding Officer

Comm's – commuinication

DEA – Drug Enforcement Agency

Deploy – move into action

Drop Short or Seven Mile Sniper – derogatory name for Artillery personnel

ETA – Estimated Time of Arrival

Forces IDF – Israeli Defence Force

G2 – Vehicle Log Book

GCHQ – General Command HQ

Gong – Medal

Goy – Non Jewish person

HQ – Headquarters

Intel - Intelligence

K's – Kilometres

L.T – Lieutenant

LUP – layup area for sleep and food

Mag – rifle magazine

Mossad – Clandestine Special (IDF)

NTR – nothing to report

NVA – North Vietnamese Army

OC – Officer Commanding

OP – Observation Post

OR – other ranks (below Sergeant)

O/S – overseas

RDR – Radio Detection Finder

Recon – reconnaissance

RSM – Regimental Sergeant Major usually ranked as a Warrant Officer

Sarg – Sergeant

SGT – short for Sergeant

Shalom – Jewish greeting and farewell meaning Peace

Sigs – short for Signal Corp

S.O.P's – Standard Operating Procedure

SRT – Special Response Team

SSM – Staff Sergeant Major (stores)

Store - supply store

TAG – Tactical Assault Group

TWAG – Tactical Water Assault Group SR10 – short range radio (500mts)

W.O.1 – Warrant Officer 1st class

W.O.2 – Warrant Officer 2nd Class

VC – Viet Cong Guerrilla Fighter

SOUTH VIETNAM
ADMINISTRATIVE DIVISIONS
AND MILITARY REGIONS
JUNE 1967

International boundary
Province boundary
Military corps boundary
National capital
Province capital
DA LAT   Autonomous municipality

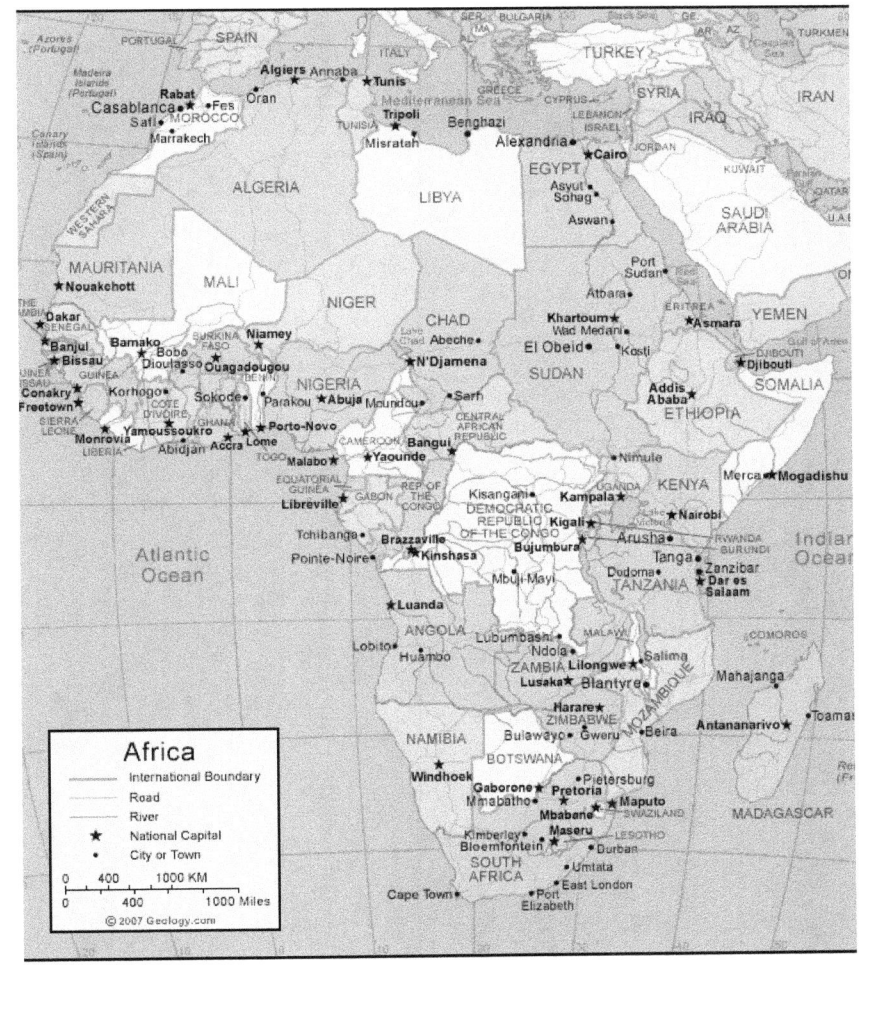

Africa

- International Boundary
- Road
- River
- ★ National Capital
- • City or Town

```
0      400    1000 KM
0      400    1000 Miles
```

© 2007 Geology.com

LEBANON

GOLAN HEIGHTS
(Occupied by Israel)

SYRIA

Har Meron
1208 m

Nahariyya   Zefat

The Baha'i gardens in Haifa

Haifa   The Sea of Galilee

Nazareth

Tantura

Caesarea   Bet She'an

Hadera

Netanya

Diamond Museum   WEST
BANK

Jordan River

> The Western Wall and
  the Temple Mount in Jerusalem
> The Church of the Holy Sepulcher

...tinian
...tories   Tel Aviv   Ramla

Ashdod

JERUSALEM

Ashqelon

> The Israel Museum
> The Tower of David

Asdod Sand
Dune Park   Dead Sea

GAZA STRIP   Masada

Beer Sheba   Arad   Masada National Park

Shivta National Park

Ey En Yahav

Negev   JORDAN

EGYPT

Eilot Area

Yotvata

Eilat

Gulf of Aqaba

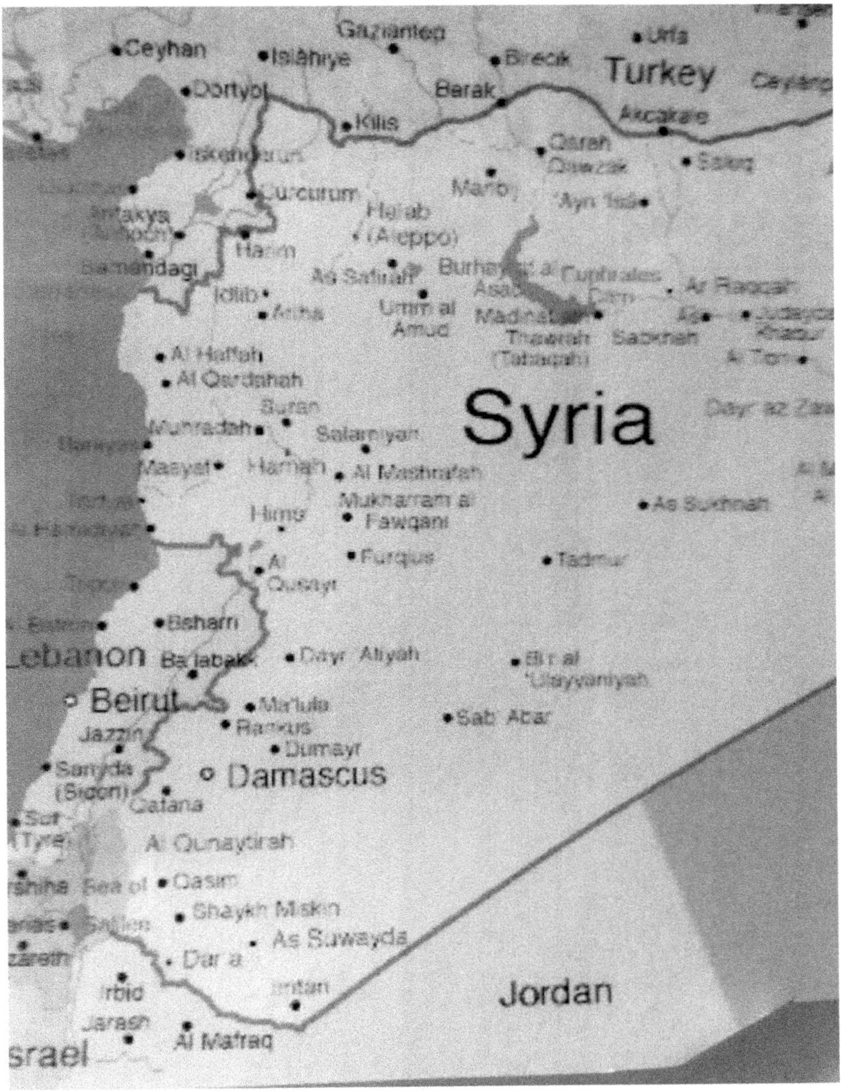
Ceyhan
Gaziantep
Urfa
Turkey
Barak
Kilis
Halab
(Aleppo)
Syria
Al Haffah
Salamiyah
Al Mashrafah
Furqlus
Tadmur
Basharri
Baalbak
Beirut
Damascus
Qatana
Al Qunaytirah
Shaykh Miskin
As Suwayda
Jordan
Al Mafraq
Irbid
srael

CHAPTER 1

Well, I found myself on the corner of Wickham and Brunswick street outside some department store called McWhirters. Three street kids, or bums, or whatever you call them, were lounging all over the bus seat. One of them asked me for some money, so I said, "Sorry guys, you're out of luck. I've only got enough to grab a cab to where I'm staying."

One of them answered, "That will do. We'll take that."

I said, smiling, "I don't think so."

One of the punks pulled out a penknife and opened it. "Give us your money now, and you won't get hurt."

Well I just laughed. This must have pissed them off because they all faced me threateningly. One said, "Take a look round, we're the only one's here. Now give us your cash before we really hurt you."

"Fuck off before YOU get hurt," I replied and tried to go around them.

One of them grabbed my arm as I walked by, so I swung and dropped him with a heart punch from my open left. As he dropped, I grabbed one of the others, smashed his head into the brick wall, and threw him through a plate glass window. The last one tried to run away, but I grabbed him by the neck, turned him, and threw him onto the bus seat. Now I'm not sure if you've ever seen an old-fashioned bus seat, but they're made with cement arms. His head hit the side; he was out cold, and as the first one I hit was getting up, I hit him with a right to the jaw, and down he went again. I legged it because the alarm from the broken window was going off big time, and I didn't need the cops grabbing me.

I ended up at a pub up the street called the Hacienda, and that is where I got my ass kicked.

Sharon was laughing as I told her. "You get your ass kicked? I'm sure that wouldn't happen unless you let it. So what happened, sweetie?"

We were driving towards Goondiwindi and talking as I drove. I had started to tell her about a night I had spent in the Valley because I was bored sitting in the motel room watching the TV. I'd taken a drive and parked to check out the so-called nightlife area while I'd been in Brisbane waiting for her to fly in.

"Well, as I said I ended up at this pub and went into the main bar. There were blokes everywhere, and I couldn't get near the bar. On the way in I had spotted a sign with lounge bar, pointing up some stairs, so I backtracked and decided to try it. Now if I hadn't been spoken for, I'd have thought that I'd hit the jackpot. The lounge bar was full of women, and no guys in sight."

"Oh honey, do you know what that pub is?"

"I do now, but just let me finish."

"Oh, this I've got to hear. Keep going."

I continued where I had left off. "Well, it was easy getting a drink, and I looked around the room for a table as I drank. There was one at the back, with an attractive blond sitting there by herself. I ordered another drink and asked her if she minded if I sat at the table. She said no, but as I put my drink down on the table, some bird grabbed me by the arm, swung me around, and said I shouldn't be trying to pick up her girlfriend. She hauls off and swings a punch at my head. Now because of the shock, or just because it's ingrained in my nature, I can't hit a female. Instead of blocking the punch, it landed on my jaw, and that girl hit hard. I fell against a big window that broke, and I ended up falling onto the footpath about eight or ten feet below. I picked myself up, and I was really going to have a piece of this bird. I stormed back up, walked over to her, but she started apologising, which took the wind out of my sails a bit. Management turned up and with some fast-talking we smoothed it all over. She bought me drink. We ended up chatting, and that's when I found out what type of pub it was. I'd never heard of gay bars, much less been in one. But I have now!"

Sharon was in hysterics, rolling around in the seat laughing. She was laughing so much that tears were streaming out of her eyes, and as she regained some composure, I said, "Well I didn't know!" This comment started a completely new fit of laughter.

After a while, I could see the funny side of it, had a little laugh, and smiled as I thought about it. It was somewhat funny. I got Sharon going again, when I said, "I was bloody sore the next morning, though!

I think that's one pub I'll stay out of, if we're ever there again." She started laughing again, which caused me to laugh at myself. I told her, "Stop laughing, it's not funny," while laughing.

We stopped the first night in Gilgandra, and the next morning cut across to the Mitchell highway and headed for Nyngan and onto the Barrier highway that would take us into Broken Hill, where we planned to stop the night. After deciding not to bother with Adelaide because we'd both been there, we cut across to Port Augusta and overnighted there, before following the coast road down and around the Eyre Peninsula and up to Ceduna, which was the start of the Nullarbor Plain.

Before we left Ceduna in the morning, I made sure both tanks were full because we didn't want to refuel before Eucla. I planned to push the car for all it was worth to see how fast it would go. I got the car up to the two twenty mark, and that was as far as the speedo went. It still had more to give, though I decided that was enough.

After stopping at the cliff's outlook, I let Sharon have some fun. We made it to Eucla in two hours fifteen, which was half the time it would normally take. The first tank wasn't near empty, which was surprising. I would have expected it to chew through fuel at that speed. Two days later, we were home, with five days to spare before I had to report.

Now, because we were two intelligent, sensible, adventurous people, we decided to have a couple of days down at the winery area of Margaret River, so the next morning we left for another trip. She drove us down the old coast road as far as Bunbury, and then we branched off onto the Bussell highway to head to our destination.

During the trip, I made the fatal error of asking, "Hey babe, what are you going to do when I start driving my car to work?"

She replied with an implied question. "Well, you could take my car?"

I laughed and replied, "So the rev head in you has fallen in love with my old fashioned Ford, and your tin box Holden just isn't good enough anymore."

She didn't reply, but the look of daggers she shot at me was enough for me to know I'd overstepped the boundaries. We did have a pleasant couple of days, after she got blind drunk the first night; from then on, I left the subject concerning the cars well alone.

Monday I returned to the barracks in my car and had breakfast in the SGT's mess before meeting Tag in his room. Together we went to HQ to report to Mark. When we were seated in his office and the door was closed, he said, "It's good to have you both back. First, you're going to need replacements, so I've got hold of all the service records for you to go through. Tiger, I'd like to make a recommendation. Because you are the team leader and have extensive explosives knowledge, that you slot into that area, instead of second sniper's role. Therefore, you'll need to find two snipers and another communication expert. Take these with you and make some selections before we reconvene in a day or two."

Tag and I grabbed an armful of records each and went to my room to sort through them. I said, "Ok, we know what we need, so just skim these and we'll put any possibles aside for consideration. That way we'll narrow it down quicker."

After about three hours, we had trimmed our list to twelve possibles, and by the time we had fine-tuned and narrowed our list down to the three men, we had agreed on, we had been at it for just under four hours. All three possibles were in three squadron, so they were off either on leave or on base. Tag was going to find out at lunch whether they were on base, and if they were, set a time for us to meet them. We headed to lunch after agreeing to reconvene in my quarters at thirteen thirty.

When I returned from lunch, I waited for Tag to join me. I went over the service records once again. The first one was John 'JJ' Jensen – Signalman, born Victoria, five eight, joined the regiment two years ago, aged eighteen, active duty, two ten month tours of 'Nam on multiple patrols, under fire on forty-two occasions, confirmed kills six, one possible, earned his nickname from his initials.

The next was Jim 'Lizard' Lawrence – Sniper, born Queensland, five nine, joined the regiment two years ago, aged eighteen, active duty, two ten month tours of 'Nam on multiple patrols, under fire on thirty-six occasions, confirmed kills eleven, earned his nickname by being able to go up a building or a tree as fast as a lizard. Notation: Sniper skills untested in combat.

The last was Cristopher 'Gecko' Martin – Sniper and Linguist, born Pretoria South Africa, five seven, joined the regiment a year ago, aged eighteen, active duty. One ten-month tour 'Nam on multiple patrols, under fire on thirty-two occasions, confirmed kills sixteen, two possible, earned nickname due to being able to somehow stick to a tree or the side of a building and even hang upside down. Notation: Sniper skills untested in combat.

"Hmm," I thought to myself, "he's going to have to show us how he earned that nickname."

Tag knocked, entered, and sat opposite me at the desk. "Okay, good news is that both Gecko and Lizard are on base, and I've arranged for us to see them tomorrow at eight at HQ. The bad news is JJ is on leave and not due to report until Monday."

I nodded and replied, "All right, we'll take these records back and see what the boss wants to do, but we need to see these guys shoot. Plus, I really would like to see Gecko in a tree."

Tag smiled and said, "Yeah, wouldn't mind seeing that myself." He started gathering the records strewn around the room. After gathering up the two piles, with our three candidates' records on top, we went over to HQ to see Mark.

As we entered his office, he said, "I'll bet that's been keeping you busy. Have you decided on anyone?"

As we placed the records on his desk, I took the top three off the pile, handed them to him, and took a seat. After perusing them, he looked at me and said, "I noticed you've picked snipers that haven't proven their skill in combat. I assume you're going to explain that, so let's hear it."

"Yeah, it's really hard to use long range shooting in the jungle, where the fighting is much more contained. However, on the other hand, they've been in combat and have accredited kills. They're going to join us here in the morning, and I'd like to take them to the range and see what they can really do before we go much further. But if they're as good as their folders say, then we'll sound them out."

I paused and Mark said, "Fair enough. Now your radio man, JJ. What's the story?"

Tag fielded this one. "He's on leave until Monday, boss, so we haven't had a chance to see him."

Mark thought this over and said, "That's ok, I'll take care of that. I'll send his pager a message having him report to me here on Monday. I'll also get onto Major Bailey, their CO, and let him know what is going on. Reg should be ok with it. I'll just say you are scouting some talent and try to leave it at that. Now, you two had better sign out a rover from transport, and also go to the armoury and clear your practise for tomorrow. Once you've sussed them out, let me take it from there."

Tag and I replied simultaneously. "Yes Boss," and left his office.

At the transport office, Tag signed out a rover, and we drove over to the armoury, where we saw the SSM. He gave us six target stakes, six crouching and six standing targets, two pairs of high-powered binoculars, the red range warning flag, and a box each of the ammo for the rifles Gecko and Lizard used.

After that, we drove to the range, and driving down the side of the range using the rover's odometer as a guide, marked one kilometre, one and a half kilometres, and two kilometres. In the morning, we would place two targets at each mark and see how they fared.

We drove back to the barracks area. I had Tag drop me off at the Q store so I could speak to the staff sergeant about getting a formal dress uniform and jacket for mess dining in nights.

He took all the measurements required and said, "I'll get this sent off to the tailor's, and they might contact you direct. I've got your pager number, but do you have any other contact numbers, in case they do need to? If there's no problem, it should be ready in two weeks. I'll give you a bell when it's here."

I gave him my room phone number, and after thanking him, headed back to my room to call Sharon to let her know I'd have to stay at the base that night.

That night I had dinner and a few drinks in the mess; the food was a little better in quality than the OR's mess, but not much. Over drinks I ruminated about the possible missions we could be sent on, and they were too numerous to contemplate. I switched tack and started to think of the time frames. We would be working and practising as soon as the rest of the team came back from leave, so there was a good probability that we would be back in 'Nam within three months, which would mean we would be there at the height of the monsoon season from May to September. This had advantages such as silent movement, easy insertions, and being less prone to ambush, but the down side was trying to keep things, and ourselves dry, which was a drain on morale. Some ground would become swamps, which meant falls and slips were inevitable.

Climbing ridges could also be hazardous, and radio communication could be a bitch, especially coding and decoding messages.

The next morning, I joined Tag, Lizard, and Gecko in the common room of the HQ quarters building. We shook hands and sat. Tag passed me a coffee, and I lit up as I said, "Well guys, what are you hoping to do now that there's a good possibility you probably won't have to do another tour of Vietnam? I think there is going to be a scale down in operations going by what the current PM, Billie McMahon is hinting at. I reckon by next year, our next sabre squadron to go, will be the last."

Lizard answered, "If you must know, Sarge, I for one will miss the action and the time away. I have no idea what I'm going to do with my war service housing entitlements, and I guess I'm waiting to see what's on offer regarding this."

Gecko spoke up. "Sarge, I do know what I'm going to do with the war service home, because I'm engaged. I'll start looking for a house to buy, but I don't want to give up my position in the regiment yet. I think I'll miss the travel as well, but who knows? Something may come up, and I think that's why we're here. You wanted to see us for some reason, so can we get to what you have in mind?"

Bloody South African trait, straight to business, I thought to myself before answering, but I liked that. Moreover, I had mentally filed the war service home entitlement issue to look into later. I was most likely eligible too, same as Tag and the rest of the team.

"Yes I do have something in mind for both of you, but it does require commitment and taking orders from me and Tag, plus being able to fit in with the rest of our team. Before I say anything else, you have to prove yourselves. Hopefully that won't be a problem."

Their heads bobbed in agreement, and Lizard asked, "So what does that entail Sarge?"

"Well, from here we collect your weapons, and I want you in full battle dress, and then we go to the range. The reason you have been picked is that I need snipers with extraordinary skills, and I assume you haven't had that opportunity in 'Nam and I want to see what you're made of. You will have that opportunity to use your skills, if you pass muster. Fair enough?" They nodded in the affirmative, so I said, "Ok, let's go then."

Tag drove to the barracks building for three squadron, and Lizard, Gecko went to their rooms and returned to the rover dressed in battle gear, and with their weapons. After they were in, we headed for the firing range. Tag dropped me at the boundary pole and continued on, while I raised the warning flag in place and trotted after them.

While Lizard and Gecko climbed out with their gear, I joined them as Tag put the targets in place. While he was away, I asked to see their weapons of choice. Lizard's was a 380 Remington with a high power infrared scope. Gecko's was a 405 Ruger, again with a very high power scope. Both rifles had five shot magazines but were not self-loading. Each were single shot bolt action, which meant they had to be manually drawn back to feed another round into the firing chamber.

"What is the most accurate distance you can fire to consistently, without any bullshit?" I asked after looking over their weapons.

Lizard answered first. "From the ground up to one and a half kilometres, Sarge, but one point eight to two K's from height."

I looked at Gecko, and he said, "The same distances under the same circumstances. I can still blow the head off a wildebeest, and they're dead before they hear the shot, Sarge."

I nodded, rather impressed. I knew I couldn't achieve anything like that. Tag returned and joined us. I said to Gecko, "There's something I need some clarification on. Your nickname, Gecko. It says in your dossier that it was given to you because you can get into any situation and stay in position."

He smiled and replied, "Sure can, Sarge."

"Ok, prove it. I want you to hang in a firing position under that second branch of the gum tree, stay that way and fire a shot at the first target when I give you the word."

He nodded and started climbing the tree I had indicated. After a moment, he was outstretched, and bugger me if he didn't look as if he was stuck to the tree branch with his back. Tag had started timing him while we were watching, and I moved to the rover to get the binoculars.

I asked Tag how long he had been in position. "Eight minutes."

"You watch him, and I'll watch the target. Tell him to fire at the ten-minute mark."

We both watched and waited. I had my binoculars firmly sighted on the target as Tag gave the order to fire. Before Tag had finished the fire order, a hole appeared in the crouching target's head dead centre, a kilometre away. Christ that was good shooting! I looked up to see him in the same position he had been in before. I was convinced and so was Tag by the look on his face. He looked at me and smiled as he nodded his head.

I called, "Ok Gecko, good shot. Come on down."

When we were all together again, I asked, "I noticed that you both use M16's for close quarter work. Do both of your rifles fold or break down when not in use?" They both nodded. "Ok, how long does it take you to assemble them and fire?"

Lizard replied, "Thirty seconds." Gecko nodded in agreement.

I nodded, moved to the rover, and reached inside, pulling out the spare ammo boxes. After throwing one to each of them, I asked, "How many spare magazines do you keep in your combat gear?"

Gecko answered, "A full mag of five in the rifle and three full spares, Sarge."

"Same here, Sarge."

I nodded. "Ok, let's go to the firing line."

After moving to the firing line, Gecko replaced the used round in his magazine. I gave them the instructions. "The first crouching target is a kilometre away, so fire a full mag for grouping in the head. The next target is one and a half kilometres away, again a crouching target. Full mag, try for body shots. The last standing target is two kilometres away. Again a full mag, and go for either head or body, whichever you can achieve. Stop after each mag change until I give you the go for the next target. Take your time and commence on my order."

Tag and I moved up to the observation platform, with Tag behind Lizard, while I was behind Gecko. When Tag was set looking at the targets downrange, I did the same and watched Gecko's first target. I ordered, "Commence firing."

Once their first mags were empty, Tag and I conferred. Both had hit dead centre with each shot, and as we lined up on the second targets, I again gave the firing order. When we conferred this time, Tag said, "I'll need to check the last shot, but they all hit within a quarter of an inch dead centre of the heart."

"Same here, but we'll check them all after the last target. You head to get the targets after we see how they do with this one, but they are doing bloody well. We may have found the guys we want. Let's get ready."

I gave the cease firing order and the shooting was finished. As soon as Tag and I had spoken, he headed to the rover to retrieve all the targets, while both Lizard and Gecko replaced all the rounds used from their magazines from the box of ammo I had given each of them and started cleaning their rifles. I watched this with an approving smile, and thought, good. Replace ammo first in case they might need the rifles again. However, they knew they didn't need them again, so they cleaned the guns. Good. Their thinking is in the right place.

I moved down to join them. "Do either of you have any qualms about shooting someone that isn't firing at you? In other words, killing in cold blood?"

They both shook their heads and said, "No Sarge."

Tag returned and pulled up as close as he could to the firing line. He got out with the targets in hand and headed to the observation platform, signalling me to join him. By the time I got there, he'd laid out the targets in two lines with pencilled names and distances on each target. No wonder he was my 2IC; I hadn't even thought of that.

Tag pointed at one of the targets. "This is the one I wanted to check. Lizard's last shot was a smidge off."

"Hmm," I replied. "See what you mean, but still its damn close. We will ask him about it. Let's have a look at the far ones." I was stunned. "Christ! Didn't both of them say they weren't too good at that distance?" Tag was smiling and nodding his head at my question as I looked at the targets. Both had holes in the middle of the head. "Bastards, they've conned us!"

I went over to the railing and called, "Ok you two, when you're ready, both up here, please."

When they reached the platform, I said, "I think you guys have been conning us. Go have a look at the furthest targets."

When Lizard saw his, he remarked, "Shit, I've never done that good before."

"Hey, that's not bad, is it?" Gecko asked.

"No, it's damned good from both of you. Can either of you give me an explanation?" I asked, looking from one to the other.

Gecko said, "I can't, Sarge, but because there's no wind, which could maybe account for it, or we both really want the job you may be offering. I can say honestly, I've never shot that good at that distance before,"

"Neither have I, Sarge," Lizard commented.

"Ok, I'll accept that. Lizard, have a look at your second target, and while you're being honest, tell me what went wrong."

He hung his head and said, "I'm sorry, Sarge. I moved my arm a bit without thinking."

"Christ," I replied, "you should know better than that. I am not saying anything more because it would have been a kill anyway. Thank you for your honesty. But don't do it again."

He looked up and replied, "Yes boss, thanks."

I smiled and said, "Right. Both of you go get your gear and we'll head back for some lunch. Both of you report to Tag and I at thirteen hundred."

After retrieving the range warning flag, Tag drove back to three squadron barracks, where we dropped them both off. When we arrived back in the parking area of our barracks, I asked, "Well, what do you think?"

Tag sat back and thought for a couple of minutes. "They're

bloody good. If we can get them working together, they'd work out really well. I think the rest would be ok with them, but I guess we would have to do some practice together. They are probably not used to working in such a big team either, but I reckon we did well to find them. If they decide to take the job on?"

"Hmm, yeah. Well, we'll find out about that later, if they are a go. I will try to get them into see the boss later this afternoon.

Leave the range gear in here. We will worry about it later. Go have some lunch and come up to my room after you're done."

CHAPTER 2

After lunch, Tag met me in my room. I got on the phone and rang Mark's office. "Boss, Tiger here. Would you be available to see a pair of troopers in a couple of hours? Fifteen hundred would be fine, boss. See you then."

I looked at my watch, then at Tag. "Well, I suppose we should head down. We'll see how interested they really are."

He replied with laughter and a smile. "Yeah. The poor fools don't know what they're really getting into." I laughed as we headed out of the room.

They were both waiting as we walked into the common room and were about to rise from the table when I indicated not to. Instead, Tag and I sat opposite them.

"Ok, guys, are you ready to see how you fared?" I asked. They nodded in response and I continued. "As far as both Tag and I are concerned, we're happy to have you, but that's up to you, and also our boss. I'll tell you what we do, what is expected, the rewards, also the down side, and then I'll ask you to make a choice to either join the team or remain where you are. I will need you to give me an answer this afternoon, so I'm afraid there is no think time. It is now or never. I hope that's fair enough, and unless there are any questions, we'll get started."

Considering there were no questions, I continued. "The team is called SRT, which stands for the Special Response Team, and we answer only to the CO of HQ Squadron, whom ever that might be. At present, it is Captain Ryan. We were initially formed by the present OC, LT. Colonel Clarke, as a rapid deployment team for any emergency operation that might crop up unexpectedly. We have already completed one mission, but it cost us some men. One was killed, so we are looking for revenge for that occurrence.

We are all multi-skilled members and can fulfill most missions within the team, but if we cannot handle it within the team, an expert can be placed in our care. So in short, we do everything from blowing bunker setups to assassinations." I paused for a bit to let that sink in.

"What is expected is that we never give up on a mission. Every mission we take on is completed. In addition, if you join the team, there is no quitting. Once you are on the team, you are in for good unless there is a damn good reason to get out. No just, doing it for a little while and then going back to a sabre squadron. It doesn't work that way, and once you're out of the team, you're out."

"There's no second chance, so you could consider that part of the downside, I guess. Are there any questions yet?" They both shook their heads, I looked at Tag, and he shrugged his shoulders. I indicated for a cuppa, and he nodded and got up to make one while I continued.

"Now, about the rewards. Frankly, there aren't many, apart from the travel that may be involved. Also, the feeling of doing a job that not many others get the chance to do; and we could end up anywhere. However, I would say that soon we'll end up pulling out of Vietnam, and its back to peacetime duties for everyone. But our team will still be on an operational footing for anything arising." I paused as Tag passed me a coffee and I took a sip.

"Ok, now for the downside, and Tag will probably help me out here, because there's a lot on the list. First off, you don't get thanked for the job."

Here Tag interjected. "Apart from our last mission. We were all promoted a rank, and we have been awarded a couple of gongs, but I think Tiger is saying that it is not announced for everyone to know. All our work is top secret, so nothing much is said."

He looked back at me, and I was smiling. "There is one point, though, that Tag mentioned. Our work is classified top secret, which means your records will be sealed, but it also means you can't tell anyone what you're doing or where you're going. For instance, my girlfriend, and yes I do have one, has no idea what

I'm doing. All she knows if I'm not at home is I'm working and I don't even tell HER, so that's what I mean about anyone. There is also the point that we may come to be hated by other members of the regiment because we'll still be operational. Therefore, secrecy is a key element. No one is to know what you're doing. As far as anybody else knows, you've been transferred to headquarters squadron.

"That's the proposition. This is your last chance to make up your mind. If you're in, your in. If not, Tag and I start looking for someone else. We're going outside for a smoke, and when we come back, be prepared with your answer. Do you have any questions?"

Lizard raised a hand. "Tiger, what happens if we're wounded on a mission?"

"Well, that's a pretty good question. If it's a minor wound that doesn't incapacitate, you remain with the team. However, if it's major, and it is going to put you out of commission for more than a couple of months, then I'm afraid that you're off the team and a replacement will be found. And that brings up something I've forgotten to tell you."

After finishing my cuppa, I continued. "We are SRT One. At present, we're an experiment. From what I gather, if we are successful on our missions, there may be other SRT's formed, but if you've been selected to join us, and refuse, then there won't be a second chance on any other team formed. Saying that, and you get incapacitated for a fair while and get dropped from the team because of that, if other teams are formed, I can't see any reason why you couldn't join another SRT once your one hundred percent fit again. Does that answer your question, Lizard?"

"Yes, Sarge," he replied.

"Ok, any other questions? No? Ok. Tag and I will be outside having a smoke. See you in five."

With that, Tag and I went outside. He already had two out of his pack, passing one to me. I lit it, then his and asked, "So how do you think that went?"

16

"Well, if that doesn't put them off nothing will. That was a lot harder than you and Pep were on me when you wanted me to make the same choice, but we are not here to win friends or influence people. It's a hard job, but someone has to do it, I guess." He paused as if considering. "What was that about revenge?"

"Don't you think we've got some squaring up to be done? Pep was a good friend, and as far as I'm concerned, the body count isn't anywhere near what he was worth."

"Yeah, I agree with you on that score," he answered, nodding.

After we finished our smokes, I looked at my watch. Fourteen thirty, and we needed to see what they had to say before hopefully taking them both to the boss. We returned to the common room, and Tag put the kettle on to make us both another cuppa. I waited until we had our coffees before sitting down at the table. After taking a sip, I nodded to Tag to ask the question.

"Well boys, you've heard what Tiger had to say. Now it is up to you. Are you in or out?"

Lizard replied without hesitation. "I'm in, boss." He smiled at me.

Gecko said, "Make that two, but what I need to know is what do we call you, boss?"

I laughed and replied, "Whatever you're comfortable with. As you have guessed, I answer to boss, Sarge, or Tiger, but as far as I am concerned, Captain Ryan is our boss. Moreover, very shortly you're going to meet him. He will get everything sorted for you, but you will be moving quarters into this building, so be prepared for that. Thanks for justifying my faith in you. Now when you're ready, we'll take you to see the boss."

They nodded, and after draining my mug and washing it up, the four of us trooped up to the HQ building. After letting one of the orderlies know we were there to see Captain Ryan, we waited to be called into his office.

After a five-minute wait, we were ushered into his office, and as Lizard and Gecko stood at attention in front of his desk, Tag and I leaned against the back wall. Mark looked them up and down, opened their record files, and asked "I take it you've been briefed by Tiger and Tag as to what you are doing here and that you're both willing to join SRT. Nevertheless, I am going to give you the choice again. Lizard, do you wish to join the team? This is your last chance to pull out."

Lizard replied, "Yes sir."

Mark looked at Gecko and asked the same question; he received the same reply. "Very well. There is one little problem, however." At his comment, Tag and I looked at each other and came from leaning against the wall to attention. Mark saw my palms up gesture of questioning. "Relax, you two," he said, looking at us. We went back to leaning on the back wall, listening intently to what he had to say.

"The OC has decided that each team member except for the team leader and his 2IC must be the same rank. Now, all the other team members are lance corporals, and you two are not, so we have a bit of a problem. One easily rectified, though. I will just have to promote you both to lance corporals. I'll get that sorted today."

Tag and I looked at each other with nods and smiles as Mark continued. "Now, I've already assigned you rooms in the accommodation building, and you can start moving your kit this afternoon.

I have also started the transfer process with your squadron commander. All you need to do is sign your rank acceptance and transfer request, here and here. These are your room numbers."

As the men signed their paperwork and took the room numbers. Mark looked over at us with a smile and signed a well done. Once the paperwork was finished, he rose and held out his hand. "Welcome to SRT, gentlemen." After all hands were shook, he continued. "I'll let Tag sort you out while I have a word with Tiger."

After they left the room, Mark indicated for me to take a seat, which I did. He explained, "Sorry to throw you both for a loop just then, but the boss and I discussed the merits of everyone being the same rank. It'll probably be of help to you in future replacement issues, unless you have some concerns?"

"I do have one. That means the highest team members can rise is full corporal, whereas before they had to come up two ranks. Now there's only one more rank to rise and if some of them want promotion that could turn into an issue in the future."

He nodded his head and said, "Yes, I can see what you mean, and it's certainly an issue we may have to deal with in the long run. Let's see how it goes first, and if need be, we'll look at it later."

I nodded my head and reluctantly said, "Ok boss."

He smiled. "That wasn't a very reassuring answer. Your radioman, JJ, is reporting here on Wednesday at zero eight hundred. I'd like you to be here when he does, and we'll sound him out together. If he's like the others, you'll be able to start training your entire team early next week after I give you a situation briefing on Monday at zero nine hundred. However, between you, me, and the gatepost, you'll be heading back to 'Nam. There's a job the yanks need doing, and it's in our AO, so we've got the job."

"Ok boss. I'd like to have some training time at Canungra with the guys, if you can arrange it."

He nodded. "I'll see what I can do. See you Wednesday if not before."

The others were waiting for me outside HQ, and Tag lit me a smoke and passed it to me. After a big drag on the smoke, I said, "Let's head back to the barracks and see if your rooms are ready. Tag will help you move your kit with the rover."

As we entered the barracks common room, Dumper was at the table having a coffee. "Hey Dumper, how are you?" I enquired.

"Hi boss, Tag. I'm fine, just got sick of nothing to do, so I decided to come back a little early from leave," he answered.

I laughed, as did he and Tag. "Well, if you're looking for something to do, I can fix that. Say hello to two more team members, Lizard and Gecko. Guys, this is Dumper. We were going to have a look at the new boy's rooms, and then Tag was going to help them move their kit. You interested in helping?"

He replied, "Sure thing, boss."

I left Tag and Dumper to look after Lizard and Gecko, and after telling Tag to see me in my room after dinner, I left them to it and went upstairs to call Sharon's work number.

We arranged to meet outside the sigs mess that afternoon after knock off for a couple of drinks before she went home. I drove my car over to the sigs mess and met Sharon as I climbed out of my car. We embraced and shared a kiss before we went through the usual routine of mess etiquette. As I got a round of drinks, Sharon found us a table away from prying ears.

After sharing our days with each other, she asked whether I was coming home that night. I told her I probably wouldn't be home until Friday because of the amount of work. I'd explain to her what was happening when I was home over the weekend.

After another round of drinks arrived at our table, she asked, "Do you think I can drive your car home?"

I laughed. "Yeah ok, but any speeding tickets, you pay them." We swapped keys, as the house keys were on each set. "What I'll do is ring you if I get held up on Friday, but otherwise I'll just head home when I'm through. I'll see you each afternoon if I can. If I can't I'll try to let you know."

When we finished our drinks, we said goodbye to each other at the cars, with a kiss and cuddle, and after watching her roar off in my car, I hopped into the Monaro and drove back to the quarters.

That evening, instead of staying in the mess for drinks, I went back to my room, made a coffee, and lit up a smoke. I had the radio tuned to a Perth radio station I'd found; they were playing a lot of sixties music. I was singing along to "Flower Girl" by the Cowsills when Tag knocked and came in.

He grinned at me. "Good song that, pity you were murdering it."

I laughed. "At least I can sing, unlike some."

"Yeah, well, even a monkey could do better than me. So what does that make you?"

"Touché." I replied, laughing. "So how did things go with the newbies?"

"Good. They're both settled in, and they and Dumper were buying each other drinks when I left. I think they'll make friends with the others, no problem," he answered.

"Good." I poured us both a scotch and put the bottle of dry on the desk. When we'd both added the dry to our drinks, we toasted each other with "cheers." I said, "The boss told me there's a job on the table for us. We'll get the briefing on Monday. I've tried to wrangle some training time at the Canungra Jungle Training Area; he said he'd do what he could."

"That would be good if we can. Did he say anything about the job?"

"Apparently it's a job the yanks want done, but because it's in our AO, it's going to become our job. After looking at the map, I think it could be up the top part of Long Khanh, or Bien Hoa, but don't quote me on that. If it is, we may be in for some hairy moments. It's pretty mountainous in those regions, but I don't want to second-guess anything just yet. Let's see what he has to say first, and then we'll have a bit of a conflab about it in detail, once we know what it is. Also, JJ's reporting in at HQ on Wednesday at zero eight hundred, and the boss wants me up there with him. Now that Dumper is back, we should expect the rest of the crew to turn up in dribs and drabs."

I opened the top drawer of my desk while we were talking and pulled out four of the lance corporal pins we had gotten hold of and passed them to Tag. "I'll leave you to keep me informed as the guys get back. Here are the rank pins for Lizard and Gecko to wear on their cam fatigues, and I'll leave you and Dumper to get them settled in and sorted out.

Also, try to give them an idea of how we do things on the team. You know what changes they have to make, as opposed to being in a sabre squadron. Now here's something to consider when everyone is back. You'll need to know how many more sets of cam gear we need to get when we get to 'Nam, because from now on everyone in the team wears only cam fatigues. They can throw out the old normal greens. How many cam blankets have we got left?"

"We've got six, and I'm keeping them stored away in my wardrobe. Why?"

"Well, I was thinking that if we've got enough, which we have, pass one each to the newbies and fill them in on how good they are. Also keep one available for JJ. Tomorrow I'll take the rover over to the armoury and get rid of the stakes and flag, and then I'm going over to the Q store to get rid of my old fatigues."

"In that case, I've done the same as you and replaced every old set with cams. So can you drop mine in as well?"

"Sure," I replied. "I've got a better idea. How about we all get together in the common room downstairs at zero nine hundred and we'll see how many sets of cams everyone one has. If they want to get rid of the old greens, I'll take the lot. Now on the cam sets we have to get when we get to 'Nam, make allowances for each of us to have at least fourteen sets, even if we don't take them all on this next trip. To give you an idea, I have five sets at Sharon's, five I leave here at the barracks, and five that I wear when we're away, unless it's going to be a long trip, that is."

He nodded and replied, "Yeah, I've got about the same number. I'll make sure to get an accurate count."

"Fine," I said as I poured us another drink. "That will have to be one of the things on your agenda, once we're there. I think I might have a fair bit on my plate. If there's anything I need, I'll let you know, but try and get some ponchos for the newbies and anything you think might come in handy. Hopefully Jock will still be there, but if not, try to get on good terms with his replacement. It's always handy to be on the good side of the stores people. You've seen me operate, how I get things done."

After that we called it a night. I had a shower, and after my usual routine, I settled down for the night. The following morning, after breakfast in the mess, I was in my room when the phone rang. Mark wanted me to be in his office at eleven hundred.

After telling him I'd be there, I rang Tag's room to see if he was there. "It's me. Can you see if you can bring everything forward half an hour? I've got to see the boss later, so I'll probably need the leeway time."

At zero eight thirty, I was down in the common room with everyone, and there was a pile of green fatigues sitting on the table. Buzz had returned from leave. I smiled and gave him a wink as I entered. "Another one that can't stay away, huh, Buzz?"

He smiled and replied, "It was too quiet without you around, boss."

"I take it you've been introduced to the new members?"

"I got in last night. They were still with Dumper in the mess, so, yeah, we've all met," he answered.

I nodded my head with a smile on my face. I learned from Tag that most of the guys had plenty of sets of cam gear but would top up when we got to Vietnam.

After the rover was loaded with all the redundant sets of greens, I headed to the armoury first to drop off the range gear to the SSM, and then drove over to the Q store. I saw the same staff sergeant. "Hi Warren. I've got some redundant greens for you."

Warren looked up. "Sure, no worries Tiger. I'll get you a box to put them in. How many sets you got?"

"Thirty,"

He laughed and said, "Surely they're not all your old ones?"

Smiling, I replied, "No, all of the guys in my team acquired cam fatigues on our last trip in country, and hopefully by the time we need new ones, maybe the army would have bought something decent like these."

He laughed again. "Don't hold your breath. Get Jock to get you some more while you're on your next tour. I've already got him sending me a few sets with his next shipment."

"You two should do better than that. Get as many sets in

different sizes and flog 'em off to the rest of the regiment. You'd make a packet, even at ten dollars a set."

We both laughed, and he asked, "Who told you we were thinking of that?"

I replied, "Well, it would be common sense."

"Hey, this is the army. Having common sense isn't allowed!" We shared laugh over the inside joke he had made, and he added, "Oh, I've had word from the tailor's. Your ceremonial uniform will be here Friday, if you want to pick it up."

"Sure Warren. That was quick," I replied.

"Yeah, well, I took the liberty of putting a rush on it because we've got the first dining in night of the year in a couple of weeks. You'll need it then, so I put the rush on it."

"Thanks for that Warren. I'll buy you a drink tonight in the mess, and I'll also see you on Friday, if not before."

By the time I saw the boss, it was quarter to eleven. As I was ushered into his office, he motioned for me to shut the door. I took a seat as he spoke. "Ok, Tiger, I can get your team into Canungra. We'll settle on dates after the Monday briefing, but the main reason I called you in is that the new construction the boss got started last year is finished and has been named "the killing house." It's full of automated targets and hostage situations and is designed for clearing buildings at night, so when you go into it you need light intensifying headsets. I've arranged for your team to be given a tour of it tomorrow afternoon by Warrant Officer Bradly, so you'll need your team at the armoury at thirteen hundred in battle dress. He may run you through a couple of scenarios. I know it'll be throwing JJ in at the deep end, but it should be ok."

"Well, if we can talk him onto the team fairly quickly, I'll have enough time to get his gear shifted and introduce him to the rest of the team. Oh, speaking of that, Buzz came in yesterday, so there's only Wires missing, but I expect we'll see him in the next day or so. According to Buzz, it's too quiet for them on leave. They prefer to be near me, where all the action is."

Mark laughed and said, "Things do have a tendency to happen around you. Go on, get out of here."

With a smile on my face, I rose. "Ok boss. I'll see you at zero eight hundred tomorrow."

I was still smiling as I walked into the mess for lunch. I saw Shooter Bradly from the armoury sitting at a table by himself, so I went over and asked to join him. "The boss tells me you're showing us the killing house tomorrow."

He replied, nodding his head, "Sure am, and you're going to love it. But you need night goggles for it. I'll be issuing them to you to keep as part of your kit before we go down. Just make sure you've got your pistols. You won't need your rifles. While we're there, we'll run through some of the scenarios it can be set for. Is your whole team back?"

"Not as yet, Shooter, but I expect the last one to turn up soon. But if he's not there tomorrow, there's always the next time."

He laughed and said, "You're a hard man, Tiger, but that's probably why they like you."

"Don't let that get around." We both had a good laugh.

After lunch, I headed to the barracks to see if Tag was around, and just as I got there, Wires was about to enter carrying his kitbag.

"What took you so long to get back, Wires? The rest of the boys have been here for a couple of days. You're just in time for something new tomorrow," I called to him.

He replied, "Sorry, Sarge, but I got held up at Melbourne airport because of a screw up. It's good to be back, though."

I laughed. "Well, come on then. I'll hold the door for you. You've got a couple newbies to meet." He walked through the open door, nodding. "The last one is JJ, and he'll be here tomorrow."

"That's great, boss. I've worked with JJ before, and he's an ok bloke," he commented.

"That's good. Let's see who's around."

I followed him down the hall to the common room. The rest of the crew were there with Tag, and the greetings for Wires were very vocal amid the laughter. He was introduced to Lizard and Gecko.

I interrupted the proceedings. "Ok guys. Wires, go throw your gear in your room and come join us. I've got some news for you all."

Wires was only gone a minute; when everyone was seated, I said, "Ok, even though some of you aren't finished with your leave yet, I've got something you may want to take part in. Most of you know about the building the Colonel had built, and wondering what it's for. Tomorrow you get to find out at thirteen hundred. We'll all be in combat gear, pistols only, at the armoury, and Warrant Officer Bradly will take us for a tour of what is now known as the killing house. Also I hope to have the newest team member with us."

CHAPTER 3

The next morning at zero eight hundred, I was in Marks' office. As JJ reported in, I was introduced. He took a seat, and I closed the door. I sat in the chair next to him.

Mark told him, "Now, JJ, the reason you've been summoned here instead of reporting to your own CO is because at the moment Tiger is looking for replacements for his team. He and his 2IC have been through the personnel records and have decided to offer you a spot. I must stress to you that if you decide to accept the offer, it will mean you would have to leave your sabre squadron. The rewards for doing so aren't many, but if you accept, because all the personnel in Tiger's team have to be the same rank, you would automatically be promoted to Lance Corporal."

At this point I interjected, "JJ, one of the reasons the captain and I are talking to you is that you've been vouched for by one of my team members already. Anything you will do will be kept under wraps because we don't advertise our existence due to the secretive nature of our missions. That is one of the rules, by the way; everything is top secret, so you can't tell anyone what you're doing. This is one of the downsides of joining my team. Another would be on our last mission everyone in my team was awarded not one, but two gongs, but that has been kept low key; not even the sabre squadrons know what we've been awarded. While I'm on the subject of the sabre squadrons, we may bear the brunt of being disliked because we'll still be on an operational footing when we pull out of 'Nam while everyone else goes to peace time duties. Trust me, I reckon within the next year, we'll be pulled out. We've been in Vietnam since '65, nearly seven years, the longest time Australian troops have been in any war. So yes it will end, the rewards aren't great, but there'll still be travel to different parts of the world and the enjoyment of doing a worthwhile job.

I need some sort of commitment from you before I go further."

JJ pondered what I'd told him for a moment, then asked, "So what do you need, Sarg?"

"A few answers. Are you interested in what you've heard so far? Do you want more info? And if you like what you hear, are you prepared to make a choice, yes or no, when I ask for a commitment from you? Let's get this straight, if you decide to take the job, it is a commitment. There's no going back. You can't just see how it goes. You're in or you're out. Do I make myself clear?" I looked at Mark, who was watching me with his eyebrows raised.

"Yes, Sarg, I'm interested," JJ answered. "I would like some more info though. And yes I will make my choice after you give me the info. I understand that there's no backing out."

Mark spoke up again. "The team was formed early last year and is top secret. At present it is known as SRT, which stands for Special Response Team, so Tiger leads SRT one. Right now there is only one team, but in the future there may be other teams formed. This is important for you to understand: you have been approached to join SRT. If you refuse, there will be no second chance at a later stage to join another SRT. Whether there are any more teams is dependent on Tiger's success."

As Mark paused to let that sink in, I watched JJ's reaction, and I could tell that he was interested.

Mark continued. "What this means to you is, one, if you accept, the first thing that happens is you move quarters into the HQ squadron barracks. Two, your service record becomes a sealed document. Three, because you're only a private, and everyone else on the team is a Lance Corporal, you will be promoted to that rank. Before you make your decision, I'll give the last word to Tiger."

Turning towards me again, JJ leaned forward in his chair. I smiled as I remembered that I was much the same way when I was first interviewed by Mark and Pep. That seemed years ago, but it had only been last year.

"This is the last word on SRT before you make the choice. Within the team there are specialists in different areas. It's a team of eight, and the usual regiment rules apply. You need to be able to fill any position, you answer to me and my 2IC, and to whoever is the CO of headquarters squadron. At the moment Captain Ryan is our boss, but he answers to the OC. If you decide to join us, things will move quickly. You'll be assigned a room in our barracks, and your kit will be moved today. Should you be asked, you're being transferred to HQ squadron, and that's all you'll say to anyone. As for the question, take your time answering. You can go outside for a smoke to think it over if you wish." I paused before asking the question. "JJ, would you consider joining my SRT team?"

Glancing at Mark, he nodded, and I continued. "Let's go outside so you can think this over. You can give me an answer when we come back in, and you can ask me questions while we're outside."

As we walked outside, I pulled two smokes from my packet and lit one for him and passed it to him. He didn't have any questions as we smoked, but he did look as if he was deep in thought, so instead of interrupting him, I let him continue stewing over his answer. In my thinking, I could understand his dilemma, so I gave him a few extra minutes before I told him it was time to go in.

Back in Mark's office after the door was closed, I said, "Ok, JJ, it's time for an answer. Are you in or not?"

He looked at Mark, then at me. He nodded. "Count me in, Sarg. But there's one thing I'd like to know first. What happens if I'm wounded?"

I smiled and looked at Mark before replying. "I'll tell you what I've told everyone else. If it's a minor wound, you stay with the team; however, if it's major, and you're out of action for months, then you'll be replaced, and once fit again, you'd be eligible to join another SRT. Does that answer your question?"

"It does, Sarg, and you can still count me in. Thanks for being honest."

Mark stood up and shook his hand. "Welcome to SRT, Lance Corporal Jensen. Now, I have some dreaded paperwork for you to sign, just here and here, and this is your room number in the barracks." JJ signed the paperwork and took his room number. "Tiger will make sure you're squared away, and I'll phone your CO and let him know what's happening. I'll leave you in Tiger's hands."

After that, we stood and I opened the door for us, and we headed out of Mark's office, JJ picked up his kitbag in the front office, and we started walking to the barracks.

On the way to the barracks, I quizzed JJ about his cam fatigues, and, like the rest of us, had heaps of sets. I informed him that he was to only wear the cam gear now, no greens.

I found the team in the common room, and made the introductions. "JJ, Tag will sort you out, and the guys will help you shift your kit to your room. Tag will tell you what's happening after lunch.

You've joined us at the right time. We're going to see something new today." I clapped him on the back and turned to Tag. "Tag, come with me please. Boys, help sort JJ out. I'll see you after lunch."

Tag followed me up to my room and I gave him another set of rank pins for JJ. "It doesn't have to be done straight away, but don't forget to give him a cam blanket. Try and get him shifted before lunch if possible. There's enough time to do it, and bring him up to speed so he's ready to go with us this afternoon. We'll meet in the common room and go to the armoury from there." I paused as I considered. "We may try to march over there. That'd be a change."

After lunch, I met the team in the common room, everyone in their combat gear, but the rifles were still in our rooms. I gave them the quick once over and nodded my head. "Looks like we're all ready. Any questions? No? Let's go then."

While we marched to the armoury, I asked Tag, "Did you get JJ shifted and settled in?"

"Sure did, and he's getting on well with the others," he replied.

"Good. Looks like the team should work out well then. Christ, I hope we don't have too many casualties. I don't really want to have to go through the replacement business again, if I can help it."

He replied with a grimace, "That's you and me both. It's bloody difficult."

When we arrived at the armoury and trooped inside, Shooter was waiting and issued each of us a set of night vision goggles. "We just got these from the states last week. You guys are the first to use them, so everyone tries them on and get them adjusted so they're comfortable. They require an hour to charge the battery, but it will last up to twelve hours. Don't forget to take the charger with you. When you're ready, we'll go out the back to the rovers. Tiger, you follow me in the second rover. Let's go."

Outside I got into the second rover, and the guys split into two groups. When everyone was on board, Shooter ahead with me following. When we arrived at the killing house, Shooter unlocked the gate and drove to a second building behind the kill house.

Once we were all in a group, he said, "First, we'll go into the kill house. I'll turn on the lights and give you a tour. Then we'll come back here, and I'll show you the control room and run some scenarios."

After we were all inside the killing house, Shooter told us, "While I close the door, put your night glasses on and turn them on."

As he shut the door, all daylight disappeared. When I turned on the night vision goggles, I was able to see again and was surprised by how much I could see.

I heard Shooter's voice say, "I'm going to turn on the lights." In the next second there was a white flash and I was blinded until I took off the glasses. I swore and wasn't the only one.

Once my eyes adjusted again, I saw Shooter standing near a switch, smiling. "Now you know what happens if you get hit with bright light while wearing those things, so if it happens, get them off immediately as you shut your eyes. Then you will be able to see when you open your eyes. Ok now, let's have a look around. I'll show you some of the different targets and friendlies."

As we wandered through the rooms, Shooter would pause occasionally, disconnect a wire, and manually lift a target. I had noticed something but kept it to myself and filed it into my mind for use later. As we moved from room to room, Shooter informed us, "From the control room, we can see everything that goes on in here." He pointed to a camera. "We can also change the room configuration as well as target and friendly positions. The aim is to enter and clear the building of enemies, and if it's a hostage situation, rescue the friendlies without harming them. Right, let's head over to the control room."

We moved into the control room building, and as Shooter powered up all the screens in the room, I noticed why he'd left the lights on. Each screen showed a different camera angle, and with a push of a button, he was able to move whichever camera he'd switched on to move.

I asked, "So if the lights are off, just how much can you see?"

He smiled and said, "Watch this." He flicked a switch, and the lights in the kill house went out. We still had a clear picture of each room, though, and he explained, "All the cameras are infra-red and work in much the same way as your night vision goggles. I'll load a hostage scenario so you can see what happens."

He went to one of the computer banks, pulled a program reel, and locked it into place. He moved to the computer keyboard, loaded the program, and as the reel started turning, I watched the room in the kill house. The targets started to show in each room, some supposedly sitting, some standing in different rooms, and then a family group appeared on a couch that had targets standing on each side of the group with guns trained on them.

Shooter said, "Tiger, if can you send one of your men to shoot one of the targets? I can show you what happens."

I nodded to Lizard and he went out of the hut. We followed his progress on one of the outside cameras. Another camera picked him up once he was inside, and Shooter said into the microphone, "Just shoot any target anywhere and then come back."

Lizard gave a thumbs up to the camera, fired a shot, and as he did, a target outline came up in the control room. The shot was marked on the outline, and as Lizard re-entered, he was able to see the result of his shot.

"That will happen with any target hit, so after an exercise the results can be replayed and seen on screen," Shooter explained.

"Bloody hell, that's brilliant!" I exclaimed. "So how does it work in the case of a forced entry in multiple spots of the house?"

Shooter laughed, held up a finger, and said, "Watch this." He tapped a button on the control board.

A diagram of the house showed on the main screen; at numerous points, there were red marks. "Each red mark is an entry point, and at each point you tap a button which simulates as an explosion. For instance, at the door, you tap the button and you've effectively blown the lock. The electric lock releases the door for entry. Cool, huh?"

"I'll say," I replied. "Now, my main question: can a scenario be repeated after being analysed during debrief?"

Shooter answered, "Sure, it can simply be rerun, or another scenario can be loaded, and there's about thirty different scenarios available."

I nodded my understanding, thinking how bloody remarkable the technology was.

I looked around; every one of the team members looked anxious to try it out, so I asked Shooter, "Do we have enough time to run a simple clearing scenario, with no hostages or friendlies?"

He looked at his watch, nodding. "Sure. Sort out what you want to do outside, and I'll load a program for you. I'll time you from the minute you approach to clear. Just give me the signal."

I nodded. "Ok, everyone, outside for a quick briefing."

Once we were outside, I said, "Ok, two teams. Tag you take the second team to the back door. Lizard, Gecko, at each side to shoot at windows, but make sure you can see me at the front. And Tag at the back so when I give the signal you pass it onto Tag. Once inside, one high, one low, clear every room, but remember we're using live ammo. Let's not shoot each other. Everybody take your berets off. All the targets wear something on their head. Don't shoot anyone without head covering, clear?" Everyone nodded. "Ok, let's give it whirl."

We made our way to the go point, and I turned to the camera to give the ok signal. "You all know where you need to be. GO!"

My team of Dumper and JJ hung back cautiously, then moved to the door. By now Tag would be in position. I gave Lizard an arm wave and hit the button. Dumper and JJ had they're goggles in place as I said go. They moved in and covered me while I put my goggles on. We moved into the front room, each killing a target. I checked behind the door before we moved to the next room. As we were about to enter the next room, a target appeared at the end of the hall and I shot it. We cleared all the front rooms, so my team moved up the stairs, leaving the lower level for Tag's team. As we climbed the stairs, we encountered two more targets that were despatched. We cleared all the upstairs rooms, despatching three more targets, then returned to go back downstairs.

At the top of the stairs, I called, "Team two, this is leader at the top of the stairs. Clear up here."

I heard Tag call, "Clear down here. Come on down."

Shooter's voice blared over the loudspeakers. "Exercise complete. Well done. Lights on in five, four, three, two, one." The lights flickered on as he reached one; we had removed our night goggles and slowly opened our eyes.

My team went down to the lower floor to join Tag's crew. As we exited, we were joined by Lizard and Gecko from each flank, and once we were all together, I said, "Well done, guys. Sorry you two didn't get much action."

"I don't know about that. I had a couple pop up," Lizard commented.

Gecko chimed in, "Same here." We all laughed.

After the laughter died down, I said, "Ok, let's go see how we did."

Back in the control room, Shooter had rewound the tape, and we watched it through. "That was bloody good considering it was your first time and you've not been trained for this sort of action. Now you've done it once, you have the chance to fine tune things, but all in all you did well. All your targets were kills, and they wouldn't have had the chance to get a shot off. I'm marking it down as perfect, and your time all up was two minutes twenty-four, start to finish." He clapped his hands together happily. "Ok, ready to call it a day?"

Outside, I told everyone we'd have a debriefing back in the common room. We climbed into the rovers and headed back to the main base area and the armoury. After thanking Shooter Bradly for his time, I headed off with my team to the barracks common room. We were all carrying our new night vision goggles and chargers. Once there, Dumper and Wires made some coffee.

As we lounged in our seats and lit up smokes, I asked, "Well, was everyone as impressed as I was with our new training toy?" By the comments I received, and the discussion that followed, I came to the understanding that they all enjoyed the killing house. I asked them for ways we could improve our performance after today's run through.

There were two stand-out suggestions, both with merit. The first one was probably the most do-able: that we do the training in the kill house at night so that we wouldn't have to wait the seconds our eyes needed to adjust to the darkness. We would already be wearing our night goggles. I thought this suggestion made complete sense and thanked Buzz for coming up with it. I'd talk to the boss about the scheduling for that area of our training.

The second suggestion from Tag was probably the best: we needed radio communication between each team member, which would mean each member would need a radio with a headset for hearing and speaking at no more than a whisper. I looked at Wires and JJ. "You're our comm's experts. What do you think? Could you two put your heads together and come up with a solution?"

Wires answered. "It's possible, Tiger, but we'd need a couple of weeks, and we'd probably need to get some parts from the sigs company, but once we've got a working prototype, it'd be easy to make others."

"Ok," I replied. "I'll leave it with you. Just let me know how you're getting on, and as for sigs, I've got a contact down there."

There were a few other suggestions about weapons, and it was decided between us that next time we'd use our machine pistols with the silencers on because the gunshot noise inside that building really reverberated through the whole place, especially my forty-five. This threw me off on a tangent that I'd been meaning to address before, but hadn't gotten around to.

I looked at Lizard and Gecko and asked, "Guys, are your rifles fitted for silencers?"

They both nodded and Gecko said, "They sure are, Sarg. We keep the silencers in our kits for when needed, but with them on it's hard to gauge accuracy at very long range."

"But good for at least a thousand yards?" I questioned.

Lizard considered before answering. "Yes, but after that it gets a bit iffy, Tiger."

I nodded and said, "Good, thanks guys."

Dumper put his hand up and asked, "Tiger, can we take these new night glasses with us on our next trip? They'd be bloody handy."

I laughed and said with a smile, "Sure, and as a matter of fact, everybody put them in their combat kit where ever we go from now on. Having these would have made our last mission a lot easier. Just don't lose them. There'd probably be hell to pay if we did." There were laughs all round, and everyone was discussing the new goggles, except for Wires and JJ, who had their heads together, discussing a drawing they were putting together. I assumed they were already working on my request.

I looked at my watch; it was almost knock off time, so I said, "Unless there's anything else, we'll call it a day. Don't forget to clean your guns. I'll see you in the morning." Before I left, I said to Tag, "I'm going across to sigs for a couple of drinks and to warn my contact that our comm's experts may be heading her way in the next day or so, looking at what they're cooking up."

He laughed and said, "Ok, I'll see you in the morning."

Over at the sigs mess, after the usual protocol routine, Sharon and I were seated at our table with drinks within arm's reach as we shared some quiet time together over a smoke. I told her about our day at the killing house, and she asked, "How were you able to see in the darkness?"

I laughed and said with a smile, "We've been issued night vision goggles. I'll show you how they work tomorrow night. I'll bring my set home with me." I paused to take a sip of my drink. "By the way, don't be surprised if a couple of my men come looking for you. Both of them are comm's experts, and I've given them a job that they'll probably need spare parts for."

I explained the job to her briefly, and she said, "They'd be better off converting an SR10 set with a headset and microphone, but I'll wait until they come and see me. I can put them together with one of our technicians."

"That'd be excellent, honey. Thanks," I replied.

"Are any of the team married or have girlfriends?"

Before I answered, I lit both of us a smoke, passing one to her. "None of them are married. One's engaged and some of the others have girlfriends. Why?"

"I was thinking that I don't know any of your team or they're girlfriends. Why don't we have a beach party and BBQ at home over the weekend, say Saturday afternoon? No shop talk, just have a relaxing social time, and if anybody gets too drunk they can stay over."

I nodded and said, "Yeah ok. I'll tell them later, get it arranged, but I might have some sewing for you to do over the weekend. I'm picking up my ceremonial uniform from the Q store tomorrow. And while we're on that subject, are you ready to swap back cars yet?" She looked at me with a wicked smile and a pout. "All right, I guess that means no."

"Thank you, darling." I just laughed, an exasperated look on my face.

That night in the Sgt's mess, Warren from the Q store came over to a drink with me. "Tiger, your uniform's in so you can grab it anytime tomorrow if you wish."

"Thanks Warren. I'll probably grab it in the morning if that's ok?" I replied.

"Sure anytime. Let me buy you a drink."

"Thanks," I said.

When he returned, I told him about the kill house and the comm's problem it brought up. He said, "Sounds like we need to get something like the US delta team's comm's setups. I can't get hold of any, but when you get to 'Nam again see Jock and see if can put his hands on anything like that. That'd be your best option."

Not long after our conversation, I called it a night, and as I went into the barracks, I called into the common room to see if any of the team were there. As luck would have it, they were all there. Wires and JJ were discussing another drawing, Tag, Buzz, Lizard, and Gecko were playing five hundred, and Dumper was watching the run of play.

I walked over to Wires and JJ. "I've had a word with my girl-friend at sig's, and she said that you may be better off converting an SR10. If you go see her tomorrow, she'll get you together with one of their technicians if you like."

"That'd be great boss. We'll go over first thing. Who do we ask for?" Wires asked.

"Private Dawsett. Tell her I sent you." They both nodded, smiles on their faces.

I looked around the room and called, "Can I have everyone's

attention?" After they quieted, I continued. "On Saturday arvo, you're all invited to a beach party and BBQ at my place starting between fourteen and fifteen hundred. Wives, girlfriends, or both are invited too, so if you want to bring a date, by all means do. Bring your own booze and some meat. This will be purely social. The girls can meet each other, and my girl says if any of you get too drunk, you can stay the night. Anyone interested?"

All the guys raised their hands with smiles on their faces. I nodded, smiling, and wrote the address on the notice board. "That's the address. Tomorrow Wires and JJ are going over to sig's and aren't sure when they'll be back, but otherwise it's a quiet day. Stay around if I need you, though. Have a good night, and I'll see you in the morning." As I headed towards the door a chorus of good nights followed me.

CHAPTER 4

As I predicted, Friday was a quiet day, apart from Wires and JJ heading off to the sig's company. The only thing I had to take care of was picking up my uniform from Warren at the Q store. When I got back to the barracks, I phoned Mark from my room first, and after confirming the time for Monday's briefing, I informed him of the upcoming BBQ and asked if he'd like to attend. He accepted and said he'd be bringing his wife.

My next call was to Sharon. I asked how she got on with Wires and JJ, and she said with a laugh in her voice, "Oh, they were absolutely charming, and right now they're ensconced with our chief tech. The way it looks they could be here for days."

I laughed. "Ok, now hold onto your hat. The boss will be attending the BBQ with his wife. I did tell him it was a low key, purely social occasion, and he said they'd be happy to come, so I guess we've got some shopping to do tomorrow morning."

"We sure have, and you'll need to buy some bottles of wine for us girls. I'll probably get away from here early today, so I'll see you at home."

"Ok," I replied before hanging up.

That night after dinner, I took Sharon into the bedroom where I got my night glasses out and put them in place on her while she sat on the bed. I told her to shut her eyes while I turned them on and turned the room light out. I went through the house turning the lights off.

"Ok, you can open your eyes and move around now. See if you can find me."

As she entered the lounge, I heard her say, "Wow, these're

really great!"

"Told you they were good. Come out on the balcony and have a look round."

"I can see everything as plain as day. Can I get some of these?"

I laughed and said, "Honey, there's only nine sets in this country, and mine's one of them, so the answer is no. If you want to see how dangerous they can be, go turn on a light while you're wearing them."

It was easy enough to know if she followed my advice when I heard "SHIT!" as she found out the drawbacks of wearing them when lights are on. She came back out on the balcony where I was having a good laugh and punched me on the arm. "You shit. You knew I'd look into the light. They are good, though. No wonder you love them. Here you go." She handed them back, and I went into the house, turning the lights back on as I went, and replaced them in my kitbag.

The next morning, we went to the butchers and grabbed a fair bit of meat for the BBQ. We also went to the pub to stock up on booze and ice.

While Sharon was sorting out the meat and salads, I went for a stroll along the beach picking up drift wood and old timber to use for the fire under the BBQ plate. After about half a dozen trips up and down the beach, I figured I had enough wood and kindling. As I was on the last trip, I had what I thought was a funny thought. I should ring Tag and have him pilfer one of the bloody poles I had to cart around for that first week at Swanbourne. I would gladly have taken an axe to it.

After making sure the BBQ was clean, I started the fire under it so I could warm it up and oil it. When I finished that, I grabbed my surfboard and went to catch a few waves before everyone started to arrive. The surfing wasn't good that day; it was somewhat flat, and the onshore winds wouldn't kick in until later in the day.

I went up the back stairs, walked into the kitchen, and gave Sharon a playful slap on the bum. "How's it going, babe?"

She replied with a sigh, "Well, it's ok for someone who went surfing while someone else was stuck in the kitchen. I've got the bare feet; all I need now is to be pregnant."

"I hope that's not going to happen anytime soon, but my heart bleeds for you, darling," I replied.

Laughing, she said, "Yeah I know. Buckets and buckets of horse piss. Speaking of that, can you pour me a drink please? But no horse piss."

As I finished pouring her a glass of wine, there was a knock on the front door. I glanced at my watch and looked at her, wiggling my eyebrows. I went to the door and opened it. Janice, one of the girls from sig's that Sharon had invited, was standing on the porch. I told her Sharon was in the kitchen and latched the door so that it would remain open. While they gossiped, I poured myself a scotch and dry and carried it to the front door when I heard another knock.

Mark and his wife Wendy had arrived, so I showed them in and introduced everyone. I made drinks for everyone. The women stayed in the kitchen, so Mark and I went out to the balcony.

Everyone started arriving at the same time. Sharon organized the food in the fridge, and I was downstairs with the men putting the booze they'd brought into an old tub I'd filled with ice. After everyone had arrived, the women came downstairs, and we headed down onto the beach after changing into swimsuits.

We swam for about an hour, but hunger got the best of us. We walked back up to the house and fired up the BBQ. We sat in the backyard, talking and drinking while the cooking was done by me, Dumper, Mark, and Tag taking turns, arguing over the amount of time required for all the different meats. As far as I could tell, everyone had a good time.

Dumper had sort of hooked up with Janice, and they must have been getting on quite well because they later left together. Wires and JJ had told me early in the day that they had sorted out the comm's problem, and I told them to let me know about it on Monday. The only one that ended up staying was Tag, mainly because he got pretty well hammered and had driven the rover. I was not going to let him drive, just in case. Mind you, I wasn't much better, but I didn't have to drive.

Sunday morning after a couple cups of coffee and a swim in the surf, both Tag and I had shaken the hangover effects. When we got back to the flat, Sharon had warmed up some of the leftover meat and fried some eggs, so we all sat down to a belated breakfast.

Over more coffee, we discussed the previous day's BBQ, and our consensus was that everyone had enjoyed themselves. The afternoon could be counted as a success.

After Tag left, Sharon and I continued our lazy day. While we sat around having drinks later, Sharon asked, "I know you've got a briefing coming up tomorrow with the whole team. Does that mean you'll be going away again soon?"

I nodded my head. "Yep. It is in the cards, but we also have some training to do up at Canungra first, so I am not sure, when we will be taking off to Vietnam again. It'll be like last time if we go, a quick couple of jobs, then home again."

Sharon looked at me sharply and stated harshly, "Not all of you came home last time." As she saw the pained expression on my face, she quickly tried to apologise, but her barb had hit home and hurt. I quietly rose and went to pour another drink without speaking.

After sitting down again, I said, "Sharon, you've told me that you wouldn't interfere or pressure me about my job, the same as I wouldn't interfere with yours. Yes, we both know things can go wrong, but those are the risks we all take. I do love you. However, please do not force me to make a choice between you or the job. You may not like the outcome."

She was looking at me. Tears rolled down her cheeks. "I won't ask again, but that won't stop me from worrying about you all the time. I promise I'll never say anything again."

I nodded and said thanks. To lighten the mood, I said, "What do you think we'll have for dinner? We have quite a lot of choices.

We can have warmed up BBQ, or we could go upmarket and have warmed up BBQ. Which would you prefer?"

She laughed as she wiped her tears away. "If you make me another drink, I'll warm up some leftovers and we can eat them out here."

After our impromptu dinner and drinks on the balcony, I cleaned up and decided to join Sharon in the shower. Our shower was quite a long one. We continued what we had started in the shower in our bed, a very prolonged session of foreplay and lovemaking that exhausted us both. We did have to have another shower before retiring for the night.

We were up early the next morning. As usual, I left Sharon to have breakfast while I drove to the barracks and had breakfast in the sergeant's mess. After eating, I went to find Tag and the rest of the team. As I entered the common room in the barracks building, I was cheered by the guys and passed a mug of coffee by Dumper.

"Well, obviously you all had a good time the other day. Next time you guys have to take some of the cooked meat home. I'm still eating the leftovers." They all laughed and started reliving the BBQ; I turned to Dumper and laughingly said, "I suppose you'll be spending a lot more time down at the Sig's mess now?"

He smiled and replied, "Very good possibility boss."

We both laughed. "Good for you." I caught Tag's eye, and motioned for him to join me outside. We lit up, and I asked, "Well, do you think they're ready"?

Tag nodded and replied, "JJ, Lizard, and Gecko have made friends with some of the others, and they've been accepted by the rest of the guys. The BBQ the other day did have a lot to do with that. It was good bonding time on top of last week. Brilliant move by the way, and thanks for letting me stay over."

I smiled. "No problem, you should know that." We finished our cigs and headed back inside. "Is everyone ready for the briefing later?" I received nods all around and continued, "Ok, now, before that, Wires and JJ have something to tell us. Let's hear it guys."

As Wires went up the hall, JJ started speaking. "What we've been able to come up with, thanks to one of the sigs techs is we've been able to modify our SR10 sets so that the speaker is converted into an earpiece and a voice operated lapel microphone can be plugged into a new jack in the top. We can still use them as normal and can still change frequencies."

"Does it work?" I asked as Wires came back holding two SR10 sets. He showed me how to insert the mic wire then turned the radio on and put it in my top pocket.

He put the other set on, turned away from me, and his voice came through the earpiece. "Can you hear me boss?"

I whispered into my lapel mic. "Yes. How am I coming through?"

"Perfectly five by five boss," he replied as he turned around.

I looked at him. "Great. So how much range do they have with the extras you two put in?"

Both he and JJ smiled as JJ said, "That's the best part, Sarg. The sets still have the normal range of five hundred metres without any loss of signal."

"Fan-bloody-tastic!"

"You two have really excelled. How long before you can make sets for all of us and a couple of spares?"

Wires answered, "If we can get down to the sigs tech after the briefing today, and can work down there all of tomorrow, we could have them ready by tomorrow night if the sigs company have enough spares. But we'd have to take everyone's SR units with us."

I thought his reply over for a minute before replying, then nodded my head and said, "Ok. Collect all the SR's and take them with you to the briefing, and as soon as it's over you and JJ head down to sigs to get started. I'll let Sharon know you're coming down, so see her first." I looked at the others. "Right guys, go get your SR sets and give them to either Wires or JJ, while Tag and I get ours."

Tag and I headed for the stairs to our rooms, and as we climbed the stairs I said, "Come up to my room and grab my radio while I let Sharon know what's going on please."

"Gotcha," he replied.

When we got to my room, I unlocked the door, went to the wardrobe, and handed my SR set to him. He left for his room while I picked up the handset of the phone and dialled Sharon's line. When she answered, I said, "Hi, honey, it's me. No, we have not gone over yet, but I wanted to let you know that Wires and JJ will be coming over as soon as we are finished. Oh yes, you have to put up with them again. They will come to you first, but will most likely spend a lot more time with your tech. Brilliant. Thanks love. I will catch you later. Ditto. Bye."

After the phone call, I went back down to the common room. As I got there, Wires came up to me and said as he patted his backpack, "Got them all boss."

I nodded and after looking at my watch, said, "Right. Everyone ready for the briefing?"

Lizard responded. "I just need to get another notepad, boss. My old ones full."

JJ piped up. "I've got a couple of spares in my room, Sarg. I'll go grab one if you like." I nodded. He returned a moment later and brought back a notebook, which he passed to Lizard, who nodded this thanks.

"Right. Everyone ready now?" There were nods from everyone. "Ok, let's move!"

When we arrived at the lecture room, I stood at the door as they all moved in and took seats. I mentally noted that each specialist pair sat together. Tag was seated beside Buzz, Lizard and Gecko were side by side, same as Wires and JJ, and Dumper had pulled out a chair for me to sit down beside him. I thought to myself that this was probably a good arrangement and would make it easy to compare notes later because each specialty would concentrate on what was important for them. That way we would get a good all-around view of what would be required.

I saw Mark coming up the stairs with the OC Lt Col Clarke. I called "Attention!" as Mark and the OC got to the door. Because I still had my beret on, I saluted. Mark had his cap under his arm, so just nodded; the OC was still wearing his cap, so he returned my salute and made his way into the room. I moved to my seat beside Dumper.

Mark looked towards the OC, who removed his cap, and said, "Ok everybody, sit please. I just wanted to say a few words before your briefing with Captain Ryan." With a smile on his face, he looked at us and then toward Mark and remarked, "You really do look like a fine bunch of scoundrels. This next mission is very important, and that is why I wanted my best men for this job. This mission isn't for us, but because it's in our operational area, General Command wanted Australian soldiers to undertake this job. It's for the yanks, and you will be saddled with one of their mob as a liaison and observer." Although none of us groaned outwardly, our faces spoke our displeasure. "Sorry men, but that's the way it has to be."

He took a moment before continuing, "But it does have a plus side. If we can convince them of our capabilities, you may find that you won't only be confined to our operational area of the country. You could find yourselves working in different parts of the country, doing work that our yank cousins can't manage for themselves. And of course, adding to our reputation of being the best tactical soldiers in the world, so please be careful not to fuck up. If you do, at least do it out of eyesight of the observer. I know you will do us proud. Thanks gentlemen."

He turned to Mark and said, "I'd like to see you and Sgt Davis in my office after the briefing, Captain."

Mark replied, "Sir."

As the OC put his cap back on, we all stood at attention. With a wave of his hand, he left the room.

"Ok, as you were, be seated," Mark murmured and started to unroll and hang a couple of maps, one of the whole country of

Vietnam and one of Long Khanh and Lam Dong provinces, both very mountainous areas.

I had a hunch this wasn't going to be an easy mission, and I was proven right by the end of the briefing.

Mark started the briefing by saying, "You heard the boss. This isn't one of ours, but it's become our job. The target is a radio tower that the NVA has built here," He used his pointer and touched a spot on a high ridgeline that marked the border of Lam Dong and Long Khanh provinces. "According to intel reports, it's situated three hundred metres inside the Long Khanh border, and that's why it becomes our job.

"Over the next couple of weeks, I'll be receiving high altitude recon photos of the layout and all the accumulated Intel reports on the facility, but my guess is that getting power to the site will be a major problem. I would expect they use a couple of generators, but how they got them there would be anybody's guess, same as the steel for the tower."

Buzz put his hand up, Mark acknowledged him, and he said, "Knowing the slopes, boss, they would have carried them in there in pieces and then put the whole thing together from scratch. Same for the generators. And they probably lug fuel up there as well."

Mark thought this over. "You're probably right, Buzz, but how they got it there isn't our problem. It's our job to blow it to hell and back." We all laughed at his comment, and then the job was put up for general discussion, the main question being how we were going to accomplish it.

After half an hour of open discussion, Mark called a halt. "All right, let's continue. The planning I'll leave to you guys, but I'll need a feasible plan before you leave on the mission. However, take into account you are going to have enemy personnel on the ground. I have all of you booked into the Canungra Land Warfare Training Area for the next two weeks starting Friday, so you'll be leaving here on Wednesday. I'll let Tiger know when, and he can fill you in with timing." He paused briefly. "Now on a personal note I'd like to add my thanks to Tiger and you guys for a very enjoyable BBQ the other day."

"My wife and I enjoyed it immensely, and I hope most of you recovered from your hangovers, which I imagine there would have been." The men nodded their heads and murmured a few sentences. Mark said, "Tiger and I have to see the boss, so we'll close the briefing. Thank you gentlemen. I'll schedule another briefing when you get back from Queensland. Dismissed."

As they filed out of the room, I told Wires and JJ to get going, and told Tag to have everyone else in the common room after lunch so we could all get into working out a couple of plans for the job so we could find out what worked better while we were at Canungra. Mark and I headed to the headquarters building to see what the boss wanted with us.

Once we were inside the Col's office and the door closed, he had us take seats across the desk from him. "Davis, I hope the briefing went well considering the scanty information we had available."

"Yes sir," I replied.

"Good. I hope that our cousins across the way will have supplied as much info as they can before your team gets back so you can have a proper sort of briefing instead of this airy-fairy stuff that they have given us. Now, I hear that you and your team had a run through my kill house. What did you think?"

I replied, "Sir, first off it's a cracker of a place, and state of the art."

He interjected, "Look, I'm not here to be buttered up, lad. Ryan said you had a few problems, so I want your honest opinion. Let's hear it."

"Yes sir. As I said, it's great, but where we encountered what I perceive to be a major problem is in the fact that the night vision goggles we use require at least a minute to adjust to from daylight. My suggestion would be to hold off any training in the kill house to a nighttime exercise or have the lights on during daylight training. Another problem we encountered was with how to communicate when we used a multiple entry technique, but my radio specialists have that problem solved and are making adjustments to our SR10 units, with the aid of technicians at the signals corps."

He seemed to think this over. "I'd be very interested to hear what your radio specialists have come up with. This could solve a lot of communication problems."

I replied, "Certainly sir." I filled him in on what Wires and JJ had come up with, and finished with, "We intend to trial them while we're in Queensland under combat conditions, sir, so I'll probably know more after that."

He sat back in his chair and said, "Good, good. Keep me informed on that. Now back to the mission. I've been on the blower to my opposite number in the states. Because you'll be working predominately with officers, you need to be at least equal in rank or above them for this to work. Due to our ranking structure being different to theirs, I've been able to secure you the rank of honorary major in their army. Your liaison officer, a Captain Fredrick, will meet you at Nui Dat soon after you arrive, and he will have your rank insignia with him. Only wear them when you're in the company of yank officers, though. Don't wear them around our lot, or you could get shot for impersonating an officer." He laughed. "That wouldn't do at all, would it?"

Both Mark and I laughed, and I replied, "No sir."

"Hopefully we'll have more info for you when you get back from Canungra. Isn't that right, Captain Ryan?"

"Yes sir," Mark answered.

"I'll also be waiting to hear how your radio adjustments work out, Davis, so keep me informed," the OC said. "For now, that'll be all gentlemen."

Mark and I stood to attention and marched out of his office and into Mark's. He closed the door, and I took a seat and looked at him with raised eyebrows. He laughed and said, "Well doesn't that beat all? You got away with telling him his pet project had major flaws, and how to improve them, and he's made you a Major in the yank army!" He laughed loudly. "Christ Tiger! You keep doing this; you'll outrank me without going to officer's school. Shit!"

I laughed and replied, "No chance of that, boss."

He laughed as well. Then he got down to our other business. "Ok, at zero nine hundred Wednesday I'll have two rovers and drivers outside your barracks to take your team out to Pearce RAAF base. There's a Herc heading to Amberley at zero ten hundred. You'll overnight there, and the following morning they'll transport your team to Canungra. You'll have to arrange with them to take you back to Amberley after your time there. I'll have arranged for a flight to get your team back here, but I'll send you further info through your pager, ok?"

"Yes sir," I replied and left his office.

I went into the common room back at the barracks, hoping that most of the guys would be there. Considering we used it as our operational area while on base, I made a mental note to have Mark try to find us a building to use as our operational headquarters. We were lucky at this stage that most of the headquarters staff that lived here were working most of the day, so we'd had no interruptions as yet. Tag and the rest of them were there discussing some aspects of the upcoming mission.

I watched them a moment before interrupting. "Right. Have we got anywhere near to an operational plan yet?"

Tag replied, "We got quite a few ideas, boss, but were waiting to run them by you."

"Good, but we'll leave that discussion until after lunch. For now, I need you guys to concentrate on this. We leave the base here at zero nine hundred on Wednesday to go to Pearce and onto Queensland. We'll be overnighting at Amberley before being taken up to Canungra. We've got an hour before lunch, so I'm going to take Dumper with me. We'll be taking the rover over to the engineer's company. Tag, the rest of you start thinking about the move on Wednesday. Right, Dumper let's go!"

As we drove over to the engineers' company, Dumper asked,

"Do you mind if I ask why we're coming over here boss?"

I replied, "No, not at all. I want to have a discussion with Te about those generators we'll be facing. I've got something sneaky in mind, but need to talk to Te about it to see if it could work." I pulled the rover up in front of the building that the demolition team used as they're office.

"Tiger, Dumper, come in. What can I do for you?" Te asked as he saw us at the door. We sat down in chairs brought in for us, and I explained what I had in mind. After a quick rundown of what we'd be doing, without going into specifics, I told him, "What I had in mind for the generators is to cut the power lines to the installation and smash the control boxes. However, I was thinking of putting some ammonium nitrate into the fuel tanks and squirting a mix into each cylinder so that they would blow themselves and the generators to shit when they started them up again.

Do you think it could work? Otherwise we'll just blow up the generators ourselves, but I thought my idea would add a nice touch."

Te and his crew were smiling, and with a laugh he said, "I don't know about the nitrate in the fuel. It could work, but putting a mix into the cylinders would certainly work. You're a sneaky, crafty bastard, Tiger! Come back over in the morning and we'll work it out."

Dumper and I got up to leave and received pats on the back and comments of "Well done," and "See you in the morning." We climbed into the rover, and headed back to have lunch.

CHAPTER 5

The guys were waiting for me as I walked into the common room after lunch. Tag had managed to get some area maps, and as we all sat around the table with notebooks to jot down any notes, the planning session got underway in earnest.

The first point we discussed was the insertion. Because the terrain was dense jungle, we'd probably need to rappel to ground level. Because of this, we'd have to carry all our supplies with us; therefore, two choppers would be required to get us in. Getting out presented another problem. We would need to make our way to a clearer area for extraction.

There were many comments going backward and forward, so in the end I decided to stop all the wrangling. "Ok, there's only two ways this can be determined. One, from the aerial photos we'll get to see at the next briefing, or two, by me making my mind up when I do the flyover recce. Agreed?" They all nodded. "Right. What happens when we're on the ground? Let's run that around a bit."

It was eventually decided that once we'd established an LUP, we'd look for an observation point close to the facility and take turns watching the target for forty-eight hours. Because we had the night vision goggles, and the improvements to the SR sets, the job would certainly be easier.

We moved to the plan of attack. Lizard and Gecko would go into the trees with silencers on their rifles and cover the assault team, which would include the rest of us. Once we'd killed the enemy, Tag would supervise the destruction of the radios and collect any codebooks and papers while Dumper and I rigged the aerial tower and booby-trapped the generators. After we cleared the facility, we'd set the tower charges off and bug out. What we did after that and how we would be extracted would be determined by the Intel reports at the next briefing.

Just as we finished, Wires and JJ walked in because it was close to knock off time. JJ said, "We've got five sets done, boss, and we'll be able to do another seven tomorrow. After that we'll have to wait while the sigs get some more parts."

I nodded and replied, "That's good, guys, but twelve sets ought to be enough. The rest of the boys will fill you in on what you've missed. Now, in the morning after breakfast, Dumper and I'll be with the engineers, and Wires and JJ will be working down at sigs. The rest of you can start getting yourselves ready for Canungra. That's it for the day. I'm going down to sigs for a drink. Dumper, you want a lift?"

"Please, Sarg," he replied, and we left to go down to the sigs mess.

Down at the sigs mess, I was able to walk right in because after a word with their mess committee it had been decided that due to my living with one of their members I didn't require going through the normal protocol routine. So after ordering a couple of drinks, I joined Sharon. Dumper had already taken a seat with Janice across the room.

As Sharon and I sipped our drinks, I lighted both our smokes. She asked, "So when do you go?"

"Wednesday morning," I replied, taking a drag before continuing. "We're off to Canungra for two weeks, and back again, but it should give us plenty of time to try out the new radios. JJ and Wires will be back down here tomorrow finishing the rest of them. Can you drop me at the barracks in the morning? I'll leave my car at home because I'll have to stay on base tomorrow night."

"No problem, honey. I was going to leave at the same time you do tomorrow anyway." She caught my eye and nodded so I would look at Janice and Dumper. "Janice came and talked to me at lunch today. She's a bit smitten with Dumper, I think. She couldn't stop talking about him."

I laughed and asked, "A bit like you were with me?"

She looked at me coyly, laughed, and said with a smile, "Yes darling."

At home that night we talked about my trip to Canungra and the possibility of leaving on a mission soon after. She asked, "How long do you think you'll be gone?"

I answered her after giving some thought to the question. "It'll be back in 'Nam so what could be just one job might turn into a few others, but I think maybe only three or four months. You know how it turned into a longer trip last time."

The next morning after saying goodbye to Sharon and breakfast in the mess, I joined some of the guys in the common room. When we were all gathered, I sent Wires and JJ off to finish the radios after they handed me a pair of the new working sets. Tag and Buzz were going to the Q store for last minute supplies, while Lizard and Gecko were going to the armoury with their rifles and silencers for checks with the armourer. That left Dumper and I clear to go down to the engineer's section.

As soon as we arrived, Te said, "Good you're here. The crew and I found that one of the old trucks in our demolition field has a motor in it, so we'll go down with a battery and long cables and some witches brew to test if what you want to happen will really happen." We went out the back door and climbed into their truck, the tailgate left hanging.

When we arrived at the demolition field, Loni, who was driving the truck, kept going and pulled up at an old Wiley's four-ton truck from pre-World War Two days.

From the back of the truck, Te said, "This should be perfect. It's an old diesel, so what we'll do is remove the glow plugs, squirt some of the brew in, give it time to dry a little, replace the glow plugs, run a set of cables from them to where we'll be with the battery, and that should set it off."

While Box and Jonesy started work to remove the glow plugs, Te, Dumper, and I made up a mix of ammonium nitrate and diesel and put the mix into a plastic squeeze bottle. When all was ready, we poured some of the mix into each cylinder of the motor, and

Loni connected the cable up to the glow plug control. He played out the cable to a small hillock fifty yards away. We all jumped onto the truck and Loni drove over near the hillock, placing the truck side on between where we would be on the ground and the target.

We decided to have smoke while we waited for the mix to dry and sat around talking and smoking while a water can was put on the small gas stove to boil for coffee. After an hour, Jonesy and Box walked across to the target and replaced the glow plugs. Everything was right to go. Te nodded to Loni, who started to attach the cables to the battery, and while he was doing this, he said, "We'll probably have to wait a bit until the plugs warm up before we get..."

He was interrupted by the detonation of the explosive mix.

We all stood and moved around the back of the truck that had shielded us from the blast. There were whoops of delight and laughter, and Te clapped me on the back, laughing, and said, "Well I think your idea works, Tiger!"

Looking at the remains of the truck, I had to agree. The whole front section of the truck cab had disappeared, and what was left was the smoking and smouldering rear section of the truck and some twisted metal and burning rubber.

After loading everything up, we got back into the truck, and Loni drove back to the shed. Once inside, Te gave me another squeeze bottle and a plastic bag half full of nitrate. "This should be more than enough to do the job. You'll have to siphon some diesel out of the tank to mix it so you won't have to carry any with you. Good luck and thanks for the entertainment." I thanked him and the crew, and Dumper and I drove back to the barracks.

Both of us had smiles on our faces as I drove back, and Dumper said, "Well boss, I have to admit you get some really smart ideas, and what a pearler of a booby trap!"

I laughed and replied, "Pity we won't be around to see the results."

Back in the common room, Buzz, Lizard, and Gecko were sitting around waiting, and Tag came into the room behind us. I passed the bag of nitrate to Dumper. "You know what to do with that." He smiled and went to his room. I continued. "Ok, what's the score?"

Tag filled me in. "I've got all the supplies we need. Lizard and Gecko have had their rifles and silencers checked and are right to go. Most of the packing for Queensland has been done, so barring last minute stuff; we're all ready to rock."

I nodded. "Dumper and I have the extra punch we needed, and he can fill you in on that later. Apart from me needing you to come with me, the rest of you can have the rest of the day off, unless anyone wants to go down to sigs and give Wires and JJ some help." They all wanted to do that, so I said, "Buzz, you're in charge. When you get down there, ask to see Sharon. She'll know where they are. Also tell her I'll come down for drinks later, and I would like to see either Wires or JJ here after lunch please. I'll see the rest of you here after lunch as well, so off you go. Tag, let's go."

I grabbed the two radios from the rover, and as we walked toward the Headquarters building, I passed one of the radios to him and explained what I needed him to do. "Put this on and in place, then turn it on. You'll need to stay outside the building, but be ready for instructions as the other unit is turned on. Don't be surprised if the Colonel comes through. He wanted an update on these, so now is as good a time as any. But first I'll have a word with Mark."

As we reached the building, Tag peeled off towards a bench seat in the shade while I continued inside. In Mark's office, I asked for two things: one was to see the Colonel, and the other was a request that he find the team a building we could use as our base of operation during work hours.

Mark agreed. "I've been thinking the very same thing, and I might be able to come up with one. I've got to get permission from the boss first, but I'll need some sort of sweetener from you guys."

"Well, I might have just the thing; shall we go see him and show him the modified radios?"

"They're ready? Good! Let's go." He stood up and led the way to the Colonel's office.

After knocking and receiving permission to enter, we marched into Lt Colonel Clarke's office and stood at attention in front of his desk, waiting until he was ready to hear what I had to say. He looked up and said, "Right, gentlemen, what can I do for you?"

"Two things, sir. The first is Sergeant Davis would like to show you the progress made on the radios," Mark said.

The Colonel's eyes lit up and he interrupted Mark. "Well, Tiger, let's see what you got."

He was looking at me like a kid at Christmas as I showed him the SR set. I showed him how it worked and helped him with it. I turned it on and raised my voice so Tag would hear me through the lapel mic. The Colonel's eyes lit up when he heard Tag answer. He yelled into the mic, "Hello!"

Even I heard the cry of pain through the earpiece. "Sir, these mics are designed for whispered conversation. That cry you heard was my Corporal having his ears blasted, so either speak normally or turn your head toward the mic and whisper. Go ahead try again, sir."

After playing with the radio for five minutes, the boss ordered Tag to come into his office. A minute later Tag was at attention alongside Mark and me. The Colonel came around his desk and shook Tag's hand. "Sorry about the shouting, Corporal. Let's put it down to first timer trouble." He faced all of us, and with a beaming smile, said, "Damn good job, first rate. You've made my day, thank you. Do you have any spares you can leave with me?"

"Well sir, I've had a dozen made up because the sigs company didn't have any more spares for more than that. I'd like to keep enough for my team and a couple of spares, so I could leave these two sets with you, sir."

He answered immediately. "Yes, that would be good. Please do."

58

Tag took his set out and turned it off while I helped the boss, and we put them on his desk side by side. The boss said to Mark, "Now Captain, you said you had two things. What's the other?"

Mark answered, "Perhaps that could wait until the men are finished, sir."

"Yes, yes is that all sergeant?" the boss asked.

"Yes sir," I replied.

"Very well done. Thank you. You're dismissed."

"Sir," I replied as both Tag and I came to attention and marched out. As we went, I heard the boss say, "Now Captain, what can I do for you?" I smiled as we made our way out of the building.

"What the hell was that all about?" Tag asked.

I replied with a smile on my face. "We've made the old man happy, and now Mark is going to screw him for what we want, of course."

"Oh? And what do we want?" he asked.

"We want our own operations building. Unless you'd prefer to keep using the common room as our office."

He replied, "Shit no! It'd be better to have our own building where we could spread out, have a store, a gunroom, a workshop, and our own offices. So which building does he have in mind?"

"Not sure yet. He has to get the old man's approval first, but anywhere would be an improvement."

Tag laughed and replied, "You're not wrong on that score. You could have let me know before, though."

"How could I? I'd only just thought of it while I was in Mark's office," I answered.

Tag started laughing. "Now I know why I enjoy being on your team. You come up with some half brained schemes, and you get away with it. I've stood beside you, when you've done it, and I'm buggered how you do it, but watching you operate is great to watch. You have the confidence that nothing will go wrong, and it doesn't."

I smiled, turned to him, and answered, "That's the whole trick. Confidence in yourself or what you're doing and the bravado to carry it through without backing down. How's that for psycho-babble?"

By this time, we'd reached the barracks and went into the common room, but none of the others were there. We went up to our own rooms. While I was in my room, I got my gear ready and packed for the trip the next day. I unlocked the safe and pulled out my weapons, gave them the once over, and checked on my ammo supply. I had more than enough, the only thing I didn't have was my SR10 set, and that would be rectified as soon as Wires returned.

Just as I was about to leave the room on my way to the mess to get an early lunch, my phone rang. Mark wanted to see Tag and me at the briefing room at fourteen hundred. After telling him we'd be there, I rang Tag's room and told him we had to be there.

"What's going on?"

"Stuffed if I know, but if it's in the briefing room, something must be up."

"Yeah," he agreed. "Ok I'll see you after lunch in the common room with the rest of the guys."

"Roger that," I replied.

Everyone gathered in the common room after lunch. As I sat down, I said, "All right, around the table discussion starting with Wires. Where are we at in regards to progress?"

"Thanks to the help JJ and I have had, we've only got two more radios to modify. Should only take us an hour boss," Wires answered.

Dumper was next to him, so he spoke next. "Apart from helping with the radios, I stored the bag of nitrate in my stuff ready to travel at any time, boss."

The rest had completed everything to do with preparation but were still willing to help with the radios, and of course, Tag had to be with me later. After some thought I asked, "Wires, do you need any extra hands this afternoon?"

"No boss, JJ and I can handle it," he replied.

"Did you bring the completed radios with you?" I asked.

JJ answered. "Yes Sarg. Do you want me to get them?"

I nodded, and he went to get the radios, returning with the eight converted ones, and laid them on the table.

I reached down and picked one out. "Ok, everyone takes one and put it with your gear. Now don't lose or bust them because we'll only have one spare. In case you've forgotten, we'll have a passenger along on the operation."

My last comment received questioning looks from a few of them. I looked at Wires and said, "The last two you're fixing this arvo, keep them with you and they will be the two spares. The first two have gone to the boss, and he's quite chuffed about them, so maybe we can expect some upgrades at a future date. You two can head off when you're ready. The rest of you stay close in case we need you later, but for now consider yourselves off duty, unless Tag or I call."

After that, I took my radio up to my room, put it with my operational gear, and went back down to the common room to kill some time before meeting Mark. Shortly after Tag joined me, and after looking at his watch, he said, "If we go now we'd be a little early, but I've only seen the briefing room and nothing else in that building. I thought I might go over and have a sticky beak. What about you?"

"Count me in." I got up and we walked to the lecture building.

As we entered the building from the veranda, the first two doors on each side opened into what could become offices. The next door on the left opened into a lounge area with a small kitchen area and large fridge at the far end. The room on the right was another entrance into the briefing room. The door behind the lecture/briefing room opened into another office-sized room, and the door opposite was another entrance into the lounge area.

The next doors opened into large rooms with nothing in them, and the last four doors, two on each side, were toilets. The door at the end of the hall led outside to a large parking area.

My thoughts were racing with ideas; I wondered if I could talk Mark into letting us use this building. It was ideal for our purposes. A bit of furniture, some benches, a gun rack, a large safe, shelving, desks and chairs, some filing cabinets, and working phones, and we could really turn this into an operations office.

Tag stated the obvious and must have been on the same wavelength as I was. "Christ! This would be ideal. What do you think?"

"You're reading my mind. I wonder if I could talk him into it. Mind you, we'd need some stuff, but yeah it's more or less purpose-built for us. I've just got to convince Mark, so get ready for some fast talking on my part when he gets here."

We went back outside to wait for Mark, and shortly we saw him heading towards the building carrying a clipboard. We went inside to the briefing room, and as we sat he said, "Have you two seen the rest of this building at all?" We both nodded, and he continued. "Good. Do you think this would serve as an operational building for SRT?"

Tag and I looked at each other, then back at him. I answered, "Yeah, but it would require a fair bit of different furniture. Why boss?"

Mark replied, "This is the building I had in mind for your team, and the only other time it's used, apart from your briefing sessions, is for the odd lecture for new personnel. But that could be done elsewhere, and the OC has granted me permission to use it as the SRT building. So what we are going to do is go through each room, and you can tell me what you'd use it for and what you require in it. Let's get to it."

Tag and I rose with smiles on our faces, and I quietly remarked to him, "Well, that took a lot of convincing." He burst out laughing.

"What's so funny Tag?" Mark asked.

I answered, "Nothing boss. It's just about something we were going to talk to you about, but we don't need to now."

Mark had drawn a mud map of the building. He wrote what each room was and what each room required in the way of furniture and shelving. While we were in the lounge area, I asked, "Would it be possible to get a large TV and cabinet for this wall for news updates and so on?"

He nodded and said, "Good idea." He wrote it down.

In what would become the weapons room, we discussed the gun rack and safe size. All up, the time taken to tour the building and Mark to write down our requirements was an hour and a half, and when we were finished, Mark said, "All right, now, I can get most of the stuff you want and put into the various rooms. The phone lines can be installed while you're away in Queensland. The safe I'm not too sure about, but I'll do the best that I can. The furniture and shelving will be put into the rooms. You guys will have to sort out and place everything after your back. Is that understood?"

"Yes boss," Tag and I said simultaneously.

Mark smiled and said, "Well in that case, welcome to the new SRT building, gentlemen." We all laughed.

After Mark had handed us each a set of keys to the building, he started back toward headquarters while we walked around to the carpark area for a proper look. I decided that when we came back, we'd sign out two rovers from transport as permanent vehicles. I told Tag what I'd decided in that regard, and said, "You'd better warn them of that when you take the rover back today."

We headed back to the barracks to inform the rest of the crew of what would be taking place once we came back from Canungra. When we got there, Wires and JJ had finished with the radios, so everyone heard the announcement at the same time. The news generated cheers of delight from all of them.

I let them know the downside. "I'm glad you all like the idea of moving to a permanent work area. Work being the operative word. When we get back, the boss said he'll try to have all the furniture in, but we're the ones that have to put everything into place, so be prepared for some real work when we get back."

It was almost knock off time, which meant Dumper and I would head down to the sigs mess, but before that, I said, "Tag, it's up to you to make sure everything's ready for tomorrow. Don't forget, you lot, that the transport will be here at zero nine hundred, so be ready. And no hangovers please. Right now I'm off to my usual place, but I'll see some of you later."

Dumper and I headed to sigs, and as we walked, we discussed the amount of C4 we'd probably need to blow the radio tower. It was all speculation until we saw the actual photos, but it gave us a starting point.

At the mess, Dumper bought me a round of drinks while we waited for our girls to come in, and as the barman was setting up the next round, Dumper let me know the girls had arrived. I added to the order, and with a smile, the barman said, "Already ahead of you Tiger." He put down two full wine glasses with the other drinks. We headed to the table where the girls were sitting together, sat down and had the first sip of the drinks before lighting up smokes.

Sharon said, "You're looking rather pleased with yourself. What have you been up to?" I told them the whole story of getting our own operations building. "So after all the reasons I had prepared as arguments for Mark to let us use that building, it was the one he was going to give us anyway."

Janice and Sharon had a good laugh over that, and Janice asked, "What time do you leave tomorrow?"

Dumper answered her question, and then because she lived on base, she asked him, "Are you coming back down after dinner to see me?"

Dumper looked at me, as if seeking permission, so I nodded my head, and he replied to her, "Sure, but only for a little while, dear heart."

Sharon and I smiled as we listened to this exchange. Soon after that, Sharon and I went out to the carpark to say our goodbyes with kisses and cuddles, and I laughed as she asked coyly, "Do you think I could drive your car while you're away?"

I nodded my reply and said exasperatingly, "Ok."

The next morning after breakfast, I was dressed in full battle gear and took my kitbag down to the entrance to the barracks to await the transport. Tag joined me, and because we were alone, I said, "There's one thing I've had on my mind that I wanted to ask you about. When we move into our building, we're going to need someone to look after all the stores, including ammo and explosives. I don't want you doing it. I was thinking you could make Buzz our unofficial storeman and teach him the ropes both here and in Nam."

He replied, "Sure. Good idea. That way he'll have something productive to do when we're not on operations. I'll sound him out about it when we're on the plane."

I nodded and said, "Good."

The rest of the crew started to assemble, and we were waiting as the two rovers turned up. After arriving at Pearce, we were in the air by zero ten hundred and landed in Amberley at sixteen hundred kilo local time. We were billeted in the guests' quarters above the mess that night, and after breakfast, we climbed into the truck that took us to the Canungra Land Warfare Centre up near Springbrook in the Gold Coast hinterland. We arrived there at zero thirteen hundred, and after having lunch, they showed us our quarters for the duration of our stay.

CHAPTER 6

The following morning after breakfast, I went to the camp headquarters and discussed a training area we could use after the base orientation and training course later that morning. The main instructor for the training and orientation was Sergeant Mick Webb, and he suggested an area where we could train. It was close to a high-tension power line tower that was over two hundred feet in height. He did warn me that it wasn't accessible by road, due to the denseness of the bush, and we would have a two-day walk to get near it. This sounded to me as if it would be perfect for the practising I'd like to do before the real thing.

During our orientation lecture held in a room similar to our briefing room was in the main headquarters building of the base. Sgt Webb decided to forgo some of the usual routine he normally ran through with soldiers that hadn't been to Vietnam before because all of us had completed at least one tour. To train us on what to expect during jungle warfare was a little superfluous, so he skipped over most things, but did warn us about the types of snakes were prevalent on base, which was rather handy to know.

We continued with the base orientation, and he asked, "So how long do you guys want to spend on your training exercise, taking into account that it'll take two days to walk into the area from our closest crossroad?"

His question started a discussion of how long we were all happy to stay in the bush and train, and it was decided that we'd stay in the general location of the training site I'd picked for a week. Allowing for the hike in and out, after ten days we'd be back at the pickup point, spend that night in camp, and then be transported to Amberley the day after.

Sgt Webb agreed to organise our trip back to Amberley and would organise transport to our drop off point. We were to be ready to leave at zero eight hundred the following morning. We then adjourned.

Tag and Buzz went off to the Q store for supplies for the following days, while the rest of us went back to our quarters. Once there, I organised Wires to make enquiries in regards to communication with base while we were in the field. He left to find out. The rest of us relaxed while we waited for the others to get back. Wires was back first and had the comm's sorted out with base. Shortly after Tag and Buzz returned carrying a stack of stuff that included ration packs, rope, climbing gear, and camouflage cream. Once sorted, we made our way to the mess for lunch.

The following morning, we were transported to the closest crossroad to the area we would use to train. After orientating ourselves with the map, we set off in the required direction as if we were going into action, which meant we practised our combat patrol techniques. We were now wearing our modified radios. Buzz was the scout and lead man for the first couple of hours, and then we would alternate in rotation.

One of the things we discovered was the terrain was much worse than we'd previously encountered in Vietnam, and it was hard going trying to move silently because of the dryness of the jungle and lantana we were moving through. That first night we all praised Wires and JJ for their work with the radios because trying to use hand signals in that scrub was next to impossible. The radios made it so much easier.

I will not bore you with the details of the training we did over the next few days, but we practised quite a few scenarios we were likely to encounter and worked out the best plan of attack for each of the different scenarios. What we worked out during those days included that we would have to kill the entire enemy on site because we needed at least two to three hours on site. Wires and JJ would concentrate on destroying the radios and collecting documents and the paperwork from each of the dead enemy soldiers. Dumper and Tag would team up and plant explosive charges and wiring on the tower. Buzz and I would take care of destroying the electrical control boxes on the generators and rigging them with the booby traps. For good measure, we would place claymores with trip wires around the generators, which I hoped would divert attention from the main booby traps I intended to lay in the generators themselves. The job of covering the assault force would fall to Gecko and Lizard; not only would they have to keep watch and relay information to me, but they would also kill any enemy that came near the complex.

The scenarios we practised were based on the number of buildings that may be in the complex. After some discussion amongst ourselves I decided to practise killing up to forty enemy personnel and clearing up to four buildings as well as reducing this number down at a rate of ten personnel per building. This was assuming quite a lot, but I didn't want to take the risk of over or under rating the enemy.

Probably the worst case scenario would be the forty and four, the least ten with two buildings, one being the radio room. We were really operating in the dark because of the lack of information from the yanks, but hopefully we'd know what we were facing, and strengthen our planning to suit accordingly, after the next briefing we had back at home base.

After being away for fourteen days, we returned to home base in time for dinner, and as soon as we got into my room, I phoned Sharon to let her know I was back and that I'd see her the following afternoon in the mess. I made my way to the sergeant's mess for dinner and a few drinks.

After dinner, I was sitting in a lounge chair watching the TV while I sipped a scotch. The political climate was really changing. The labour party was surging ahead in the opinion polls after Gough Whitlam had become the leader. Much of this was due to his stance on ending the involvement of Australian troops in Vietnam, and he had obviously won big points with the voting population because of this. He also wanted to reduce the voting and drinking age to eighteen.

I had to agree with his point of view. If someone was old

enough to fight for his or her country, then that person should be able to have a say in the running of the country as well as have a drink legally. However, I was torn on the issue of pulling out of Vietnam. Okay, we should not have become involved in the first place, but we were making a difference for the people who lived there, and if we pulled out too soon, the other side would win easily. Everything we had done, and the soldier's lives we had lost, would be in vain. Also, pulling out could be viewed as a defeat, which would not sit too well with a lot of serving members of the defence force, me included. There was still two years before the election, and polls had a way of giving false information; however, I did think that if he did get into power, there would be a real shake up because he seemed to be a person that would honour his promises, unlike most politicians. Little was I to know how history would prove my assumption right.

The following morning during breakfast, my pager went off. After reading the message, "Meet me at SRT at nine. Bring team. CO," I looked around at the inquiring faces and said, "No probs. Carry on."

Everyone visibly relaxed and continued eating. As I entered the common room in the quarters, Tag was making coffee, so I said, "Black, no sugar, thanks."

He made the drinks, and we sat down and waited for the rest of the team to arrive. When everyone was back from the break, I said, "All right guys, listen up. My pager went off earlier. It was the boss saying that he wants us all at our building today at zero nine hundred. Now, until then, we've got a few issues to sort out, the first being that when we move to the new building, we're going to need someone in charge of stores. So unless there's any objections, I'm asking Buzz to take that on."

Buzz smiled and said, "Sure boss, what do I have to do?"

Tag answered him. "You'll have a stores room, and you'll be responsible for everything we've got and anything that we'll need. I'll help you as much as I can, and if you have any questions or need something, come and see me, but as far as everyone else

69

is concerned, they'll be coming to you."

"Hey Buzz," Lizard called. "I need a new warmer for my rifle." This started the laughter and everyone jokingly ordered non-existent items.

I let it go on for a while. "Ok, second order of business. Debrief time. Is everyone ok with what we practised?" The debriefing went on for half an hour, and we were all happy with what we'd practised in Queensland but would be happier when we had details that are more exact.

At zero nine hundred, we were at the SRT building when Mark pulled around into the carpark at the back. He joined us out front. "Good, you're all here. Let's go inside."

He led us up the stairs and waited for me to unlock the door. We all trooped in, and he gave us the ten-cent tour. All the furniture was in the allotted rooms, including a large safe in the gunroom and a big TV set in the ready lounge.

After the tour, Mark said, "Everything you wanted is here. All you have to do is sort it out. Even the phone lines are working. How did things go at Canungra?"

I replied, "As good as it could go. We worked up a few scenarios and practised them, but until we have a clearer picture it's only conjecture at this time."

"Fine," he said. "We've got more info for you, so we'll have a full briefing Monday morning at nine. You've got enough to go on for now. Get this place in order. Tiger, come and see me tomorrow at nine in my office. Carry on gentlemen." He left the building.

After he left, I said, "Right. You heard him. We've got until Monday to make this place liveable. So Tag, you take Buzz and Lizard, I'll take Gecko and Dumper, and we'll get our office furniture in place. Wires, JJ, you guys can start moving the benches around in the workroom. Two benches to each section. Comm's, explosives, and long guns, probably place each section against the three sides. Ok, let's get to it."

Having all the guys working at once, my office furniture was in the places I wanted within five minutes, and Tag's was done a couple of minutes after that. I left Tag to organize the placing and the building of the shelving in all the storerooms while I headed to my room to get all the paperwork and files I kept there concerning the day-to-day running of the team. When I returned to our headquarters, I noticed that progress had really been made. I dumped all the stuff I was carrying onto my desk and went for a look to see how things were going.

The first storeroom had been completely finished and setup with all the shelving in place. I found the team in the second storeroom setting up all the shelving and putting the completed shelving into place at Buzz's direction.

Tag came out into the hallway and joined me. "Come and have a look at what I found." I followed him to the third storeroom, and he said, "Have a look behind all the shelving boxes."

I did as he requested and saw a dozen lockers. "Wonderful! This solves a problem I had been thinking about. Have them all moved into the gunroom, six on each side of the room. Put names on them but leave two on each side vacant. Make sure mine is opposite the safe please."

Tag nodded as I continued, "Make shifting these lockers into the gun room the next priority. After lunch, everyone brings all their weapons over. Rifles in the gun rack, combat gear and pistols in the lockers, all the ammo and explosives can be given to Buzz to sort out and put into the safe. You and I will be going over to transport to requisition two rovers as permanent detachment to our team. Anything else?"

"I've figured out that after all the shelving is put together in the store rooms, we'll have a dozen sets leftover. What do we do with them?" he asked.

I laughed and replied, "Have Buzz take two into the gun room, and the rest can go into the workroom. If Buzz needs more in the gunroom, let him sort it out. I'm going back to my office to sort some files and paperwork until lunchtime. I'll see you in the ready room after lunch." He nodded and went back to where the others were working, and I headed to my office.

After lunch, I went back to my room and gathered all my weapons and combat gear, plus a spare work uniform and pair of boots. I took all these to our operations building and sorted them out. After making sure I had all mags full of ammo, I put everything into my locker and my rifle into the rack. I noticed that someone had place nametags on the rifle rack for everyone and thought it was a great idea, considering most of us used the same type of rifle. When Tag arrived and had finished sorting his gear, we headed over to the transport office.

As we walked in, Sgt Phil Simmons, whom I'd played a few games of snooker with in the mess, greeted me. "Hi Tiger. I'll bet you're here to look at your established detachment vehicles."

Tag and I looked at each other, and I turned back to him and replied, "Yes Phil. How did you know about that?"

"Your boss put in a requisition a couple of weeks ago, and I've had them here a week waiting for you to get back."

Seems Mark was one step in front of this. I asked, "What did he requisition for us?"

Phil replied, "Two land rovers, a ten tonner, jumper cables, and an emergency jumper pack and charger fitted to a trolley. Do you have someone that'll be looking after the vehicles, first parading them each day, and looking after the G2's?"

"Yes," I replied.

"Good. You can send him down to see me, and I'll run him through everything. He can sign all the necessary paperwork. Do you want to take any of them with you?"

I nodded my head and said, "Yes, we'd like to take the two rovers."

Phil replied, "Sure no problem. They are both full of fuel. Anytime you need fuel, drive over to the bowsers and fill up, but don't forget to fill in the G2's."

"Thanks Phil and I'll send my man down to you."

We made our way to the vehicle yard, and Phil pointed out two new mark three rovers beside an International ten tonner. "There they are guys. All yours."

After thanking him again, Tag and I jumped into a rover each and left the yard.

After parking the rover, I went to the back door of the building and called for Dumper to join me outside. He came out of the building as Tag pulled up in the second rover. Tag asked, "Dumper, do you have your army licence for trucks?" Dumper nodded that he did, and Tag continued. "How would you like to be in charge of our vehicles?"

"Ok Tag," he replied.

I said, "Good. Now I want you to go down to transport, see Sgt Phil Simmons, and tell him I sent you down. He will get you to sign some paperwork and show you how to maintain the vehicles. You can go down now, and when you come back, drive the truck that is there waiting. You can park it over there." I indicated the park closest to the rear of the building. "When you come back, the charging stuff can go into the workroom for the time being. Away you go." As he left, I told Tag to check on how the work was going and meet me in my office after.

When Tag joined me in my office, he brought in coffee for both of us and took a seat in front of my desk. He reported that the work was just about finished; the boys were just putting together the last three shelves in the workroom.

As I sipped my coffee, I nodded and said, "Good. Tomorrow you need to get together with Buzz and put together a list of gear to get from the Q store. Make sure rope and climbing gear is on the list. We'll need them for the upcoming job, and lay in a good supply of ammo, cam cream, sweat cloth, rat packs, smoke grenades, gun oil and rag, and anything else you can lay your hands on."

He laughed and said, "Don't forget, I learned from the best scrounger around." I joined him in laughter when he winked at me.

"Once the guys are finished, they can knock off for the day. They've done a top job. We have been able to transform this place into ours in just one day. Bloody good, I think."

Tag replied, "I didn't think we'd do it in such a short time. If you want to take off early, I'll wait for Dumper to get back."

I replied, "No, Sharon won't be any earlier, so I'll wait to knock off, but if he's not back by then I'll get you to hang, though."

Soon after we heard the sound of a truck passing by the building, so we both went out to the back door. Sure enough, we saw Dumper reversing into the space I had allocated.

He got out with a smile on his face, and I asked, "Everything go ok?"

"Sure boss, but I was wondering if I could use one of the spare stores rooms as the transport office."

I turned to Tag and said, "Christ! Everyone's getting delusions of grandeur!" I turned back to Dumper with a grin. "You work it out with Buzz, and whatever you work out with him is ok by me."

We all shared in the laughter. Tag and I gave him a hand taking the accessories up the stairs and into the building. By the time we did this, the rest of the team had finished erecting and placing the shelving, so we adjourned to the ready room, which was what we were calling the lounge area.

After looking at my watch, I said, "Fan bloody tastic job today, guys! We have done this in less than a day! I suppose I had better announce that Dumper is now the transport officer for the team, and clap yourselves on the back. We now have an operational HQ! Therefore, everyone gets to knock off early. Thanks and welcome to the operational HQ of SRT. Now piss off and enjoy yourselves. I'll see you here in the morning."

Amid the cheers and jubilation, they started to head to either the mess or the barracks building. After locking up, Dumper joined me for the walk down to the sig's mess. Our girls treated us to cuddles and kisses when they saw us.

When Sharon and I sat down, I filled her in on what had been happening. "Now that we've got our own HQ, you'll be able to come up and visit during working hours if you can get away."

She replied, "I might just do that, and I'll get your office number while I'm there. Are you coming home with me tonight?"

"You better believe it, honey. Hope you're not too tired," I replied with a smile on my face. "Why don't we just stop and order a pizza on the way home. That way we can have an early night."

She agreed, and as we drove home, we stopped at a pizza shop up the road from home. While we were waiting, I asked, "Can I drive my car tomorrow?"

The following morning, I drove my car into the SRT carpark before going to breakfast, and as I was walking back to our building Tag joined me, followed by the rest of the team. As we sat in the ready room having coffees, there was discussion of what to do during the day.

I asked Tag, "How many men do you need to help with your mission today?"

He replied, "Beside Buzz and me, say two more and the truck."

I smiled, knowing that he would try to come back with the truck fully loaded with supplies. "Take Lizard and Gecko. Buzz, I hope you and Dumper have come to an understanding. Dumper, you get what you need and setup the transport office. Wires, JJ, draw up a list of anything you might need for the comm's side of the workroom and see what you can get from the sigs company. Now, you all know that I will be with the boss, so I want someone here in the building at all times. You three staying put, work it out amongst you. Any questions?" The men shook their heads. "Good. Let's get on with it."

We all went our separate ways after our briefing session, if you could call it that, but I had decided a while ago that something as informal as that did the job in most respects.

At nine I was seated across the desk from Mark, and after I had brought him up to date with what we'd been doing, and had a laugh over the transport issue, he said, "I was wondering if you'd thought of that. At least I am still one-step in front of you. Now, to business. How soon can you be ready to deploy?"

I was a little shocked at the question and wondered what had happened that might bring the job forward. "Well, I could have a suitable plan of attack written up within an hour of knowing all the latest intelligence and photo layout. My guys could be ready for a full operational briefing first thing tomorrow. Following that, we could be in the air an hour or two after the briefing. Why?"

Mark replied, "Good. The timeline has moved up. This needs to done ASAP. I'm about to give you all the latest on the target. Your liaison officer will be notified when you leave on the mission and will meet you in Nui Dat. Major Chipson of two squadron will be expecting your arrival and will be appraised of the situation. Quarters and anything you require will be looked after.

Once the mission is completed, you will be at his disposal for any other missions he may need you for until you hear from us here. We will use the same codebooks as last time, and I'll arrange for your transmissions to be forwarded to us as S.O.P's. Here is everything we have so far. Take it with you and let me see what you come up with. Ring me when you have something tangible. He handed over a large manila folder, and I got up and took it with me back to my office.

As I started going over the intelligence reports, what I read astounded me. I looked at the aerial photos and also at some that had obviously been taken at ground level of the complex. The ground shots were brilliant, and no wonder; they'd been taken only a month previously by a patrol from number two squadron. My thoughts went out to the patrol leader, who had probably wondered why they had been ordered to do a recon of the installation, but they had been in the vicinity for a couple of days, as I married up the patrol report with the photos. This was perfect for the job I had to do; the intelligence from our own regiment gave me exactly what I needed, and I knew it was reliable.

As I stated previously, I was astounded at what I read about the complex. Three enemy only manned it at a time, and every three days they were replaced with a fresh contingent. There were two buildings. One was the radio building and the other living quarters. Two generators were on site, and the cabling for the radio building was laid in a pipe that went under the building from the generators. The pipe was level to the ground before going under the building. I thought to myself that this was heaven on a stick. We could obliterate this place easily. I got up and went into the hallway to call for Dumper to join me.

I handed him the photos of the radio tower, both ground and aerial shots, and said, "Take a seat and have a good look. Give me an estimate of how much C4 to blow it, if we bring it down in three sections." I pointed out each section.

He studied the photo for a while. "That would be a little bit of overkill, but maybe forty kilos."

"I was thinking fifty, which would leave us some spare."

He was nodding his head. "That should do it, and with enough left over for surprises, like to blow the buildings."

We both laughed, and I said, "Dumper, I love your way of thinking. Thanks."

After he left my office, I started work on writing up an attack plan, and this was made a hell of a lot easier by having the patrol report from number two sabre squadron, which gave me dates and location coordinates for LUP's and the OP that was used.

As I was finishing the attack plan, Wires knocked on my open door. "You've got a visitor boss." Standing behind him was Sharon, and as he walked off, I signalled for her to come in. I got up and kissed her before she took a seat opposite my desk. She was looking at the photos that were on my desk, where Dumper and I had left them. "Looks like you're busy. What are these?"

"Recon photos of a target," I replied. She looked at me with raised eyebrows, so I quickly continued, "And to what do I owe the pleasure of your company? Which is always nice to have."

She laughed, "Rick (Wires) has been putting some pressure

on my technicians to order some equipment for him that usually only signals staff use, and I needed to find out if it's been properly authorized."

I laughed and asked, "Do you have a list of what he wants?" I pulled out a book of requisition forms from my desk drawer and started filling a form out. "Do you need a counter signature, sweetheart?"

She replied, "No darling, just yours. Then I can go ahead and organise it for you. Probably take a few weeks for it all to arrive, though."

I looked up at her and asked, "Can they be left with you if we're not here and picked up when we come back?"

Her eyebrows went up again as she asked, "Is that likely?"

Knowing I was treading on dangerous ground, I sighed. "Yes, and before you ask, it'll be soon."

"Where, and how soon?"

"O/S. Probably as early as in a few days."

Her eyes started to mist over, so I got up, reached out, and closed the door. As she cried for a couple of minutes, I kissed and cuddled her. After she composed herself and had dried her tears on a tea towel that was on top of the bar fridge where I had my coffee supplies, I made a mental note to get some tissues for my office.

She asked, "So that's what you were working on when I arrived?"

I nodded. "Yep. I've got to give it to the boss as soon as it's finished."

"Ok, I'll get out of your hair. And I'll see you at home tonight, honey."

I nodded and said, "Sure babe." I kissed her goodbye as she picked up the requisition form and left.

I put the finishing touches on the attack plan and rang the boss's office to let him know I was ready to see him. He instructed me to come straight over, so I gathered everything up, but kept one of the copies of the patrol reports for myself, and headed to HQ.

CHAPTER 7

Well the only thing that worries me is the way you get out. If you head for Bao Loc, you may not find a suitable LZ for the extraction. Harass the enemy along the way, yes, but what if you run out of supplies before you find an extraction point?" Mark asked.

I was sitting in Mark's office as we were reviewing the attack plan. "I'll be flying over the area when I do the recce, so I'll look for a reasonable LZ. As you can see, I am only allowing five days after the mission is complete to bug out. If we have to climb into hovering choppers, we do it, but I'll also be leaning on the liaison officer as well, in regard to the extraction."

"Ok Tiger, I'll trust your judgement," he replied with a laugh as he continued. "Remember, it's your operation, but screw that yank for as much as you can get. I am accepting your operational plan. Briefing at zero eight hundred. You'll be leaving before the end of the week."

"Roger that boss," I replied with a smile, and got up to leave.

Back at SRT, everyone had returned from the tasks they had been doing and were sitting in the ready room. I walked in and asked, "So how'd it go guys?"

Everyone was smiling. Buzz answered first. "We grabbed whatever we could, boss. All the storerooms are full. It took us an hour to unload the truck."

I looked at my watch. Christ! I'd been with Mark for nearly two hours, and it was close to knock off time. I looked at Tag, who seemed satisfied with what had been accomplished. "Good. First off, I would like a box of tissues for my office, when you can, Buzz. At zero eight hundred tomorrow, everyone be in the briefing room. The timeline for our mission has been moved up, and we'll be leaving before the end of the week. You know what that means. Get all last minute items together. For now, let's call it a day. I'll see you in the morning. Tag, my office please."

When we were sitting in my office with the door closed, I passed across the patrol report copy I had kept so he could read "it. When he had finished, he said, "Shit! If this hadn't come from our own guys, I wouldn't have believed it. Only three slopes in residence, so what's the plan?"

I explained my attack plan to him. "We go in the same way, use the same LUP and OP. Two days to walk in, two, maybe three observing. Go in, three to four hours on site, blow it, and bug out. Head towards Bao Loc scouting for a suitable LZ, and ambush any enemy that aren't too strong in number along the way. We shouldn't be in the bush for longer than two weeks."

"Fan bloody tastic! This will be so easy. The guys will love it," he said.

"Well, let's not get too cocky just yet."

As I walked into the briefing room the following morning, I could feel the electrifying atmosphere; everyone had coffee mugs, pens and notebooks ready to go, and the guys were chatting excitedly. Wires brought me two coffee mugs as Mark entered the room. Everyone else stood until he'd grabbed a mug and gestured for us to sit. As he took a sip of his coffee and looked around, I started pinning the photos up; there was a blow up of the military map of the area hanging up that I put there the previous day.

When Mark finished his drink, he said, "You're all looking good. It must have been all that hard work the last couple of days." He waited for the laughter to die down before continuing.

"All right, this'll be the final briefing for this operation before the go order, which will come in a day or so after I've arranged transport. All our intelligence on the target has been confirmed by a patrol from number two squadron, so you know it is reliable and is no longer than three weeks old. So give the guys from number two a cheer for that when you get in country. Once you are airborne, I'll be informing General Command that you're on the way, so soon after landing in the Dat, your liaison person from the yanks should join you. When you get back to Nui Dat after the mission, you will be at Major Chipson's disposal until you are recalled or we have another mission for you. Radiomen, same codebooks as last time, but you will have to check with the comm's unit for frequencies. If you have trouble with your 64 sets, as a last resort use the enemy's radio before everything comes down. Tiger will give you the operational attack plan."

He sat down while I delivered the attack briefing, complete with all the position coordinates for the insertion, LUP, and OP. I went through our bug out route and ended with, "I will be flying a recce to find an LZ for our extraction and checking the insertion site as usual. This is a lot easier than our first mission because we'll only be taking fifty kilos of explosives, my own little surprise for Charlie, a couple of ropes, and a few claymores with us beside the usual gear. Any questions?"

Once a couple of questions were answered, Mark stood again. "I'll be letting Tiger know when you'll leave, so no doubt you'll know shortly after that. Let's make it another successful mission, boys, and try to stay safe. Thank you."

We stood as Mark left the room and went to wait in my office. I joined him after I had dismissed the team, and they went to make preparations or continued their normal routine. After we'd talked in my office, Mark wanted to have a look at what we'd done to the building, and while we were in the workroom, I warned him of the requisitions I'd made.

To say he was impressed with what we'd done would have been an understatement. He was beaming and full of congratulatory comments as he left. I had Tag get the team together back in the briefing room. There were a few points I wanted to go over that I hadn't told them during the briefing.

A few minutes later, we were all in the briefing room, and I addressed the guys. "Ok, apart from what you heard earlier, there's just the one thing I need to go over. On the way out, I will need the forward scout to be at least two to three hundred yards in front of the main body. Now that we all have our radios, communication should be just as easy as they were at Canungra. Any ambush we attempt will have to be on the run, so to speak, so the claymores we take along will be placed on the track to the target. The slopes aren't going to look favourably at us after the amount of hell we're going to give them. Any questions?"

Buzz asked, "What if you can't find a useable LZ, boss?"

I laughed and replied, "Well, I don't think we really want to walk all the way to the capital, Bao Loc, so if that's the case we'll have two options. First, I'll put the screws on our yank cousin to get us out somehow, or two, we'll just have to find a secure position to rope climb into the choppers. I don't want to walk all the way, unless you guys want to?" Comments of "not likely" and laughter met this statement. "Now, if I know the boss, he'll be on the blower trying to get our transport arranged, so assume that we'll leave within forty-eight hours. Let's have everything ready to go by knock off time tomorrow, kitbags and all. We'll leave from here so if you want to bring your gear here sometime between now and then, do. That's it for now. Tag, Buzz, I'd like to see you in my office please. You all know what needs to be done, so get to it."

Tag and Buzz followed me to the office, and I gestured for them to take seats as I sat down behind my desk. "Ok, assuming we can get most of what we need from the Q at the Dat, what else do we take from here?"

"I think we should take our own rappelling gear just in case, and what about a set of night goggles for the blow in?" Buzz answered.

"Nah. As you said, he's a blow in. If he doesn't have his own set, tough."

Tag commented, "We'll need our own climbing gear. I doubt if we'd get any over there."

I nodded and replied, "Good point. What about rope?"

Tag answered again. "No, I saw heaps of coils there last time."

"Ok, do you want any extra medical gear?" I asked.

Buzz replied, "No boss. Both kits are full, but we may need spare batteries for the SR10 sets."

"Good point again," I replied. "I'll see Wires or JJ about it. Apart from what we've mentioned, are we good to go?" They both nodded. "Ok, I'll leave you to remind the guys about the night gear, rappelling, and climbing gear. I'll go see Wires about the batteries. After that I'll be gone for half an hour or so, so Tag you're in charge. Not that there is much to do. Just keep an ear out for the phone."

We stood and left my office. Tag went to his own, and Buzz headed to the storeroom. He had acquired a desk and chair, god knows where he got them, but I wasn't about to ask questions. After seeing both JJ and Wires together in the workroom, it was decided to get spares from Buzz and pack them. I hopped into a rover and drove over to the sigs company to see Sharon.

As I walked into their HQ, Sharon saw me and gestured for me to follow her into an empty office. After closing the door, she gave me a long kiss and cuddle. "That was the good, now what's the bad?"

I laughed and replied, "You certainly know me well enough by now, but you also knew we were having the briefing this morning.

Yes, we'll be leaving within a couple of days, so we're on readiness alert after tomorrow night. I'll be going straight home at knock off today, and I may get tomorrow night in as well. I can't tell you for how long, but as I said weeks ago, it'll probably only be a couple of months."

"Ok. I'll be straight home instead of going to the mess this afternoon, just as long as you make me a drink when I get there."

I smiled and replied in my best Clark Gable impersonation, "But of course my dear." She laughed as I continued, switching to Jimmy Stewart. "And I'll get you to drive me to work for the next two days if you don't mind, dear." By this time, she was laughing so much she was crying with laughter, and I joined her in the laughter before giving her a kiss and leaving.

Before going back to SRT, I walked into my room in the barracks and collected my kitbag after making sure it had all the stuff I'd need O/S. I drove back and took my kitbag into my office. There wasn't anything in my in-tray, so I went into the gunroom, gave my combat gear a check, and took everything, including my rifle, into the workroom, where I started stripping my guns for a clean and oiling. I ejected all the rounds from my spare magazines, pulled them apart, and did the same with them. After reassembling the magazines, I reloaded them all and took them back to my locker. After making sure, I had everything squared away and ready, then came the worst part of all: the waiting for the go order.

The following morning, the whole team spent most of the day in the ready room, and the anticipation in the air could be cut with a knife. I decided it was time to teach the guys some of the relaxation techniques that Pep had taught me. An hour later, everyone was either ragging on each other or more relaxed. The tension that had been in the air was now next to zero. Tag had started a game of five hundred with Wires, Lizard, and JJ; I was playing a chess game with Gecko while Buzz and Dumper alternated between watching the game of five hundred and my chess game.

The previous night, Sharon and I had spent the night full of intimate talk and cuddling, and we enjoyed a marathon of love-making in anticipation of my impending departure. When she pressed me on the issue of my departure, I told her that I was more or less expecting not to be home with her the following evening. I had no idea why I had told her that; it was just a feeling I had. My feeling was right.

Just before fifteen hundred, the phone rang in my office. I had swapped places with JJ and was half way through a hand in the five hundred game. I dropped my cards and told Dumper to take over my hand. Mark wanted me to come to HQ immediately. As I grabbed my beret and left the office, I yelled, "I'll be back!"

Having gone straight to HQ, I walked into Mark's office, and as soon as I arrived, he said, "That was quick. There's a shuttle run from Pearce to Tindal tonight, with wheels up at nineteen hundred. It will arrive at zero two hundred India (local time), and a transport to Vung Tau leaves at zero four hundred India. I have your team on both of them. I've also arranged your transport from SRT to Pearce; it'll be there at eighteen fifteen. Sorry for the short notice, Tiger, but it's all I could do to get you there. I hope your team is ready to roll."

I replied with a smile. "Yes sir, they're chomping at the bit."

He held his hand out and we shook. He said, "Good luck, and come back in one piece." I left his office with a beaming smile. Finally, I thought.

As I walked into the ready room, every eye fixed on me. "We're a go! Early dinner tonight, guys. Transport is laid on. We saddle up at eighteen fifteen." Comments of "great, yes, yahoo, and finally," preceded cheers.

I went into my office and rang Sharon. When she answered, I said, "I'll join you for drinks in the mess, darling, but I can't stay too long."

"Oh. It seems your sixth sense was working last night."

"Yep. See you soon."

Dumper came down to the mess in the rover with me because he wanted to say goodbye to Janice. We parted company in the mess; he joined Janice and I went to the table in the corner where Sharon was waiting. She got up and gave me a kiss and cuddle when I joined her with the drinks.

"How long until you leave, honey?"

I looked at my watch and replied, "Two hours before we leave the base to Pearce, and then straight onto a flight."

As she answered, she looked over at Janice and Dumper. "Ok. Umm, I think we'd better go over there and lighten the mood a little with them."

I glanced over at them, nodded my head, sighed, and replied, "Ok."

After another round of drinks and smokes, I glanced at my watch. Sharon saw me look at my watch and looked inquiringly at me. I nodded. She knew it was time for us to go.

"Don't worry about Janice, John; she's coming home with me tonight for some girl time. You and Tom get going. You've got a job to do." She got up and gave Dumper a kiss on the cheek before giving me a kiss and cuddle. Janice was doing the same with Dumper, and as we turned to leave, she said, "Love you, darling. Please take care."

I dropped Dumper at the OR's mess before continuing to the sergeant's mess for an early dinner. Back at the SRT building, I put my combat gear on, with a final check of my pistols and ammo, put my grenade bandolier into my backpack, picked up my kitbag, and took it all out onto the veranda. I saw the rest of the team heading towards the building.

When the two rovers arrived, we were all outside on the veranda, casually talking and smoking. My kitbag and rifle went into the back with Buzz, Wires, and Gecko and I climbed into the front with the driver. Tag's voice came over my radio earpiece. "We're all ready to roll, Tiger."

I told the driver, "Right, let's go."

At Pearce RAAF base, we walked up the ramp of the Hercules transport plane that was taking us on the first stage of the journey. It was warming up, and the crew chief told us to spread out so we would be able to lie down and sleep during the flight if we wished. We had ten minutes before take-off.

We arrived at Tindal Air Base in the Northern Territory with plenty of time to catch our connecting flight. After talking with the operations staff, we were escorted to the crew's mess, and told someone would come get us when it was time for loading. After an enjoyable, relaxed breakfast of ham steaks, scrambled egg, hash browns, and tomatoes and as much coffee as we wanted, we settled down to a game of five hundred before being called for our flight.

Dawn was just tinging the sky as we walked across the tarmac to the Herc warming up as we reached the ramp. The crew chief met us and said over the noise of the engines warming up, "I hear you're going all the way with us, so here's the gen. The first hop is to Butterworth where we'll overnight.

We'll take off the following morning at zero six hundred and arrive in 'Nam at thirteen hundred golf. Feel free to spread out, and I'll show you where the coffee and sandwiches are after we're in the air. Go and make yourselves comfortable." With that, we trooped onto the plane and sorted out places for ourselves.

Two long and boring flights later, we arrived at Vung Tao, where we transferred into a chopper for the flight to Nui Dat. We walked to our HQ from the chopper pads, and I went inside to report our arrival to Major John (Chips) Chipson. He was about six foot, had black hair, and was wearing a starched set of cam fatigues. It did not take me long to work out he was not going to be anywhere as easy going as Trader had been when he was in charge. Chips was a little too much by the book for my liking, so I decided to warn the team to brush up on formal army etiquette. This was only my first impression. The way he came across was that he thought SRT was a waste of time, but he had to go along with orders. I knew I would have to tread carefully.

When the formalities were over, he said, "I know this isn't the first time your team has been here, so I've billeted you in the same tent you were allocated last time. Your liaison, Johnnie, hasn't arrived yet, but he'll be put into your tent when he does get here. Apparently, your mission takes some priority, so you just let me know what you need, and I will take it from there. If there's any report you wish transmitted, have it ready and back here in half an hour. That's when I'll be sending word of your arrival to base HQ. That's all."

I saluted and marched out, and as I left the building, I let out a sigh of relief. "Same tent, guys. Pick up your shit and let's go."

Inside the tent, I was seated at the table coding a report for HQ to go with Chipson's after I'd sorted out my gear near the same bunk I had used over six months ago. My coded message was not overly critical of Chips, but I did state that he might become a stumbling block due to his attitude towards SRT. Once it was complete, I took it up to the HQ, marched in, and saluted Chips. I handed him the message and said, "It's ready to go with your message, sir. Thank you."

"I can't read this," he commented, looking at me.

"That's right, sir. It's already coded."

"All right. I'll make sure it goes. If that's all, you're dismissed."

This second meeting did not do anything to change my opinion of him, but I was rather intrigued with the thought that he had wanted to read what I was sending. I decided to keep my suspicions to myself. Back at the tent, I had a discussion with the team regarding Chipson and his apparent dislike for SRT. Everybody agreed to tread carefully whenever he was around. It was decided that Tag and Buzz would go on the scrounge the next day for supplies we would need, and if they needed a hand to call on anyone else. We were all to use our SR10 sets while on base.

After our informal briefing, we headed to the mess for dinner and relaxed over a few drinks, but most of us were back in the tent by twenty hundred, either playing cards or relaxing on our bunks reading. The radio was tuned to the US station armed forces radio. Every now and again, someone broke into song if a good one was playing. The favourites were any Beach Boys song, House of the Rising Sun by the Animals, Wild Thing by the Troggs, some Donavan songs, and anything by Steppenwolf or Bob Dylan. As far as I was concerned, though, any of the Beatles songs or the Rolling Stones were good.

Half way through the next day, an orderly arrived escorting a Yank Captain. I took a look at him and noticed he was wearing a seal recon patch. He was about five nine, lean, looked fit, and had sandy coloured hair. He put his hand out, and I shook it.

He spoke with a Californian or west coast accent. "Hi, my name is Captain William Fredrick, but most call me Bill. I'm looking for Major Tiger Davis."

I laughed as I replied, "Well hello, Bill. You've found him, but most people call me boss or Sarg. Come on in and we'll talk."

Because I was wearing my radio, everyone knew what was happening, so as we entered the tent the team had formed a line at attention. I nearly burst out laughing at how ridiculous they looked, but I introduced all of them to him.

Just as I finished, I heard Tag in my earphone. "Boss, I need two bodies at the Q."

"Gecko and JJ are on their way." I motioned with my head for them to go.

Bill looked as if I had gone mad until he saw the earphone, and he laughed and said, "I was just wondering what sort of loony bin they'd sent me to until I saw that earpiece. What a top idea. I didn't know you guys had headsets."

I was actually starting to like this yank, and after showing him what bunk area to use, I said, "Ok Bill. We do things a little bit differently than most Aussie units, which are most likely far removed from your army as well, and we're going to go over this shortly."

After he was squared away, we went up to HQ. I asked for a room we could conduct our business in. He checked with Chips. The orderly came back and showed us to an office at the far end of the hall. "The boss said you can use it for the duration." I smiled and thanked him, and he left us to it.

When we were seated, I said, "Ok Bill, the first thing you can do is drop the sir. On my team, we work on a nickname basis, so I'm referred to as Tiger, Sarg, or boss. Rank means bugger all to my team, so if you don't like being told to do something by a lowly private, say so now. By the way, none of my men are privates. They all hold rank".

He started to laugh and asked, "Can we speak freely, sir?"

"I thought I told you to drop the sir routine, and yes you can speak freely. All members of my team do, so if you've got a problem get it out there so it can be fixed, understood?"

"Yes s... Tiger," he replied. "First off, I have to give you these, Tiger." He held out his hand with two oak leaf major pins. I took them and placed them in my pocket. At the same time, I remembered to turn off my radio. He continued. "At first I was apprehensive about this job, but after meeting your band of cutthroats and you, I must say, I'm looking forward to working with you and them. You will no doubt need to know some of my background, so here is a quick version. I'm twenty-two, joined the army at eighteen from ROTC (Reserve Officers Training Corp) at college. Because I'm from Coronado in California where the seals are based, I applied and passed the training. I'm Special Forces trained, but have yet to go on a mission where those skills are needed. That is why I took this job when I was asked, because your people wanted someone Special Forces qualified, and I was the only one nearby. That's it in a nutshell, boss"

I was impressed with his candour and honesty. I definitely liked him, and because of this, I decided I would treat him as an equal. To do that I had to straighten a couple of things out for him. "All right Bill; to start with, I like you so I'm going to give you a crash course in dealing with members of my team. As I said before, we don't hold any store with rank, but give respect where it's due. My guys will respect your rank, but it's up to you to win them over. Also, we live very close to each other and know we can trust each other. That's what you have to achieve with them. They have to be able to trust you. Now, we don't make a thing of rank. We eat and drink with all the other soldiers, no officers' privileges. Go with the flow, and I think you'll be ok.

"Tonight you mix and make friends with them. At the present time, you're considered an upstart yank that'll need nurse-maiding. Show them you're not, but don't take any shit either. Tomorrow, anything we talk about will be done with them in earshot. No secrets, clear?"

With a weak smile on his face, he replied, "Yes boss."

I laughed, slapped him on the shoulder as I got up, and said, "You'll do. Let's get back in there."

Back in the tent, Tag asked him what sort of weapons and gear he had. He took his rifle out of one of the two kitbags he'd brought, and it was the usual M16. Sidearm was an issue forty-five colt, six grenades, ten full spare ammo clips in ammo pouches, four water bottles, combat knife, wet weather poncho and liner.

Tag said, "Righto Bill, here's the rules for what to carry. One spare set of cam fatigues, your poncho, which you'll sleep in, those fifteen ration packs that Buzz will give you, no soap or shaving gear. You'll wear your shirt inside your trousers, and around here, we always carry our weapons. If you haven't already noticed, Wires is going to give you a personal radio and show you how to use it. Silence is the key to our success, so tomorrow after breakfast we'll find a little patch of grass and see how quietly you move. After lunch we'll be having a briefing, ok?"

"Sure Tag. Say, how'd you get that name?" After being told, he commented, "Well I'll be darned." He proceeded to ask each of the others. He almost fell off the seat backward with laughter when Dumper told him his story, and I could see he was slowly relaxing their guard and winning them over with friendship.

CHAPTER 8

L ater in the mess, Bill and I were sitting with some of the sergeants having dinner. After I'd introduced ourselves (some of them already knew me by sight, some by my reputation). When Smacker Harper introduced himself, I asked him if we could have a quiet word and drink later. Smacker had been the patrol leader who wrote the report on our target. He nodded his consent to meet.

After we'd finished eating, Bill joined the rest of the team to buy them some drinks while I found a table away from the noise.

Smacker joined me and said, "Uh oh. You better go rescue your boy. He's about to come to a lot of grief." I looked over and raised my eyes in exasperation. "Get him out of there, Tiger. That's one of my boys, and he's an unarmed combat specialist," Smacker warned.

Bill had bought a round of scotch, and after throwing it down his throat neat, he'd upturned his glass as he put it down, unaware of our Australian custom: an upturned glass was sign of wanting to fight anyone in the bar. A couple of men were about to show him the error of his ways. My guys were around him and Gecko stood in front of him talking to the man Smacker had warned me about.

As I reached them, I heard Gecko. "Oh come on man. He's a yank and he doesn't know the custom. Let it go."

I grabbed Bill by the arm and said to the SAS member, "Besides that, he's an officer. You do not want to face any grief about striking one. I'm Tiger Davis, and I give you my word that he'll apologise for his mistake."

Bill shrugged off my hold on his arm and reached forward with his hand. "I surely will apologise, sir. Please let me buy you a drink. I'm terribly sorry."

I inwardly thanked Bill for saying and doing that, and it diffused the whole affair. They shook hands, and after Bill had paid for the round of drinks, I guided him away to my table with Smacker.

"Well, you've got balls Captain, I'll give you that. He would have made mincemeat of you. It would have been a different story with Tiger, though," Smacker remarked, and I shot him an enquiring look. He explained, "Swifty Lewis is a mate of mine. He and three others couldn't beat you."

I nodded in understanding and corrected him. "Four."

He laughed and said, "Just testing." Bill was looking bewildered by our conversation, so Smacker explained, "Swifty Lewis is the unarmed combat instructor back at home base. He and Tiger went at it, and Tiger beat him and four other instructors at the same time."

After that, Bill looked at me with awe, which made me rather uncomfortable, and while Smacker was away getting a round of drinks for us, I asked him to quit thinking of me as a legend.

He agreed but said, "I had no idea whose exulted company I was in."

I smiled at his praise but countered. "Well, now you know why I'm in charge of such a talented bunch."

When Smacker came back with the drinks, he asked, "What can I do for you Tiger?"

I looked at Bill to explain, "Smacker here wrote the report I showed you earlier."

He looked at Smacker and nodded. "Very fine work."

Smacker looked perplexed. I laughed and said, "That radio station you looked at a few weeks ago. I'm here to blow it to shit."

Smacker laughed. "Well, you've got a cushy job then. Apart from getting in and out, it should be a walk in the park. Now the getting in, I got as close as I could without alerting suspicion, but as you'll have read, I put in the coordinates of where I rappelled in, and there wasn't any opposition nearby. If you use the LUP, it's perfect. We were there for a week, and it's only three hundred yards from where we established the OP. We left the platform in place. It's fifty feet up, so it can't be seen."

I asked, "When you came out, which way did you come? Are there any suitable LZs close by?"

He shook his head. "No, but after that we were tasked to search and destroy, which we did all the way down the mountain. It wasn't until we were near the bottom that I called in an extraction LZ, so there's no quick way if you go the way I went."

I thought this over for a bit. "What if I continue further into Lam Dong and head for Bao Loc?"

After a moment of thought, he said, "You might find an LZ if you do a flyover recce, but it's in US territory." He chuckled. "Hence the yank, good one! Yeah I'd try that way."

"Do you know where or how far away the fresh manning teams came from?"

"No, but it must be quite a distance because they looked fairly worn out when they got there. Also, they were carrying four jerries of fuel, I'd say," he replied. He looked at his watch, saying as he got up, "I hope that's been a help. I'm taking a patrol out in the morning, so I'd better hit the hay. Good luck."

We stood and shook hands, and Bill went to get another round of drinks for the two of us. When he got back, I said, "Well, looks like you and I will be taking a plane ride very soon. Do you think you can get us a flight over to your base at Bien Hoa and a Cessna recce flight?"

"Yes" he said with a nod.

I smiled and said, "Good. We'll work on that in the morning. Right now, I'm going to get some sleep. You can stay if you wish, just don't get too drunk."

He looked at me and replied, "No, I think I'll come with you. It may be safer that way." We laughed as we walked out.

After breakfast the next morning, I had Wires take Bill over to the signals unit to arrange the transport and recce flight for midday. While they were away, Tag and I went into planning mode, after which he led the team out to the area and location we had discussed. It was their job to give Bill a surprise when I took him to the location Tag would use.

Bill and Wires returned half an hour later. The three of us grabbed our rifles. As we did, I noticed Bill wasn't wearing his radio and smiled a wicked grin. I thought, without it, he was in for an even bigger surprise. Oh well he'll learn.

Whilst we were walking towards where I wanted to go, I dropped behind them to light up a smoke. I asked Tag if he was set through my radio. His reply came through: "All set and ready, boss."

Wires turned around and looked at me. He'd heard the conversation in his earpiece, and I gave him a casual shake of the head. He nodded, understanding that I didn't want him to say anything.

When I reached the area, Tags voice came through my earpiece. "You're almost on top of us, boss."

With a smile, I said, "Ok, Bill, how many men can you see?" He looked at me in bewilderment, and I said, "My whole team are in this area, except for Wires and me, so have a good look. Can you see anyone?"

After a few minutes of scanning the area, he said, "I think I see one."

"Ok. Walk over and tap him on the shoulder, but move as silently as you can," I told him. I watched as he moved slowly to the spot he had pointed to. He found nothing, and as he turned toward me and lifted his arms to indicate nothing, Dumper rose up from the ground, grabbed his head, and put the reverse side of his knife at Bill's throat.

I said into my mic, "Everyone stay put, and don't move, Buzz. I'm about to walk over you."

As I reached Dumper and Bill with a smile on my face and laughing, I enquired, "You sure you don't need to change your pants?"

Bill let go with a string of swear words. "I didn't see, hear, or feel him until the kill stroke. God, you guys are good, and you knew it was going to happen."

I stood there with a smile on my face, nodding. "Can you see anyone else?"

"No."

"Okay, stand up, everyone."

Bill's face was a sight to see, and by some of the emotions I saw flash across his face, I assumed he wasn't too pleased with himself. He looked around and said, "Christ! I've seen seals and delta squad members go to ground concealment, but you guys are really something else."

Tag replied, "Well thanks Bill. We'll take that as a compliment. Mind you, you did well in moving silently, a first rate job. What do reckon guys?" Everyone was nodding their agreement and smiling.

While we were standing there, I said, "There you go; you've got the vote of confidence from the team. However, if you had been wearing your radio, you would have heard me talking to the team members. Do I have to say anything more?"

"No I guess not," he replied.

"Ok everyone, let's head back," I ordered. As we walked back, I asked Buzz, "Did you get the ropes, explosives, and detonators from the Q tent?"

"Yes boss and I got a few spare rappelling buckles," he replied.

"Well done. Bloody good work, Buzz."

Wearing full battle gear, Bill and I arrived at the chopper pads just as US air cavalry gunship was touching down. We climbed aboard, and the gunship climbed again and banked in a turn. We put the internal comm's helmets on. The pilot looked around and said, "Welcome aboard, sirs. We'll be at Bien Hoa in fifteen minutes, and your fixed wing is ready for take-off." Bill thanked him and we settled back to enjoy the ride.

Half an hour later, we had transferred into a US Cessna fixed-wing plane that flew slowly and gave us the type of view for observation. We flew over and checked the insertion coordinates, and I voiced my agreement with Smackers assessment to Bill. As we looped around the target towards Bao Loc, I spotted a likely LZ for the extraction and asked Bill to have the pilot swing around for a closer look. We flew over it a couple of times so I could get the coordinates correct, and then circled wide to head back to Bien Hoa.

Back on the ground, we went over to the operations room to see if they could give us any information about the possible LZ at the coordinates. They had used it as an LZ but not recently, but it was reputed to be considered a quiet one without much action any time it had been used. Bill and I agreed this was the one we'd use to get out.

We had a late lunch at the air base before Bill arranged for our chopper back to Nui Dat. The worst thing I found about moving around the air base was that we were always being saluted, due to the fact we were wearing our rank pins. To tell the truth, I found it very disconcerting because, in essence, I was only an NCO, not a proper officer. It was downright tiring on my right arm as well.

When we landed back at the Dat chopper pad, I turned on my radio and called Tag to let him know we were back and were heading to the tent.

"You'd better go to HQ, boss. The major's already sent an orderly down here twice looking for you both."

"Ok, roger that, but when I get back, it's time for a natter, so make sure everyone stays put."

"Roger that, boss," he replied.

I turned to Bill. "You heard that?" He nodded as I continued. "All right, let's go see what stick in the mud Chips wants."

He laughed and said, "Yeah, he is a bit of a sour grape, isn't he?" It was my turn to laugh.

We were ushered into Chipson's office as soon as we arrived. He motioned the orderly to shut the door and for us to take seats at the same time. He leaned back in his chair and said, "Well gentlemen, it seems I owe you both an apology. I am told that your mission is one with one of the highest, top-priority operations that I've had since being here. I can see now why Trader holds you in such high esteem, Davis. Apparently the wires have been singing from Central Command here to General Command in Australia to our base HQ, and on to me, and I've been told in no uncertain terms that I'm not to interfere with this operation in anyway. I'm to make sure it takes place ASAP." He looked at Bill. "Captain Fredrick, there are messages here for you that have to be answered, and one from HQ to you, Davis. I have given instructions to the communications unit that anything being sent by either of you is given highest priority. Is it possible for you to let me know what you're up to?"

As I disclosed the mission target and parameters his face turned white, and he said, "Good god, why didn't you tell me this earlier, Davis?"

"Orders sir," I replied with a shrug.

"I take it you have an attack plan already?"

"Yes sir," I answered. "We've just come back from an aerial recce, mainly to find a quick way out, and we'll be putting the finishing touches to the whole plan as soon as my men and I get together. We will both be transmitting the plan to our respective commands after that, and I will be able to let you know the whole operation plan after it's transmitted to Swanbourne, sir. Then all we have to do is wait for the go."

He considered this for a minute. "I see. All right, don't let me hold you up. Tiger, if you need anything let me know immediately, and I'll make sure you get to see me whenever you need." He nodded. "Gentlemen, can carry on."

"Yes sir," we voiced simultaneously and left his office.

"My god, what brought that about, I wonder," Bill said.

I replied with a smile. "It may have been something I told my boss in a report I sent about him and his attitude after we got here. I'll bet he's had a real kick up the arse over this."

Back at the tent, we gathered around the table as Tag marked the coordinates on our operating map. The LZ was in a direct line between our target and Bao Loc, twelve km's inside the Lam Dong border. We were happy after that because it was perfect. This mission would be like licking ice cream, if it all went to plan.

Then we worked out how long it would probably take us to get to the target area and when our execution window would be. This was done using a calendar and Smacker's patrol report date. Calculating the three-day turnaround of enemy personnel on site, we chose three insertion windows to allow time for sending the windows and getting the go order from HQ.

After that we calculated our time for the operation, moving to our extraction point, and the extraction itself back to the Dat, our time for the mission from go to whoa was sixteen days. We had allowed two days as a buffer for any problems that might arise, and we would use US choppers for the mission.

While I coded a message to be sent to Swanbourne HQ, Tag briefed Bill on the whole attack plan. I did make one change, however, and it involved taking four jumping jack mines. After explaining why, my guys were smiling, and Bill said, "Tiger, you must really hate these commie bastards. That's positively evil."

I replied with a smile, "No, just leaving nothing to chance. Besides I like surprising people." Everyone laughed.

The jumping jacks would be placed on the trail to the complex at irregular scattered intervals. This plus the claymores would really wreak havoc should a large force investigate the explosions as we left the area.

I read the message I was sending to Bill and the team. "Boss, Major Chipson has done a complete turnaround, giving us any and every assistance. Attack plan has been revised to include extraction at LZ (coordinates). All air transport for mission by US gunships, time on ground sixteen days. Dates for window of opportunity are (I listed the dates). Will use closest window when we receive the go ahead. Captain Fredrick asks that a copy of this is forwarded to his HQ. Tiger."

I looked up at a bunch of smiling faces. Bill said, "Thanks for that. I'd better send one off to my HQ as well to request authority for the choppers, so if anyone screws with us I have it in writing."

"Love your thinking, Bill," I replied. "Let me know when you're ready and we'll go up together. Buzz, you know what I want, so go and get them."

Bill said, "Ok, Tiger, I'm ready anytime you are."

We walked up to the communication office together. Chips must have really put a rocket under them; our messages went straight away, no waiting.

Back in the tent, Buzz had returned. "They only had six, so I took the lot."

I smiled. It was two more than I had asked for, but the more the merrier. "Damned good, Buzz. What are those piles on the table?"

"I've sorted everything that we're taking into nine piles, so each man will be carrying roughly the same weight in their packs." The piles had everything we needed: Rat packs, C4 and detonation wiring, claymores, jumping jacks, and rope.

I looked at him with a smile. "Buzz, you're a marvel, don't let anyone say otherwise. You're a damned good store person."

I called everyone together to the table. "Ok, the messages have been sent. All we need now is the go order. Each man takes a pile of gear to go. Buzz has sorted them out so the weight is evenly distributed. Don't forget your night goggles or rappelling buckles."

I turned to Bill as he asked, "You guys got night vision gear? I couldn't get a set of them."

I replied, "Yeah, but they're personal issue, so I'm afraid we don't have any spares to lend you."

He laughed and replied, "That's fine, buddy, and I'll just make sure I've got a set for the next jaunt we take."

I smiled as I continued. "Now, I think we'll have three gunships each time. One will remain as cover. In the first one will be me, Bill, Buzz, Wires, and Gecko. The rest of you in the second. How about it, Bill, can you swing three choppers?"

"Sure enough, boss," he replied.

"Ok, everyone takes a pile and stow it into your combat gear. Then we are ready to go. After that, I don't know about you guys, but I'm ready to hit the feed trough and relax with a couple of drinks. We'll go when everyone's ready."

The next morning Tag, Bill, and the rest of the team, dressed in full combat gear, went out to practise silent movement and patrol drills while I stayed behind to catch up on some paperwork and go over everything again for the attack plan to see if there was anything missed. I did find one error. I forgot that I wasn't dealing with the RAAF, so I'd have to make sure Bill spelled it out to the US pilots that the choppers were to be rigged with drop lines. I'd get pretty pissed off if we arrived at the insertion point without drop lines to rappel down.

At zero eleven hundred, a communications clerk entered the tent with a message for me and one for Bill. After decoding mine, I smiled. We were a go. Also, it was at my discretion which window of opportunity was used and that HQ would be waiting word of the insertion. "Yes!" Now all I had to do was work out when to go. After looking at the calendar, I decided the insertion would be at zero six hundred the day after next.

After I had worked that out, I left the tent and headed to HQ. I sat down in Chips office with the door shut and proceeded to fill him in on the whole mission and attack plan. At least he didn't interrupt me with questions, but waited until I was finished before the questions started. He only had one or two.

After a moment of thought, he said, "Rather unsporting, but damned good. Who came up with this?"

"I did sir, from start to finish," I answered.

He looked at me quizzically. "Bloody good show. We'll have to make sure those intelligence Johnnies don't get a hold of you. So, when is this going to take place?"

"Three US gunships will be picking us up at zero five hundred day after tomorrow, sir, but we'll have messages to send and receive from Bien Hoa before that to make sure everything's perfect," I replied.

"Very well. Again, anything you need let me know. I'll be waiting for the insertion advice. Good luck and good hunting, Tiger. I'll let you get on with it."

As I arrived back at the tent, I saw the team walking up the road. They were all dusty and sweaty and were glad to get into the shade of the tent. I gave Bill his message as they stripped off their field gear.

"Tell me in a minute what it's about," I said. I raised my voice. "Well, how'd it go?"

Tag answered, "We've all decided to call him Wild Bill from now on. He's as ready as he'll ever be."

I started laughing. "That's good news, but I can top it. We're a go! Zero hour is oh four hundred day after tomorrow." That news lifted everyone's spirits. After that there was a lot more laughing and joking.

Bill joined me at the table with his message. "Same news as yours, and I've also got my authority in writing to draw on any US personnel or equipment that I consider necessary to the mission."

"Lovely, because I thought of something while you were out playing around," I said.

He looked at me with raised eyebrows. "Tell me you're joshing. That was damned hard work."

We shared a laugh. "We'll get together in a minute and nut out the request to Bien Hoa. Right now I've got to remind Wires of something."

I walked over to Wires and said softly so no one else could hear, "Don't forget the camera to take interior shots for the Intel boys and the usual of the destruction when we leave."

He smiled and said, "Already packed, and with a new roll of film, boss."

I laughed and said, "Good one, Wires."

I got together with Bill again, who had a pad out to jot things down. As I called Wires over, asking for the frequency of the SR10 sets, Bill wrote it down. I asked Wires, "Do you have the call signs and frequencies for the mission yet?"

"You know me too well, boss. We're SRT1 and here is Sabre base and the frequencies are ..." Bill wrote it all down.

When he'd finished, I said, "Thanks Wires. It's not that I know you, which I do anyway, but it's what I've come to expect from you, knowing you're always on the ball." He left with a smile on his face.

Bill said, "You sure know how to get the best out of your men."

"I just treat them with respect, like I'd like to be treated, and that's the best way to get anyone to do anything for you. We'll nut this message out at lunch," I replied.

He said in the most atrocious Aussie accent I've ever heard, "Righto old sport, no wucking forries." I nearly fell off the bench laughing, while all of the rest started laughing, yelling, and throwing pillows at him.

Tag and I headed to the mess. I told him, "You'd best have a talk with the cook staff and arrange for an early breakfast day after tomorrow. Make it zero four hundred. Most of the guys will be up, so we'll have breakfast before getting our gear on. As long as we're at the pads at five."

He nodded. "Leave it to me. I'll get it sorted."

The lunch that day was supposed to be roast beef, which it was, but I was sure they'd left the hide on it because it was as tough as leather. I could have done with a carving knife to cut it and after the first couple of chews that almost broke my teeth, before I tried the veggies. I eventually gave up in disgust, threw my eating irons onto the plate, and pushed it aside. Bill was enjoying his, so I assumed he had tender cuts of meat. When he had finished, we got down to sorting out the message to send to air operations at Bien Hoa.

I told Bill my requirements in regards to the drop lines and stated that the lead pilot of the flight be given the frequency of our SR10 sets so he could call us as they were approaching the pads for loading. In addition, he could relay a transmission to Sabre base that I would give him prior to our departure from the chopper, which included the frequency. After I gave the go ahead to transmit, the flight was to remain in the vicinity for twenty minutes in case we needed extraction due to enemy activity, as per Australian RAAF SOP's. We required an estimated flying time from the Dat to the insertion point ASAP.

Bill remarked, "That's being pretty school teacher, Tiger, spelling it out like that."

I answered without thinking, "Well, you know how stupid and dumb these yanks can be."

He replied in a heavy drawl, "Ain't it so, pal?"

I instantly knew he was not impressed with what I'd said, so in my best winning manner I smiled a weak smile and tried to mend the wound. I looked him straight in the eye and said, "Oops. I'm really sorry about that, Bill, but I don't include you in that silly statement of mine."

He smiled and said, "That's quite all right, Tiger. Sometimes I think my whole country is full of hillbillies and rednecks. Some of them are such dumbasses."

He laughed when I said, "One day you'll have to explain that to me."

"One day I will, and as you say, no problem," he replied.

The second message I wanted him to send was a request to his HQ for the radio frequencies in use by US soldiers in the area around Bao Loc. Again, this was for contingency purposes only.

After leaving the mess, we went to the communications unit. His request that the messages to be sent happened immediately, and within five minutes, we had confirmation of the messages being received and acted upon. We went back to the tent to relax for the afternoon.

Two hours later a signals clerk entered the tent, and subsequently Bill had the replies to his requests. The first one he passed to me as he read the other one. The request for the frequencies had two listed, one marked P meaning primary, the other marked S as the secondary frequency.

I gave these to Wires. "Keep a note of these just in case we need them."

Bill told me the second message was notification that his request had been approved and was being scheduled, and that the flight time to the coordinates given from Nui Dat would be approximately fifty minutes. I realised that we would need to send them a second request for the same flight to be on standby for our extraction. So we went back to the communication unit and sent the second request, giving the coordinates for the LZ. Again, we received confirmation within five minutes.

CHAPTER 9

The next day we relaxed as much as we could. At zero ten hundred, Bill received another message stating that the extraction flight was approved and scheduled. In the message was the radio frequency for direct access to air operations at Bien Hoa should we wish to amend the extraction coordinates or change when we required the extraction. Flying time to the LZ would be fifty-five minutes from Bien Hoa. He passed the message to Wires so he could copy the frequency into his book.

I woke at zero three thirty the next morning. Dumper put a coffee on the table for me, and while we had a quiet conversation, the others woke in drips and drabs, until everyone was awake by zero three forty-five. At four, we went over to the mess. For once, the cooks had excelled themselves, and we ate a hearty breakfast of toast, scrambled eggs, bacon, tomato, and hash browns.

As we walked back from breakfast, I told Bill he could give the order to get ready. Inside the tent, he said, "Gentlemen, it's a privilege to be going on this mission with you. Let's lock and load!"

I laughed and said, "Ok, Wild Bill, don't get too carried away." Everyone had a laugh.

We went about strapping on guns and getting our combat webbing on as well as our backpacks. Buzz passed around the cam cream after he had applied his, and at a quarter to five we closed the tent and silently moved towards the chopper pads.

The earpiece crackled in my ear. "Delta X-ray 79 to SRT1 over. Do you read, SRT1?"

I answered "SRT1 to Delta X-ray 79. Copy you loud and clear, over."

The reply came immediately. "Delta x-ray to SRT1. Captain

John Calhoun at your service, sir. We're two minutes out, over."

I replied with instructions. "SRT to Delta x-ray. Good Morning John. Keep one bird in the air and land two. Once landed we'll load in less than a minute."

"Delta x-ray to SRT. Roger wilco number one will be in front. Number two will land behind and to the left. SRT, over."

"SRT to Delta x-ray. Roger that John. We'll be waiting."

I motioned for Tag to lead his group to the left on the pads, and we held onto our hats as the downdraft from the rotors started. Less than a minute later, we were strapped in and both choppers were rising.

I put on the communication headset and said hello to John. "You know where we're headed. Is flight time still fifty minutes?"

His accent reminded me of Texas as he answered, "Surely is, sir." He turned around to look at me and give me the thumbs up signal. I nodded in reply, then sat back and shut my eyes.

I woke as soon as I heard John's voice over the intercom. "Hey fellas. Ten minutes out. Clear your guns and get ready."

As the gunners let loose with a couple of bursts each, the others opened their eyes. I held up my hands to let them know how long to go. The sky had lightened considerably while I had been snoozing; it was almost full daylight. I knew it would be a different scenario under the jungle canopy on the ground.

I said into the intercom, "John, I'm going to give you what I need you to transmit to our base. When I give you the go ahead to bug out, I've written the frequency on it for you." He looked around and stretched out his left arm; I placed the message into his palm, and he gave me the thumbs up.

A couple of minutes later his voice came over the intercom. "Just coming up on it now, sir. What do you think?"

I looked through the windscreen and out the side. "Seems ok John. Do a loop around it, and then we'll go for the drop."

"You're the boss, sir," he said.

"Drop the sir. Make it Tiger."

He turned to look at me with a smile. "Wilco Tiger. You take care down there." I smiled and gave him the thumbs up as I heard him saying to the crew, "Ok guys, get ready to drop the lines."

I took off the intercom set, put my bush hat on, got the first line threaded through my rappelling buckle, and got out onto the skid. Buzz was beside me on the skid, and Wires, Gecko, and Bill were out on the skid on the other side.

I felt a tap on my shoulder and started the descent. As my feet touched down, I slipped the rope from my buckle and saw that everyone was down.

I said into the radio, "Ok, loose circle a few yards out to cover Tag's group."

I looked up; John's chopper moved off as the lines were pulled up. A minute later, everyone was on the ground and standing to as the gunships moved away. We waited five minutes, without any movement.

"Lizard, you're first. Take the point."

"Roger boss." He started moving forward.

I said into my mic, "SRT1 to Delta X-ray 79. Do you read, John? Over."

His voice came back, "Delta X-ray 79 to SRT1. Reading you, Tiger."

"SRT to Delta X-ray. Quiet as a church down here. Have a good trip home. You can head off now."

"Delta X-ray to SRT. Wilco. You be safe people. Over and out".

The message I'd given to John to send to base read: "SRT1 to Sabre base. Insertion successful. No opposition encountered. Proceeding with mission. Will establish contact at scheduled time. SRT1 out." I was very pleased I didn't have to make any amendments to what I'd coded the day before.

We started moving in the direction that Lizard, as scout, had taken. We were approximately three hundred yards behind him. The going was tough due to the dense growth, but it also meant that our chance of coming upon any enemy was minimal. We were moving silently and any noise we made, blended with the background sounds of the jungle.

Dumper was in the lead when I said into my mic, "Dumper, find a spot for an LUP and we'll have a lunch break."

All our walking had been on an ever-increasing incline as we climbed the mountain range, and it showed no signs of levelling off yet. We stopped to brew up and have something to eat, and we all showed signs of the hard slog with red-tinged faces from hard exertion and sweaty shirts due to the high humidity.

About sixteen thirty, I started to look for an LUP area. While I was doing the scouting, the going had gotten easier over the last couple of hours.

We were on top of the ridgeline now. I found a good spot and let the others know I would be waiting for them to catch up. We established the LUP by leaving our backpacks where we would eat and sleep before standing to.

As the light finally turned the full black of night, I called a halt to the stand to, and we went to the LUP to settle for the night. While water was heating on the little hexamine tablet stove that was in each rat pack, I worked out our position on the map. We'd come two thirds of the way to the LUP coordinates, which was good going, but mainly because I had insisted on a fast pace that in the end would pay dividends.

I passed the position info on to JJ, who was setting up the 64 set to keep the twenty hundred radio sked. I also told him to pass on the info about finding no opposition at either the insertion point or along the route we were taking. After having a warm coffee to wash down the tin of cold ham, eggs, and hard tack biscuits I ate for dinner, I walked a short way off for a slash and settled down for the night.

I woke at zero four hundred and roused everyone for stand to. At zero six thirty, it was full light, and we went back to the LUP for breakfast, over which JJ told me that the radio reception the previous night had been scratchy at best. If we were close to the radio tower that night, we should get better reception as the signal would bounce from the radio tower.

I nodded and said, "Ok keep me informed tonight." He nodded, and we cleaned up the LUP and moved off with Buzz in the lead.

We reached Smacker's LUP just before midday, and it was perfect, a small depression about thirty foot in diameter.

After leaving our backpacks, we headed to the OP coordinates and found it two hundred and seventy yards from the LUP. Gecko climbed up, and after reporting the climbing rope was still there, he let it drop to the ground.

Tag tested it and said, "Still in good condition."

I nodded and asked, "How far to the camp Gecko?"

"I've got a good view here, boss. Good coverage all around. We're thirty yards from clear ground and fifty from the camp."

"Ok. Usual OP SOPs each two hours. Who's going to be first?"

Gecko replied in my ear, "I'm already up here, boss, so I may as well take it."

"Ok thanks Gecko. We'll head back to the LUP," I replied.

Back at the LUP, I went to my pack and retrieved a pack of cards. "Ok, first red jack is next." We sat on the ground, and the order came up as Buzz, Bill, Wires, Lizard, Dumper, Tag, JJ, and me then back, to Gecko. I said, "Right, let's get the house in order and then rest up. If we have a small fire for cooking and water, it shouldn't be seen. Make it a deep pit all the same. Bill, set your gear near mine, and I'll brief you on what to do at the OP. Ok guys, get it done."

I woke, grabbed my rifle, and was moving fast all at the same time. As Buzz's voice came through the radio. "Boss, OP now. Quickly."

I was up in the OP in just under a minute. Buzz stated, "I saw them coming down the track a minute ago."

I swung the binoculars onto the arriving group of three enemy soldiers, my mind racing. If this is the relief, they weren't due until tomorrow. They were sauntering along the track without a care in the world, definitely not on the alert. Two were carrying their AK47's slung on their shoulders, while the third was carrying his in right hand by the barrel, letting the rest of it hang down. A pole with four jerry cans, two front and two back, rested on his left shoulder. I thought to myself, Sloppy, and they look tired and don't show any fear of enemy soldiers around. Probably think there is no one nearby. Fools.

As we continued watching, two of the three in residence met them. The third waved from the doorway of the radio hut. I also noted that one of the new arrivals was a woman and had to look twice to make sure. Then as this was my first close look at the target, I took in as much as I could and thought those huts had been built properly and to last, not like the usual village dwellings. They had to go as well. It would be a very time consuming effort if they rebuilt this place after we destroyed it, but my main thought was that we now had six personnel to deal with. That should not be a problem; my mind was ticking over the best way to deal with the attack.

While I there with Buzz, his two-hour stint was up, and Bill had come up to the platform because it was time to relieve him. After he had filled Bill in on what was taking place, I said, "When I come to relieve you, I'll bring everyone and we'll have the stand to here."

Bill nodded and gave me the thumbs up with a smile. I smiled back, gave him a tap on the shoulder, and Buzz and I returned to the LUP.

When we returned, I told the others what had transpired and that the stand to would take place at the OP. I went to rest after a cup of coffee and a few bites of the chocolate block from the rat pack. Before I knew it, it was time to take my shift at the OP and for the stand to.

As we moved to the OP, I said to JJ, "You'll have to do the sked tonight. Just pass on that we are at the LUP and the OP is established. Once you get a confirmation, try to pick up anything from the target so we have an idea what it's used for." He nodded.

We arrived at the OP. Tag organized the stand to while I climbed into position on the platform.

While I was up there, I gave thought to how we could stage the attack, which would require everyone to be involved in the stand to. The advance party entered under the cover of dark and took up position under the radio building. After the stand to, Wires elected to stay with me because his shift was next and not very far away. Soon after I was back at the LUP enjoying a warm can of braised beef and veg, a stick of cheese with a biscuit, and a coffee and smoke.

As Dumper returned from his shift, JJ came over and whispered, "I've been listening and got the frequency, boss, but they don't seem to be transmitting too much. Just passing Intel and messages backwards and forwards."

"Ok. Get some sleep, but leave the set unpacked. Both you and Wires can listen in every now and again to see if anything changes," I replied.

As we rose for stand to, I spoke into my mic and asked Buzz if there was any movement around the area.

"NTR boss."

"Roger that. I'm going to cancel stand to. Your relief will be there on time."

"Roger that," he answered.

The rest of the team settled back down again, except Bill, who was on duty next. He put fresh wood on the fire and started boiling water for coffee, and as we drank, the daylight started to filter through the canopy of trees.

Shortly afterward, he grabbed a bar of chocolate from his rat pack and his rifle. He threw me a salute and headed toward the OP.

Soon after Buzz came back, and after having something to eat and some coffee, he lay on his poncho and went to sleep. Slowly the boys started to wake and prepare food and coffee. I opened a can of ham and egg, warmed it up, and had another coffee, before grabbing my rifle and heading to the OP for my shift.

As I climbed onto the platform, Bill said, "They got up half an hour ago. Two of them are in the radio hut, and the rest seem like they're having chow", "Ok, go and grab some shut eye, but before you do ask Wires or JJ to see if there's much traffic on their frequency". "Roger that" he replied, and then left. Nothing much of any consequent happened, until about half way through my shift.

There was a stir in the camp; three of the enemy came out of the second hut. One of them was carrying the pole, and as I followed his progress, I saw him stop at a thicket of trees that hadn't been cut down. He came out again and put two jerry cans near the stick, then came out a second time with two more. After standing them up, he threaded the pole through the handles. By the ease with which he moved the cans around, I assumed they were empty. I'd found the location of the generator.

He joined the others, and the fourth one came out of the hut. Another from the radio hut joined them. The other one in the radio hut stood by the door and watched as they started to leave the camp area, leaving the two just down from the radio hut. The ones staying were laughing and waving goodbye.

I thought to myself with a kind of pity; enjoy your day, because by this time tomorrow, you will be dead.

After all was quiet again, Wires took over. He told me the only thing that had been picked up was a bit of movement's traffic, so they weren't playing or transmitting any music, which would be handy.

"Good. The three that came in yesterday are still here, but the first lot left the camp about an hour ago. We'll take them in the am. I'll fill you in later," I replied as I left him to it.

Back at the LUP, I held a council of war. Wires was able to hear what was going on via his earpiece as I laid out the attack. When we stood to in the morning, Wires and I would move into the camp and hide ourselves under the radio hut. Lizard and Gecko would be our cover, but one would keep watch on the camp while the other watched the trail. Gecko was to kill the third one before

Wires and I took the other two in the radio hut. As we entered the radio hut, Bill would lead the rest on a sweep of the entire camp. Once everyone was dead and the sweep complete, we would meet at the radio hut. Tag and Dumper were to rig the tower for blowing while Buzz, Bill and I took care of the generators and smashed the electrical boxes. Wires and JJ were to gather all documentation, codebooks, personal papers, and whatever else they could find before smashing the radios in time for Dumper and Tag to rig both huts to be blown at the same time as the tower.

"Unfortunately, that means we've got a bit of to work to do today, which involves laying the claymores and mines. When we do this, both Gecko and Lizard will be at the OP. Everyone else will be with Dumper or me as cover guards. In the morning when we go in, rifles are to be left at the OP. Only silenced pistols are to be used. During today's sojourn, have your rifles, but if we meet any opposition, try to take them out with silent weapons. Everyone clear?"

Wires voice came into my ear, "Roger boss." The rest in the LUP nodded in agreement, and I said, "Ok, we move in two hours."

Luckily, the track got narrower further away from the camp. Placing the claymores was the tricky part because we had to find areas where the trip wire would go across the track and lay the wire very close to the ground before sprinkling dirt over the top of them. Luckily, the slopes had a habit of shuffling when they walked. The jumping jacks also had to be buried and made to look as if the track was undisturbed. Finally, when we were finished laying them, we had a killing ground nearly five hundred yards long with claymores interspersed with mines, enough to give anyone a headache getting through it. We did it all in broad daylight, with no enemy discovering us.

When we had finished, we moved back to the OP. Dumper resumed the watch roster as the rest of us went back to the LUP for a brew up and something to eat. I coded two messages from the blue book, the first to go with that night's transmission to base; the second to be sent when we were out of the area with the following night's transmission. The first one stated that I would attack the complex in the early morning, and the second stated that the target was obliterated with three enemy dead, with intact codebooks and papers seized.

I gave the first one to Wires, who wrote down what I wanted sent to base that night along with the blue code. He or JJ would code up the normal message from the red book. Then I got some sleep.

When I woke, Bill caught up with me and asked, "Hey boss, why am I not going in the radio hut with you?"

"Bill, to be brutally honest, I need my own men on this because we have to kill without hesitation, and I can rely on them to do just that. The reason being is that one of those three is a woman, and the look on your face just told me you'd hesitate."

The last comment made as his face drain of all colour. He thought about it and answered, "Thank you for being honest. You are right even though I don't like it. You would be better off using your own men, and in your place I'd probably do the same, Thanks for explaining, Tiger."

I walked over to Gecko and Lizard and sat down with them. I had some last minute changes after I recalled what I had seen in the camp that morning. "If things change a bit in the morning, I'll expect you two to be on your toes. Gecko, your priority is the last person in the second hut. They have to go first. Lizard, I don't think we'll have company, so you keep an eye on things too. If there is two near that hut, you take out the other one, but let Gecko make his shot first. Remember, they have to be instantaneous so head shots."

"Roger, boss."

Next, I moved to Wires and JJ. "Now, remember, you guys are responsible for getting all the documentation, even code books and papers from the dead. What about the transmissions we have been getting? Are they being recorded?"

JJ answered. "Sure are, boss, on a vox recorder I rigged a while ago."

"Good," I replied and as I got up and motioned Wires to join me. I moved toward the fire and asked, "Who's doing the sked tonight?"

"I am boss," he replied.

"Good. You know the routine with putting the blue code in with the normal one. Teach JJ how to do it. A word of warning: one of the three in there is a woman, but the result has to be the same. Instant death."

"Roger that, boss," he replied as he poured a coffee for both of us.

I sipped the coffee, and then said, "One more thing. What's a vox recorder?"

He laughed. "Like our radio mic's, boss." I nodded my understanding.

I woke at zero three thirty, grabbed my night goggles, and went about rousing everyone. After a quick breakfast, we moved towards the OP. Wires and I were wearing our night goggles, and I let Tag know we were on the way to him. As Gecko and Lizard went up to the platform with their silenced rifles, I took off my grenade bandolier and placed it with my rifle. Wires put his rifle beside mine.

We led the team toward the camp; they fanned out line abreast just inside the edge of the foliage as Wires and I stealthily made our way into the camp and to the radio hut. Under it we found a good spot where I thought we would not be seen, and to check, I whispered to Gecko, "Can you see where we are Gecko?"

"No boss," came the reply.

I looked at Wires and nodded. "Good. Now we settle down and wait."

My doze was cut off as Gecko spoke over the mic. "Boss, I got movement. One heading toward your hut."

"Roger," I whispered.

Just as well, Wires and I had taken our night vision gear off; the sudden blast of light coming through the floor would have blinded us for a minute otherwise. We heard the hum of the radios being switched on and warming up.

I whispered, "How long before full light?"

Tag answered. "About half an hour."

"Ok, let me know when it is," I whispered back.

"Roger that."

Soon after, Gecko informed, "Boss, one coming toward you. Wait, we've got both targets."

"You know what to do. Take 'em," I replied, and as I saw one fall, I heard "Both down." I slithered out from under the hut and boldly walked up the steps with my forty-five out. I saw that Wires had got out from under as well.

I heard a female voice speaking Vietnamese. "What took you so long?" She was sitting ninety degrees on to me as I shot her in the side of the head.

"Down inside. Bill, do your thing. Dumper, bring the backpacks." I stuck my gun into my webbing belt.

The previous night we'd transferred all the C4 and detonator wiring into one backpack and the bag of nitrate and a claymore I'd kept into another. A third remained empty, and all three packs had come with Dumper.

Wires joined me in the radio room and handed me my goggles, then went to the second hut searching the bodies and hut for paperwork. I walked outside. Wild Bill's group had completed the sweep and joined us at the radio hut. JJ moved into the radio room with the empty backpack.

"Ok, you all know what to do. Let's get it done. You two out there, nice shooting. Keep a sharp watch out. We'll be here for a while," I ordered.

Gecko replied, "Thanks and roger, boss."

Tag and Dumper had headed to the tower, and Bill and Buzz came with me as I headed for the thicket where I hoped the generators were located. Two twelve cylinder diesels sat where I had expected, and the wiring control boxes sat on the end of each motor. I nearly laughed as Buzz picked up the tool for removing the injectors from on top of one of the control boxes. He started removing them for me, and I asked Bill to find any container that wouldn't leak. I took out the nitrate bag, and Bill returned with a beat up old saucepan. I had him pour some diesel into it from one of the jerries, and then I mixed up my surprise package. I slowly poured the first batch of mix into the squeeze bottle, screwed the spout on, and showed Bill how to put two squeezes of mix into the cylinders while I brewed the next batch.

After an hour, the booby trap was set. Buzz was doing up the injectors while I pulled my knife out and cut all the electrical leads. Bill and I then smashed the control boxes with a sledge hammer from beside one of the motors. We only had to set the claymore and trip wire as my first surprise.

When we returned to the radio hut, Tag and Dumper were rigging the second hut and moving toward the radio hut. When he was in earshot, Tag said, "We left the rope hanging in the tower. Why bother carting it back with us?"

We all laughed as I said, "Why, indeed?"

As Dumper and Tag started work on the radio hut, Wires came out and called, "We're all finished inside boss. Got everything and smashed the radios."

Soon after Tag and Dumper started playing out the firing lead, taking it all the way to the fringing scrub. I ordered everyone to grab their gear. Back at the OP, Wild Bill, who'd brought all his gear to the OP, volunteered to stay and keep watch while the rest of us went to the LUP to eat, clean-up, and break camp.

Back at the OP, I ordered Bill down and said, "Get your gear on and we'll all go watch the bang."

When we got to the firing charge, I said, "Ok, Wires, go take your before shots."

Dumper prepared and wired the charge trigger and returned.

"All yours, boss."

"Technically this is a US mission, so Wild Bill, you get the honours."

Everyone was smiling as Bill put his hands on the trigger, and as he twisted the handle, he said, "Fire in the hole." The ground shook, and there was a deafening boom. Pieces of wood flew through the foliage overhead.

"Ok, go take the after shots," I told Wires after the aftershocks had settled. When he returned with a huge grin on his face, I said, "All right, that was pretty noisy. Saddle up and let's get the hell out of here before company arrives. Tag, you have the bearing. Take point and let's go."

CHAPTER 10

After walking most of the day, I told Buzz, who was on scout, to start looking for an LUP. We hadn't encountered or seen any opposition, nor in the early part of the day did we hear any explosions. We would have heard any from the claymore or mines, so there was an air of joviality as we marched along.

Buzz came through on the radio fifteen minutes later. "Found a good one, boss, and will be waiting."

That night, I was doing a mental debrief, after bringing my mission diary up to date and realised that by insisting on the heavy slog the first day of the mission we'd have never been in position to see the changeover at the target site. That first day's slog had earned us four days in front of scheduled time in the field. Not a bad return for the extra effort. Plus, we wouldn't have to hurry to make the extraction rendezvous; we could pace ourselves and look out for suitable enemy targets to attack.

The further northward we moved the less dense the jungle became, and if we moved along at our normal pace, we'd have more time for search and destroy targets.

We didn't have too much luck finding a target over the next couple of days, but about mid-morning on the third day away from our mission target, we heard gunfire in the distance and decided to investigate. It didn't take long to get close to the gunfire, and once we were closer, we were able to determine that a firefight was taking place.

Lizard moved ahead and climbed a tree. He wanted to see what was taking place and reported his findings. "Boss, there's a firefight going on. It looks like a yank patrol has been ambushed by the slopes. Wait one. Yep, a yank patrol numbering twelve men are pinned down by fourteen, make that fifteen VC. We could get around behind them and take them out."

I did some quick thinking; we'd have surprise on our side and it would be easy to get in behind the VC, but we'd be facing unfriendly and friendly fire. No, we'd be able to prevent that.

I asked Lizard, "Is it possible to get within a hundred feet of the VC without them seeing us?"

"Yes boss, but if Gecko was in another tree, we could certainly guarantee that wouldn't happen. If anyone turned, we could take them out."

"Wait one," I replied. I thought it over for a moment and said, "Lizard, guide Gecko to a suitable tree. The rest of you huddle up." Lizard guided Gecko to a tree, which he climbed and reported that they both had a clear line of sight.

I asked Wires to get his frequency book out and told him to look for the Lam Dong Frequencies. "Can you get one of our sets onto the frequency?"

He replied, "Sure boss. Channel four is the same frequency."

I turned to Wild Bill and said, "Bill, put your radio onto channel four. Here's what we're going to do guys. We'll move in behind the slopes as close as we can get, then Wild Bill will radio the yanks to train their return fire skyward. Bill's a yank, so they'll take more notice of his voice than any of ours. Then what we'll do, when I give the word, is stand up and walk forward, guns blazing. Gecko, you start taking out the left flank, Lizard you the right. Bill, I don't care what you say as long as we don't walk into friendly fire."

With a smile, he replied, "Copy that boss."

"Ok guys, get into position. You guys up top guide us in. Let's move."

We moved silently into position behind the slopes, guided by Lizard and Gecko. If anyone of them had turned while we moved in close behind them, that would have been end game, but it didn't happen. I nodded to Bill, and he started talking into his mic; a couple of minutes later, he gave me the thumbs up.

The fire from the yank patrol continued but ceased whizzing by. I said, "Right. Stand up. In line advance, fire and give them hell!"

By the time the VC realised what was happening, over half of them were dead, and the rest followed soon after. Bill yelled to the yank patrol, "Cease fire!" as we advanced on the VC and made sure they were dead.

I called, "Lizard, Gecko, come on down. The rest of you start gathering the papers. You know the drill."

Wild Bill and I stood in the space between both forces, and the patrol started to stand up. Their officer came forward to introduce himself and shake hands.

He was a young fresh faced lieutenant no more than nineteen or twenty with pimples on his face. His name was Chuck Brody, and this had been his first patrol since arriving in the country two weeks ago. As I listened to him, my eyes went skyward in exasperation. I looked around for his sergeant, who was nursing a shoulder wound, and went over to talk to him while Bill sorted out the young shave tail.

In the aftermath of the firefight, Tag and Buzz gave the yank medic a hand with the wounded, which numbered four, but all wounds were non-life threatening. A couple were only superficial. While the sergeant, Jake Rhobards, was being attended to, he told me the story of the ambush.

The salient point being that after seeing Brody's map, Rhobards didn't think they should have been anywhere near here, and he thanked me for coming along when we did. Brody's plan to break the deadlock was a frontal assault. In my exasperation at this piece of news, I exclaimed, "What! He'd have got you all killed!"

Rhobards agreed with me. "Don't I know it?"

Bill had heard my exclamation and moved over toward me. "What did you find out?" We moved off where we could not be heard, and I covered my mic with my hand and told him what I'd found out.

When I finished, he exclaimed, "Shit!" He turned and yelled, "Brody, get over here!" When he walked over, Bill extended his hand. "Show me your map."

"Yes sir." He moved to salute him before handing the map over.

Bill yelled at him, "Don't salute me, you frigging fool!"

He passed the map to me, and I compared it to mine. Sure enough, he had been following the wrong line. He was five kilometres away from where he should have been. I asked him where his base was, and he pointed to it on the map. I worked out a bearing to take him straight to his base.

Meanwhile, Bill had asked for his patrol diary and had started writing in it. Bill said with a smile at me, "Go ahead, Major, let him have it."

I gave him his map back, telling him to hold it, and then showed him where he actually was and told him how far he was from where he thought he was. I told him to listen to his sergeant, a man who knew what he was doing. Brody's face went red. Bill called out for Rhobards, who joined the group. Dumper came over with coffee.

As we drank, Bill said, "Sergeant Rhobards, my name is Captain Bill Fredrick of the 2ND Western Pioneers Company, and this is Major Tiger Davis of the Australian SAS. I want you to hear what I have to say to Lieutenant Brody so there will be no misunderstanding."

Bill finished his coffee, faced Brody, and said, "Lieutenant Brody, under the authority of the General Command, I'm cancelling your patrol and am ordering your patrol to return to base by the shortest direct route. Once there, you'll explain your presence to your CO and write a true and accurate account of your patrol, listing your incorrect map reading which resulted in this engagement. You may also mention that your life, and the lives of everyone in your patrol, are owed to this Aussie SAS SRT team led by Major Davis. A copy of your report is to be sent to my office. I've told you where to send it. Major Davis has written the bearing you require to return to base on your map. Once your needs are taken care of, you can prepare to move out."

Brody's face had lost its colour entirely, and he looked like he wanted the earth to swallow him up. He replied, "Yes Sir!"

I looked at Rhobards. "Good luck, Jake."

"Thank you, sir." He turned and strode off after Brody.

I looked at Bill after they were out of earshot. "Christ, you almost gave me a heart attack when you started throwing all that rank around."

He laughed and said, "Had to do it that way or he'd either get himself killed, or worse, his entire patrol. I'll bet his CO has him map reading for the next month, which'll do him good. He'll be out of harm's way for a while, hopefully learning."

Before moving back to our route we had a food break, and I wrote up an account of the engagement in my patrol diary. Back on our route, we continued looking for targets, but they were few and far between. We had to make do with a leisurely walk in the dark green.

We located the LZ in the early afternoon, a day after the ambush engagement. After checking the LZ for suitability, we went looking for an LUP and found a good place only two hundred yards from the LZ. We were four days ahead of schedule, and after some thought, I decided not to hang around. I had JJ break out the 64set, change the frequency to the Bien Hoa operations office, and request extraction at zero nine hundred the following morning at the cold LZ. We'd use green smoke. We received word that the request was approved, and the Delta X-ray flight would arrive at zero nine hundred.

That night during the radio sked, base was informed we would be arriving before midday next.

Everything went to plan. As I heard the choppers, I said into my mic, "SRT1 to Delta X-ray 79, do you read, John? Over."

I heard John's reply clearly. "Delta X-ray 79 to SRT1. Tiger, throw your smoke. We're a minute out."

I nodded and Tag threw the green smoke grenade. "SRT to

Delta x-ray, you should be able to see the smoke. Same routine, John."

"Wilco, first one coming in."

As he touched down, my group scrambled in, and he lifted off to be replaced by the second chopper. Once it lifted off, the flight circled and headed to Nui Dat. I heard John on the intercom. "Welcome abroad Long John's flights to paradise. We must apologise if there is any delay on service; however, the flight attendant was thrown out the window. Our flying time to the beautiful paradise of Nui Dat will be approximately fifty minutes, so please make sure your seat trays are fastened, sit back, and enjoy the flight. Bbbbbb, that's all folks."

We arrived on the pads at zero ten hundred, and after thanking John for the ride, I led the men down to our tent where we got out of our combat gear, guns and lay on our bunks for a while. No sooner had I stretched out on my bunk, then an orderly arrived with a message that the major would like to see me and Captain Fredrick in his office ASAP.

I groaned as I got off my bunk. "Come on, Wild Bill. That means now."

We followed the orderly back to HQ, and he took us directly to Chipson's office. Chips said, "Welcome back gentlemen. Take a seat. Congratulations on a job well done. It's good to have you back."

"Thank you, sir," we said simultaneously.

"Normally this would be done straight away, but because of the interest shown in your mission, the debriefing won't start until the day after tomorrow and could take several days, I'm afraid. Take the time to write the mission reports from you and your men. Now is there anything else I can do for you?"

I replied, "Yes sir. We need the photo lab to do a rush job on a roll of film, and a typist that speaks the Northern Vietnamese dialect and can type from a tape."

"The photo lab will be notified, and I'll also instruct the comm's unit to give you all the assistance necessary."

"Thank you, sir," I replied.

"Good then. Don't let me hold you up then." We got up and walked out.

Back at the tent, I told the team the good news. There were plenty of groans and complaining that went along with that news. I told Wires to get the roll developed at the photo lab, three copies of the prints and get the negatives back, and then told JJ to go to comm's and get an interpreter to type up the transmission tape.

Buzz said, "Boss, I've got a mate in the laundry that will give our stuff priority. Just put the personal bags into this big one and all the washing will be done ASAP."

"That's the best thing I've heard today, Buzz. Top idea. I don't know about you lot, but I'm heading to the showers. I want to get into fresh gear before going to lunch. Then I'll worry about the mission report."

At that time of day, the showers were brilliant. Tag and Bill had gone over with me, and after washing a few weeks of accumulated grime off and out of my hair, I felt a hundred percent. Back in the tent, I dressed in fresh gear, bundled my washing into my personal laundry bag, and threw it into the big one Buzz had brought in.

Soon after everyone returned from showers, the tent smelled of aftershave and deodorant. Buzz dropped our bag off at the laundry on the way to lunch. His mate told him to come back before knock off time to collect everything. We enjoyed a meal that didn't come out of a tin for the first time in a couple of weeks.

That afternoon was spent writing up the mission report, which meant transcribing my patrol diary into a full report. The only thing that wasn't in my diary was the extraction and our arrival back at base. The report ran over ten foolscap pages, which I'd have to get copied three times. When it was finished, I had to code it for transmission to HQ at Swanbourne. I didn't get that finished until half way through the next day.

I went to the comm's unit, and as usual it was sent straight away, but took half an hour to send. While I was waiting for the confirmation of receipt, I took the original report into HQ and had the three copies done. After going back to the comm's unit, I still had to wait for the confirmation of receipt. While I was there, Bill walked in to send his reports, and as he was being looked after, my confirmation came through. I waited for Bill to finish.

After returning our paperwork to the tent, we went to the mess for lunch. The rest of the team were already there, and they informed us of the progress on their reports and the other things that had to be done for the debriefing session.

I warned them, "According to Chips, this one's going to be a little different than the usual debriefs we have. According to him, it may take longer than the one day." My news was greeted with groans, and I smiled.

Bill said, "Also guys, because it was a joint op, most of the Intel officers will be US, so expect to see a lot of brass around."

The next day we were ready. Everything had been done, and all the copies were in the three boxes of Intel we'd collected, along with the originals. We arrived at HQ at zero eight hundred and were informed that the debriefing would take place in the spare building beside HQ that was usually used as a reception area for visiting dignitaries.

We carried our stuff over and waited on the veranda. Chipson, accompanied by a couple of other officers, arrived soon after and opened up the room. Inside, there was nine seats beside the door facing into the room, and there were six tables, three on each side of the room with three chairs each, two on one side of the tables, and one on the other side. At the far end of the room were three tables, each with two chairs facing the door.

As we went inside, a flight of choppers flew over heading for the pads, and Chips said, "Sounds like your audience is arriving, Tiger. As you can see, you'll be facing two intelligence officers at each table, one from the US at each one. Each table will deal with different aspects of your mission, but the first one is the important one dealing with the full mission report."

"Yes sir," I replied.

He looked around and said, "You men can put those boxes on the end tables if you like. Does everyone have your reports?"

Tag answered, "All in this box, sir."

"Good. Keep them with you before you put the boxes down there."

Tag took out all of the reports, left them on one of the chairs, and took the boxes down to the three end tables. I told each of the guys to grab their reports and copies. Bill and I left ours sitting on a chair each as an orderly escorted a group of twenty officers into the room. Nine of them were US officers, the rest were Australian. As Chipson was welcoming them, I had my team line up. I whispered to Bill, "As our liaison officer, you do the team introductions, which will be in a minute or so."

My prediction was on the money. After the hierarchy had introduced themselves, Chips brought the yank contingent our way and introduced Bill to them. The lead yank was a Colonel, so Bill threw him a salute.

The Colonel said, "Forget the saluting, Captain, otherwise we'll have sore arms. How about introducing your men?"

"They're not my men, sir. Major Davis is their leader, sir."

"Hmm, well, where's this Major Davis then, Captain?"

I stepped forward and said, "Major Tiger Davis, sir."

The Colonel looked at me. "Well, hi there. Tigah is it? Would you like to introduce your men?"

"Tiger sir, and certainly." Bill smiled at me, and I introduced the team with only their nicknames.

The Colonel shook each of their hands. He stood in front of us and said, "Well men, I've been told you've done a good job. Just how good is what we're here to determine. As each of you is called to the first table, you then continue on to the next in line and so on." He looked around; almost everyone was seated. "We'll start with Captain Fredrick. Let's go Captain."

He turned and headed to the first table. Bill grabbed his report and copies and followed him to the first table. Chips walked over to us as we sat waiting. "This could take a while, gentlemen, so feel free at any time to walk out for a smoke. Just don't go too far."

"Thank you, sir," I said.

He turned to me and asked, "By the way, what's all this Major malarkey?"

I smiled. "You haven't been told, then?"

"Told what?"

I sighed. "Well sir, I hold the honorary rank of Major in the US army. I thought you had been informed. Colonel Clarke arranged it before we left Australia. I even have the rank pins to wear on US safe bases."

"Where are they now?" he asked.

"In my pocket, sir." I reached into my shirt pocket and showed them to him.

"Yes, I can see how that would help when dealing with the yanks, especially officers," he said.

"That's what the Colonel thought too, sir, and that's why he arranged for it. If you'll excuse me, sir, I'm going to grab a smoke before they start on me."

"By all means, Tiger, go for it," he said and moved off.

I looked at Tag and motioned toward the door. He nodded and rose from his seat. I pulled two smokes from my pack as we walked out the door and passed one to him.

I took a drag after lighting and said, "Make sure that if any of them come out for a smoke, there's always at least one of them left inside to pass the word to the outside if needed."

"Gotcha. I'd been thinking about that myself," he replied.

Roughly an hour later, Bill got up from the first table and moved to the second; I was called to the first one. I handed the copies to each officer but kept the original. I had told everyone to keep their original reports so they could go to back to HQ Swanbourne. I waited while they read, ready for the questions that would come.

The Colonel was the first to finish reading, but waited until his Australian counterpart was finished before speaking. "Damn, that's a pretty concise report Tiger. So who planned the mission?"

"I did, sir," I replied.

"So you're saying that everything went as you planned it?" he asked.

"Not everything, sir."

"Explain please."

"Well sir, the patrol leaders in our unit plan their own operations, but we always leave a bit of leeway for contingencies that may arise. This time I pushed the pace on day one of the insertion, which allowed us to see the arrival of the relief at the target. This actually saved us five days all up. If you wish to see a copy of the attack plan, my original is here," I answered as I pulled out the attack plan I'd written up out of my shirt pocket and passed it across.

He finished reading it and said, "Not bad. So you did stick to the plan. How did you deviate, and when did you come up with your attack plan?"

"The date is on it, but before I left Australia, I submitted it to my boss, who Okayed it. The differences are: I found an LZ for extraction, the pace I set on the first day, the attack itself, and laying jumping jack mines as well as claymores."

"So you actually stuck to your plan."

"Yes sir, with a few differences," I replied.

"So how come you didn't check the bodies?"

I replied, "Sir, I don't know if you've seen the results of a sniper rifle hit, and my guys use exploding rounds. The result is virtually the same as my forty-five. Goes in small but with a head shot will take half your head off coming out. They were dead."

He laughed and said, "Damn good, boy, damned good." He turned to the Australian major beside him and asked, "Do you have any questions major?"

The major turned to me. "Do you know if the destruction was discovered?"

"No sir, but they'd be in for a few surprises if they did, and it would cost them."

They both laughed, and the major said, "That's all, Tiger. Move to the next table, please."

As I got up Bill was moving to table four, so I figured that these next ones were quite quick going.

They were quick ones and involved: whether there were any medical problems, communication, interaction with troops other than Australian forces, if we had any problems dealing with the air base at Bien Hoa, were US air personnel or equipment on a par with the Australian forces, and so on. Most of it was superfluous as far as I was concerned. The end tables were mainly about what we'd obtained. I was asked where it was, how recent it was, how we came by the radio recording, why the photos were taken, and which photos pertained to the mission. I answered what I could, and at other times had to stay with a stock answer: "I can't tell you, as I wasn't there. I was busy doing other things, and they'd have to ask my men." I did tell them who to refer to; for example, if it were a comm's question I would refer them to Wires or JJ.

By the time I was finished, Buzz, who'd been called after Tag, was just leaving the first table, and Wires was on table five. I watched as the Australian Major got up and headed toward me.

When he reached me, I came to attention. He said, "Stand easy, Tiger, we won't be calling anyone else today. It's almost sixteen hundred, so we'll call it a day. You and the members of your team who have been interviewed don't have to come back tomorrow. Could you please arrange for the rest to be here by zero ten hundred? By the way, I must say you did a remarkable job, and all the intelligence you collected are gold mines of information.

To actually get those codebooks intact, even though they have to be translated, was a feat in itself. Great work, Thank you." He offered his hand, and I shook it.

I was still quite shocked after he told me the time; it seemed as if we'd been in there for a few hours, yes, but I hadn't realised we'd been there the whole day. I turned to the remaining team members and said, "That's all they're going to do today. Sorry guys, you lot will have to come back tomorrow. Dumper, you'll have to make sure you, JJ, Lizard, and Gecko are back here at ten.

You can head off if you want. I'll stay until the other guys are finished." I followed them out and said to the others outside, "Ok, they're done for the day. You guys can head back if you wish. I'll hang in until the others finish."

As they started heading to the tent, I lit a smoke. Wires came out as I was about to stub it out, and I filled him in on what was happening. He elected to stay with me. Tag finished as we walked back in and took a seat. Buzz finally finished ten minutes later, and we headed for the tent.

That night in the mess, there was a fair bit of whinging and laughter about some of the stupid questions we were asked after submitting our verbal and written reports. The originals I'd gotten from everyone that had gone through that process, and when the other four had finished, I'd collect them and have them mailed back to HQ. Bill had already sent a copy of his to his CO, and he gave me the original to go with all the others.

When we got back from the mess, there was a note sitting on the table with a coded message addressed to me. The note informed me of the time it was received and time it was delivered, which had been five minutes earlier. I decoded the message, taking some of it in as I did, and then read the whole message again when I'd finished.

Mark had written: "Christ! Are you trying to give me a heart attack? You should have told me! The Army has found out you are under the age of recruitment, but the Colonel has been able to quash any major ramifications. He's ropeable. You'll be reporting to him when you get back here. Major Chipson will be informed and will discipline you with the following punishment, but nothing more. Your punishment is a fine of one week's pay, reduction in rank, to private for thirty days, confined to barracks with loss of privileges for thirty days, and this will be noted in your personnel file."

After reading it through twice more to take it in, I exclaimed, "SHIT!"

I had wondered how much crap I would be in when they found out about my being fifteen after I was accepted and the forging of my birth certificate. I thanked Christ the Colonel went to bat for me; otherwise, I'd probably been serving time in Holsworthy Military Prison.

CHAPTER 11

Following my exclamation, Tag came over to the table and asked what was wrong. I said, "I suppose you'd all better come over and sit. I'm in the shit big time. You'd all better read this, and I'll answer any of your questions afterward."

I passed the decoded copy to Tag and told him to pass it around while I went out for a smoke. When I returned, Bill said, "I'll talk with you later, after you finish with your men." I nodded and continued to the table.

The guys were smiling, and Wires asked, "How did you manage it, boss?"

I sat down and explained how I'd gone about getting my licence and the forgeries before applying and subsequently being passed at the recruitment centre.

Gecko asked, "I've heard rumours that you never finished basic training at Kapooka, yet you ended up with us. Can you explain that for us?"

I explained my early basic training, meeting up with Pep and Mark, the grenade incident that won me the gong, and being asked to join the regiment.

"You've already done one tour with most of us, boss. Was that an SRT job?" JJ asked.

"Yes it was, and the guys with me then can explain what happened and what it was. But, I've never been in one of the Sabre squadrons. The Colonel, Mark, and Pep asked me to be part of SRT after I'd passed the regiment training."

"As far as I'm concerned, you did a brilliant job under shitty circumstances on the last mission, and I'm saying I'll stick with you, Tiger, as my boss, even if you are younger than me." Buzz's statement echoed around the table.

The question I had been expecting at the beginning came. Dumper asked, "So how old are you really?"

I stood up and moved to the top of the table. All eyes followed me. I looked at them along the table and said, "You've all read the punishment. There is no mention of losing my rank after my suspension, or not continuing to lead SRT, so I'll understand if any of you wish to reconsider remaining under my command. All I ask is that you give me some notice so I can inform the boss and arrange for a replacement. Now, to answer Dumper's question, in three weeks I'll turn seventeen."

Tag whistled. "Shit. And, you've been with SAS for over a year! How old were you when you joined?"

"Fifteen and a half," I answered.

Dumper looked around and said, "I don't know about the rest of them, but you're the best boss I've had, so I'm with Buzz. I'm sticking with you, boss. You may be younger than me, but you're a lot older in the head department, and smarter. I'm staying!"

There were nods and smiles all around the table. I reminded them, "Just remember, the offer is still there if you change your minds, but thanks for your support, guys."

"I just don't want to be in your shoes when shit for brains Chipson finds out. He's going to give you hell!" Tag exclaimed. That started the laughter, and they all had suggestions of what to say to him.

"Yeah, I know. I'm going to cop a heap of crap from him. It'll make his day, but look at it this way, we all get a holiday for a month," I said with a laugh. This was greeted with cheers and more laughter.

After the clamour died down, Bill asked, "Can you and I go and get a drink alone?"

"Sure, just give me a minute." I quickly rummaged in my kitbag, grabbed my beret, and said, "Ok, let's go."

We walked over to the mess, and Bill got the drinks while I grabbed a table. As he came back with the drinks, he said, "I noticed you put that ring on. Why?"

"I don't usually wear it in operational areas, but I'm going to have a month on holiday after I front Chips tomorrow, so I figure what the hell, why not?"

"It's nice. Can I have a look at it?" he asked. I took it off and handed it to him. After inspecting it closely, he said, "Oh I see. It's a regiment ring. It's got your unit insignia on it. What's the black stone?"

"Onyx," I replied. He handed it back, and I replaced it on my finger.

As we sipped our scotches, he said, "I heard the entire conversation with your men, and I have to say, being around you and seeing you in action, I'm in agreement with your men. I'd stick with you, too, if I was in your unit." He sipped again and continued. "I've done the Seal training and talked to most of those instructors, and they reckon that the training we do in Seals is nothing compared to the training your regiment have to do. And you passed that as, and I mean no disrespect, but as a kid. You must be tougher and smarter than you look."

I laughed. "I've been told that before." I drained my glass and got up to get another round. When I got back with the drinks, I said, "After this, I'm heading back for some sleep."

He replied with a laugh, "Sure. I also want you to know that I'm not saying anything to anyone about what I've heard because I haven't heard anything, if you read me."

"Loud and clear," I answered.

The next morning after we'd been to breakfast, Dumper, JJ, Lizard, and Gecko were getting ready to face the debriefing. During the night the rain had started but wasn't cooling the normal heat down yet; that would take a few days. As yet, it wasn't as strong as it would get, just a constant light rain, but I figured by the end of the following day it would start pouring down. An orderly came into the tent to inform me that I was to report to the major at HQ.

I thought to myself, well here we go, time to face the music. I headed to HQ with Dumper and the boys. They went off to the debriefing room as I entered the office. The orderly that had come down to the tent went to inform Chips I was there, and I heard him yell, "Get him in here!"

This is going to interesting, I thought as the orderly came to escort me to his office. He whispered as we went up the hall to the office, "He's not in a good mood. Watch out."

"Thanks," I said, "but I think I'm the cause of his bad mood."

As I entered his office, he told the orderly to shut the door. He didn't offer me a seat, so I remained standing at ease.

"Davis, the reason you're here is because you've been caught in a lie by the defence force. You were under age when you enlisted. You are bloody lucky that you are here. If you'd been in Australia, you'd be in Holsworthy now, serving a sentence before being dishonourably discharged." He paused for effect. "As it stands, your military record reflects your outstanding accomplishments; therefore, instead of losing all the money and effort taken by personnel in training you, and also lose a person with your talent, Lt Col Clarke has pleaded on your behalf to keep you in the army and our regiment. However, you have to be disciplined. Your punishment sentence is: One, fined one week's pay. Two, demoted to private for thirty days. Three, loss of privileges for thirty days. Four, confined to barracks for thirty days. All of this will be noted in your personnel file as a matter of record. Now, military police officers will monitor you, and they will escort you to the mess at meal times and to the ablution block. That is the only time you will leave your tent. Is that understood, Davis?"

"Yes sir."

He picked up the phone and asked if the MP's were here and to send them up. There was a knock at the door, and he said, "Come." Two MP's entered the office, and Chips said, "Please escort Sgt, make that private, Davis to his quarters."

I came to attention, made a textbook left turn, and marched out of his office. As we made our way to the tent, the MP sergeant said, "Tiger, I know your reputation and I don't like this at all, but there will be an MP on duty at the entrance to your tent twenty-four seven."

I replied, "Well, that's ok if they want to be miserable, but my guard may as well be inside out of the rain. There's plenty of room inside, I don't mind, and I'll make sure my guys don't pick on him."

The sergeant laughed. "I have no problems with that as long as you're sure you won't mind."

"Positive. Besides, who wants to get wet as a shag doing nothing but standing around?" We reached the tent, and I had them come in. "If you bring a table and chair, he can sit near the doorway."

The MP Sergeant said, "I'll get back shortly with a card table and chair. I really appreciate this, Tiger. Thank you." He shook my hand and left.

The guys had been giving the MP's sullen looks, mainly because of a soldier's hate of cops, but I figured they were human and just like us in some respect, doing a job where there weren't any thanks. So I turned and said, "Right. We're going to have one of these guys here for the duration of my confinement to barracks, so don't give them a hard time. Be nice. They're just like us, guys, doing a job. Is that clear to everyone?" There were positive responses from them all, and I said, "Good."

Things got a little heated, but it was good to get it out of the way and start a trend. It came about as we were going to head over to the mess for lunch. The MP put his cherry beret on, while we had on our bush hats.

Tag said to the MP, "You're not coming with us dressed like that."

The MP replied, "My orders are to remain in the prisoner's company and to escort him back after each meal."

Tag got a little stroppy. "Firstly, Tiger isn't a prisoner. Secondly you're not going to be sitting with us, you jumped up glory hound!"

"I have my orders and I'm going to carry them out. If I meet resistance, you could face charges yourself."

I was prepared to let them sort it out, but things had moved onto dangerous ground, so I intervened. "Ok, you two, settle down and pull your horns in." I heard laughing at my statement. "Ok, let's have some compromise here. Look, you've been a good sport so far by not wearing your beret in the tent and trying to remain inconspicuous. I'll comply with what you need, but these guys don't need to be embarrassed either. So how about you wear different headgear, and we'll all get along."

The MP thought it over and said, "But I don't have anything else."

I smiled and said, "That's easily taken care of. Buzz." Buzz came forward and handed him a bush hat. "Now, you wear that, and there's no need for argument, is there?"

The MP put the bush hat on and stated his agreement. "Well, it would keep the rain off better than my beret."

"Yes, and you look good. Any more objections, guys?" There were none, and I said, "Let's go then."

The next incident occurred because of the phrase 'loss of privileges,' which meant after dinner I couldn't go for a drink but had to return to the tent. Shit! But I was determined to play by the rules so complied with my escort's wishes and returned to the tent while the team went for drinks. Bugger, that was a sobering thought, in more ways than one. So each night after dinner, I'd go back to the tent and play cards with my escort while the team drank. The bastards!

One-night Tag came back from the mess early, bringing with him a bottle of Glenffidich fifteen-year-old single malt scotch. "I was owed this. I don't drink scotch, as you know, so I thought you could do with it." As he pulled out a glass from his pocket, he continued. "Couldn't do anything about ice, though, boss."

We looked at the MP questioningly. With a shrug, he said, "As far as I'm concerned, you've met your obligations, Tiger. You have not left the tent or gone to the bar. What happens in the tent doesn't matter, so enjoy yourself."

Tag had obviously passed the word around. Every now and again one of the team would turn up with a bottle to keep me going. The prize came, however, from Gecko. Somehow, he had used his contacts, and one afternoon he presented me with a bottle of Johnny Walker Blue label, one of the most prized in their collection and worth nearly a week's wages. I drank it sparing because it was so good.

At the start of the third week, Bill came to me and showed me a decoded message from the US Chief of Staff for the Commander in Chief South East Asia, General Creighton Abrams, a US Marine Corp officer, who was, in fact, a true field commander, unlike his predecessor, Westmoreland.

Apparently, he wanted to meet the team at his Headquarters in Saigon the day after tomorrow. I told him, "No, that's not going to happen. I'm confined to quarters until the end of the following week, but any time after that is fine."

I thought Bill was going to have a heart attack. "Jesus God damned Christ, you can't say no. He is the Commander in Chief of this whole bloody war. I'll go to Chipson and get you an exemption or something."

I replied calmly, "No, you won't. I want this thing finished with. I don't want it hanging over my head. I'll help you draft a reply, but I won't go until I'm free of this punishment. Is that clear?"

He replied, "Jesus Christ, Tiger, even though I think you're crazy and could lose me my commission, I'll agree with your judgement, but you better come up with a doozy of a reply."

We threw different suggestions around, and after an hour, we had worked out the wording for the reply refusing the request. It read, "Sir, it is with deep regret that Major Davis and his team are unable to accept your kind invitation. At present, Major Davis is under house arrest for a disciplinary infraction against Australian

Military law. His team, however, are available to travel but would refuse because they travel as a team or not at all. Major Davis will be available in fourteen days' time."

As he coded the message, he said, "You're nuts, you know that. And I'm nuts for going along with this." He paused as he finished up. "Ok, it's ready. I'll go send it unless you want to change your mind." I laughed and pointed to the entrance flap.

He came back an hour later, sat down, and started decoding the message he'd received. As he did so, he said, "They made me wait for a reply." I laughed.

When he finished reading the decoded message, his face lost all colour. "I'll be damned as a redneck, and you've got some balls with the stunt you made me pull, but the man ain't taking no for an answer."

He passed me the message. "What is this horseshit, Captain? That man better not be shitting me. My schedule is clear on Friday. I will land there at zero ten hundred. You have his CO meet me. I'll give those Aussies what for over this shit, but you tell Davis if the man won't come to the mountain, then the mountain will come to him."

I cracked up laughing. "This deserves a drink. If you really want some fun, take that up to Chips. He's going to have a heart attack."

Bill started laughing and said with a smile, "You know, I think I will, just to see what he does. I'll tell him why the Commander in Chief is coming here to chew you out after you refused to go to him, but first I think I'll have that drink. I'm going to need it." After two neat ones, he copied the message and headed to see Chips.

I said to my shadow after I finished my drink. "You'd best stand outside and make everything look official, because when Chipson sees that message and grills Bill, he's more than likely to come down here to chew me out. He knows I can't be ordered up there while I'm confined."

He replied with a smile, "You just don't want me to see or hear the fun, Tiger."

I answered, "Oh, you'll hear it, I'm sure, but once he comes in, because you're guarding me you're allowed to come in to prevent any harm coming to me or him." We both laughed.

A couple of minutes after he went outside, I heard him say, "You were right. He's coming this way with your mate." I got up from my bunk and moved to sit at the table, grabbed the cards, and started a game of solitaire.

Chipson came in followed by Bill, and the MP. Chips walked up to the table and said, "What the hell do you think you're doing, Davis?"

"Playing solitaire, sir," I replied.

"Don't take me for a fool, Davis. I mean you refusing an order by a superior officer."

"I haven't refused any order, sir," I replied quietly.

Chips' temper broke. He yelled, "Yes you did! You refused the US Commander in Chief's order to go to Saigon."

I looked him in the eye. "For the second time, sir, I didn't refuse any order. If you care to read the message again, sir," I replied, my voice full of venom and sarcasm.

He snatched the message out of Bill's hand. Bill was smiling and gave me a wink, while Chips reread the message. Chips looked at me and said, "That is polite language for an order coming from a high office."

"Nowhere on that message is the word order, sir."

He had no leg to stand on; he knew I was right, so he switched tactics and asked, "So why did you refuse such an honour?"

I answered, "You should know, sir, you put me here. I'm confined to barracks, and you even put a guard on me as if I couldn't be trusted."

My sarcasm wasn't fazing Chips. "How am I going to explain this to him? He'll want answers, and now I have to arrange a formal welcome as well."

Christ, do I have to fix everything, I thought to myself. "Well sir, I always find that the truth works. I'm here because I lied about my age when I enlisted, have been sprung, and now I'm serving my punishment."

He was thinking as he answered, "Yes, that could work, I suppose."

Bill stepped forward and intervened. "Excuse me sir, but I know about him. He's a marine and they always like to hear the honest truth about everything. If I could make a suggestion? Don't organise a formal ceremony or anything else. He'll get pissed. He is here for one thing; he'll do it and leave. He hates fanfare, sir."

Chips answered with a distracted voice. "Yes I see. All right then, I'll just meet him at the pads as he requested and tell him the truth about what happened to you, Tiger." He looked around at the men in the tent. "Carry on. I don't think you need to be guarded. You've proved your trustworthiness, and I'll do something about that." He turned and left. Bill and I looked at each other and burst out laughing.

Later Tag came back with a few of the guys followed shortly by Buzz, who had Lizard and Gecko with him. They brought with them armloads of stuff from the Q tent over the road.

I asked for everybody's attention. "All right guys, you're all to be dressed in clean gear on Friday. We're expecting a visit from General Abrams, so I want you all looking smart."

Gecko asked, "Who's this General Abrams boss?"

"We're all fighting a war, and you don't know who the supreme Commander in Chief is? Surely you jest."

"I thought that was Westmoreland," he replied with a shrug.

They all laughed, and Tag said, "No, he got the sack because of his stupidity. So why's he coming here, Tiger?"

I looked at Bill and said, "Fill them in on what's been going on." Bill filled them in on the messages, my refusal, and what happened with Chips. They were in hysterics when he'd finished.

As we were getting ready to go to lunch, the MP Sergeant

turned up and told me, "I'm afraid you're losing your shadow, Tiger. Chips has cancelled the guard order."

"Well thanks for that. So I'm going to lose some furniture as well, huh?"

"Yes, and I'd like to thank you for making life easier on my men."

"No problem. It was a silly order anyway. Where was I going to go?" I replied. We shook hands, and I said goodbye to the day watch MP. As he was folding the table legs, he told me he had enjoyed his time, and that morning in particular.

After they left, I turned to the team that had been watching and listening and said, "That's how you treat people the right way. Now let's go to lunch." They were all laughing and cheering as we left the tent.

Friday came round, and after breakfast, we were sitting and relaxing around the table. I asked Buzz, "How are we with supplies?"

"I've managed to get hold of another dozen of the ponchos and liners, so we're right with having enough now. I got a dozen of those cam baseball caps like Bill wears. Everyone has a bush-master knife like yours, boss, and we have plenty of ammo. We've got about five days' supply of rat packs for everybody, plenty of grenades and smoke, so we're pretty well stocked up."

I thought about this for a moment. "Hmm ok. Stock up on anything you think we may need in the gear and clothing department. I've got a feeling we may not be coming back to the Dat again." We finished talking as three choppers flew over, and I noticed an every so slight change in the sound. The chopper had its side doors closed. I said, "Ok boys, time to get ready. Unless my ears are playing tricks on me, I'd say our visitor just arrived."

Bill was standing at the tent entrance. "Here they come."

I lined the guys up and stood in front of them. I saw Bill come to attention and salute, then shake hands with someone I couldn't see. Bill entered and was followed by a man about five ten with silvery black hair once he took his cap off and dressed in pressed cam fatigues with a single star on each collar.

I called the men to attention, and for once followed US army procedure and saluted. He returned the salute as Bill informed him who I was. He shook my hand and said, "Major, would you like to introduce your men?"

"Yes sir," I replied, and as I introduced the team one by one, each came to attention again and Abrams shook their hands. After the introduction, he moved to the front and faced us. By this time Bill was standing beside me.

The General said, "At ease men. Now, the reason I'm here is that my invitation to you to come to Saigon was refused." He looked pointedly at me, and continued. "You all did me a great service by not only destroying a headache I had but also rescuing some of my soldiers. For that I'm going to award you all with some citations."

One of his aides had come forward with an armful of stuff and placed it on the table, sorted it out, and passed the first item to him. "For carrying out such a hazardous mission, Captain William Fredrick." Bill stepped forward to stand in front of the General. "You are hereby raised in rank to the rank of Major." Abrams handed him a box with the oak leaf pins and paper scroll and shook his hand. Bill stepped back, they both saluted, and Bill stood beside me again.

Now that we knew the protocol, we would do the same as we were called forward. "Honorary Major Tiger Davis, for completing said hazardous mission, you are raised in honorary rank to full Colonel." I received a box of silver winged eagle pins and a scroll. The rest of the guys were awarded honorary ranks of Captain in the US army. I had been watching Chips, and as I got my rise in rank, he was ashen faced. I smiled inwardly.

The General said, "Now then, gentlemen, each man is going to receive the following reward for saving my men, so I'll read the citation once and come up as I call your name. For meritorious valour in the face of the enemy above and beyond your duty, you are awarded the bronze star, Major William Fredrick." Bill stepped forward as before, but this time the medal was pinned on by the General. He called each of us up, pinned the medal on, and we returned to our places with smiles.

After the awards, Abrams continued. "Gentlemen, I know you feel like celebrating, so I will buy you all a drink, but first Colonel Davis and I have some business to discuss. I am sure your Major Chipson will show you to the officer's mess. Colonel Davis and I will join you shortly. Thank you." They put their stuff on their bunks and followed a sullen Chipson to the officer's mess.

Abrams rounded on me and said, "Take a seat, Tiger." He waited for me to sit. "Now, you can tell me what the bloody hell did you think you were doing when you refused my goddamned invitation? And what's this horseshit about being under house arrest? So tell me, son, what's going on?"

I told him the story. He laughed at times and would sometimes interject with a question. When I had finished telling him the story, he laughed and said, "I'll bet there are some very red faces in your army now, and I am sure some poor schmuck is going to get a rocket up his ass. Tell me how old are you now? Are you of age yet?"

"Sir, this is thirsty work. Would you like a drink?"

"Sure son. I'll have a scotch if you have any."

I smiled and brought out the blue label, poured each of us a drink, and answered his question. "I'll be seventeen in a couple of days, sir. Eighteen is enlistment age, but they can't kick me out now."

He laughed and remarked on the scotch. "This is really nice scotch, nice and smooth." He took another sip. "Now I like you, son, so I'm going to be straight with you. If you'd have come to Saigon, I was going to see if you'd be interested in doing a job for me."

"Go on, sir," I said.

"There's a job up in the central highlands some of my people think your team would be good for. And some that think it is impossible. How about it, son? You willing to see if it can be done?"

"First I'd have to get permission from my HQ, but I could take look at what it is and see if it's doable, sir."

"I'll arrange things with your HQ, and I'll make sure Major Fredrick gets all the help he needs getting you guys moved up to Da Nang. Let's go see the others." He looked at the scotch after taking another sip. "Man, that's good."

I put the bottle away and we headed to the officer's mess.

CHAPTER 12

In the officer's mess, things were in full swing. The boys were talking amongst themselves, Bill was talking with the General's aides, and Chipson was standing off on his own, glaring at my team, looking rather sullen and miffed. I thought to myself, Good. Stick that up your jumper, you, asshole.

Abrams said to me, "If you'll excuse me Colonel, I've got a promise to honour." He raised his voice over the din. "Gentlemen, I do believe it's my shout. Breast the bar please." To me, he asked, "Was that the right phrase?"

I smiled at him. "Yes sir"

He smiled and said, "Let's get a drink. Scotch, Colonel?"

"Scotch is fine, sir."

After the guys had their drinks, I moved over to them and said, "Well, here's to another gong, you sorry looking officers." They all laughed, hoisted their glasses and drank. After the toast, I continued. "I suppose you can start to get used to this because we'll be shifting digs soon up to Da Nang yank territory. Since you're all officers, we'll be using the officer's mess up there."

Tag said, "Three cheers for Tiger."

Soon other officers moved into the mess and a little after that, a soldier dressed in waiter's gear banged a hand held gong. "Luncheon is served, sirs."

We moved into the dining room. I found my way to Chips and said, "Don't worry, sir. My guys will behave, and I'll be back to the tent to finish my confinement. After all, I'm allowed to go to the mess for lunch." I walked on with a smile on my face. The meal was far better than in the OR's mess, so I, for one, was looking forward to the shift to Da Nang.

After lunch, General Abrams asked me to accompany him to

the chopper pads, along with Chips, whose mood hadn't evaporated. I knew he would not take kindly to my team or me after this.

Just before he boarded his chopper, Abrams said, "I'll get things under way, so expect to move before next week is out. I will send everything through Major Fredrick. Thank you and I'll see you again soon, Tiger."

He shook my hand and got into the chopper, and the door slid closed. I held onto my beret as the chopper blades increased in pitch, and lifted off.

I turned to Chips and said, "If you'll excuse me, sir, I have to get back to my tent before I get arrested." I walked off, leaving Chips glowering after me.

Back at the tent, everyone was laughing and joking, and as I entered, I said, "All right, everyone put a glass on the table." I went to my kitbag, pulled out the blue label, and poured a little into each glass. "Everyone take a glass. This is sipping stuff, do not waste it. Gentlemen, to the US army."

"And its new officers," Bill added.

We sipped the scotch, and Tag called a second toast. "And to the best kid boss we could serve under!" This elicited murmurs of "hear, hear" as the team drank again.

I turned to Gecko. "Chris, if you can get any more of this, I'll take it, even if I have to pay for it." I handed him the empty bottle and raised my voice. "Ok you lot, just remember not to switch to your US rank pins until we're out of here. Oh, and definitely don't wear them back home."

A couple of days later, I was coding a report for transmission back to HQ when a sigs clerk came in with a coded message from the very person I was writing to. After decoding the message, I read it all the way through. "Tiger, received your interim message, awaiting full report. Have also received report of incident from Chips. You have put his nose out of joint, but technically, you outrank him. Congratulations on that, and to your men. The request you warned me about has come through and been approved. Need to speak to you. Will phone you at Chips' office today at sixteen hundred your time. Get that report to me ASAP. Mark."

I finished coding the report and wrote a note to Chips. I called Bill over to the table. "That was a message from home. They got the request from the General's office. It has been approved, so you can expect some stuff from your crowd very soon, I'd say. Now, I need you to do me a couple of favours. First, I need this message sent, and secondly, I need you to see Chips and give him this request."

Bill replied, "Sure thing. Sounds like we'll be out of here soon."

"Not soon enough for me, but I've still got two days left to serve of my confinement. I'd like to get that over and done with."

He replied with a smile. "I thought you were getting a little tent crazy; the way you've been tetchy of late. You ready for me to do that now." I nodded my head and passed across the report for sending and the request note for Chips. He grabbed his ball cap and left the tent. He was right; I had been getting bored because I couldn't move around freely and had been snappy and grouchy with everyone.

When Bill returned, he was carrying a message of his own. "Chipson said your request is granted. This may be the start of what we've been waiting for."

I was smiling when he told me my answer; I nodded as he sat down to decode the message. After he finished he turned to me and said, "I've been ordered to Saigon for briefings. A chopper's arriving for me at zero eight hundred. Looks like this is it. Yahoo!"

I smiled. "Great. At least I don't have to put up with your ugly mug all day."

"Ah shucks and I thought you loved my company. Now I don't have to watch your pacing and being an asshole."

Even though I knew he was kidding, I had been getting too touchy lately and longed to be out doing things. I put it down to too much inactivity. I was pleased that Bill was taking on some of our Australian habits, like taking the mickey out of someone, as he had just done, and I realised that not knowing our culture this sort of thing could have punches flying from anyone else because of misunderstandings and decided there were flaws in any culture.

I arrived at the HQ building at fifteen fifty-six and was shown into Chipson's office. We waited for the call from home. When the phone rang, Chips answered it, and as he listened, his face lost a lot of its colour. "Yes sir. I'll do that immediately. Yes. All assistance will be placed at his disposal." He put the handset on the desk and said, "I have to leave you alone." He left his office, shutting the door on the way out.

I sat in his chair and picked up the handset. "Tiger here."

"Ah Tiger, Clarke here. I'm a little bit pissed off at you. Have you any idea of the fast-talking and favours I had to pull to keep you out of Holsworthy.

You had better prove I made the right decision. It seems that you have already. Your mission report was splendid. Job well done. I have read your last report as well; it seems you impressed our yank cousins. Apparently, the CnC has taken a liking to you and wants you for a special job. I have okayed it, but after that, I want you back here. Understood?"

"Yes sir." I replied.

"Good. I'm going to pass you onto Captain Ryan to work out the specifics, but good job, my boy, and pass that onto your team."

"Thank you, sir," I replied.

Mark came onto the phone. "Tiger, the boss has left my office, so we talk freely. You have no idea of the shit-fight that went down here because of you, but I can understand it. Full marks on the mission. The boss is probably a little miffed at you because you have made full Colonel. Told you you'd end up outranking us." He laughed before continuing. "Even if it is only honorary, well done!"

"Thank you."

"I've approved the request for you to work with the yanks, which means we won't be getting copies of your transmissions when you're on an operation. If you can, try to let me know beforehand, and let me know you are back ASAP after the job. Then you can send me the mission report after that. They are going to shift you up to Da Nang, so take it easy up there and don't put too many noses out of joint. You will have to arrange transport back. Let me know if you are stuck. Good luck."

"Thanks boss." I hung up.

I left the office, and as I walked into the main office, I said to Chips, "I'm finished with your office. You can have it back now, and I'll fill you in tomorrow morning after my confinement is over." The orderlies had smiles on their faces, and one of them nearly burst out with a laugh at my last comment but was able to cover it.

Chips replied, "Yes, all right."

I walked out smiling. I entered the tent, and even though I was wet from the rain, I told the boys where I had been and what was happening, Bill had told them he was off to Saigon in the morning, and I apologised for being grumpy and grouchy the last few days. "After zero ten thirty tomorrow my confinement ends, so I'll be able to buy you all a round of drinks in the mess tomorrow night. You'll just have to bear with me tonight."

They all cheered and I heard "Thank Christ" and "About time." We all had a laugh at my expense.

That night after dinner, Bill and I returned to the tent while the team went on to have drinks. We sat at the table sipping on scotch from my dwindling supply, and he asked, "So how will it feel to be uncaged again?"

"Hopefully it'll feel a hell of a lot better. I will be able to get out and get some exercise, and with a bit of luck, something will come up that will exercise my brain. I have grown a little tired of wreaking retribution on Chips. It's no fun anymore; it's become too easy. To tell you the truth I would rather be back in action. I tend to be more alive then. All of my senses working and trying to out think the enemy." I nodded appreciatively at the idea.

He laughed. "I know how you feel. That is why I took this job with your lot. Being back in HQ was driving me around the twist. As soon as I was back in the thick of it, I felt reborn, if that makes any sense."

"Yeah Bill, it makes sense, at least it does to me, but don't tell any trick cyclist that. They'll put you in a rubber room," I replied.

"Trick cyclist? What's that?"

With a smile, I replied, "Psychiatrist."

"What, as in looney bin?" he asked, and I smiled and nodded my head as we both started laughing.

He got up, went to his kitbag, and came back to the table. "See if that fits you." He held out his hand; in it was his company ring. I looked at it closely. It had a blue stone in it and raised lettering that read Western Pioneers, the number nineteen and a pioneer soldier on one side, and the number seventy with a wagon wheel supporting a flame on the other side. The wheel had a plaque on it saying Nulli Secundus (Latin for Second to None).

I asked what the stone was, and he told me it was a Columbian Sapphire, which are very hard to get. I took my regiment ring off and tried it on; a perfect fit. He tried mine on, and it fitted him as well.

We decided to swap rings with a proviso that it was not a permanent swap and with a pledge that if either of us needed the others help, their own ring would be returned to them, and the other would come to their aid. We sealed the pledge with a drink.

Note to the reader: I still wear Bill's ring to this day, even though cancer took him three years ago. His son Jake was going to give it to me at his funeral, but I told him the story of how our rings were exchanged, and told Jake that the pledge still held true. Jake renewed his father's pledge, and he now wears the ring.

When the team started to dribble back into the tent, Bill and I had a final drink before going to bed. I said to Bill, "I'd love to come up to the pads and see you off in the am, but I've made such a fool out of Chipson that I don't want to give him any excuse to charge me with something else."

"I understand that, buddy, and hopefully my going down to Saigon gets us all out of here."

The following day was the last of my confinement. I had been sentenced at zero nine thirty a month before, so to err on the side of caution, I left it until zero ten thirty before I walked openly from the tent. The rain was only a constant drizzle now, but it felt good to be out in it.

Tag joined me. We had worked out earlier that I would go nowhere without company so that anything said to me was witnessed. We both looked at each other, nodded, and started toward the HQ building. As I entered, the orderlies smiled and I said, "I'd like to see Major Chipson please."

The orderly returned after a moment. "Go right in, Tiger."

Tag and I walked up the hall and into Chip's office; he invited us to have a seat and asked, "What can I do for you, Tiger?"

"It's what I can do for you, sir. Yesterday, with your permission, I had access to your office to take a call from HQ, and you were told to leave. I did promise that when I finished my confinement to quarter's term, I'd fill you in on the call, and since my sentence ended an hour ago, I'm making good on that promise, sir."

"Yes, that's right. You are now fully restored to your former sergeants' rank, and pay, and no longer confined to quarters. So what was it all about?"

"Well, sir, I'm not sure if you were informed of anything, so I'll tell you what I know, which is that General Abrams asked them for my help, and they approved his request. We will probably be moved up to Da Nang. I think that is why we were all given a rank in the US army, sir. At present Major Fredrick is in Saigon sorting things out."

He thought about it for a minute. "Hmm, I wasn't aware that it was that involved. All they asked me to do was render any assistance possible, but I was privy to some of the conversations you were having with the General, if you remember."

"Quite so, sir. That was all the call was about from HQ, sir, apart from SOPs regarding the change of procedure in communication with base HQ. Now, considering that you've been asked to help, if I receive any message from Major Fredrick, is it possible that I be notified immediately, no matter what time it is?"

"Yes, I can arrange that for you, Tiger. Anything else?" he asked.

"No, not at present, sir, but I'm sure I can rely on you, should something arise. That's all for now, sir, unless you have something else you wish to discuss," I replied

"No. That'll be all, gentlemen."

I found it hard to contain my laughter as we left the building, and once we were outside, I gave vent to it. Tag joined in, saying, "You're a piece of work, and an artist at putting someone down without them realising it, boss. That was a pleasure to watch. I almost pissed myself with the putdowns you were laying on him, but the worst part is he's probably too full of himself to realize what you were even saying."

"Oh, he will, probably in a day or so, and god help the orderlies or anybody around him when it happens. Like revenge, retribution is rather divine when served cold, but I think we'd better keep our heads down and not draw any attention for a while."

Not a religious man, Tag said, "Amen to that. I'll warn the boys."

Two days later, I received a message from Bill asking me to have the team ready for departure at zero nine hundred the following day. He also asked if we could bring the rest of his gear with us. The choppers picking us up would take us to Bien Hoa base, where we would rendezvous with him, and board a caribou flight to Da Nang. We would arrive in Da Nang that afternoon, where officer's quarters were arranged in a building to ourselves. The chopper flight would consist of two choppers, but Big John from Delta X-ray would be the flight leader because he already knew our procedures.

I called Buzz over and quietly said, "Ditch whatever we don't need or can't carry, or have it boxed up and arrange for it to be sent to us at Swanbourne. I want you to make sure that anything Bill left here, is packed and comes with us. We're leaving tomorrow morning."

He smiled. "Roger that boss, but I've already sent all the essentials we wanted in regards to clothing and ponchos back to base via service air. The rest of the stuff is either rat packs or ammo and grenades."

I thought this over for a tick and said, "Keep the rat packs but return the ammo and grenades. I will leave you to get it sorted. If you need a hand, yell."

"Roger that, boss," he replied.

I raised my voice so everyone could hear me. "Everyone to the table please, except Buzz." As they all gathered, I said, "Ok guys, this should brighten your day. I want you to get all your stuff together because at zero nine hundred tomorrow, we'll be airlifted to Bien Hoa to board a transport to Da Nang."

After the laughter and cheering subsided, I continued. "You need to take everything because we won't be coming back here. Now, after breakfast, we will swap our Aussie rank pins for your US ones. Wires, JJ, I will need you to check every SR10 for battery life. If any need replacing, get it done before end of business today. Tag, we have a bit of business to take care of soon. Ok, you all know what to do. Get on with it."

JJ grabbed my attention. "Boss, I'll check yours and Tag's now if you like."

"We'll leave them on the bunks for you," I replied. Tag and I went to get our gear and left our SR10 units sitting on the bed. We returned to the table, where I drafted a signal to go to HQ and had Tag code it.

We went up to the comm's room together, where I sent two messages, one to base and the reply to Bill, which stated: "Roger that. Will be waiting with bells on. You have made my day. Tiger."

We had both confirmations back within five minutes, so we headed to HQ and straight into Chip's office. He had us sit and asked what we wanted.

"Well, sir, I've come to let you know that we'll be out of your hair at zero nine hundred. We are being air lifted to where we're going, so I thought I'd take this opportunity to say goodbye."

He smiled. "Well Davis, I can't say it's been a pleasure, so all I'll say is good luck and I wish you success."

"Thank you, sir. The feeling is mutual." We got up and left his office, and I muttered under my breath about him being a jumped up sanctimonious asshole.

As we heading to the tent, a comm's clerk caught us up and handed me a message from HQ. We decoded it when we got back. Mark had written, "Message understood. Have fun in new digs. Will wait to hear from you at your earliest. Good luck, Tiger."

When we went to dinner, all was in readiness for the morning, so after dinner we let our hair down a bit in the mess, but not to the extent of getting rip roaring drunk. I felt elated at the thought of getting into action again, but as I looked around at the rest of the members of two squadron, I thought this would probably be the last squadron from the regiment to see action, in this war anyway.

After breakfast in the morning, we returned to our tent for the last time, got into our battle gear, and changed our rank pins. As I did a final inspection, I noticed that, apart from all our personal gear, we were taking three big cartons full of rat packs and a smaller one that had Bill's gear in it. I nodded and said, "Right. Let's go." We made our way to the chopper pads.

Five minutes later I heard through my earpiece, "Delta X-ray 79 to SRT1, do you read? Over."

I replied, "SRT1 to Delta X-ray 79. Read you loud and clear. Over."

"Delta X-ray to SRT. Good morning, Tiger. ETA two minutes. Over."

"SRT to Delta X-ray. Come on, John, did you stop for coffee?

Over." I heard Big John laughing through my earpiece.

We would split into our usual groups, with Tag's group taking the extra luggage. As both choppers touched down, we loaded and were in the air two minutes later. Once I put on the internal intercom unit, I said, "How ya goin', John?"

"Fine Colonel, sir, just fine."

"What's our ETA, John?" I asked.

"Oh, about twenty-five minutes, Tiger, give or take a few to stop for coffee," he replied and looked around with a smile on his face.

When we neared Bien Hoa, John came onto the intercom. "I hear you're heading north, Tiger."

"Yeah," I replied.

"They won't let me up there. Something to do with too much wine, women, and song. Whatever are ya goin' to do without me up there?" he teased.

I replied, "I don't know. Probably have to train some other dumb schmuck how to do it right."

He laughed and said, "We're coming in now, Tiger. Good luck to you, sir, and good hunting."

"You too, John, and thank you," I replied. When we landed, he turned so we could shake hands and nod to each other.

Bill was waiting for us as we walked across the tarmac. I grabbed his box of gear, and as I gave it to him, said, "I don't know what to do with you; you go swanning off and leave half your shit behind."

We both laughed. "Yeah, they keep telling me I need a nursemaid. That's our ride over there," he said, nodding towards a caribou twenty yards away with the ramp down.

"Can we stow our gear yet?"

"Sure. The crew are probably inside," he replied.

We headed toward the plane; the crew chief came down the ramp and saluted me. I asked if we could stow our gear on board,

158

and he showed us where we would be sitting and where to put our gear. Bill told him we would be in the crew canteen, and to send someone to get us when they were ready. Bill took us to the crew canteen, and on the way it was funny to watch the guys getting used to being saluted all the time, whether the person saluting wore head gear or not.

Instead of having coffee while we waited, we elected to eat large bowls of ice cream with a few different flavoured scoops in each, which was a rare treat. Getting ice cream in a military area during a war for Aussie troops was next to impossible. We made pigs of ourselves! Dumper went back for three helpings while the rest of us only managed two.

As he was finishing, a crewmember came to us and said, "We're ready to go, sirs. If you could make your way to the plane, please." We followed him to the plane and boarded.

Along the way, they had to do a couple of supply drops to forward firebases, and we watched with rapt attention at what they did. First, the ramp was lowered and the plane slowed down. As the crew got a green light, one of them pulled two parachute ripcords, and they would push toward the back of the plane. As the chutes opened up, the cargo cage was pulled out of the plane. Smaller chutes on each corner opened as it floated to earth less than fifty feet off the ground, and I thought that it was a neat piece of flying. The following drop was as the first, but this time the plane took a bit of ground fire that put a few holes in the fuselage. Cool as a cucumber, one of the crew moved up the plane smiling and placed duct tape over the holes as if it was an everyday occurrence. As I looked around at other patches in the plane, I assumed that it was.

When the ramp lowered in Da Nang, there were four open style jeeps waiting with a lieutenant standing beside them. We walked down the ramp to meet him, and he stepped forward and saluted. "Sirs, I've been sent to take you to your quarters and office."

He stepped forward to pick up my kitbag and headed to the lead jeep. He got in as I climbed in beside the driver and looked around to see the rest of the guys getting into the other vehicles.

As we moved along at a fair clip into the base area proper, just as well the driver knew where he was going because I would not have had a clue. Mostly the buildings were the large demountable type painted green. I assumed we were nearing our destination because the lieutenant started talking rapidly.

He said we had the VIP quarters, which would be handy for us as it was across the road from the officer's club with the intelligence building on one side and the communication building at the other end. Next to that was the HQ building. As we pulled up, the lieutenant jumped out of the back, grabbed my bag, and escorted me into the building. He opened the first door on the right and waited until I entered. He followed me in and put my kitbag in the wardrobe. As I took off my bandolier and put it and my rifle on the double bed, I looked around the room.

There was a desk near the windows, a two seater lounge and two armchairs opposite a wall mounted TV, a fridge with coffee making stuff on top, and beside a counter that was stocked with all types of spirits, the fridge had beer and drink mixers as well as fresh milk. The lieutenant showed me the bathroom, which had a bath as well as a shower. I nodded and walked out of my room.

Across the hallway, Bill was squaring away his gear, and I went to see how the others were getting on. There were two more rooms behind Bills and mine; Tag was in one, Dumper the other. Then there was a large lounge and bar area. The bar area was equipped with fridges and spirits; the other side of this was more accommodation, and at the far end a huge room with a conference table for twenty with maps hung up around the walls.

On the way back to my room, I ducked into see which room Buzz had chosen. All the rooms were like mine, so everyone was going to be comfortable. Back in my room, I dismissed the lieutenant before going inside to square away my gear; Bill had told us earlier that weapons weren't carried on base, so I stripped off my combat gear also.

After walking down to the lounge, I raised my voice and

ordered, "Everyone into the lounge now, please!" I told them all to take a seat as they arrived, but I remained standing. "Now, try to remember, your officers now, so act like one. I will bet you we are going to be scrutinized by everyone here. You have all seen the accommodations we have been given, so rank has its privileges, but to keep what we have, you have to act like gentlemen. Soon we will be going over to the officers' club, so I am going to get Wild Bill to fill us in on the dos and don'ts. I don't know whether we look after our rooms or not, or what the go is regarding the bar or the booze in our rooms. Maybe Bill can help us on that as well." I looked over at Bill. "Bill, we're all yours."

CHAPTER 13

According to Bill, as far as the quarters were concerned, a cleaning staff looked after the rooms when they were in use, and the booze was gratis. I told the people to keep their rooms reasonably clean, which meant at least throwing the sheets and covers up and locking away the guns and ammo. Bill told us the bar in the club was on either a tab system or pay as you go, but the booze was as cheap as Chips'. I told the people to stick with the latter, no setting up a tab. The mess part of the club operated most of the time, but closed between midnight and zero five hundred and was open seven days a week. We could expect to get most things on the menu. Unless stocks were low, it meant we sat and waited to have our orders taken.

At the officers' club a short while later, Bill introduced Tag and I to one of the intelligence officers, Captain Jake Carson, who we would be speaking with in the morning and the boss of his operational planning office, Colonel Reg Price.

While we were having a drink, Price asked, "Tell me, Tiger, is my boy looking after you well?"

"Couldn't be better, Reg. That's why I got him promoted." We laughed at my joke; everyone he knew was aware of the circumstances under which Bill was promoted: for taking part in an extremely hazardous mission, even though as far as we were concerned it was easy mission.

I asked, "Reg, do you mind if Bill is my liaison on any mission that may occur?"

He replied quickly, "That is a certainty, Tiger. By all means." I thanked him.

A little later we went into eat, and my eyes lit up as I perused the menu and decided the fresh Alaskan lobster would be swimming in my stomach tonight. I started to wonder why I didn't take the officer training when I had the chance. Rational thoughts entered my mind; even officers in our army wouldn't get to eat this well. The yanks really did things in style I could give them that.

The following morning after a big breakfast, we went into the lounge. Bill gave us some idea of why we were being called in. The mission was to find and, if possible, destroy a radio station used nightly by the enemy somewhere close to the Quang Ngai, Kontum province's border, up in the highlands, and about one hundred and fifty kilometres from firebase delta. The briefing we were having with Captain Carson was to give us a closer area to focus on, and to let us know what the yanks had been able to come up with and how to go about finding it.

I thought to myself that this could go either way that the job was right up our alley, or it could be a major waste of time. I decided I would have to get Mark's approval once I had heard the extent of the knowledge available. At zero nine hundred, we entered the Intelligence building and were greeted by Jake Carson, who showed us to a briefing room he had setup.

Once we were seated, he wasted no time getting into the mission objectives, which was to locate and destroy the target if we could. He showed us the area where they thought it was located. The closest it could be pinpointed with flyovers and radio triangulation was within a square kilometre.

Tag said, "That's an awful lot of ground to cover in that terrain. Can you get us any closer?"

Carson replied, "We've been waiting for some portable RDF's (Radio Detection Finder) to arrive from the states. They got here last week, finally. The plan is to send a team into the area and sweep it all, but there is a drawback to that. The station only operates during the night."

"Why don't you just listen in if you have the frequency they use?" I asked.

"We don't have a copy of the code they're using, but we're

hoping one of the books you recovered in your last mission will get us closer."

"First off, I need a slow fixed wing to have a look at the area myself. Have any of the flyovers caught ground fire?"

"No. They may be trying to remain inconspicuous," he answered.

"Let's hope so," I murmured. "Can you get me that plane today? I'll do a run over it, and we meet up same time tomorrow. Meanwhile, I have to send a message."

He replied, "You'll have priority, Colonel. I'll send a corpsman to the Major when I have a time for you, sir."

"Very well. Ok men, back to the quarters. Thank you, Captain," I replied.

Back in the quarters, I wrote the message I wanted to send to Mark and gave it to Tag to code and send. I asked Wires, "How good or reliable are these portable RDF's?"

"If they're the ones JJ and I think are, they'll be good and accurate enough to put us within two hundred yards," he replied.

I nodded and said, "Ok, all we have to do now is wait."

Tag returned half an hour later with a reply from Mark, which read: "Don't spend any more than two weeks searching. If you don't find it, call it off. If you do, then do what you do best." I smiled at his last comment.

A young corporal entered the barracks soon after to announce that the flight I wanted had been arranged and could take off as soon as I was at the airfield. The Captain was sending a jeep to take me there in ten minutes. I looked around and said, "Thank you, corporal. Bill, gear up. You are coming on this one. Tag, you're in charge."

After passing over the firebase, we started the area sweep, flying low and slow. Both Bill and I had the side doors open on each side, and we were lying on the floor with binoculars to our eyes as we swept the terrain below. Fifteen minutes later, I was just about to turn to the pilot, when I caught a glint out the corner of my eye. I yelled, "Circle!"

After five minutes, when nothing was spotted, I had the pilot mark our position. I had an overwhelming feeling that this was the place. I told the pilot to expand the circle and said to Bill, "Look for a possible LZ. I think we might have found it."

Two minutes later we circled what looked to be a good spot we could use for insertion and had the pilot keep looking around a bit. I did not want to alert the enemy that we may have found where they were hiding. After another ten minutes, I had the pilot return to base.

On the trip back, I explained to Bill what I had thought I had seen. "Don't ask me how I know, but it's a strong feeling I have. Even though we didn't see it again, it was like the sun glinting on something shiny and metal."

He replied, "Well, your hunches usually have a habit of being right. Anyway, it gives us a place to start if you're wrong."

With a smile, I replied, "Thanks."

Back at base, I called everyone together and filled them in on what I had in mind. "Bill, you'll need to organise some transport because you'll be taking Buzz and Dumper with you. Dumper, fifty kilos of C4 and wiring. Buzz, I want enough rations for three weeks, so top up what we have and anything else you think we'll need. The rest of you start cleaning your guns. Wires or JJ, go to comm's and sort out frequencies and sked timing. All right, let's get it done!"

I went to my room, sat at the desk, and wrote up what I had in mind in a report for HQ. I coded it, and just as I finished, Wires knocked on the door and entered to tell me he was about to go to comm's.

"Good. Take this with you to send to HQ and get the answer before you come back, please."

After lifting the phone and dialling zero, the operator came on. I asked for Captain Carson. When he came on the line, I asked him to come straight over and bring two RDF's with him. While I waited for him to arrive, I pulled out my weapons and started cleaning them, ready for action.

Soon there was a knock on the door, and I looked up to see Carson standing there. I had left the door open. I got up from the bed and invited him in. We moved to the desk, and as he sat down, I asked, "Captain, the gunships I saw at Delta when we flew over, do they stay there?"

"Yes sir. They fly recon patrols and can be used for medical emergencies as well as Evac if needed."

I nodded. "Good. I may have found your target, but if not, I have a search point to from which to start. Here's what I have in mind." I filled him in on everything, including the plan I had formulated coming back in the plane, which was to have two choppers recalled from the firebase to pick us up and take us back to the firebase. We would have the choppers take us to the LZ as part of a normal recon flight. We would make our way to the position I had noted, and if we found the target base, we would observe for a couple of days and either move in and destroy it or call for reinforcements. After that, we would have the firebase choppers extract us and fly us back here. If it were not the target, we would search for three weeks; after that, we would have to abandon the search. Hopefully with the RDF's we would have a good chance of finding the target, even if my hunch were wrong.

Captain Carson said, "That's one helluva plan, Colonel. When do you want to start the ball rolling?"

"Tomorrow, or the day after," I replied.

"That soon! In that case, sir, I'd better get the wheels turning." As he finished his sentence, there was another knock at the door.

Wires had returned with the signal. I beckoned him in, and he handed it to me. I asked, "You get everything else sorted, Rick?"

He smiled and said, "Yes boss. Ready to go."

I nodded and said, "Good. Captain, can you go with Wires and show him and JJ how to use the RDF's please. That'll be all for now. Captain, get back to me later please. Dismissed gents." The Captain saluted, Wires nodded, and they left my room.

I reached for the reply from HQ and started decoding it. The message from Mark was to the point. Carry out the plan, get everything wrapped up, and return to Australia ASAP. I finished cleaning my guns and rifle.

After I had finished doing that, I walked into the lounge to find nine bundles sitting on the table, and as I inspected one bundle, Buzz came in, saw me and said, "All the gear we need to pack, boss. Man, I could have had a field day in their Q store."

I smiled and said, "I'm sure you could have, Buzz. I'll take my bundle and get it packed."

After I had packed my load, everything was in readiness. The phone rang before I left the room. Carson informed me that the choppers from Delta would arrive at zero ten hundred, and he had organised transport to take us to the airfield at zero nine forty-five.

As I walked toward the lounge again, I called into Bill's, Tag's, and Dumper's rooms to see if they were all packed and asked them to join me in the lounge when they were ready. I continued down the hall checking everyone else and telling them the same.

Once they were all gathered, I held a quick briefing about when we were going, what I hoped to achieve, and how we would go about it. "Our transport will be here at zero nine forty-five, so after a relaxing breakfast, we'll slowly get ready. No nice cosy beds for us tomorrow night, boys. We will probably be on stretchers at the firebase. I'm heading over to the boozer, so I'll see you in there." Bill, Tag, and Dumper joined me as I walked across the road.

The following morning, we took our time over breakfast and went back to the VIP hut to get ready. I put on some cam cream before strapping on my side arms and combat webbing, followed by my radio, but not switched on. Next, I put some cam sweat cloth around my neck and tucked the ends into my shirt, replaced the silver rank pins with the black set, put my bandolier over my head and right arm, picked up my backpack and rifle, and shut the door of my room.

I walked down to the lounge where Dumper passed me a coffee. I asked, "Do you think we have enough explosives, Dumper?"

"I should think so, boss. It's not as if we're bringing down mountains again," he said with a laugh.

I laughed, remembering our first mission. "I hope not, Dumper, I hope not." Our laughter continued.

When everyone was in the lounge and quietly talking to each other, I looked at my watch and announced, "All right, the transport should be here soon. Let's head outside."

They grabbed their backpacks and rifles and followed me as I walked toward the door. Just as I got outside, three jeeps drove up, so three of us jumped into each jeep. I nodded to the driver, who pulled away headed for the airfield. The driver parked next to two gunships whose crews were standing close by.

An air cavalry Captain stepped forward, saluted, and asked if I was Colonel Davis. I nodded, and he introduced himself as Tangles Holden and told me they were ready to leave when we were.

I nodded and said, "As soon as we're loaded, Captain. Why Tangles?"

"Well sir, if there's a firefight around, I'm usually tangled up in it."

I laughed and said, "Ok Tangles. Let's go."

"Yes sir," he replied. Having split into our normal groups, we boarded and soon the rotors were at full pitch, and we lifted off.

After an hour, we landed at firebase Delta. The camp commander, Major Tim Wright, met us and escorted us to our quarters, pointing out the Q store, mess, slit trenches, our quarters, and HQ. We followed him down the steps of the sandbagged building, which was a timber frame with a sheet tin roof.

"Charlie's been quiet lately, but use the trenches if he calls," he told us.

I liked his devil-may-care attitude as he showed us around. The building had twelve bunks, and he said the ablutions were at the back and showed us the doorway. He faced me and asked, "How long you here for, sir?"

I looked at my watch and decided it was too late to start today. "The mission we're on is time sensitive, major, so I'd like an insertion flight scheduled to reach these coordinates by zero nine hundred tomorrow, if you can arrange it. I would like to use all four choppers as a normal routine patrol flight. I don't want to alert anyone to what we're doing." I passed him the coordinates of the LZ.

He replied, "Yes sir, I'll get right on it." He headed for the doorway.

As I settled down on my bunk, Bill showed me his latest acquisition, his own pair of night vision goggles. "The General made sure I had a pair before I left Saigon. Hell knows where he got them, but I wasn't about to say no."

I laughed and replied, "You'll certainly need them on this job."

The following morning, the insertion went smoothly. We didn't encounter any enemy. We were five hundred metres from our target coordinates an hour later, and I had half my team out scouting as we moved toward the coordinates.

Two hundred metres further up, Lizard's voice came through my earpiece. "Boss, Lizard. Come up slowly toward me."

We converged on Lizard's position. When I reached him, he pointed something out. I trained my binoculars for a closer look, and then I saw it: one hundred yards away was a tree that had a very thick antenna pole tied to it. The pole was easily eighty feet in height.

I whispered into my mic, "The cagey bastards. No wonder we couldn't find it. Bill, get over here and look at this."

Once everyone had a look, I had JJ scout origin of the antenna feed wire. His voice sounded in my ear, "Found it, boss. I'll come back and get you."

We followed him over a rise the tree was standing on; we moved another fifty yards forward and saw a small clearing. As

I saw the other side of the clearing, I groaned; the mouth of a bloody cave. Shit! As we watched, four figures appeared at the cave mouth, one an NVA officer and three VC. The officer was obviously instructing them to do something, so I followed their progress with the glasses.

They went to the clearing and pulled up a bamboo-framed cover with leaves and dirt on it, and bugger me, sitting in the pit was a generator motor. The crafty little shits! They pulled out a jerry can and refuelled the tank. After they replaced the cover, the only visible thing was the top of an exhaust pipe.

After assigning Tag to keep watch, I took the rest of the men back down into the gully and over a slightly lower rise to the bottom. We had a good look around and decided this would be our LUP. After we set up house, I asked Wires what our sked time was. "No set time, boss. It's operating twenty-four hours."

"Ok. Set up the radio and send the code word for finding it and that we're observing with an intention to attack in a couple of days," I replied.

The next day I concluded, after hearing the reports of each OP shift, that there were at most ten enemies present, but more likely only six, two NVA officers and four VC. I started to formulate an assault plan, which did not take me long. It seemed that the two officers were the radio operators and the VC were there to do the grunt work and guard the place during the day while the officers slept.

I planned for Lizard and Gecko along with JJ to cover the assault group. JJ would remain with them because once we had knocked out everything inside, it would be up to them to cut down and destroy the aerial. The assault would be at zero two hundred the next morning. Wires and I would take the radio while Tag led the rest to nullify the VC. It wasn't the best of plans, because once we were in the cave we had no idea of the layout, so I was trusting luck and hoped the only ones awake would be the officers. I wanted to time the assault for when they would be at their weariest and while the others slept.

We rested as much as we could during the remainder of the day and most of the night.

When it was time for the attack, we all geared up, put our night vision on, took our rifles and the two backpacks of explosives, and moved to the OP, which was the rise where we first observed what was going on. We left our rifles and explosives with Lizard, Gecko, and JJ.

I led the assault team silently toward the cave mouth. About ten feet from the cave, I heard Gecko say, "Halt. Go to ground!"

I saw one of the officers coming out for a smoke. As we went to ground like shadows, I whispered, "Dumper." I watched as he slowly moved up behind the officer, grabbed his head, sliced his throat, and then slowly lowered him to the ground.

Gecko gave the all clear, and we continued. At the mouth of the cave, we split into two groups; luckily, the next officer was in the radio room. Wires did as I had done previously and walked boldly into the room. He shot the startled officer stone dead.

Tag took his team further into the cave, and a few minutes later I heard, "All down."

"Dumper, Buzz, the explosives. Wires?" I asked.

He replied, "Yes boss. Getting the books and paperwork together."

"Roger that," I replied. When Buzz and Dumper returned, I said, "Give me two blocks, and give the empty pack to Wires, then rig the place to come down."

I moved outside and called to JJ. "How's it going, JJ?"

"It's coming down now, boss. Soon there won't be much left of it."

"Good man," I replied. I moved to a spot so I could see the generator exhaust showing just above ground level. I reefed the cover off and placed a block of C4 each side of the motor with the detonator wiring attached. I grabbed a stick, stuck it in the ground and wrapped the detonator wiring around it so it could be attached to the main wiring as Dumper paid it out. Dumper came out of the cave with the rest of the team around him, feeding out cable; he spliced in the charges to the motor and continued towards the rise.

Dawn was about an hour away, and I had to make the decision to blow it now or wait for daylight. I decided to wait. I sent JJ to the LUP to send a message to Firebase Delta to extract us from the LZ at zero six thirty and pack up the radio. I sent Lizard and Buzz with him, instructing them to get all their stuff and return. When they came back, I had the next two do the same and so on until we were all back at the rise with all our gear and ready to move.

As soon as it was light enough for Wires to take photos, he did. I flicked the firing switch; the only real noise was from the motor blowing to bits, but there was no longer a cave. It had imploded.

While Wires got his shots, Lizard said, "We've got company boss. Ten VC heading this way at a run."

"Shit!" I exclaimed as I thought quickly. "Ok, we'll wait until they're close, and we'll engage and withdraw to the LUP and hit them again."

As it turned out, we did not need to withdraw in a hurry because I then stood up and fired a grenade that took out four of them while accurate shooting took out the rest. As we moved to collect papers and make sure they were dead, one of the group that fell from my grenade was able to fire a round that hit my right side. I stumbled to my right, the rest of my team opened up, and he was cut to ribbons.

Tag was at my side instantly and ripped my shirt open to have a look at the wound. He put a bandage on it and said, "We'll go back to the LUP, and I'll fix it properly. Meanwhile just hold the pressure on this pad, ok." I just nodded.

Bill made sure all the papers were collected, that there were no survivors, and then helped me back to the LUP. After the shock wore off, I stripped off my gear and Tag bandaged me up while the guys ate.

After pronouncing it as only a deep flesh wound, I said to him, "Did you really have to rip my shirt?" I fished a fresh shirt out of my combat webbing bum bag, grumbling.

He replied with a smile, "No, but I knew it would piss you off."

We had some breakfast and coffee. After that, I announced it was time to go after everyone had finished. We reached the LZ with five minutes to spare, and as we heard the choppers, Bill threw a green smoke grenade. We arrived back at firebase Delta fifteen minutes later. We trooped toward our quarters, and Buzz disappeared into the store and joined us in the quarters a few minutes later.

He passed me two new shirts in my size. "You may as well throw the other one away after you grab your rank pins off it, boss."

Smiling, I thanked him. I told Wires to send the destroyed code word to Da Nang, and Bill to see if the camp commander could join us. While I was waiting, I brought my mission diary up to date and started drafting a message for home that I would send from Da Nang. Wires returned with an acknowledgement from Carson to say well done and to let him know when we would return to Da Nang.

Major Wright and Bill came in shortly after that, and I asked, "Major, how soon could you get my men and I back to Da Nang?"

He replied, "I could get you back there after lunch, say thirteen hundred take-off."

I smiled and said, "Thank you. Go ahead and arrange it please and thank you for all your help."

He returned the smile and answered, "My pleasure, sir."

We landed back in Da Nang at fourteen hundred. Carson and transport were waiting for us. As the jeeps rolled to our quarters, Carson and I arranged for the mission debrief to take place the following morning at the Intelligence building at zero eight thirty, and we anticipated, it would only take an hour since this was an intelligence mission in the first place. That left me free to have

Bill get a hold of his boss and arrange a flight back to Australia for my team. As soon as we reached our quarters, I had Bill start working on it.

An hour later, I was finishing the coding of the message for our HQ, which included a detailed report on the mission we had undertaken and the successful conclusion. Bill came into my room to announce that Colonel Price had arranged space for us on a Star lifter cargo plane, which was twice the size of a Hercules, leaving Da Nang bound for Tindal the following night at twenty hundred and due to arrive at Tindal at eighteen hundred the following night after stops in Hawaii and Guam. I included this information in my message; meanwhile, JJ had been at the intelligence photo lab having the camera photos developed. We would keep two copies and hand over one copy and the negatives to Carson during the debriefing session the following morning. The team worked hard to get their mission reports written and copied.

By dinner that night, everything was ready for the following morning, and my message sent to HQ. I decided the boys could let their hair down a little that night in the officer's mess. Later, Bill and I had time to have a quiet talk and say our goodbyes to each other.

"Somehow I've got the feeling we'll be working together again soon, so I won't say goodbye, just that we'll see each other again," I said to him.

He replied, "Well, I've learned to trust your feelings, but besides that, you'll have to come back again to accept your Purple Heart."

"What the hell is that?" I asked.

"Any soldier wounded in combat automatically receives the Purple Heart medal. Carson recommended you get one after he found out you were hit on the last mission."

"What a lot of bullshit!" I shook my head. "Well, you'll just have to accept it for me, and I'll tell him so." I remarked.

The next morning the debrief went as expected. We tendered

our reports, the photos, the codebooks and the enemy papers, and as with the last mission, everyone was amazed about what we had come back with, and what we had accomplished within the short time we had been there. I also had a word with Carson about the Purple Heart nonsense, but he remained adamant. I informed him that Bill would accept it in my name.

That evening, we were all back on the tarmac waiting to load and shaking hands with some of the officers we'd come to know. The team gave Bill a fond farewell, shaking hands, and Tag presented him with a regimental beret complete with insignia on behalf of all of us. As he climbed the ramp, tears formed in his eyes, and I gave him a final handshake and nod before boarding. As the ramp started lifting, I gave him a salute and made my way to my seat. Ten minutes later, we were in the air heading home.

CHAPTER 14

After arriving at Tindal, I went to have a chat with air operation and found out that a shuttle flight was leaving for Pearce in an hour. After being told there was room to take us, I told them we would be having something to eat in the crew mess. We finally arrived back in Western Australia at zero ten thirty local time, and I rang Mark so he could arrange to have us picked up. An hour later, we walked into our building. I dropped my gear in my office, told Tag I was going over to HQ. I knocked on Mark's open door and walked in. He told me to take a seat and said, "You look beat. I guess I don't have to ask how the flight home was."

"No. After thirty-six hours flying, we are all pretty well done in, and we didn't get much time after the last mission to settle down before we were on our way back. So what has been happening here? And what's next?"

He replied and started laughing, "Well, what's next is you have to front the OC. And what's happening, apart from you're getting us into so much shit that it wasn't funny, and the yanks wanting to keep you full time. Not a lot."

I laughed. "Yeah, Abrams did hint along those lines, but I wasn't having a bar of it."

"Just as well. However, seriously, at the end of the week, I am going to stand your team down for six weeks leave. You've been away for nearly five months, and most of that time was in action, except for your little enforced holiday. By the way, I do like the way you turned the backlash of that onto Chipson. He can be a right arsehole at times. The signal from Abrams wasn't too complimentary at all toward him, but that's OC's problem. Speaking of which, are you ready to face the music?"

"Yes sir," I replied, "but before we do this, could I ring our building and talk to Tag?"

He lifted his handset and passed it to me while he dialled. Tag came on, and I told him to take the guys to lunch and I would see them afterward. Mark and I stood, and I waited for him to take the lead as we went to the OC's office. After knocking, we entered and stood at attention in front of his desk.

He looked up and said, "Sit Captain. Sgt Davis, you can remain standing. Now then, boyo, you have caused me no end of grief, and high praise. Thank you for ingratiating yourself with our yank cousins and doing such a splendid job, but more on that in a minute. You're very lucky you were on assignment when all this shit about your true date of birth became known; otherwise, I wouldn't have been able to help you." He took a drink of water.

He continued with a slight smile. "Whenever there's a war on, men will try to join the services even if they're underage, but you've taken it to new heights. Not only were you underage and still are, but also not even a citizen of this country! That has to be fixed very soon. I must say, I admire your ingenuity and craftiness, but because of your devotion to duty and your previous gallant actions, you are able to remain in the army without further disciplinary action, and to stay with us. I guess the bean counters have worked out that your worth too much to throw away."

I was about to speak, but he held his hand up. "However, like I said, these things are going to be rectified tomorrow. Captain Ryan will have one of the legal people come see you, and he'll make sure all the paperwork you need for citizenship and a passport is filled out correctly and a rush is put on your application." He paused, shaking his head. "Damn it Tiger, you're too valuable to me. You really should have told us. Yes, I know you weren't too sure what would have happened if you did, but at least we would have been forewarned and possibly able to short cut it. Anyway, it's done now, so we'll forget it ever happened. On another note, your work with the yanks was superb. You have shown them our capabilities, and for some reason, they love you. Don't be surprised if SRT doesn't get more work involving them. All I can say is thank you for fulfilling the role I gave you. I understand you and your team are going on stand down, so make the best of your break, because the jobs are already lining up for you." He stood up and reached across to shake my hand. "Well done, thank you."

When I returned to SRT, Tag took me over to the base medical unit to get a doctor to have a look at my wound, which was still bandaged. After looking at it, he said I was lucky; another smidge and the bullet would have pierced my liver.

He asked Tag if there had been any greyish colour in the wound when he cleaned it, and Tag said, "Just a little."

"Hmm. It seems the bullet may have only just nicked your liver. You may end up with a scar on your liver, but that would be all. Nothing to worry about. This doesn't need a bandage now. It's healing remarkably well, so I'll only put a plaster gauze on it. Come back and see me in two days."

"Ok doc," I replied. As we left, I asked Tag, "What did you make me do that for?"

He shrugged. "I know you've got a high pain threshold and wouldn't complain about anything unless you were at death's door, but I wanted to make sure that you're all right."

"Fair enough," I replied.

Back in our building, I gave the guys the good news about the stand down for leave and told them to fix any travel warrants with Mark before the end of the week. I went to my office and rang Sharon to tell her we were back and that I'd see her at the usual time before I started sorting my gear out. During the flight time coming home, we'd taken the time to clean all our weapons, so my guns went into the gunroom, the rifle in the rack, and the pistols into my locker. I made a coffee in the ready room before going back to my office and thought about the stuff the legal eagle could possibly bring up.

At knock off time, I took my kitbag with me down to the Sig's mess. It only had a couple pairs of cams, and I left it beside my car that Sharon had obviously been driving while I was away.

Inside the mess, she rushed into my arms and gave me a prolonged kiss. "God it's good to see you. I've already got the drinks in, so come on over to the table." She pulled me to the table where our drinks were waiting.

I smiled at her. "Been having fun with the car, honey?"

With an innocent look on her face that broke into a smile, she said, "No, I drove it today so you could drive me home."

I laughed and replied, "Ah huh, and how did you know I'd be home today?"

Laughingly she replied, "I took a lucky guess." We laughed as I fished out a smoke.

When we got home, she took my washing to sort out while I opened the place up. She came out to me holding the bloodied shirt. "What don't I know? Get up and take your shirt off."

I turned to her. "It's old. Just throw it away."

She insisted I take my shirt off, and I did as she asked. When she saw the bandage pad, she said, "Christ Tom, you didn't tell me you'd been shot!" She rushed to put her arms around me and got a closer look at the pad. "That's been bleeding, and that's where I would normally have my arms around you. Oh darling, you should have said something. I'm sorry."

She turned away to finish sorting the washing, but not before I noticed a tear falling from her eye. From the laundry, she called, "You go and get changed so I can have that uniform. I'll make us a drink when I'm done, and you can tell me everything that's been going on. I want to know what these rank pins are doing in your kitbag."

I changed out of the uniform I was wearing, minus the shirt that was already off. I put on shorts and a T shirt and took them into the laundry. I exchanged my stuff for the two sets of Eagle pins, which I took back to the bedside table.

When I came out of the bedroom, Sharon was making the drinks, so I went out to the balcony, lit up, and filled her in on what I had been doing. I told her about the trouble with Chipson, and that I had the CnC visit us, and what happened.

She couldn't contain herself. "So that's why you have the Eagle pins, but just because you are a Colonel, don't go trying to throw your weight around here. Am I clear, Colonel, sir?" We laughed together at her comment. "Why did he come to you? Usually you get summoned to them."

Now we came to the subject that could rip apart our relationship, but I told her exactly what had happened, and why the CnC had come to me. After the shock at what I told her wore off a little, the questions came. I told her the whole truth about my age and how I went about getting my forged documents. I wasn't sure whether she was pissed off with me for not telling her my real age or the fact that I hadn't told her before. Eventually she calmed down. I was only three years younger than her and we loved each other, so why should something like that upset our life together. The subject was dropped after I told her what happened when I fronted the boss this morning, and the visit coming from legal the next day.

The following afternoon, after Dumper and I made our way down to the Sig's mess, Sharon said to me, "Honey, you look as if you're only half here. Didn't things go all right today with the lawyer?"

As I took a sip of my drink, I replied, "What? Oh yeah, everything is fine. I should get my Citizenship Certificate in a couple of weeks, but the passport will be longer coming. I do have a matter we need to talk about at home. I filled the guys in about it earlier, but it's rather important and something we need to talk about."

"If it's that important, we can go after this drink." I just nodded my head.

At home, we changed into comfortable, loose clothes. I made drinks while Sharon opened up, and we went out onto the balcony table. I lit both smokes.

Sharon began the conversation. "Ok, what's so important?"

"As you know I'm entitled to a war service house after each tour. The lawyer told me there is a wrinkle with that. They don't accumulate! If I don't buy a house before the last tour is added, instead of buying two, I can only get one. That means we've got to buy a house within the next month or lose the next one."

"Shit! Then we better start looking for a house," she replied.

I nodded and asked, "So where would you really like to live?"

She thought about that as I freshened up our drinks. When I came back, she said, "Darling, I would like a house in Brisbane, but on the south side out toward Ipswich where there's some newer suburbs."

I thought about it. I didn't know Brisbane and decided I needed to learn. "Ok, I'm on leave in a day. I could fly up there, look around, and see if I can get one, and then we'll have a house up there."

She sipped her drink slowly before replying. "If you fly up, you could stop at my parents' place while you're there. Dad will probably let you have Mum's car to drive around in. They could even pick you up from the airport. I'll ring them soon and see if it's all right."

I nodded my head. "Yeah ok. Tomorrow I'll see Mark and get a travel warrant, ring army housing, and get things started."

The following day, I saw Mark. He wrote out a travel warrant for me. Back at SRT, I rang the local office of Army Housing and started the ball rolling. They told me when I'd found a house, all I had to was go to the Army Housing Office in Brisbane, and as I was approved up to fifty thousand, they'd write out a cheque to be paid to the Real Estate company handling the sale. I thanked them and hung up. I let out a whoop of delight.

I went into the ready room and told the guys how much I'd been approved for with Army Housing. Gecko chimed, "Well, it looks like Anna and I are going house hunting while I'm on leave."

Most of the guys were nodding in agreement. I wished them

well on their leave and told them, "I'll see you guys when you get back. Take it easy and be careful. I've been told the jobs are backing up, so be ready to get into some work when you get back. Until then, have fun."

The next morning, I felt like death warmed up, so I went back to bed. When the fever started to hit me, Sharon realised I had come down with a case of the flu and nursed me most of the time. I was beyond caring at that stage. I would drift in and out of sleep. At one point, I woke up as she was saying, "You know, seeing you're buying us a house, it's probably about time we got married."

To save any argument or conversation because I just wanted to go back to sleep after being disturbed, I answered, "Sure honey, whatever you want." I didn't realise the implications of what I'd agreed to.

When I was better a couple of days later, I was reminded of the agreement. I had no option except to say, "In that case, I guess we're now engaged. I'll get you a ring while I'm away."

With a smile, she went to the bedroom and came back with an old ring. "That's the size you will need to get."

The next day I went into the Ansett office and arranged my return ticket. Sharon rang her parents with my flight times. Everything was arranged, and her father was going to give me his car to use instead of her mother's. They would pick me up at the airport. She gave them the news about our engagement, so naturally they were happy about that.

Three days later Trevor and Jenny picked me up at the airport at fifteen hundred, and after settling in, we had a nice dinner together.

The next morning, I consulted the street map and decided to start searching a suburb called Wacol. Now, I won't bore you with the details of days on end looking at houses; most of us have been there and done that. Suffice it to say, after three weeks, I found one that I liked in a place called Gailes; it was massive, only five years old. On a quarter acre of ground, faced the west, had four bedrooms with an ensuite in the master bedroom. A games room with enough room for a pool table, a separate three-car garage. Best of all, it had a spa and swimming pool in the backyard. All the rooms were air-conditioned.

I took photos of everything on Sharon's camera. I sat down with the agent and told him I would take it. We arranged a deal that worked for both of us. The agent would pay for the inspections I wanted and the transfer into my name, at Trevor and Jenny's address. We shook hands on the deal, and off I went to the Army Housing Office, which was at Gallipoli barracks in Enoggera. I told them I needed a cheque for thirty-nine thousand and the realty company's name; an hour later, I headed back to Gailes with the cheque. The agent gave me the two grand cash I had asked for, and we signed all the paperwork required. He arranged for the inspections I wanted for the next day so the reports would reach me in a couple of days.

The following day I caught the train into the city, and while the photos were processed, I went shopping for an engagement and wedding ring for Sharon. The engagement ring had a half-carat square diamond with cubic zirconia stones going down each side band, and the wedding ring fitted behind it nicely. They were able to resize them, if I gave them an hour, so after getting the photos and coffee, I picked the rings up and headed to the train station to grab a train that would take me back to Banyo. Unfortunately, I had just missed one, so I whiled away the time by going next door to the pub to have a scotch.

Naturally, when I got back to the house, Sharon's parents looked at the photos of the house, which they thought were great and would be a good place to live. Jenny went gaga after I showed them the rings and asked, "Why haven't you bought a wedding ring for yourself?"

I explained that I would switch my dress ring to my left hand after we were married, which mollified her after I went to my room, took it out of my bag, and put it on for her to see. Three days later, the inspection reports and deed to the house arrived in the afternoon mail.

They had cut it a bit fine considering I was due to return to Perth the next day. After perusing the reports, we decided I had made a brilliant purchase.

I had been talking to Sharon most nights, keeping her up to date, except for telling her I had bought the engagement and wedding rings, and that night I let her know when I would be arriving so she could pick me up.

After saying goodbye to Trevor and Jenny at the airport, I boarded the plane and watched a couple movies during the flight home, Rio Bravo with John Wayne and Day of the Triffids, a low budget English horror film. The flight wasn't nearly as bad as it could have been, thanks to the entertainment.

Sharon picked me up and we drove home. She was like a cat on a hot tin roof until we were home. I no sooner had my bag on the bed for emptying than she wanted to have a look at the photos and keys to the house I had bought. She was in seventh heaven when I placed the engagement ring on her finger.

After another week of filling my days by running on the beach, swimming, and surfing, it was time to go back to work.

During the next few months, number two squadron returned from Vietnam, and no other sabre squadron took their place. As far as the regiment was concerned, our days there were over. Sharon and I spent Christmas apart because she wanted to go home and visit the house, while I had to work as the team was on standby. This caused some intense arguments before she left, and when she returned at the start of February, the hammer came down rather hard.

Her next posting came through; she had to report to the Signals Company at Sananandah Barracks Wacol by March fifteen. This really started some huge arguments, but we were two rational adults; we compromised and worked it out. I would move all my stuff back to my barracks room, and she would arrange the movers for the removal of her furniture at the flat to our house at Gailes. We would be married two weeks before she had to report, have a week's honeymoon at Rottnest Island before she drove her car and clothes back to Queensland. I deposited ten thousand into her account for more furniture for the house.

We went to see the army chaplain, who told us we could be married at the barracks chapel. When I brought up my age, he said, "That's all right. I can make a declaration that you will be on an overseas operation at that time so you have to be married early. It won't be a problem."

The day the movers came for the removal, Sharon moved into base quarters for two nights prior to our wedding, and on the first of March we were married in our dress uniforms. Dumper served as best man and Janice as maid of honour. All the team and their partners, Mark and his wife, the Colonel and his wife, and Sharon's company CO and his wife, attended. At the reception held in the sergeants' mess, Sharon's CO announced that now we were married, her next posting would be at the same barracks where I was stationed.

After the honeymoon on Rottnest, where we had a few arguments about my work, we spent our last night together in a motel before I drove her to her car in the morning. With a last kiss and cuddle, she started the Monaro for the long drive to Queensland.

After she left, I drove over to SRT to begin my day. Four nights later, while I was in my room, Mrs. Davis rang to tell me she had arrived safely and the following day the furniture was arriving at the house. She and her mother were going over to meet them and would probably do some shopping before she had to report for work the day after. She would let me know the new phone numbers when she knew them.

The team and I had been putting a lot of time into training with different scenarios at the kill house, and we varied our training from nighttime to daytime and back again. Sometimes we would finish a daytime scenario, and I would then pull a snap operation after hours, just to keep everyone on their toes. One morning after we had pulled an all-night training exercise, I stood the team down until the next day. I was finishing some paperwork before heading to bed myself when my office phone rang. Mark needed me to go see him, and after telling him I would be right there, I locked up, grabbed my beret, and went to HQ.

Mark had me sit after closing the door. "I know that you've been putting a lot of time in at the kill house. Is that because you're frustrated not having your wife around, or does the team need all this extra training?"

I smiled as I answered. "We've been at it a bit hard lately, but no. I miss Sharon not being around, but this is more work orientated. We need to be doing something to keep ourselves from getting bored."

"I might have something for you to get your teeth into, but this will be the type of operation that never took place. We were never involved. What do you think? Are ready to give it a go, or do you want to pass it up?"

I looked at him with a smile. "You certainly know how to keep me involved, don't you? Ok, say I am ready to see what it is. Can you tell me a little more to help me make up my mind?"

Now it was his turn to laugh. "This will be absolutely top secret. Only the boss, your team, and I will know anything about this. It is for the yanks again, but this time it is a little different. It will mean going into a country with whom we are not at war. If any of you are caught, we will deny knowledge of your existence and try other avenues to get you out after the heat dies down."

I thought a few things over before asking, "Will I have use of Major Fredrick on this op?"

"I'll have to take that under advisement."

"How sensitive is it really? Apart from being in a foreign country, and I'd have to assume it's either in Laos or Cambodia, because we still have troops in Vietnam."

He smiled. "Damn your intuition. Yes, it is one of the two you mentioned. If you'll give me an ok, anything else concerned with this will take place off base in civvy attire."

"Ok, I'm hooked, but in the end it's up to majority decision from the team when we're told the whole story."

"Agreed. Our cousins have a man in the air at present on route to us, so it should be tomorrow or the day after that we'll be taking a trip into town."

After leaving HQ, I left a note on Tag's door that I wanted to see everyone at SRT after dinner but before they went into the boozer. I finished it with something's on. I set my alarm for dinner and crashed out.

After dinner at the Sgt's mess, I went to SRT and opened up. I made a coffee in the ready room while I waited. By the time I had a smoke, the rest of the team had assembled. I addressed them while they sat, filling them in on everything that transpired in Mark's office. "In the end, the decision is by majority vote whether we go or bypass it, but I'm going to give you a choice now. Do we bypass, or do we want to know more? So who's for knowing more?" Every hand went up; I smiled. "People would think you're all sick of training. Ok, all we can do is wait until I hear something from the boss.

From now on, absolute secrecy, not a word to anyone. Remember, your life, and more importantly, mine, could hang on this. Any questions?"

Buzz, the joker of the team, raised his hand. "Is it all right if we go to the boozer now? I think I need a drink."

I smiled and replied, "Yeah Buzz, go have some fun. I'll see you in the morning."

Tag stayed behind, and after everyone had gone, asked, "Are we going to have Bill in on this one?"

I looked at him and replied, "Well, you heard what I said about that, but it would be nice to have him along. If things go tits up, the yanks will move heaven and earth to get him, and hopefully us, out of where ever we'll be."

"Yeah, that's what I was thinking too, but someone not wanting the yank army to know what's going on stinks."

He was right; I had had the same thought. "All we can do now is wait and see. If I don't like the smell of it, I will likely vote to pass it by. However, if I am given a legitimate reason, I might go with it. Right now, all we are doing is theorising. We will know more soon. I mean to keep my word; this will go to a majority vote. If we don't have that option, I will pull the pin straight away. Now let's go have some drinks, have fun, and worry about it when it happens."

He smiled and replied, "That's one order I can go along with. See you in the morning, Tiger."

We locked up; he headed to the OR's mess and I stopped to enter the Sgt's mess. As I sat in the mess contemplating all sorts of connotations about the mission, I became quite blitzed. I stumbled back to bed to let tomorrow take care of itself.

CHAPTER 15

In the morning, I went to breakfast with a grade seven hangover, and by the time I'd had something filling and two coffees, it had dissipated to a grade two. After opening up SRT and having another coffee with a smoke, I was more or less back on top of my game, which is just as well because at zero eight ten Mark rang to inform me that the meeting was booked for eleven hundred at the Plaza.

Mark and I arrived in the first taxi of three, with ten minutes to spare, and as we gathered in the foyer Mark rang the room number he had been given. We went to the eleventh floor conference room and found seats. A couple of minutes later, two waiters came in with huge platters of sandwiches, danishes, pastries, and three jugs of coffee, which they set in the middle of the table and left.

As they were leaving two men came in dressed in suits carrying briefcases. The first one was about six one, with brown hair and brown eyes. He pulled out what looked like a toy car controller and moved about the room. The other was about five ten with blonde hair and blue eyes. He sat at the head of the table and watched the other one, who had closed and locked the door. He nodded.

The one sitting at the table spoke. "I'm sorry for the inconvenience, gentlemen, but we needed to sweep the room for bugs. We don't want any of this getting out." Mark and I exchanged a look. "My name is Alex Stein, and my partner is John Mosely. We are agents of the US DEA (Drug Enforcement Agency). I understand that Colonel Davis is here." I put my hand up. "Am I to understand that the rest of these gentlemen are your staff, sir?"

"Yes, as well as my boss, General Ryan." Some of the team laughed, and Mark nearly choked.

Stein continued, ignoring the commotion. "Thank you, sir." He addressed Mark. "And thank you for taking the time, General." Mark nodded. "Now let's get straight to business."

"General we've come to you, because Colonel Davis and his staff have developed a reputation in our military of being the people who handle the impossible in the shortest amount of time, without casualties. You aren't from the US, which brings us to the mission." He cleared his throat. "Two years ago the CIA (Central Intelligence Agency) thought up a plan to weaken Charlie with an idea to supply his army with free heroin, and so formed a detachment, code named Air America. Perhaps you've heard of it, Colonel?" I nodded. "What they did was establish opium fields in Laos farmed by the local peasants."

He halted to pour a coffee for himself. "Feel free to enjoy the refreshments gentlemen." He gestured to the food and drinks. "Now to continue, eventually the CIA dropped the operation, but some rogue members of Air America remained and continued farming and processing the opium into heroin. Instead of supplying Charlie with free heroin, they started dealing it as a commodity and have since started smuggling it into the US, using corrupted army and air force personnel on a grand scale. The reason we have come to you is we want to stop the supply but have no idea who in our forces can be trusted and who cannot. Therefore, we need a totally non-US force to destroy the fields and interrupt the supply."

"Why not just bomb the fields? Surely you know where they are," I asked.

He looked at me with a small smile. "Yes we know where they are, but to bomb them risks starting a war with Laotian forces, and quite frankly, sir, our country is tired of war and can't keep it up. Soon we will pull out and leave Vietnam to fend for itself. The other problem with bombing is that it will not destroy the fields for good; we want to make the ground infertile while at the same time destroying whatever crop is in the ground. We can air drop the chemicals to our ground forces when they're ready to destroy the fields. So how about it? What do you think, gentlemen?"

"Where are we getting our support from?"

Stein replied, "We have our own agency operatives running a base beside the airfield at Da Nang complete with two caribou transports and four gunships, but no US personnel outside of our agency is allowed access, sir."

"Agent Stein, I want one US soldier in on this, or I say no," I said. "He is completely trustworthy, and I'd need him along in case we have to deal with any US forces."

Stein nodded his head. "In that case, sir, we could bring him into the loop, but I'd need his name."

"All right, Agent Stein, if you and Agent Mosely could give us a few minutes. I need to confer with my staff."

They rose from each end of the table, taking their briefcases, and Stein said, "We'll wait at the end of the hall until you're ready, sir." I nodded and they exited the room.

I looked at Mark. "What do you think, General Ryan?"

Mark was laughing with the rest of the crew. "I think it's a reasonable request, and it has merit. Whatever goes to the States invariably ends up coming here, and we already have enough junkies in this country without adding to the flow. I made you a promise, though; the decision is yours and that of your men"

I looked around the table and said, "I'm with the boss on this, but it's up to you guys. Majority rules. Those for the mission, hands up." Without any hesitation, all hands went into the air. "Ok, looks like we're a go. Let's get those two back in here and go through everything." Everyone nodded in agreement while I went to the door and beckoned them in. They took the seats they had vacated moments ago.

"Gentlemen, you might want to write some of this down. First, Major William Fredrick, 2nd Western Pioneer Company, will be bought into the loop. If his boss gives you any grief, just say Tiger Davis needs Bill's help. Two, we need to know what sort of explosives we will be using. Three, what is our tactical backup? Four, do you have parachutes available? Five, how do we get there, and six, when will we have full access to your intelligence? Until all these questions are answered, none of us leave this room." I sat down and reached for a sandwich.

Stein watched me eating before he spoke. "We'll bring Major Fredrick into the loop as soon as we get to Da Nang. All of the DEA Personnel at Da Nang will be your back up. Yes, we do have access to parachutes, and the explosives you will be using are thermal charges and detonators. The chemical agent in napalm will be poured over the fields, and then ignited, which will render the ground infertile for years. You get there with us in our jet, and as far as taking a look at our intelligence, if you agree to accept the mission, we can get into that now." He held up his briefcase.

I grabbed another sandwich and took a bite before answering him. "Having your personnel as our backup doesn't thrill me too much. Let's face it. You're really policemen when it's all boiled down, not military. However, we have decided to accept the mission, but we'll need to meet our liaison agent with your agency as soon as possible."

Stein smiled and replied, "That's easily taken care of, sir. I am your liaison agent. Ex captain 1st battalion rangers. John is also an ex ranger. In fact, out of the whole force in Da Nang, there's only one civilian."

I laughed. "Touché, Captain. Allow me to withdraw my comment about policemen. It seems we will have military style backup if required. My compliments, Captain."

He smiled and replied, "Thank you, sir. Now, let's get into what we've got." He took everything out of his briefcase, and we started what became an impromptu briefing. I had been impressed with his businesslike manner to start with and found myself warming to him. He certainly believed in what he was doing, which came through in his manner and tone of voice. I liked him.

When we discussed what to expect in the way of opposition, he looked at it in a military context and wasn't squeamish.

"Whoever you come across on this mission should be considered an enemy and killed."

Tag interrupted. "What if they're only unarmed peasants?"

Stein looked him in the eye. "Sir, don't forget you're going to destroy their livelihood. They will not take kindly to that, so you will have no choice but to kill or be injured yourself. If any escape, they will hightail it to their masters to report your presence, and you will find yourself in a real firefight with ex-military renegades. That's something you'll need to avoid because you'll be outnumbered ten to one." Stein made sense, and I think after explaining it to them, the team agreed with his kill policy. I know I did!

While Stein filled his coffee cup, I looked at the other agent. "Ok, John, you haven't said much. Tell me about this jet Alex mentioned."

Mosely grunted, "It's a humdinger, sir. A new Boeing 737 it was seized when we arrested one of the Mexican drug lords last year in Los Angeles. Rather luxurious. Just the thing for flying a lot of miles."

I nodded and turned back to Stein. "Ok, when do you want to get started?"

"As soon as you guys are ready, sir."

Mark asked, "Where's your plane now, Agent Stein?"

"At the air force base, General," he replied.

I leaned back to eat a sandwich. After swallowing the bite, I said, "Ok let's leave the rest of this stuff. It has mostly to do with operational planning. We have a long flight ahead and can look at it then. Right now, we can stop for the day. Meet us at zero nine hundred at your plane and be ready to take off as soon as we're loaded." I looked at Mark as I made this call, and he nodded. I stood and said, "Gentlemen, thank you. We'll see you in the morning."

Alex stepped forward to shake my hand, and I shook John's as I left the room and headed to the lifts. In the foyer, Mark ordered three taxis and we headed back to base.

The cabs dropped us at SRT, and while Mark and I went into my office to finalise details, Tag sorted the guys out getting ready and came in to get my locker keys. He left us to it; he took care of cleaning my guns along with his and made sure I was fully stocked up with ammo.

In my office, Mark arranged for our transport at zero eight thirty. He rose and shook my hand. "Take care. I'll inform the new OC about your mission. Once it's over, let me know. You might be required to stay up there for something else. Good hunting, Tiger."

The next morning our transport was on time, and we reached Pearce at ten to nine to meet both the DEA agents. Once we were aboard, the plane took off, and we spread out and took off our combat gear. John had been right; it was luxurious and just the thing for long flights. Alex and I spent a fair bit of the first leg of the journey pouring over locations as a battle plan started to take shape and form in my mind.

The first refuelling stop was in Darwin, and the next stop after that would be at Manilla in the Philippines, and then on to Da Nang. By the time we landed in Darwin, I had worked out the plan of attack and confirmed with Alex what I would need would be available. In addition, he told me I would be leading a larger force than my own. I vetoed this, using the argument that my team worked faster and better without having too many passengers. A larger force would not be able to move silently, and the resupply of rations and ammo would be kept to a minimum as well. His argument was that I was going to be taking Bill with me, and I countered with the fact that Bill was Special Forces trained and had already worked with us and knew our ways. However, it had taken weeks for him to prove himself to the team and me before being accepted.

He said, "In that case, John and I go with you. We used to be Special Forces and know the risks."

I thought it over. "Do you have night vision goggles and cam gear?"

194

"Yes we do."

I nodded and said, "Ok, but first let's see how good you are. Block my attack."

I stood and we squared off in the aisle. I struck; he was good, but not fast enough to prevent me slapping his forehead. I struck again; this time he was able to block my right hand strike. His smile was wiped off his face when I indicated to look at my left, which was holding my knife a fraction of an inch from his kidney. He indicated for me to look at John, who was standing with his automatic cupped in both hands pointed at my head.

"Your knife would never have struck," Alex said.

Tag piped up, "Oh I think it would have."

Alex and I looked; every member of the team had their guns trained on the DEA agents. I laughed. Alex and John joined in as I sheathed my knife, and all the guns were put down. Still chuckling, I asked, "Wires, how many spare radios do we have?"

"Beside Bill's set, we've got three more, boss."

"Thanks," I replied and nodded. "You lot should get some sleep. We will be on the ground in Manilla for two hours so we can get some breakfast. After that, I'll want you all for a briefing during the flight into Da Nang. Before you drift off to the bunks in back, let's make the proper introductions."

Alex didn't have a nickname, but John was called Mose. The guys introduced themselves and started heading to the rear of the plane, where there were a dozen bunk beds before the toilets each side. After that was a stateroom each side. I'd been assigned the port side stateroom while Alex was in the other.

After the team headed to the bunks, I motioned for Alex and Mose to join me at the table. "Ok, I'm going to allow both of you to go on the mission, but no one else. Who is in charge of your base? That will have to be made plain to him."

John answered me. "He's our boss, and he'll go along with your wishes. He was also my captain in the rangers, so he's used to dealing with Special Forces personnel, Tiger."

"Good. You will need night vision gear, cam fatigues, rifles, plenty of ammo, and combat webbing. We will supply you with inter team radios, but don't break them, please. Wires and JJ will be really pissed if you do. Anything else before I crash out?" They shook their heads. I smiled and yawned, said my good nights, and made my way to my stateroom.

We arrived back in Da Nang after twenty flying hours. Our quarters weren't as luxurious as the VIP quarters at the army base, but it was good enough considering we'd be sleeping on the ground over the coming month. The DEA commander John Stockton and I liked each other from our first meeting. He was six three with greenish eyes and cropped brown hair. He looked as if he frowned a lot; he had creases in his forehead.

He met us in the mess hall. "Thanks for coming, gentlemen. As one of your conditions in coming, I've arranged for the person coming in to meet you."

We turned to see Bill walk into the room; he was treated like a long lost brother with hand shaking and arms around each other as he was greeted with enthusiasm by the team. When he got to me, we saluted and clasped each other.

We turned to Stockton, who said, "Major Fredrick has already been put into the loop and is raring to go. I'm glad to have him. I will let you guys settle into your quarters and catch up. We'll meet again over lunch. Alex, Mose, let's leave them to settle in."

In the quarter's lounge room, Tag started making coffees for us all. Wild Bill excused himself and returned with a flat box, remained standing, and said, "Colonel Tiger Davis, on behalf of the President of the United States and a grateful nation. I would like to present you with the following medal as a token and recognition of your being wounded in action during a mission that took place in July of last year."

He stepped toward me, and I rose. We saluted each other, and he pinned the medal in place on my shirt. There were cheers from the team as we finished the presentation ceremony.

Bill said, smiling, "I've been waiting to give you the Purple

Heart since I accepted it on your behalf October last. Congratulations, Tiger."

"Thanks Bill, but this is the first time I've been given a medal for my own screw up. I didn't make sure they were dead before moving toward them." We laughed as a group at the memory.

Lunch in the mess was more like an introduction fest. We were greeted, and introduced to everyone, which took a fair while. Lunch took over an hour and a half. That afternoon, John, Bill, Alex, and I spent most of the time in John's office. I outlined the proposed plan of attack, which I was able to fine tooth with the aid of all the current aerial photos of each target that John had. He was a little put out when I reiterated that the attack force was my team, his two agents, and that was all.

"Hmm. Your reason for that is sound, I'll agree," John said, "but I'll have the rest of my men that are combat ready on standby to move at a moment's notice if you find yourself in trouble. All you'd have to do is hold on until we arrived."

I nodded and agreed. "Fair enough."

I requested that the next day the attack force, except Wires and JJ, spent our time with his explosives personnel learning about the Napalm based chemical we'd be spreading as well as the incendiary charges and timers. Wires and JJ would get together with his comm's people and work out call signs, frequencies to use, and a communication schedule so that a delivery plane with our air drop was close by after we took over each field.

He approved my request. "Don't get me wrong. I want this to work, but please, find yourself in trouble. I'm itching to get back into combat again."

We started laughing, and I commented, "I'll take that in the spirit it was intended. I'll be going out of my way not to accommodate you, but it's handy to know you won't be far away if needed." I looked at my watch. "Well gentlemen, the sun's over the yardarm, and I do believe drinks are on you, John." More laughter as he nodded and we made our way over to the mess for drinks.

When I seated myself at a table and was sipping on a nice scotch, I thought over my plan of attack, which was a simple hit and run strategy. Observe for a day, hit the first target, leave everything in ruins, bug out to the next target, and then do it all over again. I didn't like what we were going to do, but I knew it had to be done. Everyone had to be considered an enemy and killed, even if they were unarmed.

The aerial photos had shown that the terrain was likely to be mild bush, which would wouldn't slow our movement from place to place. What worried me was the numerous vehicle tracks I'd seen in the photos.

Bill sat down and asked, "Are you coming to watch the movie after dinner?"

"What movie?" I asked.

"These guys have their own movie theatre next to the mess. Tonight they're showing The Mechanic with Charlie Bronson. The rest of the guys are going."

I replied with a smile, "Count me in. I've been waiting to see that."

The next day, while Wires and JJ spent the day in the communications room, the rest of us were with the chemical team, learning about the thermal charges and the modified napalm. Apparently, what we would be using was napalm in its purest state before being jellified for military use. It would soak in instead of adhering to things in globules. We were taken to an area that had been used for experimentation with the stuff when the DEA area had been first constructed five years earlier, and it was devoid of anything. Not even grass grew in that area. The next patch we were shown was where some had been dumped but not activated by explosion. There was grass growing and some of the jungle was reforming around the fringes.

The chemical technician told us, "This lot was dumped just over two years ago, and, as you can plainly see, the regrowth is forming. That is why the chemical constituents have to be activated by heat from fire or explosion. If you would like to come over here. I'll show you how it works."

We moved over to another patch of ground that was marked off with stakes and a plastic tape. His assistant stood in the patch and upended a one-gallon container, pouring some stuff around the edges and sloshing the remainder over the whole patch He came out and picked up a stake with a rag on it. "I'd move back if I were you guys."

He came over to where we were standing, lit the rag, and underarm tossed the stake into the patch. Instantly, flames erupted with a quick whoosh. Within five minutes, the flames had gone out, leaving bare ground. To say we were impressed would have been an understatement.

"We'll be spreading this stuff. What if we get any on our clothes?" I asked, curious.

He looked me in the eye. "Don't. When you spread it, you will be using twenty litre drums. As you saw, a little goes a long way, but with each shipment sent to you, I will make sure there is a box of disposable overalls. They will protect your clothing. Wear them and throw them into the field when you're finished."

That afternoon after lunch, we were back out in the fields with thermite charges that looked like a tennis ball on a spike with a time dial on top. They were bloody deadly tennis balls. He told us we'd only need six per field and that they could be spread in any pattern as long as one was near a corner.

"How good are these compared to C4? We will also have to destroy some buildings in each area as well. Could these be used instead of the C4?" I asked him.

He talked to his assistant, who trotted off as he answered. "That's a good question, Colonel. If you would like to follow me to the remains of a small village just up the track here, we will put them to the test. My assistant has gone to get a standard block of C4 and detonator as well as another thermite charge."

While we waited for the assistant to catch up, I picked a hut for Dumper to destroy and looked for another target for the thermite charge. I'd settled on the second target as the assistant joined us. Dumper took the C4 and detonator and moved toward the hut I'd picked for him. Three minutes later, it was a pile of rubble. The assistant gave Dumper the thermite charge, and I showed him which building. It looked a little sturdier than the first target, but five minutes later, it was a ruin. Everything had been consumed in the blast and fire. That settled it! We would destroy the buildings with thermite as well; it certainly saved us lugging C4 around.

During the day, one thought had been nagging at my mind, so after we were finished, I addressed that thought and sought John. I found him in his office. As I sat down, I approached the subject head on. "That was a pretty productive day. What sort of parachutes have you got available, John?"

"We've been supplied with the new wing cell chutes. I've used them, and they're great. Why?"

I nodded my head and replied, "Well, we're used to the old canopy type, so it looks as if I've got to schedule some parachute training and someone to instruct us on their use."

"That's easy. Alex has used them a number of times and can instruct your guys on the difference. I'll arrange a couple of jumps for tomorrow at the beach cove we use for training," John told me.

"Great. I'll let Alex know he's got a job first thing in the morning. Thanks."

"No problem. Anything else I can do?" he offered.

"No," I replied with a smile. "But you can join me for a drink later."

He laughed and replied, "Sold. Now get outta here."

I found Alex with Bill, and informed him of what he'd be doing in the morning, and he nodded with a smile, and said "At last something for me to do, Tiger".

I laughed and replied, "Can't say I don't give you anything to do."

"Sure can't. You're going to love these new chutes, though. They're great. And jumping into the cove is awesome! Where do you want me to set up in the morning, boss?"

I smiled at the use of the word boss, and I knew he meant it with respect. "Our barracks in the lounge. We'll keep it as informal was possible, but we start after breakfast."

"Gotcha," he replied.

We enjoyed training with the new chutes, and as he had predicted, the cove as the drop zone was bloody great. I must admit I liked it for the jump, and the wing cell chutes answered a lot quicker than the older canopy style. The redline was only two thousand feet as opposed to five for the canopy style chutes. At the end of the day, I felt it was time to go on the mission. There were only a couple of things to work out and organise, and they could all be done the next day. I could schedule the insertion for the start of our mission for the day after next.

I informed John of my decision, and he was pleased it was getting done sooner than he'd anticipated. He said he'd have one of the pilots in his office the following morning at ten so we could arrange the time of insertion, which I wanted as close to dawn as possible, after accounting for flying time and base take off time.

That night I called everyone going to a meeting in our barracks and informed them that the mission would take off the day after tomorrow in the early morning hours. The next day, Buzz was to organise rations and ammo, Wires and JJ the comm's. Alex and Mose had been wearing cams for the last couple of days and informed me that apart from their automatic handguns, they would be carrying M16's on the mission.

CHAPTER 16

We took off at zero four thirty; the darkness was slowly giving way to the light in the east. Our destination was the mountainous region one hundred miles northeast of Sara Vane, Laos, and just west of the Thua Thien province border of Vietnam. Our flying time was approximately two hours. We would be jumping at zero six thirty to our drop zone fifteen kilometres west of our number one target, which was the furthest from base. We would move toward the east and the Vietnam border, destroying the target fields as we moved toward the border.

Our pilot was a Texan named Josh Brochus, who was proud of his heritage. His great grandfather had been Curly Bill Brochus, one of the heroes, or outlaws, depending on which side you backed in the Civil War, to emerge as peacetime reparations swept across America after the war ended. Josh was six three and had the same curly red hair his great grandfather had been reputed to have, with green eyes and a wicked sense of humour. I had met him the previous day in John's office and instantly took a liking to him. He was so proud of his heritage that his side arm was a forty-five calibre colt peacemaker revolver. He wore it in a holster butt forward, so he had developed a twist draw or could draw and shoot with his left hand. I think the only thing he loved more than his heritage was his caribou airplane.

When he'd left John's office the previous day, he'd turned and warned me in heavy Texan prose, "Any of those damned Yankees, or any of your lot, upchuck on mah plane, they'll be polishing mah Mabel for a month, y'all cleah?"

I had smiled at him and replied holding my hand palm up as if swearing, "As mud, Josh."

Once he'd left the office, John had remarked, "He loves that plane." We had both laughed.

As we approached the drop zone, Josh's voice came over the internal PA in the plane. "Time ta git ready, guys. Happy hunting, and smoke some of them varmints for me. Green light soon, y'all."

We stood, checked each other out, and turned on our radios. We made sure our slung rifles wouldn't impede the chute deployment. I quickly checked the altimeter built into my watch; we were at fourteen thousand feet, so we'd have roughly twenty seconds of freefall before pulling the ripcord to slow our descent.

The plane depressurised and the ramp lowered, and I moved toward the opening. I heard the go bell and felt a tap on my shoulder. I ran forward and launched myself into open sky. The others could probably hear my elated call of "Yeehaa!" I spotted the clearing that was our targeted drop zone as I neared the ground.

After checking my altimeter, I banked my body into the turn needed toward it and watched my altimeter closely. As I neared redline, I said into my mic, "Ok about to pull. Now!"

I pulled the ripcord; it only took a seconds for the chute to jerk open. I guided the chute by adjusting the control lines, enjoying the quick response that made these chutes far superior to the older canopy type. I glided in and pulled hard down on the lines as my feet lightly touched the ground. I turned toward the chute itself, reefing in the lines so it wouldn't drag me off my feet. Once the chute was bundled at my feet, I released the harness and let it drop from my body as I surveyed the perimeter, rifle pointed and ready for action.

There was no opposition to our landing, and I sent Gecko and Lizard on a scout while the rest of us buried the chutes as best we could, using our knives for digging implements. Just as we finished burying the chutes, Lizard called through my earpiece. "We're four hundred yards in, boss, and have done a sweep. NTR."

"Roger that. Our bearing is … we'll stay this distance behind you. Call out if you find something. Let's move!"

The terrain was made for easy going; most of the time it was light bush, but as we neared the edge of the ridge the forestry grew denser. Our target was situated close to a ridgeline, which would give us more cover due to the denser foliage. We reached the target at mid-morning the next day. Gecko scouted for a suitable OP, so we withdrew down the ridgeline a little and found a cave that was in a natural depression one hundred yards from the top of the ridge and two hundred yards from the closest side of the field. It was for a perfect LUP. Gecko returned to report that he had found a reasonable tree in which to establish an OP, which was fifty yards due west of the LUP. He'd marked it with a bit of red ribbon.

After I had been there, I knew why he'd chosen it. Higher up in the tree, a commanding view of all the cleared area on the ridge was visible. If anyone moved in that area, they'd be seen. Beside the field itself, there were three ramshackle huts, and I assumed they housed the fifteen peasant farmers I'd counted. During my watch, I didn't see any evidence of weapons. I decided to use the extra time we had to observe the movements and see what routine had been established by the peasants. We didn't want to attack too soon.

However, after my first watch, I started to formulate the attack in my mind. During my second watch, which was between zero five hundred and seven the next morning, and after hearing every-one's reports between both of my watches, I decided I was on the right track and was able to solidify my attack plan. During that day, I made sure that whoever was on watch had their radio on and could hear what was being said to the rest of the crew.

When they'd all gathered, I outlined the assault. We would hit them at dawn, which meant Gecko and Lizard would be up high covering our approach. We'd move in while it was dark in three teams. Team one was myself, Alex, and Buzz; we would take hut number one. Team two led by Tag, would have Mose and Dumper, who would take the second hut. Team three was Bill, Wires, and JJ, who would have the third hut. I ordered no burst firing, but single shots only to kill, except where necessary. Once we'd taken over, we'd move to the field hopefully where our air drop ended up, unload the cage, and start prepping the field for detonation. We'd blow the huts and the field, and then bug out toward the next target.

I had a word with Wires and JJ. "When you do the sked, I want you to let the pilot know our working frequency. His approach has to be west to east, as low as possible, and we need the air drop no later than zero six thirty. I need this sent on." I handed JJ the coded message to be relayed to our HQ, which told Mark I'd commenced operations and would contact him when they were completed.

Wires replied, "We'll make sure of everything, boss."

I smiled and thanked them. As I turned away, I remembered something, turned back, and said, "Oh, also add another half dozen thermite charges and detonators to the supply list."

"Roger that, boss," JJ replied.

I headed to my gear and lay down to crashed out for a while.

At zero five thirty the next morning, everyone was in position; all three teams were under the huts waiting for my word. We'd already removed our night vision, and I was waiting for a little more daylight. Fifteen minutes later, I gave the command to go. Each team opened fire at the same time. We weren't using silenced weapons this time; we were using our rifles.

The huts were cleared of live enemy. The only living things in the area were us. I ordered that all the bodies be placed in the field where they could be cremated when we exploded the field. Once that was done, we waited for the plane. At six twenty Josh's voice came through my earpiece. "Mabel to Broadsword, do you copy? Over."

"Broadsword to Mabel, loud and clear. Over," I replied.

"Morning, y'all. Swinging round to approach now. Over."

"Roger that."

I watched as he swung around, the ramp lowering as well as his wheels. I warned him through my mic, "Broadsword to Mabel. Your wheels have come down as well."

"Roger that. I am comin' in lower than a snake's belly."

I'd seen low flying before, but Josh's flying really took the cake. He came in so low that his wheels were actually touching the ground, and the ramp dug a two-inch furrow in the ground. As we all watched, amazed, two parachutes appeared and filled, dragging out a long cage filled with twenty litre drums with some boxes sitting on top.

As soon as the cage was out, the ramp started lifting, and Josh called, "Mabel to Broadsword. Y'all enjoy the bar be que. I'm outta here."

I smiled as I answered, "Broadsword to Mabel. Roger that. Thanks for the picnic gifts. Have a safe one home."

"Roger that. Over and out, y'all."

The cage had come to rest ten feet from the edge of the field. The guys started unloading while I'd been chatting with Josh. Dumper, Alex, Mose, and Tag were putting on blue disposable overalls with inbuilt boots.

Buzz brought a box to me that had six thermite charges. "The other box has the six for the field. These are the extras you asked for."

I gave him three and said, "Keep these as spares." I put the three other charges down and enquired of Lizard, "How we going, Lizard?"

"Still all clear, boss."

Tag poured some of the napalm over the bodies and dropped the empties. JJ passed him a fresh one. Once the cage was empty and the field completely doused with the stuff, I said, "Make the timers thirty minutes."

I did the same with the charges I had and placed one in each hut. As I came out of the last one, I saw them taking the overalls off and throwing them into the field. When everyone was ready, we moved back to the OP and then the LUP to pack everything. We were back on the ridge at the OP when the charges went off. The field erupted in a ball of flame with three quick explosions a second later that obliterated the huts.

We waited, watching, a bit awestruck at the power of the raw napalm, until the flames had diminished. We moved off in the direction of the next target, which was ten kilometres away. Tag was scouting the route two hundred yards in front, because the forestry had gotten denser. He called on us to halt and come up quietly. When we joined him we discovered that we were only fifty yards from the two huts that were beside the second target field. I detailed Gecko and Lizard to find an OP a little further back.

I took the rest back to a deep depression we'd passed one hundred yards back with the intention to use it as an LUP. As it turned out, a tree was ten yards from the depression in the direction of the camp was the one Gecko had been in and declared ideal as an OP. When he came down after attaching the climbing line, he said, "Just as well we moved back, boss. There's only four in camp, but two of them are white, wearing military uniforms and armed."

Instantly I thought of Lizard still out scouting. I radioed and asked where he was; he didn't bother answering as he walked into the depression smiling. He quietly said, "You must be getting old, Gecko. Didn't you see the Air America patches they're wearing on the uniforms?"

We all a quiet laugh. I said, "This doesn't change anything. We're still here to do a job regardless of who's in there. Now, whose turn up the tree is it?" Alex put his hand up, and I passed him the binoculars.

While everyone ate, I was doing some hard thinking. I chewed a can of cold bully beef and veg followed by a cereal biscuit. By the time I'd finished eating, my mind was made up.

I quietly asked into my mic, "Can everybody hear me?" I looked around and received nods.

Alex replied, "Loud and clear."

I looked at Gecko and asked, "Gecko, is Laotian the same as Vietnamese?"

He looked at me nodded his head. "Virtually the same, boss. However, if they speak in the Tai-Kadai dialect they'll know its Vietnamese"

I nodded. "Ok let's take a gamble Bill can you speak Vietnamese or Laotian?"

"Sure can, Tiger," he replied.

I thought for a minute. "Ok here's what we're going to do. We're going to start the attack after midnight. Bill, you and I will creep into the Laotian hut and kill the slopes with silenced weapons. Now, Gecko, Lizard, into the tree before first light. Have your scopes set on the white's hut. As soon as both are out of the hut, pop them. Tag, as soon as everybody's dead, move in with the rest of the crew. Any questions?"

"How do you know they'll both come out at the same time, boss?" Lizard asked.

"Because Bill and I are going to start a ruckus in Vietnamese that should draw both of them out." I heard laughing and Alex's voice. "I like it." Everyone else was smiling too.

I looked at Wires. "Wires when you radio in tonight, give them the appraisal and what we're going to do. Schedule our delivery for the same time. Buzz, how's our food supply?"

Buzz replied, "We're good for a few more days, boss."

"Good, so it's only that tonight, Wires." He nodded.

After that, I told them I was going to get some sleep. I lay down, wrapped my poncho and liner around me, and slept until just before midnight. I came instantly awake and started brewing a coffee on the hexamine stove. As I got into my combat webbing, I screwed the silencer onto my colt and made sure I had a round in the chamber and the safety on. In the dim light, I saw Bill preparing as well. When he was ready, I poured half the coffee into his mug, and we drank and shared a chocolate bar.

I asked if he was ready after we'd finished out coffees and chocolate, and he nodded as he put his night vision on. I did the same and asked, "Who's upstairs?"

Buzz answered, "Me, boss."

"How we looking?" I asked.

"Quiet as the grave. There's been NTR since I got up here, so you're good to go, boss."

"Thanks Buzz. You and the guys know what to do. Just keep an eye on us as we go in. About to move now." Bill and I left our rifles at the base of the tree and moved silently toward the camp and target hut.

The worst moment was breaking cover to climb the steps of the hut. As we silently ascended, I peered at the entrance. The next step creaked as it bore our weight; we froze. When there was no noise or movement, we continued into the hut, seeking our targets. They were on each side of the hut in the second room, so we split up and shot each of them in the head while they slept.

I said into my mic, "Two down, Buzz. Bill and I will get some sleep and start the ruckus just after five. That way there'll be enough light for Liz and Gecko. Pass this onto Tag so he's aware of what's happened."

Buzz replied, "No probs, boss. He's my relief. Have a good kip. I'll be watching."

At five, Bill and I started an argument in Vietnamese, stifling our laughter in between yelling at each other. It had the desired result. Lizard warned us, "Both out, coming your way. Wait. Second one's not out the door yet. Tracking both now. Both down."

We had continued the shouting until we heard they were both down. We raced out of the hut to make sure they were dead as Tag's group moved in. Bill grabbed the dog tags from their bodies to give to Alex.

The bodies were thrown into the field, and I placed two of the thermite charges we'd kept. All that had to happen now was to set the timers. Everyone waited for Josh to plough another field in the clearing, which he did ten minutes later, then disappeared into the east. I thought and smiled to myself, damned stupid southerner, doesn't he know that cowboys ride into the west!

The next three fields went to plan, but, of course, I made up the attack plan as the situation turned out. Eventually we approached the last target, and after watching for two days, initiated the assault. Everything was going well until Josh was about to make his delivery. I had warning from Lizard and Gecko that a force of white soldiers was making their way toward us in a convoy of three trucks, and they looked armed to the teeth.

As Josh lined up for his drop, I yelled into my mic, "Make the drop, then get the hell out of here. Get us some help ASAP. Looks like we're going to get caught in a shit fight!" I returned my attention to my men. "Everyone, defence positions! Wires, get a radio up and yell for help!"

I heard Josh yell, "Keep your heads down. Looks like they've got a gunship with them. Oh shit! He's coming after us! Climb baby climb!" His voice faded as he flew out of my radio range.

Wires yelled into his mic as the gunfight started, "Cavalry's on the way, boss. ETA, hour and a half!"

My instant thought was Fuck! I furiously nodded my head. "Ok boys, you heard him. If this is our last stand, so be it, but let's give 'em hell as we go down!"

We had instinctively gathered into a defensive ring under one of the closest huts. As the trucks approached, the lead vehicle turned side on. Mounted in the back was a tripod that had a fifty calibre machine gun. As it stopped, the gun crew swung it in our direction and started firing. As they paused in the firing to reload another ammunition belt, I took the chance, fed a grenade into the tube of my rifle, and fired. This was one of those times I was grateful for my instinctive accuracy with weapons. My grenade landed at the base of the tripod and exploded, killing the gun crew and destroying both the machine gun and truck in the explosion.

Taking care of that threat, was pivotal in our defence because now it reverted to rifle fire and accuracy. Once the machine gun was gone, I was confident it improved our chances of survival, knowing what each of my team were capable of. Lizard and Gecko were still up high, accounting for anybody moving too close to us and relaying information to us as to what the enemy was doing. As yet, they hadn't come under fire, which led me to believe the enemy was unaware of their presence at the moment. However, should they be discovered, they'd be in a very vulnerable situation, so I was determined to keep their presence unknown to the enemy as much as I could. This was achieved by each time either of them killed someone, they let us know and we would open fire toward the given direction.

After the first half hour of hard fighting, the firefight reduced to sporadic firing by both sides, but that didn't stop them from trying to attack us from different sides. Each time we were hard pressed from one direction or the other, we had prior warning, thanks to Lizard and Gecko. During a lull in the fighting, again thanks to my snipers, I was able to estimate that half the force that hit us were either dead or severely wounded. However, we hadn't gotten off easily; Alex, Dumper, and JJ had received minor wounds, Bill had taken a round in the leg, and I was nursing a shoulder wound. Even though Tag had given me a painkiller, it still hurt like hell, and what's worse, that meant I'd lost another bloody shirt.

The fight was nearing the hour mark when Gecko said, "Shit, boss, that frigging gunship's heading back this way!"

"Oh Christ!" I exclaimed. I fed a grenade into the tube, with the thought that I could keep it from doing too much damage if I launched a couple of grenades at it. The guns it had would rip the hut above us to splinters and in all likelihood bring it crashing down on us.

I said to my two snipers, "Liz, Gecko, if you get a chance to nail any of the crew, take it."

It started heading toward us, low to the ground, so I fired a grenade that exploded on the ground in front of the gunship with the desired result. The gunship turned away, climbing. I said, "Keep an eye on that chopper, guys and let me know what it's doing." It passed out of my eyesight.

"Tiger! Looks like it's going to give this side a crack," Bill called, so I shifted to my left. I fed another round in the tube and fired again directly at the gunship, but it was too far out of range. The grenade exploded harmlessly on the ground; quickly I fed another round in and tried again. This time the grenade struck it but bounced off, and the chopper climbed sharply before the explosion could do any damage. The chopper pilot didn't seem to be able to think much because he kept trying all four sides. Each time I was able to hold him off, but my grenade supply was running low. It backed off from another repeated attempt and moved to within range of Gecko. I heard him say, "One gunner down" as the chopper moved away from the trees.

While my fight against the chopper was taking place, the enemy ground troops hadn't stopped. They tried rushing us a couple of times, but our accurate and deadly fire held them at bay. We were all starting to run low on ammunition. During another lull, Mose checked his ammo, tossed his rifle down, and drew his handgun, ready to make every shot count.

Our eyes locked and I gave him a resigned nod because I knew that if we didn't get help really quick, we would all die here. The chopper made another attempt, but this time the pilot had woken up; it came in higher and started firing into the hut. I loaded the grenade tube again and tried to get into the chopper's side door, but it was hovering too far away.

At the same time, Gecko said, "Damn boss, they know we're here somewhere and are looking for us. We're going to be busy for a while and won't be able to help you guys."

"Ok boys, do the best you can. Try to stay alive, that's the main thing!" My mind was racing; if I could get rid of the chopper, then we'd have a chance, slim, but a chance.

I made my mind up as to what I was going to do. I reached for my last grenade, fed it into the tube, and prepared to make a run toward the chopper. I told the guys what I was about to do. My intention was to get under the chopper and fire my grenade up into it.

As I was about to launch myself out from under cover, I heard one of the sweetest things I ever heard: "Hammer to Broadsword, Hammer to Broadsword. Cease fire, I repeat cease-fire. We're coming at you."

With relief in my voice, I warned, "Broadsword to Hammer. Watch out, John, there's a gunship in the air."

"Not for long," he replied.

As I watched, I saw a rocket hit the gunship, which exploded, and then the four gunships from base came in line abreast firing toward the ground as they came. Their fire took out the last two trucks. After ten minutes of our gunships strafing the ground, the enemy knew they were outgunned, and one by one, they stood up, threw their guns to the ground, and raised their hands in surrender.

We came out from under the hut and were soon joined by Lizard and Gecko. The enemy had started walking towards us until I called on them to halt and lie face down on the ground with their hands behind them. My men moved around them, securing their hands with the cable zip ties we all carried. There were twenty-two left alive of a force we were told numbered one hundred, minus the chopper crew that were now ash.

The gunships landed, and John and ten of his force made their way toward us, while the rest of his force spread out and searched and collected dog tags from the bodies. John ordered the prisoners split up into two gunships, with guards, and the gunships were to take them to base and then return. While we rested and ate, John's force prepared the field for destruction. Tag blew up the huts, and everyone rested until the gunships returned. Because this was our last field of the mission, we would return to base.

When the other two gunships returned and we were ready to pull out, I gave the remaining thermite bomb to John. Dumper and I had wired all the others to this last one so that the timer would set the whole lot off. John planted it into the field corner and turned the dial to five minutes. We walked casually back to where everyone was grouped and stood to watch.

My team had gotten used to the sight of what the bombs and napalm mix did, but exclamations of surprise and awe came from

John and his men, as the explosion and resultant fire appeared. We waited until the fire extinguished itself before boarding the choppers to return to base.

As we boarded, I said to Bill, "Well, Wild Bill, looks like you've earned a Purple Heart."

We laughed, and he replied, "I don't think so. This wasn't an army sanctioned action, so looks like I miss out again."

John piped up. "Nah, I don't think so. I'll make sure you get one, and a promotion as well. Damn that was fun! Let's go!"

As we neared Da Nang, three of the choppers headed for the DEA base while ours carrying the wounded landed at the air force base to be met by a jeep with Colonel Reg Price and two ambulances. All the wounded were put into the ambulances and driven to the hospital. I saw John get into the jeep with Reg, and they drove off together.

CHAPTER 17

Every one of us was forced to stay the night for observation. The next morning, I was dressed and wearing a sling, much to my disgruntlement, but after removing the bullet and sewing me up, the doctor who treated me told me after I complained that slings were for girls, "Well, this girl is going to wear that sling, at least for a couple of days. I don't want those stitches tearing. Come and see me in a week, and I'll see about taking them out."

We were sitting in the canteen later when John came in and said, "Are you lot ready to do some work yet?"

"Hell yeah," we replied simultaneously and stood up. Bill was supporting his leg with a walking stick, I had the sling on my left arm, but we were ready. We walked out the front entrance, where he had two jeeps waiting, and we were driven to the DEA base.

The jeeps dropped us at our quarters. John said, "I've got a debriefing session set up in an hours' time. That should give you time to get cleaned up and into fresh uniforms. When you're ready, we'll meet in the mess."

When I walked into my room, I found that my guns had been cleaned and all my ammo clips were full again. I silently thanked whoever was responsible. I took the sling off gingerly and stripped off my shirt. I grabbed a towel and headed to the shower. After over a month in the field, I wasn't going to let a little wound interrupt the joy of a long shower. I did try to keep it as dry as possible.

As I was walking back to my room, Buzz was just coming out. "I just got back from the Q, boss. I've put a fresh replacement shirt in there for you."

"Buzz, you're a marvel. How could I do without you? Thanks. Oh, and thanks for the ammo and gun clean."

He smiled. "The ammo I made sure of, boss, but Tag cleaned your guns. He wouldn't let anyone else touch them."

Before we set off for the mess, I yelled for Tag. When he arrived, I thanked him for cleaning my weapons. "However, you have to stop ripping my frigging shirts up. Buzz has enough to do without trying to find me new shirts."

Looking contrite, he replied, "Yes boss." We burst into laughter.

When everyone was ready, we headed to the mess to start the debriefing. Reg Price was in attendance, as well as a couple of Intelligence officers from Central Command, a DEA analyst, and two CIA agents, one of whom we would be seeing again in the future by the name Jerry Hogarth. He was one of the team responsible for dismantling the Air America project. Of course, John was there also. They sat and listened while I outlined the whole mission from start to finish, at times referring to my mission diary. After I'd been questioned, Bill was called.

The whole debrief took about three hours, and I'd had the foresight to have Wires record the whole thing. I would have it sent to our HQ in a sealed package along with the mission statements I wanted my team to write and I had started writing. I would code it and send it over the wires, but my written one would be enclosed with the tape and team members' reports would go by mail.

While we were having drinks after the debriefing, Reg and Hogarth came over to me and asked, "Tiger, I've got something that may be up your alley. Because all our special forces have been withdrawn, your team may be able to fill in for us. What do you say?"

"First, Reg, my men and I need rest and recuperation time. Secondly, any mission would have to be approved by my HQ. Thirdly, I'd need to know what the mission was as well as the parameters I'd have to deal with. But yes, I'd be willing to hear the details if it is approved by my people. I'd need to use Bill, as usual."

He turned to Hogarth; I detected a slight nod, and he turned back to me. "Good man. I'll start arranging everything. In the meantime, you and your men will have the use of the VIP quarters again while you recuperate, and if you need anything, have Colonel Fredrick call me. Oops. You weren't supposed to hear that yet."

I smiled. "I'm glad he's being promoted. I'll keep quiet. Will he get the Purple Heart as well?" Reg nodded and I grinned. "We'll move over as soon as we're finished here. You can rely on me to stay silent."

I informed my guys and Bill that there was another job on the cards and that we'd be moving into the VIP quarters until permission came through from HQ.

While we were eating dinner that night, I said to Bill, "Looks like you won't be flying that desk for a while, buddy. You're stuck with us." Everyone laughed.

The following morning after breakfast, I was sitting in John's office with him, Alex, and Mose. He asked whether we were heading back to Australia, and I informed him that another job was in the wind so would be staying over at the army base until things were finalized.

"So what happens with the guys we caught?" I asked, curious about their fate.

"They're going to be shipped stateside in chains and interrogated thoroughly. After that they'll probably be doing long sentences in a federal prison, if they aren't executed as traitors."

I nodded. "Well, at least they won't just be set free."

With a wicked grin on his face, he said, "Oh no, that's not going to happen, Tiger. How do I thank you for what you and your men have done? You all deserve medals."

I laughed and replied. "Well, there are a few things. Send my bosses a glowing report, have your guys transport us over to the army base, keep Bill Fredrick on your trusted list, come and shake everybody's hand when we leave, and buy me a bottle of top shelf scotch. That should do it, I think." Laughter filled the room.

Alex and Mose stood and faced me. Alex said, "Tiger, it's been an experience I wouldn't have missed. Thank you."

I stood as he shook my hand. Mose stooped forward and shook hands, saying with a grin, "Likewise, boss."

I faced John. "John, thanks for everything. We'll be ready to pull out in half an hour." I reached forward to shake his hand.

"No, thank you for everything, Tiger." I left his office to get the guys ready to move.

When we came out of the quarters carrying all our gear, there were three jeeps waiting for us. We put all our gear in the last one; Buzz and Dumper would ride with it. John came out followed by Alex and Mose to shake everyone's hand. John said a few words to each of us, Alex got into the driver's seat of the lead jeep, and Mose the second. After all the goodbyes were done, we loaded up and drove off toward the army base.

When we arrived at the VIP quarters and unloaded, I said to Alex, "If you guys or John miss us too much, you'll find us here or across the road in the officers' club." We shook hands again before they drove off, and then we moved back into our normal rooms.

The rest of the morning was spent writing mission reports. Tag was responsible for making sure they were written. He put them with the tape in the dispatch bag and would get it sent to Swanbourne. After I'd written mine, I had it copied so the original could go with the rest. After lunch, I would code the copy to be sent over the radio, plus inform them of another job in the wind. After my message was coded, I took it to the communications building next door and waited for the acknowledgement.

When the acknowledgement came, the operator said, "Sir, it says that a lengthy message is to follow. When it's complete, I'll deliver it to your quarters, if you like."

I thanked him and returned to my room to ponder what news would precipitate such a long message. I would have to wait and see. Half an hour later, the comm's clerk brought me the message, which was three pages long. I moaned, knowing this would take me the rest of the day to decode. I put it in the desk drawer after deciding to tackle it after some lunch. Tag came to tell me he had sent the dispatch bag, which would reach Swanbourne in three days.

While eating, I let the rest of the guys know about the message coming in. I'd probably take the rest of the day decoding it, so Tag and Wires volunteered to take a page each and help with the decoding. After lunch, I gave them each a page, and they went off to their respective rooms to start the decoding process. A little after fifteen hundred, the message was complete, and I read it prior to taking it into the lounge to pass on the news.

It read, Congratulations to all on a job well done. Messages of high praise for your work are still being received. The political climate here has changed dramatically since you left; everybody knows that Whitlam will win the election in December, so McMahon, in a last effort to win support, announced that 8RAR would not be replaced and that a phased withdrawal from our commitment to Vietnam will be completed by election time this year. However, you will remain in country to fulfil other duties with the Americans. Their request for your help has already been received and is being taken under advisement. You'll be contacted as soon as we know the decision. Thank you all.

The message was signed off by Lieutenant-Colonel McFarlane, our new boss. There was a postscript added by Mark: By the time you return, I may not be here, as I'm expecting a new posting soon. I've been promoted, largely due to your efforts, so to each and every member of SRT, I thank you. It's been a pleasure knowing and serving with all of you. I wish you luck with your next mission, which may involve sneaking into Cambodia. Tiger, I know Pep would have been proud of the way you turned out. Good luck in the future, Mark.

I felt a little sad after reading Mark's postscript. I was glad he was getting the promotion, but it seemed as if the end of an era had come. We'd known each other from the beginning of my army life; he had been the one constant figure and I would miss seeing him. However, I also had to laugh, because he was still trying to warn me. He gave me an indication about what was coming up on the next mission. I'd certainly miss his doing that and sent out a silent thought: "Thanks for everything, Mark. Hopefully we'll meet again sometime and get drunk together. Love Tiger."

I took the message into the lounge and was passed a scotch by Tag. After taking a sip, I read what McFarlane had said. There were cheers, laughter, and comments of about time and good old Gough after I'd finished reading. I told them of Mark's postscript. I held up my glass in a toast. "Gentlemen, to our friend and colleague, Mark Ryan."

After the toast, Dumper called for three cheers for Mark, and we all joined in enthusiastically. I said, "I don't know what our new boss will be like, but I hope he continues to give us a heads up. Mark's still looking after us by giving us the heads up on Cambodia, so it looks like we know what we can expect on this next mission."

While enjoying drinks before dinner, I grabbed as many magazines as I could get, including a Time Life, about Cambodia and took them back to my room. I'd decided to do some research. I left them on my desk and returned to the officers' club to finish my drink and have dinner. After eating a lovely meal of fresh salmon, calamari, and fries, I told the boys to enjoy themselves and that I was going back to my room to do some work. I grabbed a bottle of scotch on the way to my desk, where I placed a writing pad and pen, poured a drink, and leaned back to read the magazines I'd picked up.

After returning to Cambodia from university in France in 1965, Pol Pot had whipped up the peasantry with his communist propaganda and formed an opposition force to the monarchy led by Prince Sihanouk. Using the name that Sihanouk had disdainfully called them, Khmer Rouge, they established close ties to the North Vietnamese government and supplied aid to Viet Minh soldiers, allowing them to move freely and establish bases within Cambodia. In 1970, the Khmers' ousted Sihanouk, and Pol

Pot was able to freely establish a purge of all western thinking. Money was abolished, books burned, schools closed. Teachers, merchants, and almost all the intellectuals in the country were arrested and murdered. This preceded a reign of terror and murder, eventually becoming known to the general public in 1978, which was now called the Killing Fields Era. However, all that started back in 1970. Between then and '78, nearly two million people were murdered without provocation. In '70, the US started a carpet-bombing campaign against Cambodia to weaken the help the Khmers were giving to the Viet Minh, and even conducted cross border raids using their forces in Vietnam. Because of the US intervention, an opposing force to the Khmer rouge eventually rose, led by Lon Nol, but years would pass before they became effective.

To gain this insight into Cambodia, which made me realise it was going to be just an extension of our war in Vietnam and that anyone one could be a threat, took about four hours of reading through five different magazines.

In the morning, I replaced the magazines in the officers' club and gave the guys and Bill an appraisal of what I'd learned while we had breakfast. Two days later, Bill was summoned to Central HQ in Saigon, and we took time out to go into town and explore, but we were ever watchful. Two weeks earlier, a suicide bomber had exploded himself in the central market place while it was full of US marines on leave and doing some shopping, killing six soldiers and three local merchants.

When we found the beach, it was pristine and the water was as calm as a mirror. It had a bar set up at the edge of the sand, and the walkway was quite popular. We decided it was an ideal place to spend a few hours paddling or swimming, and I was determined to come back after the stitches had been removed from my shoulder and swim and sunbake. I knew the salt water would help my wound heal more quickly.

The next morning, I went to the hospital. The same doctor had a look at the wound and declared that I was recovering remarkably fast. He removed the stitches and warned me not to overdo any exercise. Hah! As if, I thought.

That afternoon we went back to the beach, and after having a thoroughly long and enjoyable swim, I dried off in the light breeze while sipping a drink at the bar.

That night we were visited by John Stockton and Alex Stein from the DEA. They were carrying two cartons. John gave me one, saying it was for me. I put it in my room, and Alex took the carton he was carrying into the lounge and opened it.

John called out, "Gentlemen, for you all to share, with my thanks." He pulled out one of the bottles, which was Johnny Walker Blue Label scotch. "Would someone like to pour?"

Tag got up and took the bottle from him with a smile. He carried it to the bar and started pouring it into glass tumblers that were passed around. When everyone had a glass, I toasted, "To the DEA, who knows what to drink. Cheers!" We gratefully sipped our drinks.

There were sighs, of satisfaction all around. John filled us in on the latest after refilling his glass from the open bottle on the coffee table. During the initial interrogation of the prisoners we'd captured before they were flown stateside under custody, it was discovered that it had taken three days to find the damage to the first field, and they had been behind us all the way. Apparently, their commander was obsessed with capturing us to exact revenge, so much, so that he wouldn't even entertain the thought of getting in front of us and ambushing us. I shuddered at the thought of walking into that much firepower in an ambush; we wouldn't have had a chance. The fields we destroyed were the only ones; there were no others.

The estimated loss in money terms to Air America was in the hundreds of millions, and the flow of drugs into the US had been halved, not that anyone would know about it except the select few. John also told us that their job in South East Asia was now over and plans were being made to dismantle the base and ship personnel back to the states.

After visiting for a couple of hours, we once again said goodbye to them. The Blue Label was put into Buzz's safekeeping, and the next morning I had him ship my box back to Australia in a kit locker he had scrounged, which was packed with foam and sponge. I hoped it would arrive there without a bottle being broken.

A week later, a message was sent to me from HQ from Mark: Hello Tiger. Hope you are recuperating well. You have been cleared to undertake the mission being proposed. Note my comment from last transmission. Good luck, Mark.

That afternoon Bill returned, and he was wearing his silver Colonels eagles. I was glad that now I was able to let on that I already knew about the promotion. I asked him about the Purple Heart, and he smiled and said he'd been presented with it. I took him into the lounge where everyone was vegging out. I asked Buzz to grab a bottle of the good stuff.

Once the glasses were filled I said, "Gentlemen, let me present from 2nd Western Pioneers Colonel William Wild Bill Fredrick, Bronze Star and Purple Heart recipient, Colonel Wild Bill!"

"Cheers!" Bill was actually blushing as he thanked us.

That night in the officers' club, after we'd ordered dinner, Bill told us we'd be going to Saigon in the next day or two. A whole floor was being put at our disposal for briefings. The floor would have all our rooms on it and a conference room. Meals could either be by room service or we could eat in the restaurant on the first floor. Also, access to our floor would be guarded twenty-four hours a day for the duration of our stay. The operation we were going on, even though being carried out by the military, was a CIA mission of vital importance. Apparently the CIA guy we met a little while ago, Jerry Hogarth, was behind it and specifically asked for my team to carry it out.

For some reason I wasn't surprised by this news; lately, nothing really surprised me. I contemplated that thought over drinks when I was alone later. Was I too old for this? That was a laugh. I was only eighteen! Had I seen too much? No, I don't think so. Was I battle weary? Again no. This was only my third tour of duty. Was

I sick of the bullshit and class distinction that went on?

Yes, I think I was. A whole team of poor schmucks that were only enlisted men and not officers would be guarding our safety while we were in Saigon. I thought this was a joke. We're supposed to be a team of elite soldiers, yet men we could easily kill without hesitation would be guarding our safety? The whole thing was a bloody stupid exercise. Just let us get on with the job, whatever it was, so it could be finished and we could go home. Then a thought came into my mind, and I laughed out loud.

I replied to the thought by silently thinking out into the ether, "Yeah Pep, and you thought I was a cynical bastard before you met me. Well, look at me now!"

The next day we made preparations for leaving. I called Wires into my room and said, "From now on, anything that's said to us, either in a briefing, or privately, needs to be recorded. Are you able to manage that?"

"Can do, boss, as long as you wear your radio. I can set mine up to record whatever is said, plus I'll still be able to talk to you. I'll just need a steady supply of tapes."

I nodded. "Good. Get onto Buzz about the tape supply."

He replied with a smile. "Roger that boss." He turned and left.

That afternoon we were on a transport plane to Bien Hoa and were met by jeeps that drove us into Saigon, the capital of South Vietnam. This was the first time any of us had seen it. Most of the traffic was either pushbike or moped type scooters, but every now and then either a military vehicle or a car that belonged to the very rich upper class passed by.

Our drivers pulled up at the Saigon Hilton, where we must have looked a sight, armed to the teeth, carrying our kitbags with our rifles slung on our shoulders, plus all the other weapons and handguns strapped all over us, but no one gave us a second glance, not even the hotel staff. I wondered if we were part of the landscape now. After talking to the reception staff, we were escorted to a private lift where two US MP sentries stood guard.

I smiled and nodded to them. "Has anybody fed you guys?"

"No sir. We're not allowed that luxury," the MP Sgt replied.

"Bullshit!" I instructed the manager of the hotel that our guards were to be fed regularly by the hotel staff.

As the lift opened, I gave the MP a wink, which was returned with a nod and smile as I entered the lift. We ascended, and the duty manager informed us that we were one floor down from the penthouse that was reserved for the CnC, who was in the states at that time. We had a private swimming pool, sauna, and gymnasium on our floor, and each suite had its own spa pool.

That cynical Tiger surfaced. "If there wasn't a war on, how much would these rooms usually cost?"

"Three thousand dollars US a night, sir."

I laughed. We are all country bumkins from a flyspeck in the ocean, and we're being treated to accommodations like this. Oh how the rich live! He showed us around one of the suites and winced as I threw my rifle and kitbag on a lounge suit. He told me all the suites were the same on this floor and that there were twelve of them. We could take our pick of which ones we used. He showed us the conference room, pool, and gymnasium before leaving us to it. As soon as he entered the lift, we all started laughing.

I went back to the room where I had dropped my gear and started making myself comfortable by getting out of my combat gear. I ran the water into the spa bath. I fixed myself a drink and oozed into the spa bath. I sat back into the warm water as I sipped my scotch and let the jets massage my back and body.

Much later, instead of bothering to go down to the restaurant for dinner, we decided to have room service bring it up. The waiters served our dinners in the conference room.

Late the next morning, after having a very lovely breakfast of pancakes with the works, which included bacon eggs and hash browns, tomato and mushrooms, I received a call from reception asking if I would receive visitors. I got back to business and accepted the fact that two people were on their way up to us.

As Jerry Hogarth exited the lift accompanied by an army officer, I called the gang together. We went into the conference room. Surreptitiously glancing at Wires, I received a slight nod and knew that everything was being recorded.

Hogarth was just starting a selling speal in regards to the mission that required doing and how important it was. I cut him short. "No offence Jerry, but we don't need the hard sell. Just tell us the mission, why it's so important, what we have to look out for, what sort of terrain we're going into, how much opposition we can expect, and how are we going to get out. Fair enough?"

He was rather taken back by my no nonsense approach. He recovered from the shock of my interruption quickly, though. "Basically, the whole purpose of your mission will be to rescue one of our top agents and bring her out of the situation she's been put in, which is certain death if she's caught.

It will have to be done with finesse and in secret, without arousing the general populace to her location. She's been in hiding for a while now, and she is being hunted by the regime as an intellectual. That was enough to earn her a death warrant."

He paused in his rhetoric for some coffee and continued. "Your job will be to go in, find her, and bring her out with you. Here's the kicker: since she went into hiding, we've not been able to contact her, so she won't know you're there to rescue her. All I can give you is the code phrase she will respond to."

Thinking this over, I nodded. "Fair enough. Where is she? What's the code phrase? And how do we get out?"

The army officer unrolled a map on the table. "She's hiding out in a set of ruins just outside the village of Chbar here." He pointed to an area on the map. "It's about twenty-five miles north of Senmonorom and twenty miles from the Vietnamese border. The terrain is, to say the least, rather hostile, with steep mountain-side, deep ravines, and dense jungle."

I smiled. "Jerry, leave me the map and give me a few hours.

Come back about fifteen hundred. I might have thought up a reasonable plan of attack by then."

He nodded and said, "Wilco. I'll call back later."

Tag escorted them to the lift. I sat back in my chair with the map and thought while the rest of the team shuffled out to leave me to think. Such was their faith in my ability.

CHAPTER 18

By the time Hogarth returned at fifteen hundred, I had worked out an attack plan. It was rough, sketchy, and full of variables, which would require fine-tuning, but it gave us a starting point. While we were in the conference room, I turned my radio on so Wires could record what was being said. The plan involved a parachute insertion to a plateau that was four kilometres north of Chbar, which had a clearing. We'll head for the ruins, find the agent, get her dressed into cam fatigues, and strike out on foot east toward the Vietnamese border into the north of Quang Duc province. Once over the border, we'll turn south toward Gia Nghia and look for a suitable LZ and LUP along the way to call in for an extraction by gunship back to Bien Hoa.

He nodded and said, "Sounds good. How long do you think it'll take?"

"I think two weeks at the most could see us back at Bien Hoa, but I need some information from you. Her name and description for one, and the recognition phrase that lets her know we're friends."

"Yeah, I thought that may be the case," he replied. "Her physical description is on the back of her photograph." He passed her photo to me. "The recognition phrase is your eagle has come to help. Her name is Kami Phuong. Is there anything else you need?"

I nodded. "Yep, just hang a minute." I went to the door and yelled, "Buzz, front and centre!"

When he walked in I gave him the physical height and weight of Kami and asked what size uniform fatigues and boots would fit her. As he answered Jerry wrote down his answer on a note pad. I asked Buzz, "If we were to double our ammo supply, what would we need? Again his answer was written down, and the same for the amount of rations. I thanked him and he exited the room.

I turned to Hogarth. "Make that two pairs of fatigues, one pair of boots, and a black backpack. I'll also need this floor kept for us. When we get back, we'll come straight here. I'll contact you. Now, I need all of the gear by tomorrow night and transport to take us to Bien Hoa, plus nine of the new wing cell parachutes and a caribou to fly us to the drop zone. Work out with them the take off and flying time, but I'd like to be inserted by zero nine hundred at the latest."

He replied, "I'll have your ammo and rations tomorrow morning. Take your liaison man to the air force offices for your flight timing. I can arrange your transport whenever you wish to go to Bien Hoa."

"That'll work. I'll need a number so I can contact you, and somehow we'll have to arrange transport back here from Bien Hoa."

"Oh that'll be easy. Throw your rank around and demand transport," he replied, and I nodded as I laughed. As he passed me a card with his phone number on it, he said, "If we're done I'll see you about ten with your supplies and pick up Colonel Fredrick."

I nodded and he left the room heading for the lift. That night we decided to go down to the restaurant for dinner, and I told the team what had transpired with Hogarth. I let Bill know that he'd be working out the flight and take off times I let everyone know the insertion time and that we'd be parachuting in.

The next morning, Hogarth arrived with the supplies. He and Bill left to check flight times. Buzz went through what we'd brought, announced his satisfaction, and started distributing it into piles. Hogarth had managed to get a whole slew of magazines, and after Buzz split them up, we started filling the magazines in our respective piles from the boxes of ammunition. Any live rounds left over went into our packs as extras, and the ration packs were packed into our backpacks.

Buzz put the two pairs of fatigues and the pair of boots into the black backpack I'd asked for and said, "I'll carry these in my gear, boss."

I thanked him. Buzz then placed Bill's pile in his room.

Bill returned about three hours later, and we went into my suite to talk over what he had learned. Flying time to the drop zone would be in an hour, so if we boarded at zero seven thirty, we'd be a little earlier than my ETA. This could work to our advantage. Travel time to Bien Hoa was forty-five minutes, so if we left the hotel at zero six thirty, we'd have plenty of time to make the flight.

I made my mind up to go the following day and remarked, "All we have to do is get the radio frequencies and call signs organised."

Bill smiled. "I'm getting used to the way your mind works. I already got them while I was there, and the plane is scheduled for take-off at zero seven thirty tomorrow."

I laughed and said, "Good." I turned my head and yelled, "Wires, JJ!" They were in my room as if shot out of a cannon.

Bill gave them the call sign of the operations room at Bien Hoa, which was Mother Goose, and the call sign we'd be using, Lone Wolf, as well as the frequencies we'd use. I said, "Pass the word to the guys. We'll be eating in tonight in the conference room while we have a final mission briefing. So figure out what they want for dinner, and we'll call room service a little later. Tell them breakfast will be the same."

After they left, I said to Bill, "I suppose I'd better get onto Hogarth and let him know when we want our transport." Bill started laughing again, and I continued. "Ok, you fixed that too huh? Good man. Am I that predictable?"

"No, not by a long shot, but when you get the bit between the teeth over something, you want to get it done yesterday. Didn't you know that's what I love about you? Too bad you're an ugly cuss, or my wife wouldn't stand a chance." We burst out laughing again.

"Buzz has doubled your ammo, left it in your room, with the

rations to pack. Now get outta here and decide what you want for dinner," I ordered him jokingly.

When I ordered dinner from room service, I was assured that if I sent down the breakfast orders prior to midnight they would be delivered at the time I requested, which was zero five thirty. After that I spoke to the front desk, informing them we'd be away for a couple of weeks but would return to our floor and therefore were leaving our bags in the rooms. I was told it was perfectly all right since the floor had been booked for an indefinite stay. They also asked if we ordering breakfast, and I told them we were ordering it for five thirty. I was told the kitchen staff started at five so that it would be no problem what so ever.

During dinner in the conference room, I outlined the mission briefing. "On the way back, once we're back over the border, if we find targets worthwhile, or not too large, we'll probably try to do a little damage on the way home. Now, after this job, I'll see if we can be sent home. We've been here nearly a year. Yeah, time flies when you're having fun, but I think it's time for a rest. I'll see what I can manage. All in favour, hands up." All hands went up.

Bill announced, "This is likely to be my last mission with you guys. I was scheduled to return stateside a month ago and then this came up. I'll probably be sent home after we complete this one."

The next morning after breakfast, we geared up in our combat gear and webbing, and as the lift reached the ground, I turned to the senior MP on guard. "Look, we're off on a mission and could be gone a couple of weeks, so pass on to your boss that we won't need guarding. There's no need for you to be here."

He replied, "Oh no sir, this lift only services your floor and the CnC's, so it is always guarded."

"Oh, ok. See you in a couple of weeks, then," I replied.

With a smile, he said, "Good hunting sir."

I smiled and nodded. I went outside to the guys and had a smoke while we waited for the transport to arrive.

After the five-minute warning and applying the cam cream to my face and neck, I placed the normal sweat rag around my neck and checked Bill's gear to make sure there was no obstruction to his chute. We reversed the procedure, and he checked mine. The plane started depressurizing, and I walked toward the ramp as it lowered and launched myself into space as the green light came with a tap on the shoulder. While in freefall, I reflected on how much I enjoyed the sensation of flying. As my feet touched down, I started pulling in the chute lines and surveyed the clearing fringe for possible enemy.

We followed SOP's once everyone was down, and I sent Tag out as forward scout. It was heavy going in the jungle, and I reduced the distance from Tag to one hundred metres. About half an hour later, Tag hissed a halt. I silently joined him and noticed we'd started to enter the ruins. Where the jungle ended and the ruins began was hard to tell, but the foliage slowly gave way to stone.

I decided to split the team. Tag would take his group and circle around the ruins to the right, while I took the remainder left, giving Gecko the scout position. Half way around, I spotted movement the same time as Gecko. A figure was running on a tangent to us, so I took off.

I caught the figure with a flying tackle and rammed my arm into the mouth at the same time we hit the ground, I let go my rifle, pulled my knife, reached over to the figure's neck, and lay the edge against its throat. The figure stopped struggling.

As the rest of my group caught up, I had my knee in the person's back and my blade against the neck with my other hand across their mouth. While the group kept their guns on the captive, I took my knee out of the person's back, leaned down, and quietly asked in Vietnamese, "How many of you are there?"

The reply stunned me for two reasons. One, it was in, English and two, it was a female voice. "Just me."

I took the knife blade away from her throat and asked, "Are you Kami Phuong?" She nodded, so I let her roll over while I sheathed my knife. Buzz passed me my rifle.

When she faced me, we were still on our knees. I got up and extended my hand to lift her up. I pulled her photo out of my pocket and compared the two. I must admit her photo didn't do her justice; she was quite pretty, with long black hair and green eyes, and she was dressed in a black VC ensemble, minus the straw hat.

"Well, this is your lucky day, Kami. Your eagle has come to help in the shape of me and my men." I smiled at her, hoping to disarm her. "Sorry I almost sliced your throat."

She smiled and replied, "It wasn't the knife that hurt, but the way you threw me to the ground." She started rubbing her side and bum.

Gecko, who had been maintaining watch, said quietly, "Tag's coming."

I looked up; Lizard was just in front of Tag's group, and as they joined us, I looked at Kami and asked, "Have you got somewhere we can get out of sight?"

She nodded and replied, "Follow me." She led us to what looked like a wall with grass foliage growing up it, but it was actually a lift away doorway to a room that had once been a temple.

I muttered into my mic, "Last man in replace the door."

She must have heard me. "Thanks."

She moved to a bowl of water and scooped some into her hands. She bent to wash her face. Gecko got my attention and handed me an AK47. As I took it, his face went white and he lifted his rifle. I turned; Kami was aiming a forty-five automatic at me with two hands.

Instantly measuring distance, I said, "If you shoot me, my men will tear you apart. If you're going to point a gun at someone, be ready to use it."

She replied, "Oh I am. Now who are you?"

I ignored her question. "Well, if you're going to, you need to take the safety off."

She invariably looked toward the safety catch, and as she did, I kicked up with my left foot to connect with her right hand with force enough that the gun dropped out of her hand. I smashed the side of her head with my right palm punch, which literally lifted her off the ground. She was lying unconscious in a heap.

I said to no one in particular, "Tie the bitch up."

When she regained consciousness, I was sitting across from her with my rifle and the AK47 leaning against the rock. I sipped on a cup of coffee.

She put her tied hands up to the side of her face, rubbed it and said, "What did you hit me with?" I laughed and showed her. "No way. Nobody can hit that hard. How long was I out?"

"Fifteen minutes, give or take a couple. Are these yours?" I held the AK and automatic up. She nodded and I said, "Why were you going to shoot me?"

She looked me square in the eye and said, "Because I don't know you, and you're Australian, not US army."

I laughed again. "Well, thank you most to death for noticing, but do you often shoot rescuers who give you the right recognition phrase. I imagine that would make it harder to get rescued, don't you?"

She laughed despite trying to look haughty. "Yeah I guess so. Who are you?"

Bill came over to me with a warmed up can and a fork. I took it and started eating. "Colonel Wild Bill, tell this crazy bitch who we are."

He smiled, and with a wink said, "Yes I surely will, Colonel Tiger." I smiled.

As he told her, who we were and why we were here, her eyes widened. She said, "Let me get this straight. You're an Aussie Sgt with a US Colonel's rank."

I smiled, nodding my head. "Yep, and did you miss the part when Bill said we're here because Jerry Hogarth asked us to rescue you?"

She lifted her hands, indicating the bonds, and said, "Rescue me."

I laughed. "That's just for my protection. Are you going to try to shoot me again? Next time you might not fall for that old trick."

She laughed and shook her head. "No, I guess not."

I leaned forward, pulling my knife, and sliced the zip tie around her wrists. I passed her the knife butt first, and she cut the straps on her ankles. She returned the knife and rubbed the side of her face again.

"Come on, I'll introduce you," I told her and gave her a hand up.

After being introduced to everyone, she was passed a cup of coffee and a warmed up tin of ham and egg. She walked over to her weapons to sit and eat. Every now and again, I would notice her watching me out the corner of my eye, and when I had my back to her, I could sense her still doing it.

After I'd finished eating, I grabbed the spare backpack with the uniforms and boots and took it over to her. "There's a couple of sets of cams and some boots in there. I hope they fit. You're going to need them. I don't want you wearing those black pyjamas while you're travelling with us. We need to blend in and move silently."

"Thanks. I was getting sick of wearing them anyway. So what's the plan?" she asked as she reached for the backpack. I told her, and she nodded. "Sounds good. I'll be ready."

We left the ruins after an early breakfast the next morning at zero six hundred, and considering the mountainous terrain and dense jungle, by late afternoon, I estimated we were only eight kilometres from the border. It was time to look for an LUP; we found a good spot about half a click further on and settled in. We then stood to until full dark. As we settled down for the night, Kami, who continued watching me, had put her gear next to mine, I just looked at her, nodded, and smiled.

I don't know what, but something woke me at zero three thirty. I silently grabbed my night vision gear and rifle and quickly but silently moved out about fifty yards from the LUP to scout around. About a quarter of the way round the LUP, I spotted something moving twenty yards further on. I moved in slowly. I saw a twelve-man patrol, all VC settling down for sleep. As I pondered the variables, there was no way around it; they had to be taken care of. The best way was to give them an hour to fall asleep and kill them with silenced weapons. I silently moved back to the LUP and quietly woke each man. I used sign to tell them what was up, and they nodded.

After waking Bill, I whispered close to his ear what was going on. We didn't dare use our radios, because even with earpieces, in the stillness of the night, they'd be heard enough to give warning. I woke Kami and whispered in her ear. I told her to stay put and stay quiet. After checking and putting our silencers on our pistols, I passed Bill my Ingram to use because he didn't have a silencer.

In our night vision gear, we silently surrounded the encampment and moved to within ten feet of the VC. We shot every one of them and moved in to make sure they were all dead, collected papers and whatever they had on them.

We returned to the LUP. Our night's sleep had been shot to hell now, so we stood to until it was light enough to see, had a quick breakfast, and moved out of the area. By zero sixteen hundred we were back in Vietnam, seven kilometres inside Quang Duc province, without spotting any enemy activity. We found a suitable LUP that gave us good cover from the rain, which had started a couple of hours earlier. That was probably because we were near Tuy Duc, which is the northern most point of the demarcation line that governed the wet season in the south.

Just after dark the rain stopped, which was a little better for eating. The terrain hadn't changed much since crossing the border, but the foliage was a little less dense. I did toy with the idea of pushing the pace a little the next day but rejected it due to the terrain. I was also worried that Kami wouldn't be able to manage if I increased the pace. I glanced at her; she was staring back. She was lying next to my gear looking rather worn out. Maybe sleep would soon claim her and that nagging feeling of being watched would disappear.

Halfway through the next day, we spotted, and were spotted, by three VC. After killing them, we were bounced by a larger force of six a little later. After a three- minute firefight, they were all dead and accounted for.

About an hour later, we came across a force of twelve that looked as if they were getting ready to lay an ambush for someone. Going high, Lizard couldn't see anyone that could be a possible target, so after a quick discussion it was agreed to take them out of the equation. Gecko screwed the silencer for his rifle on and climbed to join Lizard, and the rest of us prepared our pistols and sub machine gun. We left Kami behind and moved silently in behind them. Bill had swapped to my rifle and had a grenade in the tube. When were within twenty feet of the enemy, Lizard and Gecko started at opposite ends killing the enemy; once they realised they were under attack, we opened up from behind them.

Bill lobbed the grenade right in the centre of their line, killing three. Against my team they stood no chance and were soon dead. After that, we saw no further activity for the rest of the day and decided that night to keep someone on watch all night in two hour shifts. After standing down once, it was dark.

Even though the terrain had grown less arduous, we had only managed fifteen kilometres that day due to the enemy activity and firefights. The next day we didn't see any enemy activity and made about twenty kilometres.

During the next day, we found a clear area that could be used as an LZ and worked out our exact position. While I was doing this, Tag had gone scouting to find an LUP. Gecko had gone high to guard our position, and I worked out that we were only halfway to Gia Nghia. After some discussion it was decided to wait and call in for an extraction. Everyone except Kami had heard that Tag had found an ideal LUP three hundred yards uphill from the LZ, which allowed a good view of it.

Gecko came down and led the way to Tag; he'd been watching

his progress from the tree. As we settled in, Wires and JJ lay out the aerial for the radio. Wires told me they were ready.

I passed him the coordinates. "I want an ETA and three jeeps and drivers ready to take us into Saigon when we land. Pull rank if you have to."

He smiled and started transmitting: "Lone Wolf to Mother Goose…"

After Wires had finished, he came over to me. Smiling, he said, "ETA an hour thirty. They want blue smoke unless we have to go red, and the jeeps will be waiting. I had to throw some rank around before they wanted to comply, but they've come to the party, boss."

"Good. Thanks Wires. You heard him, guys, one and a half. Time for a brew."

Kami, who'd heard what had been said, laughed. I said to her, "It'll be dark when we get in, but keep your hair up under your hat. I don't want anyone knowing there's a female travelling with us."

She replied with a smile, "Yes boss."

This had me looking at her intently, was she trying to be friendly or sarcastic?

We moved down to the fringe foliage when it came close to the choppers ETA. Everyone spread out, keeping an eye on our rear, but Bill kept Kami beside him. I heard the choppers, popped and threw the blue smoke.

I heard, "Delta X-ray 79 to Lone Wolf."

Before I answered, Bill laughed and said to Kami, "If you want to hear something funny, listen to this."

I answered: "Lone Wolf to Delta X-ray."

"Make that SRT Big John," he replied. "Well hi, y'all. Colonel Tiger sir, have your smoke in sight. Touchdown in three. You been pissin' in Charlie's backyard again Tiger? Hope you smoked some. I'll land first."

I replied, "Roger that, John to both. Did you stop for coffee?"

"Nope, but we can get some on the way back if'n you like, Colonel."

We heard laughter. Kami laughed with us, as she removed Bill's earpiece and handed it back. I said to everyone, "My group, and our passenger in the lead, Bill you go with Tag's group."

"Roger that boss," he replied and told Kami what I had said.

When John landed, my group started moving. As the other two choppers rose into the air, I took my customary seat with Kami not far from my side. We switched off our radios and put on the intercom sets.

John looked around, gave me a smile and the thumbs up, and said, "And away we go, folks." The chopper lifted and circled to take the place of the second chopper while it loaded, and then we circled once and headed back to Bien Hoa. John's voice came through the intercom. "Y'all sit back and rest. Sleep if you wish, and I'll wake when we stop for coffee."

Kami was the first to doze off, her head against my shoulder. The others smiled and smirked. I gave them a dirty scowl. Before long, I was dozing as well.

John's voice over the intercom woke me. "We're about five minutes out, Tiger."

"Roger that," I replied as I looked outside at the darkness. I could see the glow of lights from Bien Hoa, so I woke the others.

When we landed, John and I shook hands. He said, "You'll have to keep that filly quiet or she'll give the game away."

"Thanks John. Have a good night."

"Oh I will. Y'all do the same." We smiled at each other and nodded.

After returning to the hotel, we trudged straight over to the lift with Kami in amongst us. The senior MP on guard pushed the lift button for us and said, "Welcome back, sirs."

We crowded into the lift and rode up to our floor. As the lift door opened, the boys headed to their respective rooms. I told

Kami, "There's a couple of spare rooms. Just pick one. They're all the same."

"What about that one?" she asked, pointing to my room.

I shook my head and said, "No, that's mine."

"That'll do then," she replied.

"Oh no it won't. Find one of the spares." I turned to walk into my room, and she pushed back her head and went to a spare room next to mine.

After a nice, long soak in the bath, I turned the shower on to clean off. I walked naked to the wardrobe and pulled out some fresh clothes. I started unpacking the leftover rations and the spare ammo I kept as replacements when I cleaned my guns, which I planned to do in the morning.

There was a knock at the door. Tag was standing there. "We're ordering from room service. What'll you have"?

I ordered a medium steak Diane and fries with a banana split for dessert. I left the door open, gathered up my dirty washing, placed it in a laundry bag with my name on it, and left it at the door.

I made my way to the lounge area and bar, and then went to Buzz's room, which was open, and asked if we had any of the good stuff left. He smiled and brought me a bottle that was three quarters full. "After that one, we've still got nine left, boss."

I smiled and nodded. I made my way back to the lounge. I poured a glass and put a block of ice in when Kami walked in dressed in jeans and a T-shirt, a towel wrapped around her head and barefoot.

"Can I have one of those?" she asked.

"Sure. Did you order dinner?" She nodded her head, and I passed her a tumbler.

She took a sip and her eyes lit up. "My god, that's really good. What is it?" I turned the bottle around so she could see it. She whistled and remarked, "You guys really know how to live, don't you?" I just smiled.

240

When dinner arrived, we had it placed in the conference room. I asked one of the waiters to take my laundry bag down for cleaning; he nodded and said he would. The meal was excellent. We laughed and joked with each other.

After eating my banana split for dessert and waiting for the others to finish, we adjourned to the lounge. I poured Kami, Bill and myself another glass of the good stuff, and as we lit smokes. I told Kami I'd ring Hogarth the next morning to let him know we were back and that she was here with us. At this news, she seemed a little put out and disappointed. Christ! Women! Go figure.

CHAPTER 19

Later that night while I was sipping some Blue Label and writing up the mission report at my desk, Kami walked in and closed the door, which had been open. She was wearing, or should I say nearly wearing, only her fresh cam shirt, unbuttoned. As she stood across the desk from me, I could not help but see her lithe, lean, and perfectly contoured body. My body reacted at the sight of her beautiful figure.

"Tiger, I think it's time we released some of the tension between us. I want you to take me, and I know you want to as well," she said huskily.

She was damned right on that score. I resisted the urge to get up from the desk, pick her up, and throw her on the bed to make passionate love to her. Instead, I sat back in the chair, ignoring my impulses. "Kami, I'm really flattered, and even though I'd like to, I'm married."

She looked a little shocked. "No one would ever know."

"I'm sorry, but you're wrong on that score. I would know, and so would you, I'm sorry, but I won't risk my marriage for what could be an enjoyable and very good roll in the hay. I'm really sorry; you don't know how sorry I am, about that." For a spy she didn't know how disguise her feelings much, I thought as I watched a whole gambit of emotions cross her face.

"When you're talking to Hogarth tomorrow, please let him know that I'm ready for my next assignment." She turned while buttoning her shirt, went to the door, and walked back to her room.

After sleeping in the following morning, we went down to the restaurant for breakfast and enjoyed a relaxed meal. Kami had reverted to her normal self; she kept her eyes on me, but nothing was mentioned about the previous night by either of us. Back on our floor, I rang Hogarth to let him know we were back and had picked up his parcel along the way. He told me he'd be over in thirty minutes to see what we had to say and to pick up his parcel. I informed everyone that the debriefing would be in thirty minutes in the conference room.

I said to Wires, "The usual please." He smiled and nodded.

I escorted Hogarth into the conference room from the lift, where everyone was waiting. He greeted Kami, "Boy I'm damned glad to see you alive. After that little stint, you'll be heading home stateside for a while."

"Thanks boss. It'll be good to get home to some normalcy."

Hogarth shook everyone's hands, thanking us for the great work. I asked, "Did you bring any intelligence officers with you?"

"Nope, just me, but I'll tape everything." He suffered a fit of coughing before continuing, "As I said I'll tape everything and pass on all the relevant data to the right offices."

I dubiously agreed, and as he took each report, asked us to name ourselves. Luckily, all the guys had written their reports and referred to them occasionally. Hogarth wanted to take the written reports, but I vetoed that by informing him they would be going back to Australia with us when we went, which I hoped was soon. He told me whom to see at Central Command in regards to going home, and then the debriefing was over.

He waited for Kami to pack her things to leave with him. On the way out, she said goodbye to the team and came to my room to thank me for getting her out. She kissed me on the cheek and hugged me as she whispered, "I still want you, and always will. I'm in love with you, you dear, sweet, ruthless man."

I was shocked and bewildered by her bold statement. She smiled at me one last time before leaving.

After shaking off the moment, I asked Wires if he got everything, which he had, and then told everyone to have their reports ready in half an hour in the despatch case. I turned to Bill and asked, "Can I see you for a minute?"

He nodded and we went into my room to the desk. I sat down and said, "I think you and I had best go to your headquarters and see someone there about what my team and you will be up to. Can I send a message from there as well as the despatch case?"

"Well sure. The whole bottom floor is the communications room. As for what we'll be up to, probably no one will be able to tell us for a week or two."

"That's fine. It'll probably be a week before I hear from home anyway," I replied.

"We'd best be in good uniforms if we're going. There is usually a lot of brass hanging around down there, and we'll see reception when we go down. They've usually got some jeeps hanging around for military use," he told me.

I smiled, nodded, and replied, "Sounds like a plan, Stan. Let's get ourselves ready."

Thirty minutes later, we were dressed in clean uniforms and shaved wearing our silver eagles on each epaulette. My beret was curled up and jutting out of my trouser pocket, and I had the message I'd coded for HQ in my right shirt pocket. I carried the despatch case. The reception desk was able to supply us with a jeep, one of four that were permanently at the hotel for military use. They were going to have it delivered to the front entrance; while we were waiting, I used the house phone to ring Tag upstairs.

Once he answered, I informed him about the jeeps being available at reception and told him everyone was on R and R until further notice. If they wanted to go sightseeing to go right ahead. Bill climbed into the driver's seat as the jeep was brought around, and we headed off to the Central Command Building, which, according to Bill, was the old city hall. We parked in an empty spot near the main doors, and Bill pocketed the key as we left the jeep to go inside to the communications office.

We left our headgear on as we went into the comm's office, and a sergeant asked what he could do for us. I gave him the message I'd coded and asked for it to be sent ASAP. He passed it to a clerk that got straight onto sending it. I handed him the despatch case and asked for it to be sent in the mail plane.

He placed it in a bag labelled Australia. "That'll go on tonight's transport, sir." Just then, the radio clerk had a word to him and passed him a piece of paper, which he passed to me. "That's the confirmation of receipt, sir, but they want you to wait for a reply communique."

"I have to go upstairs, so I'll collect anything on the way out, if that's all right, sergeant."

"Yes sir," he replied

"Thank you," I answered as Bill and I left to go upstairs.

First, we went to Bill's HQ to see if they had heard anything, and then we were passed up the line from one office to another and so on. In the end, I got so frustrated that I demanded to see the CnC's undersecretary, and we were immediately escorted to Major Dan Firman's office. The Major knew who Bill and I were, and we were ushered into his office straight away. Major Firman had met both of us during my second tour while I was confined to barracks.

He stood at attention and saluted, as did we in return. After taking seats, he asked what he could do for us, and I explained the situation. After I'd finished, he said, "All right, gentlemen. I will do my best to find out what is going on for you. It may take me a few days, but leave it with me and I will see what I can do. You said you were at the Hilton on the floor below the CnC's penthouse?" We both nodded. "Anything I find out I'll pass along to you there."

We stood and I said, "Thank you for trying to clear this up for us, Major."

"Not at all, Colonel. It is the least I can do. Your exploits are one of the General's favourite reads when he hears you're back in the country."

There was a lengthy message awaiting me in the comm's room. I was informed that if I needed to send anything further or received more messages, all my communications could be handled at the hotel.

Bill dropped me back at the hotel because he wanted to do some shopping. I went up to my room. Most of the guys were out; only Gecko had stayed behind, and he was in the lounge doing a complete strip of his rifle. I left him with it and went to decode the message I'd received.

It read, Congratulations on another brilliantly executed mission, Tiger. Lt. Colonel McFarlane is happy and has said it is time you and your team came home for a well-earned rest. Therefore, as your new CO, I'm ordering you to not accept any more assignments. If the Americans can get you back to Australia, that would be fine. If you can't get a transport from Tindal, let me know and I will arrange it. I leave to you to do as you want regarding getting back to base. If I can help, just inform me. Major John Hallorhan.

That was a turn up for the books. I had it in writing: no more missions. I considered that as yet the yanks weren't aware of this, so we'll use the time taken by Major Firman to find out as R and R. We deserved the comfort we now had, and we may as well take advantage of it since the Australian government wasn't paying for it anyway. We could afford to have a week off. Besides, I wanted to do some sightseeing as well. I coded up a reply that read, SRT to Major Hallorhan, received last communique and will arrange to be transported back to Australia with Americans at their earliest convenience. Will advise once transport is finalized. Welcome to your new posting, Major. Will request to see you as soon as we get back on base. Sgt Davis.

A week later, we heard from Major Firman asking Bill and I to see him at Central Command. We got hold of another jeep and drove over to HQ. When we walked into his office and sat, he told us everything had been sorted out. My team had been recalled to Australia, and Bill was going home to the states on three months leave after which he was to join his own company. Firman asked if we wanted to fly into Hawaii together or separately from Bien Hoa. We chose to fly into Hawaii together and say our goodbyes there.

Firman nodded. "Fine. There is a passenger jet leaving in four days for Hickham Air Base in Hawaii at zero nine hundred. From there at eighteen hundred, a transport is leaving for Tindal and can take your team, Tiger, and Bill; you can make the following day's flight for California. Would you like me to arrange those flights, Colonels?"

We looked at each other and back to Firman. We replied simultaneously, "Yes please, Major." While we were in his office, he and his secretary arranged and booked our flights. His secretary wrote all the flight details on two different pieces of paper and gave them to us as we left.

Back at the hotel, I coded a message for HQ and went down to the foyer to have it sent. While I was there, I arranged with the manager to supply the jeeps we had been using to transport us to Bien Hoa after breakfast on the designated morning of our flight. That evening before going to the restaurant for dinner, I told my guys when we were going home and they cheered. That night we were full of excitement at the prospect of heading home.

In Hawaii, we had an hour to say our goodbyes to Bill before catching our connecting flight to Tindal. He had fought and lived with us for nearly two years over two tours, and it was difficult saying goodbye to a comrade in arms. Everyone was going to miss having him around, and as we parted, he passed me a card with his home address and phone number as well as and his home base numbers.

Close to tears, he told me, "You guys keep that, and if you ever get the chance to come to the states, you call me and I'll come running."

With final handshakes and embraces, we walked up the ramp of our transport in silence, thinking our own thoughts.

At Tindal, it was easy for me to get a connection to Pearce, and we landed there at eighteen thirty. After asking, I found out a truck was heading into town in fifteen minutes, so I arranged to catch a lift to Swanbourne. We eventually arrived at SRT at nineteen thirty on the sixteenth of August, 1973. We dumped our gear and made our way to our respective messes. The next morning, we would start work at eight, and our days of living the rich life were over for a while.

The next morning, we made sure the building was ship shape, with everything put away and cleaned. After checking our weapons and ammo, we realized we'd come home with twice our magazine supply, which were all full. We still had some ammo, which Buzz took care of. Our radios were placed in the workshop for Wires and JJ to check over, and everyone's pagers were handed out after fresh batteries had been installed.

At zero nine hundred, I rang Mark's old number, and Howler came on the line. I introduced myself and asked permission to see him and was told to stay at SRT, that he would join us here shortly. I warned my guys he was coming to us and to look busy even if we had nothing to do. I did ask Dumper to give the vehicles as well as my car the once over and start them up. I passed him the keys; all of them had been sitting idle for over a year.

As I was walking back up the hall, I spotted two officers entering and yelled, "Attention!" This was the first time we'd seen either of them.

One was Lt. Colonel McFarlane the OC. The other was wearing Major's pips, so I could only assume this was Hallorhan, our new CO. McFarlane was five ten with salt and pepper hair, which was reasonable as he was in his late thirties. He had piercing grey eyes with a lean, well-muscled body, and then I remembered he'd already been with SAS as a platoon commander before becoming the 2IC, and then he'd been posted to 1RAR.

The Major, however, was close to six foot with blue eyes and blonde hair, lean but not as muscular as the Colonel. I put his age around twenty-seven or eight. Rumour had it that he had commanded a commando unit prior to his posting here.

They followed me to my office. Before sitting down, the Colonel leaned forward to shake my hand. "Tiger, when I took over this command, I wasn't too sure of your old boss's decision to form your team and was considering disbanding it, but I must say, both you and your team have proved your worth time and time again. Plus, you have heightened our fighting reputation to quite a lot of people, not only here but overseas as well. Well done, and know that you have my full confidence."

"Thank you, sir," I replied and sat down behind my desk.

The Colonel stayed quiet as Hallorhan shook my hand across the desk and introduced himself. "Most just call me Howler because of my habit of yelling a lot, especially when I'm in a bad mood. Your old CO Major Ryan told me how you met and what you have achieved in SAS in general and with this unit. I hope we can form a good working relationship like you had with him, but I am not naïve. I'm aware that I'll have to prove myself to you and your men."

The Colonel told me they'd both heard the tapes and read my reports thoroughly but wanted me to go over everything, from leaving on the original mission to returning the previous night. Therefore, for the next three hours, with short breaks for coffee and smokes, I filled them in. Every now and again, they would ask a question, laugh, or comment "well done" or "good show."

After I'd finished, the Colonel said, "Damned fine report. I must say you've got a very remarkable memory. That's all for now, except I'm placing your team on three months stand down. You deserve the rest. You can work out the details with Major Hallorhan. Now let's go out and you can introduce us to your band of rogues."

So as we exited my office and went into the ready room, I yelled, "SRT, Front and Centre move!" Once they were all assembled, introductions were made and hands shaken.

After the Colonel left, Howler and I went back to my office to work out the details of when our stand-down was to take effect and who would require travel warrants. Because it was Thursday, our leave would commence at knock off time the following day, and we wouldn't be back until the first of December.

I commented, "Looks like we'll be working another Christmas."

"I'm afraid so Tiger. I've already had one request for your services, and it's a three- month stint."

I nodded and replied, "Ok boss. The best way to find out who'll need travel warrants is to ask them while they're all together, probably in the ready room in a minute, but first I'll need one to fly to Queensland and back."

He nodded. "Done. Now let's go see the others."

I had decided not to call my wife to tell her I was back. I would just show up and surprise her. She'd hate me for doing that but would be glad to see me. I'd also decided to buy another car while I was there, probably as soon as I arrived so I'd have transport at each end.

On Monday I drove into town to see Wendy at the Ansett office, but it wasn't Ansett anymore. It'd been taken over by Compass Airlines. Thankfully, Wendy was still there, and she arranged to get me onto that night's overnight flight, which would arrive in Brisbane at zero seven thirty the following morning. She also gave me an open return ticket; all I'd have to do was arrange my flight when I was close to returning to Perth. So with that all sorted, I went back to the barracks to pack my gear for my trip. The last thing into my bag was my gun tucked into the shoulder holster, as per SOP's. I rang a taxi that night to take me to the airport. I had decided to fly in shorts and a T shirt with my running shoes.

When I landed in Brisbane, I grabbed a cab and had him take me to a big Ford dealer. He took me to Metro Ford at Spring Hill; they were already open, and as I looked around at the new Fords, my eyes focused on the showpiece on a raised platform. I had to blink to make sure I wasn't seeing things. I started moving forward, my eyes fixed, on the beautiful Shelby Mustang Fastback, grey with wide black stripes.

I was in heaven as I oozed my body into the driver's seat, looking at the gauges and T Bar auto shift. I popped the bonnet and went for a look. Well hello rev head heaven! I drooled over the massive four hundred and fifty cubic inch V8.

My reverie was interrupted by a salesman asking if he could

help me, so without taking my eyes off the powerhouse, I asked, "How much?"

"All up with interest, it may be more than you could afford."

His attitude and statement got up my nose immediately, and I gently secured the bonnet before facing him. I looked him up and down as he did the same the same to me. If he'd known me, the deadly gaze I gave him would have been enough warning. I was already irritable from the long flight. Business class had been full, so I hadn't been able to stretch right out and sleep, only doze.

My voice lowered as I said, "I didn't ask about finance. I asked the price. That was all."

"Oh, I think it would be out of your price range, sir."

Inwardly seething and ready to do this prick some mischief, I asked quietly, "Does your sales manager work on commission like you do?"

He laughed. "No sir, he only gets sales bonuses."

"Good," I replied, "Follow me."

I marched over to the sales manager's office and boldly strode in. The salesman tried to apologise and make excuses. The manager held his hand up to silence him as I sat down after placing my kitbag beside the chair.

"Can I help you?"

I nodded. "I was prepared to let this idiot sell me a car I've already decided to buy so he could have his commission if he'd agreed to my terms. Instead, I've been insulted with finance terms and told the car is probably out of my price range. Because of this little prick's attitude, he's not getting this sale. You do not work on commission, so if you come up with the right price minus any commission add-ons, I'll pay cash. If you meet my other conditions."

He leaned back in his seat, looked at the salesman, who'd gone white, and asked, "Which car?"

The salesman replied, "The Shelby."

The manager whistled and started looking at his stock book.

He played with his calculator, looked at me, and said, "I can have it registered and on the road for you by three o'clock for nine thousand nine hundred."

I did not really have to think about it, so I made a show of it. "Make it by midday, and I'll give you five grand deposit and get the rest when the bank opens across the street."

"Done."

"While I get the money out of my bag, tell this dickhead how much commission he's just lost because of his attitude, please."

The manager laughed and started playing with his calculator again as I unzipped my kitbag. To make things easier, I put my gun on his desk and noticed their stunned looks. "Sorry. I'm a sergeant in the army and have to carry that thing everywhere I go."

The manager raised an eyebrow and said, "Make that price nine thousand five hundred. Call the other four hundred a service-man's discount."

"Done," I replied as I started counting the money.

After counting the five thousand, I asked if I could kip out somewhere while I waited. The manager took me to a waiting room with a couch and told me it was the best he could do. If I hadn't stirred before the car was ready, he'd come and wake me. He asked for my name, licence number and address for the registration. I asked him to wake me at eleven instead to give me time to go to the bank, which he said he would do.

At twelve thirty, I drove out of Metro Ford with a full tank of fuel in my new Mustang. All I had to do was find my way to Gailes. An hour later, after getting lost a couple of times, I was on familiar streets and easily found the house. I parked on the road because there was an unfamiliar car in the driveway behind the open garage door where the Monaro was parked. My sixth sense screamed something wasn't right.

My kitbag was on the passenger seat, so I unzipped it and pulled out my pistol. I walked into the yard to the door under the breezeway that led into the garage or into the house through the laundry. The door to the house was unlocked, so I walked in, moving quietly. As I moved in further, I could hear Sharon talking to someone in the bedroom. I assumed she had a friend over but couldn't work out why she was home unless she'd taken the day off. So I tucked my gun into the back waistband of my shorts and walked boldly to the bedroom door.

What I saw was enough for me to find my gun in my hand and pointed at the bed. She was naked in bed with another guy, who was also naked. She was mid-sentence when she saw me and froze with her mouth open.

The guy was looking at her as she froze and turned to look. He saw me and the gun and froze also.

My mind was all over the place, debating whether to shoot him, her, or both of them. Rational thought returned to me. "You have ten minutes to get this fucker out of my house, and you'd better pray I calm down fast. I'll return in fifteen."

I dropped the gun down and walked away, hoping he'd try to jump me from behind. He would have been shot. I walked back to my car, my brain in a fog. I drove down to the local pub and knocked back two doubles without even tasting them before slowly sipping the third. Through the turmoil of my thoughts, I rationalized that I was to blame, choosing my job over my wife, but she had known what she was getting into. I realised that our marriage was over, because even if she could convince me otherwise, I'd never be able to trust her again. I made my mind up about what I was going to do.

When I got back to the house, the other car was gone, so I drove into the driveway and stopped behind the Monaro. I walked into the house, and she stood in front of me, mouth open to speak. I held up my finger, signalling her to wait because she knew sign language. She knew exactly what I meant. I went in the bedroom, found my clothes, and tossed them onto the bed. I pulled out all my other stuff and went systematically through every room, gathering any of my gear. After I'd finished, I found a strong enough carton and started filling it with my things. Eventually all my stuff was packed into two cartons, which I took out to the car and placed in the boot.

She had watched me walk my stuff out and walk back in, not speaking. She finally spoke. "Bought a new car, I see."

"Yeah, this morning when I got in. It was for you while I was away." She looked away, tears running down her face. I continued. "Our marriage is over. I will never be able to trust you again. I'm taking my stuff. You can have everything else, even the house. Get me the deed and I'll have it signed over to you in your maiden name, and I'll send it back to you along with divorce papers. Please sign them. If any mail comes for me, please send it to me at Swanbourne." I paused, looking at her. "That's all I've got to say except goodbye." I turned and walked to my car.

CHAPTER 20

I was pissed off. What I was really pissed off about was that I'd been stupid enough to knock back what I'm sure would have been a great time with Kami. While I drove aimlessly, trying to sort out my emotions, I realised I was heading in the general direction of the Enoggera barracks and made the decision that Brisbane seemed to be a good place to live. I could try to get another war service house. With that in mind, once at the barracks, I headed for the army housing office.

After an hour of talking with a female sergeant, I discovered I was eligible for up to seventy-five grand, and if I didn't use all of it, I would be given a cheque made for ten grand to buy furniture. I asked her as we were doing the paperwork, because I didn't know Brisbane all that well, where was a good place to live. She told me that Mitchelton or Keperra were popular with army personnel. Both had a few schools not too far away, if I had kids; I replied ironically that I wasn't even married anymore. She told me they were still great areas to live, so that sorted that. I asked if there were any motels in the area, and she recommended the Mitchelton Tavern, which was right beside a big shopping centre. After all my paperwork was processed, I asked her directions. The directions she gave me were spot on, and I took a room at the tavern for an indefinite stay.

The following day, I went to the shopping centre to see if I could find any real estate agents in there. I did find one from an LJ Hooker franchise, but before going to see him, I wandered around and found a furniture and electrical outlet that was part of Walton's. I also found a waterbed shop. Wondering what they were like, I wandered in, and after lying on one decided, they were reasonable. I shook off the sales clerk by saying I'd think about it and left to continue my wander around.

I headed to the realty agent. Over the next few days, he showed me houses in his area of Mitchelton, but they weren't my style at all. Just as I was ready to give him away as a dead loss, he showed me a house in Keperra that he warned me was a little on the pricey side.

When I first saw it, I had the feeling this one was right, and after inspecting it, I asked about air conditioning because it didn't have any. He said he knew someone that could give me a reasonable quote if I took it. The house was two stories with a swimming pool in the backyard.

With a spa pool inside near the games room, and a bar downstairs. Upstairs there were four bedrooms, a kitchen dining area, and lounge. The master bedroom had an ensuite with a bath as well as a shower. There was another bathroom and separate toilet upstairs, and the same downstairs. The place was huge, but I liked it.

Back at his office, we dickered on price and finally settled at sixty thousand neat. I hit him with the kicker; he was to get the quote for the air conditioning to be installed and add it to the sale price, but the quote had to done within the next three days. I required the house keys, as I'd be there to tell the air con guy what I wanted. I also needed a carpenter to give me a quote on things I wanted done, so if he could arrange that it would be great.

He rang me the next morning and asked to see me. It only took five minutes to walk over. He gave me the keys and told me the air con guy was coming at ten. He asked why I wanted quotes for work to be done without the sale going through until after he could give me the final price. I explained to him that I was on a very tight schedule and would be going back overseas within two months. He accepted this and said he'd have a final price for me the following morning. He'd also lined up a builder he used to see me at the house at eleven. I thanked him and left to collect the car so I could drive up to the house. I wanted to make a list of furniture to buy.

The sale went through, and I'd been given the two cheques,

one made out to the real estate company for sixty-three grand, and the other was ten grand for me to purchase furniture. The air con work had been started, and I phoned the builder to start ASAP. I went furniture and electrical shopping, plus bought a king size waterbed that was to be installed the following day. By the time I received the house deed a month later, all the work had been done and furniture delivered, so I moved into my new house.

I did introduce myself to my neighbour and his family, and as it turned out, he was the RSM (Regimental Sergeant Major) of the drop short (Artillery) battalion based at Enoggera. After telling him my regiment, he had a fairly good idea of what his new neighbour did. He told me he'd keep an eye on the place whenever I was away.

I made my return flight booking to Perth the following week, which would give me three weeks to organize everything I needed to, before having to report for duty. I got back to the barracks a week later.

At seven hundred after taking the night flight from Brisbane. This time business class was almost bare, so I was able to stretch out and sleep most of the trip.

After breakfast in the mess, I made my way over to SRT and unlocked the building. I went out and fired up my XP, which caught on the first couple of turns. I let it run for a while, knowing I'd have to take it for a run very soon to blow out all of the cobwebs. Perhaps I'd go down to Bunbury on the weekend. I called the army lawyer who had helped me out before and made an appointment for ten hundred.

When I'd finished explaining things and what I wanted to happen, he explained, "Yes, well, some of it will be more difficult than others, but I can sort it all out. Just one thought, though: why not try for an annulment rather than a divorce? You have good grounds. You were under the legal age for marriage, you never spent any time in the marital home, and you were overseas for all but one week of your marriage. And your wife committed adultery."

"What's the difference?"

"Well with a divorce, you could end up paying spousal support, but we could negate that by the fact that you are willingly giving her the house. With an annulment, the marriage is deemed never to have taken place; therefore, you aren't obligated to give her anything. We could take back the house, but it will be harder to fight if she decides to contest the case."

I thought it over for a couple of minutes and said, "No, go for the divorce. Christ, I gave her the house, so surely they wouldn't come at me for more money considering she's working as well."

"That's another valid issue. Do you think she's likely to contest the divorce?" he asked.

"Not unless I give her cause to, I guess. Why?"

"Because we could go one of two ways. One would be on the grounds of adultery, or we could try out the new no fault divorce law, which I think would be the way to go. If we go on grounds, she could deny everything, and you have no photographic evidence to support your case."

I nodded. "Ok, go that way then, and also transfer the house deed into her maiden name."

"All right. I can start work on this immediately. She's not in your will, by any chance?"

"No, we hadn't got around to doing that yet," I replied.

"Good."

Then he said, "I'll get things moving. I will need you to sign some documents. Let's see, I can get all that filled out tomorrow. Ok, come and see me at ten the day after tomorrow, Tiger, and everything you need will be completed. Once you sign them, I can lodge them that day, and it should only take about six weeks until we get a court date. You will not need to appear. I can take care of all that, and copy the new house deed as well."

After leaving his office, I went to lunch at the mess and whiled away the afternoon in my office bringing all my paperwork up to date, but I found it boring. My mind wasn't in tune with what I was doing; I suppose in one way I was sort of feeling sorry for myself. I knew of only two ways to fix that, one was to get really hammered, and the other was to go for a long, fast drive.

I chose the drive option and headed north out of town. Once I was on the northern highway, I put the foot down. I hadn't been to Geraldton before so decided to go have a look.

The only trouble with a car that's capable of two hundred plus is that I made the four-hour trip in next to no time, so I didn't have much time to clear the shit out of my head about what had happened over the last couple of months. I drove around the town and beaches aimlessly, and then headed back south to Perth.

I drove slower on the way back and was able to sort a lot out in my mind. Once I had achieved that, I was able and ready to move forward with my life again, before finally crashing out in my room around zero four hundred. I had decided to have a couple of days in Bunbury after I'd seen and signed all the paperwork the lawyer needed.

A couple of nights later, I was in a beer garden bar listening to the live music when the barmaid I'd been flirting with sat down with me. She said, "I hope you don't mind, but I'm trying to get away from a clown that wants to buy me drinks. To get away I told him I'd seen my boyfriend and was joining him."

I smiled. "Well that's a step up. I'm your boyfriend! I was only flirting earlier, but let's give him a real show." I leaned forward and kissed her.

After her initial shock, she relaxed and enjoyed our kiss. As we parted lips, she whispered, "Wow, you can definitely be my boyfriend. You really know how to kiss a girl." I smiled at her.

The turkey she was trying to duck was standing in front of me when I looked up. "Do you know your girlfriend is a tease?"

I smiled and answered, "Yeah, and I love her for it. But I'm the only one she goes to bed with. Now do yourself a favour and go away."

The fool was not going to go away. "You and what army are going to make me."

I leaned over and said to Karen (thank Christ she still had her name tag on), "Will you excuse me a moment, Karen love?" I gave her a kiss as I stood up. I faced the turkey. I touched each bicep with a hand. "This army and this army."

He sneered. "Think you're good, do you?"

I smiled, as I answered, "No. I know I'm good."

"You, arsehole. I'm going to make mincemeat of you." He swung.

Since I could not talk him out of it, I struck, hard and faster than he could see. The next minute a security bouncer was there. Karen had a word with him, and he and his mate dragged the unconscious turkey off.

Karen and I spent more time together. She was a cute little blonde, about five five, with blue eyes, and she and I spent the night together. After numerous orgasms on her part, I finally emptied myself inside her, which sent her into orbit once more. When she surfaced dreamily the next morning, we went out to a café for breakfast before she went home.

Now that I'd broken the drought, so to speak, I got back into the swing of things. I had a different girl in my bed every night for the duration of my stay in Bunbury. Karen was able to have a repeat after dropping by my motel room one afternoon prior to going to work. After our lovemaking, we had a shower together, and when she was ready, I drove her to work and had a couple of drinks.

The following morning, I headed back to work. I'd finally gotten over Sharon's betrayal and was once more my usual self without any demons haunting my thoughts. While I was waiting for the rest of the team to come back to work, I concentrated on staying in peak physical condition. I spent two hours in the gym every morning, then would run the beach for an hour and swim for two more hours. Sometimes I would vary the routine by timing myself on the assault course or join Swifty for some martial arts training. Occasionally I would have a couple single soldier scenarios run at the killing house to keep my speed and accuracy up to par.

One morning, Howler joined me on the beach run. As we were running, he said, "Sorry to hear about your marriage, Tiger. Seems to be the thing with this regiment. My first wife left me while I was there the first time."

"That's ok, boss. I've gotten over it and am just waiting to get back to work now."

"How'd you like Christmas in the states? That job I was telling you about is on, and it's for a three-month stint. If your team leaves in the second week of the month, you'll be there for Christmas as well."

"It sounds good to me boss. What's the job?" I asked.

He laughed. "You're going to love this. Some idiot in the hierarchy thinks that SEAL training in the states is far harder than any training in Australia, so you will be going over and assessing their training methods of a fresh intake, from start to finish. It's got to be accurate and truthful. I want comparison notes of everything, what is useful, what's not, all that."

He was right; I loved it. "Will we be taking weapons?"

"Only pistols, no long arms," he replied.

I nodded. "Sounds good, boss. Shall I prepare the team with a pre-brief when they're back?"

"Yes, go ahead and do that. I'll get everything teed up and will give you a briefing a day or so before you're due to go."

By the time we finished our conversation, we were back at our starting point, and while I stripped down for a swim, he went for a shower and changed to start work again.

As I was walking back to the barracks, my pager went off: Howler asked me to ring him, so when I got into my room, I dialled his number. He told me he had forgotten to tell me one major piece of the assessment we would be doing, which was that two members of the team were to take part in the course.

The following week the whole team was back, and I briefed them as to what we'd be doing for the next few months. When I asked for volunteers to do the SEAL training course, all of them thought it would be a hoot doing it; they all volunteered for it. I went over to Howler's office at HQ and asked if we could fit four into the SEAL training course. He agreed that we could.

After getting back from HQ, the guys were still gathered in the briefing room, so I walked in and said, "After further discussion, there will be four of you taking part in the training, and the lucky ones are JJ, Wires, Gecko, and Lizard. You four will have to have personal tape recorders because I want you to record your thoughts on the training, whether it was any good, the good points and bad. In other words, everything is recorded. Use a tape for every day, and date the used ones. Once the course is over, you'll have to write a very concise report about the whole thing. Wires make sure each of you has a recorder and plenty of blank tapes."

He nodded. "We've still got dozens of the little Dictaphone type ones, boss, and a stack of blank one-hour mini tapes."

"In that case, we'll all use them instead of trying to write while we walk. Buzz, get with Wires and make sure we've got plenty of batteries and tapes." After he nodded, I continued. "Now the observers, which is the rest of us, we'll get together at the end of each day and compare notes. You four doing the course, you may be captains, but you'll be going through everything with the trainees, so it'll mean dorm living and eating, no special favours. Apparently, the course starts on January second, but we'll be leaving for the states in a week or so. If he's lucky, Wild Bill might let us drop in on him for Christmas. He lives in San Diego and that's where the Coronado SEAL training unit is also." They all laughed.

Howler gave us our briefing before we were due to go and told us that our US liaison officer would be awaiting our arrival at Pendleton Air Base in San Diego. We'd then be accommodated in quarters at Coronado. On our trip out, we would be transferred to

Pearce to board the usual transport to Tindal, but at Tindal, there was a US Air Force jet waiting to take us the rest of the way.

I asked, "Who's our liaison officer, boss?"

Howler said, "I have no idea. They haven't supplied his name. All I know is that he knows the workings of Coronado fairly well and will be waiting when you arrive at Camp Pendelton."

I nodded and smiled; I had a feeling we'd be seeing Bill earlier than we'd imagined. We were going to be transported to Pearce at sixteen hundred the following day. Our transport plane was due to be wheels up at seventeen hundred.

We landed at Pendelton three days later after losing a day due to overnight stops and crossing the International Date Line. Local time was fourteen hundred. Our liaison was waiting at the bottom of the exit stairs with three jeeps. The way he stood and moved was a familiar sight. I was first down the stairs and dropped my kitbag at the bottom.

We saluted each other, and then I rushed forward to embrace and shake hands with Wild Bill. Cries of joy came from the rest of the team as they saw whom I was with, and each embraced him as got to the bottom of the stairs. After loading our kitbags into the last jeep, the drivers waited for us to climb abroad the jeeps and we were driven to the officer's club.

After ordering the drivers to wait, Bill said, "I thought you could do with a beer before we head down to Coronado where you'll be staying."

While we had a couple of beers, we were introduced to some other officers before we hit the road. We arrived at Coronado just under an hour later and were shown to the visiting VIP quarters. Bill told us he'd also be staying with us at Coronado but would be going home each night. He'd arranged for us to have vehicles available for our use with the base commander, and as he was telling us this, two staff cars and a jeep pulled into the parking area. A young lieutenant came over, saluted, and passed me the keys to all of the vehicles.

Bill told me, "The base commander wants to introduce you tonight in the club, so I'll leave you to it for the rest of the day. I'll join you in the morning. On the weekend, we will have a party and BBQ at my place so you can meet the family and some friends. We can catch up and relax at the same time, so take it easy and I'll see you guys in the morning." He hopped into one of the jeeps and drove off.

I turned and said with a smile, "Ok, you four doing the course don't forget this is only temporary. In a couple of weeks, you'll be in the dorms, so while we're chatting with base personnel later, see if you can get into one and reserve your bunks before the intake arrives. Let's go settle in."

That evening we were welcomed into the officer's club by the base commander Fleet Commander Adrian Ross, and we were introduced to all his staff. After the introductions, the training chief of staff asked, "So Colonel, I understand that four of your staff will be joining the next intake. They do know they'll have to live in barracks and won't be allowed to come in here once the course is underway?"

"Yes they do. Will they need weapons? We only brought our handguns."

He laughed and answered, "No, all the stuff we do here is physical and mental, but I won't be easy on them. It will be tough on them. We train our people hard here."

I laughed. "Well, they think it'll be fairly easy compared to the training we do in our regiment. Even the rawest recruit has to carry a telephone pole everywhere they go, even the dunny and showers, so it should be a breeze for them."

His face belied the fact that he thought I was joking. "Surely you're kidding."

I called Tag over and asked, "Do you still have that photo of your recruit days when you joined, Tag?"

He nodded and pulled it out of his wallet and gave it to me. I passed it to the training chief. His face went white. The photo showed Tag and three others carrying their poles while running on the beach. I watched the man as he stared at the picture. "I don't joke about solid training, so I kid you not, we carry those poles everywhere. Correct Tag?"

"Yes Boss," he replied as the photo was passed back to him.

I turned back to the training chief. "But we're to observe your training, and also see what my guys think of it. At the end of the day, a little training is good, don't you think?"

He agreed, but I think he was a little relieved when I was called over to another conversation.

The next morning after breakfast and Bill joining us, we were given a tour of the complex by jeep. Our guide, the same lieutenant that had delivered the transport to us the day before, turned to me after the tour and said, "Sir, I've been told that some of your staff wish to see the barracks where they'll be staying when the next course begins?"

I replied, "That's right, lieutenant."

He suggested, "Well, if you like, sir, I could take you over there before we go back for lunch."

I smiled and replied, "That's a good idea, lieutenant, let's do that."

He smiled and answered, "Yes sir." I gave Bill and Tag a wink.

After pulling up to a barracks building, the lieutenant unlocked the door. The four course candidates went in for a look. I guess they weren't impressed because when they came out, Wires asked me, "Is it too late to change our minds, boss?"

I laughed and replied, "It sure is, boys; you're stuck with it now."

On Saturday we drove the staff cars to Bill's. I drove the lead car, with Dumper doing the navigating, following Bill's written instructions, while Tag drove the other car and followed us. After stopping to buy some booze and steaks, we arrived at eleven. A big fuss was made over us by Bill's wife, Mary, and his two children, Jake and Emily. We were welcomed with open arms.

I think Bill had embellished some of our accomplishments. Mary thanked me for everything I'd done for Bill. When I told her it wasn't much at all, she admonished me for being modest and said, "He wouldn't have had his last two promotions if you hadn't had a hand in it. I thank you all the same."

During the course of the afternoon, we chatted, drank, ate, and generally relaxed, talking about times gone, the present, and possible future. I spoke of my pending divorce without any bitterness, and Mary said, "Well, Tom, it's a shame. I know! I'll ring my friend Moira to come over. You'll like her."

Laughing, I shook my head and said, "I can look after myself, thank you, but if you want us to meet as friends, that's all right. Don't expect anything else to happen. I'm only here for a short time, and I do have a job in Australia."

Mary said, "I was only kidding with you, Tom, but I must confess, I did invite some of my single friends over to meet you boys. That'll be some of them now." We heard the doorbell, and she went to answer it.

Bill commented, "You're in trouble now. Some women just don't understand that a man can do things for himself. She'll try to get you married off to every single or unattached girl she knows. Don't be too hard on her, though. She means well, but I'm stepping out of it." We all had a long laugh. "C'mon Dumper, you and I are on KP duty. You can show me how to cook Aussie style."

Everyone laughed and moaned, "Oh no!"

Mary reappeared with a group of about a dozen women. "Ladies, you can all introduce yourselves after, but this is ..." She introduced all of us, and the ladies seemed to gravitate to whomever of us they were interested in. I instantly thought how do they do that, settle their focus on someone, and then move in for the kill, so to speak?

A cute brunette with hazel eyes and a shapely figure came and sat on the arm of the chair I was sitting in. "Hi, my name is..."

I cut her off. "Let me guess. Your name is Moira."

She looked surprised. "Yes! How did you know?"

"Because I'm physic."

Mary, who'd sat down in her seat, leaned across and lightly slapped me on the arm. "Tom, behave yourself. He's playing with you, Moira. I've already told him about you." She turned her head and raised her voice. "Charlene, you know better than that. He's my man!" Bill turned from the BBQ with his arms spread out, and we all laughed.

All in all, it was a good afternoon and evening. Everyone had a good time. Moira and I spent a great deal of time chatting and flirting with each other, and at the end of the evening when everyone was getting ready to depart, Moira asked if I'd like to join her for drinks and talk at her place. Not one to turn down an opportunity, I told her I'd love to as long as she could get me back to Coronado the next day. She agreed, saying "Not only that, I'll make sure you have a good breakfast with all the trimmings before we head back to the base.

So with a smile and acceptance on my part, we decided to make a night of it. I gave the keys of the staff car to Dumper, and as the team left, Moira and I said goodbye to Bill and Mary also, as she drove.

CHAPTER 21

Over the next few weeks, Moira and I spent a lot of time together, but we'd agreed in the beginning that there was no commitment from either of us; we'd just enjoy our time together and when it was time to part, there'd be no hard feelings. We did spend Christmas together at Bill's place, and that year the team spoiled his kids rotten. Some team members had formed relationships with the girls that had been introduced to us by Mary. I had warned all of them that this could happen on any job from now on. And to make it clear that the relationship would only last as long as we were there. Unless of course they wanted to keep in touch with the female involved.

After New Year we got down to the job we were there for and soon discovered they trained their soldiers by dehumanising candidates and intimidation with a sort of brainwashing, which didn't really sit well with me. This could have detrimental effects on the mental state of a soldier and make him believe he could do no wrong. The physical training wasn't any more than what recruits got at basic training in Australia but without the constant drilling. I was sorely tempted to lay down a challenge to the instructional staff to come to Australia and attempt admittance into the SAS by passing our training regime. None of the SEAL instructors would be able to pass our strict requirements. My team members were having a really easy time of it; however, there were times, I think, when they were sick and tired of constantly being yelled at. At one point, Gecko told the instructor what he thought of him and challenged the instructor to take him on.

The instructor ordered him down to the beach for a little one on one discipline, assuming, I am sure; he was going to show Gecko who was boss. As they were about to get into it, the instructor saw us watching, and Bill yelled down to him, "You go right ahead,

Master Sgt, pretend we're not here."

Gecko turned to look at us, and I could see his mischievous grin from where we were and groaned to Tag, "Oh shit. Get ready to go and stop him if he goes too far."

Tag replied, "Roger boss, but you may be the only one good enough to stop him."

I thought this over quickly and yelled down, "Gecko, remember to behave!"

I heard his reply as he faced the instructor, "Roger that, boss."

Bill leaned over and asked, "Aren't you worried?"

"Only about how much damage Gecko will do. Watch."

The instructor tried a swing. Gecko decked him and dropped him with one hit. He waited for him to get up and knocked him clean off his feet again.

"That's twice. Gecko will finish him off the next time," I mumbled.

As we watched, the instructor got up, and Gecko let him take a couple of swings before driving his left fist into the guy's stomach. He then slammed an open palm strike to the solar plexus, and the instructor crumpled. Gecko put him in a headlock, ready to snap his neck. We saw the instructor nod; Gecko let him go and gave him a hand up. Then they walked back up to the training area.

Bill exclaimed, "That Master Sergeant is the strongest instructor here, and look how small Gecko looks compared to him. How did he do that?"

"We've all been trained by the best unarmed combat expert in the business, and Tiger's the only one that's ever beaten him," Tag commented.

"God yes, I remember hearing that." Bill muttered, looking at me.

With a cheeky smile, I said, "Just Tiger will do."

We all laughed and started following them back. For some reason the master sergeant didn't do too much yelling around my men after that.

Each evening the observational group sat around in the lounge in our quarters, writing up our reports of each day's events from our recorders and discussing what we thought about the training style. The consensus of opinion was just the same as my earlier thoughts.

Saturday while Moira and I were there for Mary's birthday party, I interviewed Bill with the tape recorder, asking him how he honestly felt and thought about the SEAL training, having done it himself. Instead of spending the night with Moira on Sunday night, as was my routine, I went back to Colorado, and drove to the barracks to see my men and asked them to interview some of the intake, record their thoughts and ideas as well. I went to my quarters, where I relaxed in the bath with a drink.

The training course was nearing its end, so that weekend I started preparing Moira for my departure. As we talked after a furious bout of lovemaking, lying naked in each other's arms, she remarked, "I'm going to miss having you around. You do things to me that I never thought possible. What would you do if I followed you to Australia?"

I laughed. "Moira, don't get me wrong, but you'd be lucky if you found me there. My job keeps me on the move, and I've learned from my first marriage that long distance relationships just don't work, no matter how hard you try. I'm not ready to settle down like Bill has, not yet anyway. Give me ten years or so and I might change my mind, but not just yet."

"Yeah, I know what you mean. I'm not either, but I must say I wouldn't have missed our meeting for the world. You're not gone yet, so I get to have you a few more times."

One night during the course's last week, I asked Bill if I could come around for dinner. I wanted to talk to both him and Mary. He replied, "Sure. Why not make it tonight? I'll warn Mary when we go to lunch. Better still, stay the night. There's a spare room. Then we'll drive in together the following morning. How's that sound?"

"Sounds fine to me," I replied.

Before Bill and I left that afternoon, I had a quick word with Tag to let him know what I was up to and that I'd see him in the morning. After saying hello to his kids and spending a short time with them, Bill made drinks for the three of us, and we went out onto the back patio to talk. I told them of the situation with my relationship with Moira, and even though we were both of like mind about my impending departure, I'd still like for them, particularly Mary, to keep her involved in things and keep an eye on her and be a shoulder to cry on if she needed it. I also admitted to them that I would miss Moira, but at present, my job took precedent over anything in my personal life.

Mary confided in us that she and Moira had had numerous talks about what would happen after I left and how much she would miss me, but she was resigned to the fact that I would be leaving. She seemed as if she was determined to cope with me no longer being involved in her life, even though she had very strong feelings for me.

Mary continued. "It's sweet of you to be worried about her, Tom, but I think yes, she'll miss you for a while, but she'll bounce back all right. Besides, I will definitely be keeping tabs on her, and she knows that she wouldn't have what us girls all want: a nice marriage with a person that makes us feel special. She knows she can't have that with you, at least not in the foreseeable future. When your wife did what she did, even though you try not to show or admit it, she hurt you deeply, maybe deeper than even you realise."

I knew her well enough now to know when to change the subject with some humour, so I said, "Well, thank you, Madame Freud."

We shared a laugh while Bill freshened the drinks, and we continued chatting. Bill asked if I knew what I'd be up to next.

"No, I'm not sure, but I have the feeling they want to keep us out of the country, and considering we've done this appraisal, we might be looking at other Special Forces training, maybe even in Britain."

"Well, don't forget if you ever get over here again, you let us know," Bill told me.

Mary interjected, pointing her finger at me playfully, "Oh yes you better, because we all love you, you big lug."

I promised I would do so, and while Bill and I had another drink, Mary went into prepare dinner.

The SEAL training course finished on a Friday and we were due to fly out back to Australia the following Monday morning. A farewell party was organised at Bill's for Sunday, so after breakfast on Saturday Moira picked me up and we spent the day together doing the tourist thing. After having a nice meal at a restaurant, we went back to her place and spent most of the night making love to each other or wrapped up in each other's arms, saying our own goodbyes until we drifted off to sleep.

The party at Bill's was a great affair. People that had met us came and went throughout the day; Moira had not strayed too far from me during the day, unless Mary asked her for a hand. When it was time to head back to the base at Coronado, we got ready to say our goodbyes. Bill we would see in the morning, because he'd be bringing our transport to Pendelton Air Base, but this was our last chance to say goodbye to Mary, the kids, and our respective girlfriends.

As Moira and I kissed and cuddled for the last time, with tears running down her face she said, "You take care, Tom. I love you."

I glanced at Mary over her shoulder, who'd been watching, and nodded. Mary came over and said, "C'mon Moira, don't monopolise him. It's my turn."

Slowly she let her arms unfold from around my neck, and Mary kissed me and whispered in my ear, "Don't worry, I'll take care of her, and you take care. Come back when you can, you hear."

I nodded and joined the team. Dumper drove us back, all of us in silent thought.

The following morning, we were all packed and ready when Bill arrived with four staff cars. After our goodbyes to the Base

Commander and staff, we started the journey back to Pendelton and our waiting aircraft. Along the way, Bill said, "I made Moira stay over last night. She was quite blitzed after you left, but she will be ok. Mind you, I wouldn't like to have her head today if she's woken up yet. She was still zonked when I left." We both laughed weakly.

The cars pulled up to the bottom of the stairway up to the jet, and then it was time to say our goodbyes to Bill. We all shook hands and embraced him before picking up our kitbags and climbing the stairs into the jet. I was the last to say goodbye, and I told him to look after himself and the family and that I'd catch up when I could. After a final embrace with backslaps, we saluted each other, and I climbed the stairs. As I entered the plane the stairs were withdrawn, and the door shut. We all gave Bill a final wave from the windows as the plane slowly started to taxi out to the main runway. The engines whined with full forward thrust, raced along the runway, and took off.

Most of that first flight to Hawaii we pondered our own private thoughts or were busy writing up our reports. We overnighted there and flew on to Tindal the next morning, where we landed at sixteen hundred. There wasn't a connecting flight to Pearce until ten hundred the next morning, so we were accommodated at the overnight flight crew barracks.

The next morning, I had a message sent to Howler advising him of our ETA at Pearce and requested that transport be waiting to meet us. When we arrived, one of the drivers gave me a message from Howler that read he'd see us in the morning in our briefing room at zero nine hundred. We got back to base at seventeen hundred and went to our quarters to change and get showered so we could be ready for work the next morning.

The next morning, all the reports and tapes from each team member were laid out on the briefing room table, and we waited for Howler to put in an appearance. When he entered we moved to stand, but he waved us down and looked at the table.

"Cripes, is this everything?"

"Yes boss. They're in different piles because each team member has written his own report and conclusions. We all had different access to different people. Each report also has a corresponding tape, with interviews, but all our conclusions overall are on the top of each pile. You should find a lot of interesting reading in that lot, but it'll take a while."

He looked at me and smiled. "Christ, it'll take me month to go through it all. Ok, here is what we'll do. You lot can have a month's leave, and by the time I've gone over this, you'll be back from leave on the first of April if I have any queries. I may have a job for you after that. Something's brewing at the moment, but I'll know more at a later stage. Who needs travel warrants?" We all put our hands up. He smiled and said, "All right, you can all follow me down to HQ and help me carry this lot."

When I was back in my office at SRT, I rang Wendy at the Compass office; she was able to get me on the overnighter to Brisbane. I also booked the return for the twenty eighth of March, again on the overnight, and she told me that my tickets would be at the pre-booked flights counter waiting for me and that I could give them my travel warrant to send to her. I told her she was a darling; she laughed and wished me a good time on leave.

After that, I closed up the Building and headed to my quarters to sort out my clothes to take on leave, which was mainly civvy attire, two fresh sets of cams, and after placing my holstered pistol on top, I fastened my travel bag.

I had breakfast in the airport after I arrived in Brisbane. I grabbed a cab to take me home. An hour later I was home, had changed into shorts and a T-shirt, and opened the garage. I was about to start the mustang when my neighbour showed up at the garage door in uniform. He invited me to join him and his wife at the Gaythorne RSL that night for dinner, and I accepted graciously. He headed off to work, and I cranked up the car and sat in it listening to the pleasing rumble of the V8 motor.

That evening I followed John and Joanne Burton to the Gaythorne RSL. I was able to join as a serving member and given a temporary membership card until mine was sent to me in the mail. As I have said earlier, John was the RSM in a gunner's regiment, and his wife Joanne was a former army nurse who had not reenlisted, preferring to be a housewife. We had an enjoyable meal while getting to know each other. All I could really tell them was that I'd only be home when I was on leave, which wouldn't be all that often due to the nature of my work.

They departed soon after dinner, but I decided to stay for a few drinks. While I was sitting on my own sipping a scotch, I contemplated the turns my life had taken. I was almost twenty, and I'd been in the army for five years. I laughed at my thoughts, thinking I'd really been playing with fire when I first left home, but I had been young, headstrong, and arrogant. Since then I had enjoyed my life, living by my wits and natural abilities, but I'd also taken some knocks in the shape of Pep being killed, getting shot up a couple of times and, more recently, the breakup of my marriage. I philosophized that maybe this was divine retribution trying to show me that for every success there were also failures.

As I was about to go up to the bar for another drink, a girl tripped in front of me. I was able to stop her falling completely by circling my arm around her, but as I did that I inadvertently grabbed one of her breasts, which was nice and firm under her clothing. I placed her upright on her feet.

"Did you enjoy your feel?" she asked rudely.

I looked at her. She was lucky to be five four, had sandy blonde hair and blue eyes, and, as I'd felt, was quite lean but nicely proportioned. With a smile on my face, I replied, "Well, yes I did, as a matter of fact. Now if you'll excuse me." I continued to the bar and could feel her eyes on me as I walked off.

A little later, she walked over and sat down beside me at the table. "I hope you don't mind if I sit down. I'd like to apologise for being so rude after you stopped me from falling. I was caught by surprise."

I laughingly said, "Oh you sure were. Sorry about that."

She laughed. "I do apologise, and thank you for helping me.

My names Darlene, Darlene Smith."

She held out her hand, I shook it and said, "Tom Davis, but most people call me Tiger."

"Pleased to meet you, Tom. I'm here with my girlfriend. We live over at The Gap, but she wanted to see her boyfriend. He's in the army."

I smiled and replied, "Well, I think most people in here are in the army, or have been."

"You know, you're funny, in a good way I mean," she reassured me with a laugh.

"Well, thank you, Darlene. You're pretty good yourself. Now, can you tell me where The Gap is? I don't know Brisbane too well yet."

She asked if I knew where the Drive-In was, which I did, having driven past it earlier in the day, and she told me it was in the road that went over the hill into The Gap.

After she told me, I asked, "So tell me, what the Darlene Smith story is?"

She told me she was a student at the university, was nineteen and living with her girlfriend. "So what do you do, Tom?"

I replied with a laugh, "You're not going to believe this, but I'm in the army. Not in Brisbane though. I work in Western Australia."

She was laughing. "Why are you here then?"

I told her I was on leave and that I'd bought a house at Keperra so I come here whenever I get leave. We chatted and flirted with each other for the next hour and a half. She smiled and said, "Christ I'd like to talk to you more, but I'd like to go somewhere quiet where I can get a coffee."

I replied, "Well, I could take you to my place. I can brew up there, and it's quiet. When you're ready to go, I could drop you home if you like."

She looked at me while she thought it over. "Sure, let's do that. I'll just tell my girlfriend Linda that I'm going."

I watched as she went over to a table with a couple. I watched her talking to them and then head back to me. I downed my drink and stood up as she said, "Ready to roll. Let's go."

"Wow, you own a Mustang?"

I unlocked the doors and opened the passenger door for her. I hopped in, fired up the beast, and headed to the house.

After I closed the garage door, I took her into the bar and games room. "I can make coffee down here, or we can go upstairs to the lounge."

She asked, "You going to give me a tour?" So I did, starting with downstairs, and then we moved upstairs. When we got to the master bedroom, she spotted the gun and said, "You've got a gun?"

"Yeah. Part of the job, I'm afraid."

"Your house is fantastic, and I love the furniture," she told me while we were in the kitchen. I put the kettle on, and as I did, she asked me why my bed was so huge.

I laughed and told her that it was a waterbed, which led to more questions. "What's it like to sleep on?"

"It's great. Takes some getting used to, though," I told her.

She said, "Most soldiers I know don't carry guns like yours. Mainly rifles. Are you telling me the truth when you say you're a soldier?"

"Yeah, I am, but a special type of soldier. My team and I get to go all over the world, spying on people, sometimes shooting them. I carry a rifle as well, but we have to carry a weapon all the time, and a rifle is hard to hide."

She nodded, and with a laugh said, "Yeah, I guess it is."

We talked more, and soon we'd had three coffees each and it was nearly midnight. She expressed concern that it was too late to go home and wake Linda up to let her in, so I offered her the use of a bedroom.

"You just want to get me into bed," she said to my offer.

"Well yes, that's a nice thought, but you can have one of the other rooms if you'd like." I stood up to take the mugs back into the kitchen, and she rose as well. She put her arms around my neck and kissed me, and as I started returning her kiss, she moaned.

Our lips parted, and she said, "I think I'd like to try your waterbed."

I laughed and she giggled a lot with all the sloshing around and riding the waves as we christened my bed. She tensed and let out a small shriek of joy as the throes of her first orgasm of the night erupted within her. After four more of these waves, as she was peaking for her next orgasm, I emptied myself deep inside her. Her orgasm was so intense that she was hardly able to breathe. As we lay together spent, the waves in the bed slowly subsided, she exhaustingly muttered that that was one of the best bouts of sex she'd ever enjoyed. In my mind, I silently agreed with her and wondered if it had something to do with the bed.

She didn't have a class the next day, so we lazed in bed the next morning and did some more lovemaking before we both went downstairs and got into the spa. The bubbles and jets really did their job, and after twenty minutes or so, I was wide awake and refreshed. When we were dressed, we hopped into the car, and we drove over to The Gap and had brunch before I dropped her off at her place. We exchanged phone numbers, and we spent a fair deal of my time on leave with each other when she wasn't at school. I did some exploring when she wasn't with me and found a place I liked out at Samford, the Samford Valley Country Club, and I learned to play golf, which I enjoyed immensely, so much so that I ended up buying a good set of golf clubs.

I had the clubs customized for my size and swing. My game improved greatly, or at least I thought it did, but most of the time I only played by myself. One afternoon I was going to pick Darlene up, and noticed that Thunderbolt and Lightfoot, a Clint Eastwood movie, was showing at the drive in. I asked her if she would like to see it, and she agreed. We arrived at the drive in as they were opening the gates, so we had dinner in the kiosk before going back to the car to watch the movie. It wasn't one of his better films, but it wasn't terrible either. After that, we went back to spend the night at my place.

While we talked in bed that night, I broached the subject of my upcoming departure. She asked, "How long will you be gone?"

I replied, "Well, I don't really know. If a job comes up, dependent on what it is, I could be gone for a couple of years. I just don't know."

"Will you be able to stay in touch?"

I laughed and answered, "Well I hope so, but if you get a better offer and want to settle down with someone, don't let me stop you. There'll be no hard feelings."

She laughed quietly. "No, I don't think so. I'm too footloose and fancy free, you know that. But if you're able to stay in contact, who knows? We could hook up again when you come back. So when are you leaving, and how?"

"I have to be at the airport at twenty-two hundred." She looked confused. "Sorry, ten pm. I was going to take a taxi. Why?"

"You'll do nothing of the sort. I'll pick you up and take you. That way you'll have someone to say goodbye to."

"Ok," I replied.

Thursday I had disconnected the battery in the car, done some washing, and put my uniform out to wear. Instead of cooking anything, I'd walked around to the shops and had dinner at one of the take away cafes. I was dressed in my uniform when Darlene picked me up as promised at twenty-one hundred. I put my kitbag in the car, and we left for the airport after I locked up.

We said our goodbyes at the airport, promising to try to stay in touch, and then I boarded my flight. I was the only one in business class so I could really stretch out and got top class service from the flight attendant. The inflight movie was The Odessa File. I watched it before settling down for some sleep.

I grabbed a cab at Perth airport and was back on base by zero eight hundred. After unpacking and sorting out my washing, I fired up the XP and drove over to the base laundry to drop off my washing, which would be ready that afternoon. I then drove over to SRT to find the building open. Tag had returned the previous day and was catching up on some paperwork. After putting my pistol back in my locker, I made us both coffees.

I took them into his office, sat down, and we compared notes about what we'd done on leave. He'd gone into Adelaide and caught the Ghan railway to Darwin. He'd explored the Katherine Gorge area and had flown back from Darwin. Apparently, he'd picked up a Swedish tourist while on the train, and she had stayed with him on his wanders. We laughed and joked about that, and I told him what I'd been up to. We were really laughing as I described having a romp in the waterbed for the first time.

The rest of the team filtered back over the weekend, and after breakfast on Monday, we were all back on deck at SRT. Howler came into the building at nine thirty, and we gathered in the briefing room so he could address us all.

"Gentlemen, I only just finished going over all your reports and tapes last week, and I must say they were excellent and have since been passed on to the higher ups. You've made me proud of each and every one of you. Your job was so well done. I'll be sending you off to do another. An easier one next time. However, before that happens, the Foreign Affairs Dept. have a little job for you. They will be sending a representative to us to brief you on the situation early next month. In the meantime, I want you to keep up your physical standards and spend more time going over different scenarios at the killing house. Once again, well done. Now, I'd like to see Tag and you in your office, please Tiger. Dismissed gentlemen."

CHAPTER 22

When we were in my office, Howler said, "This next job could be a nightmare; you'll be going into a country with no embassies and no extradition treaties with any country. You will have to be on top of your game. What's worse is that it's being passed to ASIS (Australian Secret Intelligence Service) to control, so be very careful before you commit to anything."

"It could be even worse, boss. I think I'd have said no just on principle if it was one the screw-up jobs that those ASIO (Australian Secret Intelligence Organization) fuckwits DIS-organize," I interjected with a laugh. We all shared the same distaste for such an incompetent agency.

Howler continued, "Just to let you know, I've put both of you up for promotion. Tag, you up to sergeant, and Tiger, you up to WO2 (Warrant Officer 2nd class), but I won't know for a while yet if it'll come through. I'll keep you informed."

We simultaneously said, "Thank you, sir."

He looked at us and said, "You both deserve it, and it should have been done before this. Schedule whatever time you want at the killing house, but I'd suggest you keep with the routine you've used before and vary your times to cover both night and day. That's all. I'll see you later." He left my office with a little wave.

For the next few weeks, we concentrated on our fitness regimes and spent half of each day working out in the gym and running the beach in front of the base or doing actual laps of the base fence line. Because the base area was so immense, we would time those laps. On the other hand, we must have gone through at least half of the killing house scenarios and even got together with the technicians on a routine maintenance run to suggest improvements in the design of new scenarios.

There is a downside to trying to stay at peak physical and fighting standard in the form of losing endurance capabilities and just getting plain weary. I went to Howler and asked for an actual focus for what we were doing. He asked for my suggestion.

"Devise a war game. Not long. Two days or so, with a make believe enemy and objective." He told me he would take care of it.

The next day the team was ordered to report to our briefing room ASAP through our pagers. We gathered in the briefing room where Howler was waiting to give us a briefing. We were going to the Pilbara region to engage an enemy fortification, capture it, and then hold against all comers until relieved. The enemy was one sabre squadron.

I got what I asked for, but going up against our own, and a whole squadron, that was going to be a big task. All of us were under a major handicap because we couldn't use our normal weapons because they were not adapted to firing the plastic practise rounds. Everyone was issued the traditional army assault rifle, the SLR with an attachment at the end of the barrel to allow firing of the plastic rounds. We consoled each other with the fact that one squadron was faced with the same problem.

We were transported to the Pilbara region by truck, which was handy because I was able to brief my team on the attack plan I had thought up along the way. "As soon as we get to our drop off point, we need to move to get into a place where we can see what's going on before dark. The idea is to slip into their camp one by one, and this is why we'll get away with it: we'll all be in the same uniforms, all wearing face paint, have the same weapons, so it's not easy to spot an extra man in those conditions. Now, once we've infiltrated, some of us will integrate into the perimeter guards while four of us will stay up the HQ area, keeping in touch by radio." I looked at Wires. "Which reminds me, Wires; find us a frequency that nobody else uses." I returned my attention to them all. "When the time is right, we'll strike both the perimeter and the HQ area at the same time. Here's the important part, guys: I don't think we're meant to win this one, but we'll give them a good show. The way this has been set up, even if we take over the place, we've still got to contend with God knows how many counter attacks. If we have to, we keep pulling back to a point of our choosing where we put in our last stand. Everyone clear?" I received nods of agreement from them all.

From our drop off point, we moved to where we could observe the camp fairly quickly and watched from an OP in two trees that were close together. Around midday, the first thing we saw was plenty of guys wearing observer jackets. They were all over the place.

Lizard remarked, "Hey boss, the cunning bastards are using sweeper patrols. You can see the observer moving with them."

He was right; by following the progress of one sweep, I was able to tell that apart from the observer, there were four in the patrol. They were using a two sweep system. Each patrol would cover a one hundred and eighty-degree arc of the perimeter.

A thought came to mind. A sweep was done every fifteen minutes. If we could knock off one or two in a patrol, we'd be able to walk into camp as part of the sweep, or if we really wanted to be bold, take out a whole sweep patrol and replace them. But I assumed there would be a password code to get in past the perimeter.

With a small laugh, I figured out how to counter that. The first thing to do was take out two of the sweep, take their place, find out the code, take out the next sweep patrol in its entirety, and just walk straight in. After a bit of discussion, we revised the plan; four of us would split into two and take out two members of each arc of the sweep. That way it would only require the remaining four to take out the sweep.

As the afternoon wore on, it was time for the first group to attack. Tag and Dumper headed off to the furthest sweep, while JJ and Lizard moved to the closer group. Whoever had designed the sweep patrols had made a mistake. Each sweep patrol covered the same ground as the last sweep, instead of varying the sweep area, which meant we could pick our takeout points. As we watched, JJ killed his man and infiltrated, and then Lizard followed suit. The observers, always at the rear of the sweep, would rule the man dead by indicating with crossed arms, and he'd stay in place until the sweep was finished and then move off to a prearranged dead area away from the camp. No one was any the wiser.

Tag's voice came into my ear. "Password is Tom Price." I laughed and acknowledged.

Just as the light was failing, my group got into position to take out the next sweep, and then we were all inside the camp. We met up when dinner was being dished up. We'd had time to cruise around the camp and observe the defence strategy, and I devised the take-over plan. Dumper, JJ, and I would remain near the HQ area while the rest fanned out around the defence perimeter points. We carried all our normal guns, but empty. Our grenades were still live, so we would make pretence of using them. After having dinner, compliments of our enemy, we made ready, and the go signal for everyone was when I uttered the words, "You're all dead."

While the team drifted into position, JJ was near the radio tent and Dumper stayed with me. We saw that the routine we had watched earlier in the command tent was the same, an observer stayed in the background behind the CO of the camp and a runner.

Indicating to Dumper to stay put, I walked up to the command tent and said, "Sir, one of the sweeps just captured one of the enemy and will bring him soon."

"Good man soldier." I started to move away, I heard, "Get all the other officers in here. We'll hear what he has to say when they bring him in."

The runner replied, "Sir," and raced out of the tent.

I smiled. Tag said, "Oh you're devious. I nearly had kittens when I heard one of us had been grabbed." I just chuckled.

When all the officers had arrived, Dumper and I made our

move. With our Ingram's behind our backs, we walked into the tent. As everyone faced me, I said, "Sirs, he got away, but you're all dead."

Dumper and I were holding the Ingram's as if being fired, and the observer said, "I concur. Down you fall, sirs. You're all dead."

JJ reported radio was secure, Tag and everyone else reported secure, so I got JJ to send the message that we'd taken the position. The entire camp took their weapons and vacated the area, heading to the dead holding area. I reported the whole of my attack to the observer in charge, who was the CO of three squadron, which was being used as observers.

"That was pure tactical genius, absolutely brilliant," the CO commented. "You took down an enemy stronghold with eighty personnel in under five minutes, and they knew you would be attacking. You should all be proud of yourselves. Well done. Now you have to hold it against counter attacks. Do you think you can do it?"

"We can only try, sir," I replied.

When JJ had called in our success, he had also called for urgent assistance to hold the position. A relief force was on the way; all we had to do was hold. As soon as we'd finished the attack debrief, we went on the scrounge to find as much ammo as we could because there was an overabundance of observers. Each of the team was accompanied by two observers at any one time. We also had a big problem in that we had a large area to defend with only the eight of us. On our first line of defence, the perimeter, we were stretched very thinly, and each of us had to cover a large arc. The second line was the outer ring of the main encampment, and the last line, which we called the Alamo, was the eating area. All the spare ammo we'd found was placed at the Alamo, because if we had to withdraw there it would be our last stand. And if we got there we'd all be low on ammo.

It was after midnight before all of our preparations were completed. We had time to get some sleep before standing to. I woke everyone at zero four hundred, and after a quick munch we took up our positions for stand to and the attack we knew would come.

The first counter attack came just after first light. It was only a probing attack on all fronts. The next one was more concerted, but we were still able to hold the perimeter. On the third one, we were really hard pressed, and during the fourth, Wires was 'killed' and we had to withdraw to the second line, which we were able to hold for three very concentrated attacks. We were getting low on ammo and tiring. We'd been fighting continuously for five hours. The fourth attack resulted in Buzz, JJ, and Lizard being 'killed' and Tag 'wounded.'

I supported the 'wounded' Tag, and Dumper and Gecko covered me as we made our way to the Alamo. Once there, we replenished as much ammo as we could and prepared for the next assault, which came soon after. During this attack, Tag was finished off and deemed 'dead,' and Gecko was 'killed.' This left only Dumper and me. The last attack hit, and after running out of ammo, it came down to hand to hand combat. I was 'killed' by a bayonet in the back, and Dumper was 'killed' by rifle fire.

With the game declared over, I thought that even with the foregone conclusion, we'd accounted bloody well for ourselves; we'd lasted most of the day after ten hard pressed attacks, and the Major from one squadron told us so. According to him, we'd gone down only because of sheer weight of numbers hard pressing their attacks with no reinforcements arriving to help and lack of ammunition.

As far as he was concerned, we'd done a bloody marvellous job of defence. Even though we'd all 'died,' he was giving the win to us for our sheer brilliance of taking the objective and our stubborn defence once we had control of the position.

We ate with grins plastered on our faces, and we were bought drinks that night by our opponents. The following morning the camp was broken down and all personnel transported back to Swanbourne after a successful exercise.

Back at base the next day, we were busy writing up our reports.

I was in my office when I heard Tag call "Atten...shun!"

The OC, Lt. Colonel Smethurley, had walked into the building. I greeted him, and he asked to see everyone. We gathered in the ready room.

"From all I've heard from the squadron commanders that participated in the last exercise, you boys did a bang up job, and I wanted to personally come and offer my congratulations to you. I look forward to reading the reports I know you are writing. That is all, gentlemen. Thank you and carry on."

As the guys drifted back to what they were doing, Smethurley walked into my office followed by myself and Tag. After sitting down, he said, "Howler told me about the promotion he wants for you two, and I've endorsed it. I'm pushing for it all I can. Personally, I think they will be approved, but we will not know for a couple of weeks. Until then, keep up the good work. By the way, we will be getting the visitors you're expecting from Foreign Affairs on Monday. That's all for now, boys."

He got up to leave but stopped at the door and said, "Oh by the way, Tiger, you're doing remarkable work as a master tactician. You should follow that up. You're damned good at planning."

I thanked him and he left the building. Tag looked at me; I smiled and shrugged my shoulders, and said, "I suppose I'd better finish that report." We laughed as we headed into our respective offices.

On Monday of the following week, Howler brought two guys in civvies into my office. Introductions were made; the taller of the two by a couple of inches with blackish hair starting to grey and brown eyes was John Callaway of ASIS, whom I would have a lot of dealings with in the future. The other was about my height but was starting to go podgy.

He already had a fair bit of grey hair mixed in with traces of ginger and green eyes. He was Terry Dumthy with the Special Services department of Foreign Affairs, and at the time this meant bugger all to me.

After everyone had taken seats, I asked if anyone would like coffee or tea, which they all accepted, so I yelled to Tag. He came in, took the coffee and tea order, and went to make them. While we waited for the coffee, I asked, "Ok Foreign Affairs I know, but the Special Services Dept. you'll have to enlighten me, because that means bugger all to me."

So Dumthy explained their role. The Special Services Dept. was responsible for overseeing the work of all ASIS departments, including the Black Ops section. Callaway was the 2IC of that section, which raised my eyebrows a little. Callaway's section did not always have the resources to fulfil an objective and would at times call in for trusted outside help, which was why they were both here. Dumthy was here to authorize the legitimacy of the job, and Callaway was here as the reporting authority for outsiders to answer to. This meant my team, I finished for him in my thoughts.

I was about to ask another question when Tag knocked and came in with the drinks and a plate of biscuits on a tray. I motioned for him to close the door. I looked at the phone; he caught my glance and gave a slight nod. I reached for my mug of coffee and accidently flicked the intercom switch on. Then I asked my question. "So obviously you have a job that needs doing but ASIS can't do it or won't get involved, and you need my team. So what is it?"

Callaway spoke up. "At the present ASIS doesn't have anyone with the tactical knowledge and ability to plan and run an operation of this sort. It requires both. If you accept the job, your team would be going into a foreign country illegally, and if you were caught . . ." He left what he was saying hanging.

After drinking a bit of his coffee, he continued. "As I was saying, if you were caught, we would deny all knowledge of what you were doing, other than the fact that you are Australian citizens. The country you'd be going into doesn't have embassies or extradition treaties with any country. They impose the death penalty rigorously, so if you're accused of spying or trying to overthrow the government, you and your men would be hanged.

We wouldn't be able to help you in any way."

I thought quickly. "You just stated overthrowing the government. Can I assume that's exactly what you intend? And that you have ties or links to someone who could be put into place to lead the country? If they agreed to what we want in return? Would that be a yes or no?"

Dumthy took up the answer. "We've been in secret negotiations with a suitable candidate who's in hiding in a neighbouring country at present, but he's willing to open up the borders to trade and establish embassies and treaties with the western world and to impose law reforms, if he's given the chance."

I laughed. "Mr Dumthy, I didn't come down in the last shower, just the one before. Now, this country wouldn't be doing this for only that sort of return, so you can either tell me the whole, truthful story, or you can get the hell out of my office. No one takes me for a fool, and you have exactly thirty seconds to make your mind up. Otherwise I'll throw you out." I made a show of holding my watch up; meanwhile Howler was looking at the floor, a grin from ear to ear.

As I put my arm down the desk and pushed my chair back to get up, Dumthy said, "All right! Shell has been looking for somewhere to site a new refinery closer to its resources in East Africa, and this country is in the ideal location. You've got to understand that it would mean millions in revenue for Australia and the other country involved."

I smiled. "There. Isn't it better to tell the truth instead of conning people? I hope you've learned that in case you ever have to come to me again, and I hope I'm making myself very clear." Dumthy nodded. "Now, what have you got in the way of intelligence, recon photos, entry and exit points, dirt on ministers in the present government that could be used as leverage? And what assets are available to me?"

"Does that mean you'll do it?" Callaway asked.

"No it doesn't. I'll make my mind up when I've got a clearer picture after I've seen all that you can supply me."

Callaway warned, "That will take hours to go through, but I've got everything with me."

"It would be quicker for me to make my mind up. It's almost lunchtime now. How about you come back at thirteen hundred with everything you've got, and we'll meet in the briefing room and start going over everything," I suggested. "Done. But you may as well have your 2IC join us since he's been listening all along," he told me, looking pointedly at the phone. I laughed, and we smiled at each other as I nodded to him.

After lunch, Callaway, Tag, and I reconvened in the briefing room, and after introductions had been made, Callaway said, "At least I won't have to go over anything with you, Tag. You were listening to the whole conversation." He looked at me. "By the way, Tiger, that was pretty slick the way you did that. I almost missed it, and that is saying something. We ready to get down to business?" Tag and I nodded. "Ok. Probably the best way for this to happen is you ask me what you want, and I will supply the answers and paperwork. How's that?"

We nodded again, and I asked, "What's the target and objective in clear terms?"

Callaway told us the target country and the name of the capital, Kigali, which was where the government had its offices and the presidential palace. The mission was to topple the countries president, Kili Mon-Mon, who was also head of the Tutsi tribe, and replace him in a coup de tat with Juve Hali-mon, a Hutu tribesman with sympathetic ties to Australia and a democratic penchant. Moreover, all of this with as little possible loss of life as we could manage.

"Does Juve have any allies in the present government?" Tag asked.

According to Callaway, Kali Bon-non, the present Prime Minister, was rather sympathetic to his cause as they were from the same tribe. Also, the army's junior commander in chief Bon-hon as well as anyone in the current regime that was of Hutu heritage would be sympathetic to Juve.

"Where's Juve holed up at the moment? How do we get there and what ground assets are available?" I questioned.

"He's in a small village near the border in Burundi. These are the map coordinates," he answered and passed across a photo of the village with map coordinates written on it. He also gave us a photo of Juve. We would have the use of a private twelve seater jet that ASIS had seized under the Proceeds of Crime Act; it had the fuel capacity to fly direct to Durban in South Africa.

If we refuelled there, we'd have enough fuel to make Nairobi in Kenya, but we'd be better landing at Arusha in Tanzania because ASIS had two agents there that could transfer us to the village by four-wheel drives. The plane and both vehicles had secret cargo areas where we could store our weapons; the plane would be flown by ASIS personnel.

"Do you have any aerial or recon shots of Kigali? More importantly, the president's palace? How close are the military barracks?" I asked after looking at the photos.

Callaway shuffled through the attaché case he'd brought and pulled out some photos. He passed them over, explaining what they were. The first one was the presidential palace, which showed a two story, white brick rectangular building with wide upper verandas. On the back, someone had drawn the upper floor plan.

"How reliable is this floor plan?" I asked.

"Very. It was drawn by one of our men posing as an air con technician three months ago," he answered.

"Good," I replied as he passed across a town map and aerial shots of the town and military barracks, which he said was five kilometres from town. "How long do we have to accomplish the job?"

"As long as it takes, but once you're there, it has to be done before you leave," he replied.

"Ok. Leave all this stuff with us, and that area map, and let me think about it. Come back and see me tomorrow afternoon, and I'll be able to give you an answer."

"That's fair enough. Do I bring Dumpy with me?" he asked.

Both Tag and I laughed. I replied, "I was really tempted to call him that. You better. He'll probably have to approve what we'll need."

His eyebrows shot up, but he didn't say anything except, "How about three?"

"See you then." He stood up, and with nods to both of us left the room and building. I turned to Tag. "What do you think?"

"Well, it's doable, but if it went pear shaped, we'd have to get out of there in a hurry and we'd be fighting for our lives," he said with a shrug.

I replied, "My sentiments exactly. But when have not been fighting for our lives?"

He laughed. "Good point, but I guess it depends on what you come up with. You're the tactician. That's why you get paid the big bucks. If I know you, you've already got something devious running around in that head of yours."

We both laughed. I said, "Tell Wires I want a copy of that tape before we knock off."

JJ yelled from the other room, "Already working on it, boss."

We had another laugh, as I said, "Let's see who didn't hear what was going on."

That night after dinner, I went back to the desk in my quarters, poured a drink, and started writing attack plans as they came to mind. I also poured over the map, thought of any variables, looked up the moon cycles for the estimated time for the mission, made a list of what would be needed, and by the time my contemplations were over, my work pad looked like a jumbled mess with lines running to circled areas and stuff crossed out or written over. I ripped off the top page and started writing again, putting things into a semblance of order.

I looked over what I'd written while sipping my drink, thinking maybe I'd change the order or cross something out, maybe add a bit.

By the time I had finished the third rewrite, I had it all down pat. The plan of attack was formulated, equipment requirements listed, and my list of demands for ASIS.

It was after midnight when I finished, so I had a quick shower and crawled into bed. I laughed as I continued to run things over in my head. My list of demands would wipe that stupid grin off Dumthy's face when he saw me next. I'll teach him try to con me. The little shit!

CHAPTER 23

The next morning, I rang Howler and asked if I could see him. He asked whether I wanted him in my office or the other way round. I chose to see him at HQ. When I was seated in his office, I showed him the attack plan. He said, "Brilliant. How long did this take you?"

"Overnight, boss."

"Simply amazing. Can I keep a copy of this?" he asked, holding the paper up.

"That is your copy, boss. This one could rock your socks off. It's a list of what I want from Foreign Affairs to do the job." I passed him the list, and as he read his eyebrows went up and he started laughing.

He looked up at me when he was finished reading and said, "I don't think you'll get him to agree to this, but if you can, you'll be the old man's pride and joy. Can I keep a copy of this to show him?"

"Again, that's your copy, boss. Do with it what you will," I replied.

"By the way, what's the two hundred grand for?"

"Expenses boss, like hotel bills, clothes, bribes, all the usual stuff."

He nodded his head and muttered, "Yeah ok, I'm with you." I told him about the meeting set for fifteen hundred and asked if he wanted to be there. He answered, "I wouldn't miss this for the world. I'll be there."

As I was about to leave, the OC came in. I snapped to attention, and he waved me back down and joined us. "How's that thing progressing, Tiger?"

"That's what the Major and I have been discussing, sir."

Howler passed him my attack plan. As he read, he glanced at me every now and again. Howler told him I'd come up with the plan after dinner the previous night, and he looked at me again. "Absolutely brilliant. It's pure magic."

"Only if it works, sir," I told him with a smile.

Howler passed him the demands list, and the OC turned to me and said, "Bugger the WO2. If you get this, I'll make you a bloody officer."

I smiled and said, "Thank you, sir, but just the normal promotion is fine."

The OC stood up, still laughing, and handed the sheets back to Howler. I left to go back to my office.

Back at SRT, I had Wires and JJ set up my office for taping the meeting. I needed them to make two recordings at the same time. I required two more copies straight after the meeting was finished. Apparently, what they did was run the four recordings at once on four machines, but that was their area of expertise and I left them to get on with it. By the time of the meeting, my office was all wired up for recording. Tag had been briefed about the attack plan and demands, and extra chairs had been brought in.

At fifteen hundred, Howler showed them into my office. Tag had been introduced to Dumthy, and as we were at about to start, I pulled my tape recorder out of the drawer. "For everyone's peace of mind, I'll tape our discussion. You'll get a copy as soon as they can be made." I made a pretence of turning the little recorder on. "Now Mr Dumthy, as you know, Agent Callaway met with me yesterday afternoon to discuss the mission you would like us to go on, and I told him I'd consider my answer and give it to you now. Well, last night I thought it out, including some of the variables, and decided it can be done. However, whether my team does it for you or not now rests with you. I'll give you what I require one at a time, and you tell me if you're able to accede to my request. I will give you reasons for each request. Is that fair enough?"

Dumthy nodded his head. "Yes, that seems fair enough to me, but what if our points differ?"

"In that case, we negotiate. Or we don't take the job on," I replied with a shrug.

"That seems fair. What your first point?"

Now we came to the crunch. If he caved in on the first demand, I'd get everything else. "The way we go in and act will be as dumbass rich businessmen out for a good time on safari. That'll also explain our transport in, so I'll need two hundred thousand in cash to act the part. That should cover hotel bills, meal expenses to go with the part, the odd bribe, and so on."

He looked me in the eye and said, "No problem. The money can be available as soon as you accept the mission."

"Secondly, even though we get paid by the army, your department pays the equivalent of our wages into the regiment emergency slush fund while we're on the mission. It's one of your jobs we're doing, and I've estimated the job will last two months. If it takes longer, then you're in front, aren't you? This is one of the variables I spoke to you about earlier. Major Hallorhan will be able to give you those figures. What do you say?"

He tried to stare me down, which didn't work. He caved, but the glare I got from him promised my next demand would be harder to achieve. I had him over a barrel, though. There wasn't anybody else that could deliver besides my team, and both he and I knew it. His answer was short and sweet. "Yes, agreed. What's next?"

Time to go for broke. "Thirdly, our training facilities here, particularly the killing house, were built on a shoestring. Our own regiment went without things so it could be built because the defence department at the time thought we were just another army unit to fund and had no idea of our capable role in the army. The facility requires upgrading." I took a drink of water before continuing. "So our facilities do require upgrading. I'm not asking that you fund those upgrades just that your minister puts some pressure on the defence minister about our issues, and should there be a change of government in the near future, which is in the cards, that our deal is also incumbent on those new ministers to uphold."

He smiled, and I knew why; he thought he had me. "We can't force ministers to do anything. They determine our policies, so what I agree to may be overturned by the minister himself." He was still smiling, thinking he had me.

I quietly said, "Oh come on, Terry, we're not idiots. It's the department that informs and advises the minister. He just signs off on whatever is advised unless there is a direct conflict of interest, correct?"

"Yes," he agreed hesitantly.

Then I snapped the trap. "So whatever deal we make; he's going to sign off on unless you advise him otherwise. Correct?"

He realised I had him by the short and curlies and had no option but to agree. I watched as the fight went out of him. "Yes, you're right, and yes, I agree to your third demand. Are there anymore?"

I decided to twist the knife a little further. "No, but please remember that this entire conversation is being taped so no one can make excuses and back out of the deal. Not only do you agree to these terms, but also that I have overall control of the mission. Believe me when I say this: should anything jeopardise the mission, or my men, I'll call it off immediately. In other words, say our ground transport is not where it's supposed to be, then I will scrub the mission. Also, these terms you agree to need to be put in writing by you, signed by everyone present, and relevant copies distributed. Are we agreed?"

He glared at me. "Yes. Is there anything else?"

I thought for a moment and said, "Yes. You give me the direct phone numbers for yourself and John Callaway, and that both of you are present at our debriefing when we return after a successful mission. That should be it, unless you have anything."

He sat up and asked, "If I agree to all of your demands, will you carry out the mission?"

I replied without hesitation, "Yes."

He smiled. "All right then. I agree to all of your conditions, but I'll need a copy of the tape so I can write it all up and have it ready for signing at, shall we say, ten am?"

"I'll have you a copy of the tape before you leave my office, and ten will be fine." I smiled at him. I looked at Howler, and he nodded with a smile on his face as well.

I made a show of stopping the tape, got up with it in my hand, and said. "I'll just get this copied for you. Tag, can you organise some drinks please? I'll have my usual scotch, thanks."

I opened the door and closed it behind me. As I was walking down to the workroom, JJ came out with a tape in his hand. I motioned for him to go back inside the workroom. They had all been listening, so I said, "I only brought this out because I don't want them to know the room is bugged. Give me ten minutes, come knock on the door, and give the tape to me." I looked around at the smiling faces. "I hope you all approve of what I screwed them out of. There'll be a briefing for you guys first thing in the morning. If you want to knock off, go right ahead."

Once I was back at my desk, I asked, "Agent Callaway, are you free at zero eight hundred?"

"Certainly," he replied.

"I'm having a briefing for my men. Would it be possible for you to attend?"

"Of course, no problem. I'll be here," he replied.

Then JJ knocked on the door and I called, "Come."

JJ entered. "Here's the copy you wanted, boss."

I thanked him and he walked out, shutting the door as he went. I leaned across my desk, holding it out to Dumthy. "There you go, Terry. I hope that makes your writing easier."

"Thank you," he replied as he stuck it in his shirt pocket.

After they'd finished their drinks in silence, I opened the door for them. "Until tomorrow, gentlemen."

As they trooped out, I passed another copy of the tape to Howler, who had a grin from ear to ear. He leaned over and said with a laugh, "What officer's rank do you want?" I just laughed as they walked away.

The briefing the next morning was quick. All the guys knew what we were going to be doing and where. We'd have a final briefing before we took off.

Dumthy arrived with Howler, and on time, and once all the paperwork was signed, Howler took it for copying and returned fifteen minutes later with the copies. When he came back, Callaway said he would have the plane here in a week's time.

"Good. Just arrange with the Major to have it flown into a hangar at Pearce. I'll be in touch in regards to the ground transport. Thanks John," I said.

He'd already given me his number, and Dumthy gave me his. "I've got to make a few calls and collect the cash for you, so it'll be a couple of days before we leave. If you need either of us, the Major knows how to get hold of us."

I replied, "Well thanks, Terry. Meanwhile I'll work on a plan. See you when you have the money." We shook hands before they both left with Howler.

After they all left, Tag said, "I thought you'd already made the plan."

"Of course, but they don't know that," I replied, and he burst out laughing.

Three days later, Howler, Callaway, and Dumthy came into my office; Dumthy was carrying an attaché case. Tag joined us, leaving the door open. Once they were seated, Howler said, "Tiger, we couldn't get the plane into Pearce, so hangar twenty-one at Perth has been rented for the next three months by John's crew."

"You know where you can load up. It's down the end of a row, so it's private," Callaway explained. "It'll be here sometime on May thirty. The pilots will have instructions to ring you when they arrive. The crew will be staying here." He passed over the name, address, and phone number of a motel near the airport.

"Thanks, John. I'll contact you the day before we leave so you have time to get your men ready to meet us at Arusha." I looked at Dumthy, and he took a key out of his fob pocket and unlocked the handcuff on his wrist, which was attached to the case. He placed it on my desk. I said, "I'll keep the key, thanks."

He passed me the key and a piece of paper with the combination to the case. I unlocked the case and opened it. Inside were bundles of cash, each with a paper band on it that read ten thousand. On top was a bank cheque for one hundred and fifty thousand. I picked the cheque up and closed the case.

"I took the liberty of rounding up your wages before tax," Dumthy explained.

I passed the cheque to Howler, who raised his eyebrows when he saw the amount and nodded. I unfastened the cuffs off the case and said, "Thanks. I'll check this later. Tag, can you put it in the safe please? I'm going to assume this won't bounce," I said, waving the cheque in the air. Tag took the case out of the room, and Howler put the cheque in his pocket. "Looks like it's all done and dusted. I expect to be on our way during the first week of June, but I'll confirm that later. Thanks, gentlemen."

As they left the office, Howler murmured in my ear, "Give me fifteen, then come and see me." I nodded.

As Tag entered with a smile, I swept the handcuffs into the desk drawer and said, "Well Mr Wilson, do you think we're ready?"

He smiled again and replied, "I think so."

After twenty minutes had passed, Tag and I headed over to HQ and went straight to Howler's office. He was smiling as he said, "Good, you're both here. I've already told the old man about Dumthy coming through with the money, and he's rapt and wants to see both of you when we're finished. Are you going to stick with your plan?"

"Yes boss," I said.

"Good. It's a sound plan, very good work on your part, Tiger. When are you planning to go?"

I thought for a moment, looking at the calendar on the wall.

"I was thinking of loading the truck with our stuff, taking it to the plane, and stowing it the day after it arrives. We'll fly out on Sunday, which'll be the second of June, and all being well, we should have the job done and be back around the twenty second of July, give or take a few days."

"That's cutting your operational time close. You sure you'll have enough time?" he asked sceptically.

"The only hold up will be making sure the opposition is nullified by talking to the junior chief of army. Getting to him may take a bit of time, but otherwise everything should fall into place. If we can, I'll try to have the mission done ahead of time. I want to get in and get out ASAP."

He smiled and remarked, "Very well. You know what you're doing and haven't been wrong yet, so I'll trust your judgement. Let's go see the old man."

Howler led the way to Smethurley's office, and as we marched in his face lit up with a smile. "Well, if it's not my favourite extortionists. Well done, you two, very well done. I have heard the tape, heard the way you trapped that Dumpy fellow. Excellently worded. Now, I know I promised to make you an officer, Tiger, but that can't happen, I'm afraid, until you apply to join the officer's training school. I know you're not going to do that, so the best I've been able to manage, with a bit of cajoling and shouting, is that your promotion to Warrant Officer second class has been amended to first class and approved. Congratulations." He reached across the desk and shook my hand, and as he stood he'd opened one of his desk drawers and pulled out an Officers cap. He handed it to me and said, "It gives me great pleasure to hand you your first cap. Wear it well."

I was dumbstruck and a little emotional. "Thank you, thank you very much, sir."

Tag and Howler were smiling, and Smethurley said, "And now for you, Corporal Wilson." Tag braced to attention. "Your promotion has also been approved, Sergeant Wilson. Congratulations." They shook hands, and he handed Tag a set of gold leaf sergeant stripes for a dress uniform.

"Thank you very much, sir," Tag said quietly.

The OC said with a smile, "You both deserve your rank, and I'm proud to have both of you under my command. Now get out of here, you two pirates."

We proudly marched out of his office. Down the hall near Howler's office, he stopped and turned to us and offered his hand to each of us in turn. "You two deserve this. Congratulations. Now go enjoy yourselves."

Before going back to SRT, Tag and I called in at the Q store. Tag was measured for his dress uniform, and I had a word with the SSM about having to get so many WO1 crowns for my uniforms. He told me about the new detachable type that were made with Velcro patches, and he gave me a dozen of them and a roll of the Velcro. All I had to do was get the laundry to sew the patches on. He also gave me two of the gold leaf crowns for my dress uniform jacket and four for my polyester dress shirts as well as a regiment insignia badge for my cap. He had a spare cap in my size, so I took it and another cap badge with me once Tag was ready. We walked back to SRT with smiles on our faces, and I was wearing my new officer's cap instead of my beret.

When we went to lunch, I introduced Tag as the new sergeant into the mess, and he was congratulated and welcomed. As we ate, I said to him, "If you don't have enough cash to cover what you'll be up for tonight in the way of drinks, I can lend you some, or you can arrange a slate with the bar staff later."

"I'd rather pay as I go, so if you can help me out, that would be great. Thanks, Tom," he replied.

After lunch, we went back to my office, and I gave him my entire lot of sergeant's uniform pins. I took one of the rovers over to the barracks and collected as many uniforms shirts as I could, including my dress jacket. I took them to the laundry, and they sewed the new patches onto a clean shirt.

I switched it for the one I was wearing and was told to come back the following afternoon for the rest.

The following week all my shirts had been converted to my new rank. Buzz made sure that we all had extra ammo and grenades and had laid in a supply of rations for each man for six weeks. There were quite a few cartons of rat packs stored up in the stores rooms in our building.

Around ten hundred Thursday morning, I had a phone call from Agent Ross Higgins, the senior pilot of the ASIS plane. He told me they'd landed and the plane was in the hangar, so I made arrangements to meet him the next day at eleven to stow our weapons and load our gear. Then I informed the team of a meeting after lunch in the briefing room.

The following morning, we were all in the truck with all our gear, even our packed kitbags, I had taken the cash from the case and transferred it to my kitbag and for once had put a lock on it. We arrived at the airport and drove into the hangar to be away from prying eyes.

The weapons and combat gear were placed in the false floor; we loaded everything. We met the pilots, Ross Higgins and Bob Walsh, and cabin crew, Ross's wife Jenny and Bob's wife Maree. The wives were going along as extra cover, as this was a holiday flight. I arranged with Ross that we were to leave at nine on Sunday morning and fly to Durban to refuel and overnight. He told me that rooms for everyone had been booked under my name at the Savoy in Durban, and also rooms at the Safari Lodge in Arusha. Both of these were up market hotels frequented by the rich and famous and was in line with our cover. I told him that I liked doing business with such an efficient agency and that we'd see him Sunday morning.

Sunday morning, we arrived at the airport and drove into the hangar at eight forty. The whole team were wearing civvies. After Ross taxied the plane out, we left the truck parked in the hangar and locked it up. Ross was given permission to taxi out to the runway, and we lifted off at eight fifty-five. After a six-hour flight, we arrived in Durban at zero nine hundred, so in essence due to the time difference we arrived at the same time we departed. After South African customs clearance for the plane, we had to wait for immigration processing. While we were waiting Ross had the jet refuelled and moved into an overnight hangar.

After the immigration processing, the staff called three taxis from the main airport to pick us up. I gave the staff a sizeable tip and asked them to look after our plane.

At the Savoy I had the hotel pay the cabs and put it on our bill. We checked in, but our suites wouldn't be ready for occupation for another hour. I was smiling and casually flirting with the reception girl, so she arranged for us to have breakfast in the main restaurant and our luggage held at the reception holding area until our suites were ready. She'd have someone collect us. I slipped her a twenty-dollar tip (which was equivalent to two hundred rand, SA currency, thus ensuring we were well treated), as we moved toward the restaurant.

After a three-hour flight the next day, we arrived in Arusha, which is just south of the Kenyan border in Tanzania. We went through the customs and immigration procedures again, but after refuelling, we hired a hangar to put the plane in, which cost us three thousand shillings a month. I paid them for a two-month stay. That wasn't bad when you consider that one Aussie dollar equals one thousand schillings. After being given the keys to the hanger, we arranged transport to the hotel. There was a message waiting for me at reception, and I read it as we were checked in.

The message was from the local ASIS agent Tim Carr, who would call on us in the morning. I leaned over to Ross and asked, "Do you know Tim Carr?"

He whispered back, "He's one of the agents here. The other's Bill Turner. They run a safari business as a cover for their other work. I've met them a couple of times."

"Good. They're joining us tomorrow," I replied, and he nodded.

I sweet talked the reception girl and let her know we'd probably go off on a safari in the next day or so. I wanted to ensure our rooms would be looked after, and she assured me that after they cleaned the day we left, they wouldn't be touched again until our return. I thanked her and slipped her a twenty-dollar tip, which was equivalent to twenty thousand schillings. After that, she couldn't do enough for me.

The next morning while we were in the restaurant having breakfast, we were joined by Tim Carr, who was close to six foot with brown hair and eyes. He was wearing khaki shorts and shirt with ankle boots, much like the GP boots we wore when working.

After breakfast, he, Tag, and I went to my suite to discuss business. As we sat in the lounge, the first order of business was to sort out getting our combat gear from the plane and placed in their vehicles, which we'd do that afternoon. He showed us the map of the village where Juve was hiding. Tim told us that it would take us three days to get there, if we were to leave early, around six. We'd spend the first night camped near Lake Victoria, then skirt the lake before striking out for the village. We'd reach it about mid-morning of the third day.

We arranged to meet at thirteen hundred. His partner, Bill Turner, would be driving the second vehicle that afternoon when we went to get our gear. He asked, "So when do we head out?"

"I'd like to get going ASAP, so six tomorrow would be good."

He nodded and replied, "Can do."

Tag informed the guys when we were going to the airport as I walked Tim out of the hotel and watched him leave in a white Toyota four-wheel drive troop wagon with zebra stripping on it. After having a smoke, I went inside to the receptionist to arrange an early breakfast for eight at five am the following morning. I told her that if I had to pay any extra for the early service to put it on the bill. She told me that everything would be all right because they did start serving at that time.

After lunch, Tim and Bill met us, and we all went to the plane and cross loaded our gear into the troop wagons. Tim said we could probably keep the rifles out until he saw mine. "That one, however, we'll keep hidden until we're out in the bush."

We told Tim and Bill breakfast was arranged for five and that they were welcome to join us, and they said they would. That way we could start the trek as soon as everyone was finished eating. We left the hotel at quarter to six the next morning, dressed in our working gear of cams and boots, minus any rank insignia. I was carrying ten grand in cash in case we needed bribe money. The rest I'd left in the safe in my room.

As we drove, we caught glimpses of some of the wildlife, like lions, gazelles, monkeys, a few zebras', and at one point, we even pulled up to let a herd of elephants wander across the dirt track we were using. Later in the day, we pulled up to watch a cheetah stalk a herd of elands. I knew they were quick, but it was lovely to watch the cheetah as it sprang into full speed to bring down the unfortunate eland that became a meal for the cheetah's family. Just as we were about to start off again, Tim spotted and pointed out a cow and bull white rhino pair off to our left moving slowly in the sparse thicket.

That day we made camp near the shore of Lake Victoria. It was quite breathtaking, and because we were near a waterhole, as the sun sank low, we watched every manner of wildlife come to drink. We watched as the giraffes clumsily steadied themselves to drink. Wildebeest and hippos came out from the shady areas they'd been staying in, and none of the animals flinched as a pride of lions moved in to drink. We were able to spot some sets of eyes that belonged to the crocodiles in the water looking for an easy meal. As we watched, a gazelle walked too far into the water, and with a quick great surge of water, a croc launched itself out of the water. The gazelle, try as it might to get out of those jaws, was doomed.

Another croc moved in to help with the kill. The first croc went into a death roll and dragged the unfortunate gazelle into and under the water while the other croc tore at its hindquarters.

CHAPTER 24

The following night we camped not far from the Burundi border, and during the day, the terrain had become denser. When we stopped to make camp, we were into full jungle canopy foliage. We were openly wearing our guns and combat gear. Earlier in the day, we had spotted a gang of animal hide and trophy hunting poachers, and Tim and Bill wanted to discourage them from killing an elephant they were getting ready to kill. We moved closer to them and fired a couple of shots into the air to spook the unsuspecting elephant. It trumpeted and moved away, and we peppered the area around the raggedly clothed poachers with ground shots close to them. They threw down their guns and raised their arms in surrender as we moved in on them; they watched us in fright with our guns trained on them. Tim went forward to question them, and Bill was stood next to me and interpreted Tim's Swahili. Tim told them we were game wardens and demanded their names and village.

Apparently, they were just opportunists; they could make money selling the hide and tusks, but the meat they were going to keep for their village. They weren't one or part of the usual gangs of poachers, just ordinary villagers trying to feed their families and make a little cash. Tim put the fear of God into them by telling that if we saw them again trying to kill animals, they would either be shot by us or hanged as criminals. He told them to leave their weapons and go. We took the weapons with us and dismantled them as we drove, throwing bits out the windows. We threw the remainder in one of the streams we crossed.

On the morning of the third day, we pulled up outside the village confines, which was defined by a collapsing timber wall and outward facing stakes driven into the ground. I took off my gun belt and hung Wires' camera around my neck. Tim and I went into the village to make contact with Juve, who said he'd come to our camp later on and talk with me but had a few things to do first. I remarked to Tim on how cultured Juve's English was, and Tim told me that he'd been schooled at Eton College in England.

We set up our camp within easy walking distance of the village, close to another campsite that had been set up by a group of mercenary's who were fighting in the Congo with Mike Hoare's old company in an ongoing war that had raged for the last twenty years. Even though Mike Hoare, an Irish mercenary, had long been retired, the war and his company still went on, but 'Mad Mike,' as he was known, rose to prominence for his exploits in the Congo during the sixties.

Juve visited us just after lunch, and he and I moved into my tent to talk. We discussed why he agreed to our government's proposal and the terms he'd have to live up to. He had learned a lot from his time in England and wished to move his country forward in terms of educating his people, living with modern technology, and moving forward to embrace modern culture and machinery. He wanted to establish trade with countries worldwide and not be a closed off nation living on handouts from the World Health Organization and United Nations. I found him to be well educated, and he did have a genuine desire to see his country better off rather than in its present state of dictatorship. He wanted to establish law and order and freely elected leaders, but not at the point of a gun.

He and I had a debate on that subject, considering what I was there to do, but we both agreed that my team's involvement was only a means to an end. We would get the ball rolling on his commitment to his country. I decided that at twenty-eight, he still had a bit to learn but could very well turn his country's fate around from a jungle backwater dictatorship.

We discussed my operational plan as well as his trust in the junior army chief and who else could be trusted to render assistance if required. We decided he would accompany us to Kigali in disguise, and we'd take the entire top floor of the Royal Kigali Hotel. Juve told me it was the best hotel in the capitol but would only be rated as four stars at best. We would use it as our base of operations, while I decided when to attempt the coup.

"So tell me, Warrant Officer Davis, when do you wish to leave for Kigali?" he asked me.

My ears still hadn't gotten used to my new rank, and I winced as I heard an outside source say them. "Call me Tiger. How long do you think it'll take us to get to the capitol?"

He smiled and said, "In your vehicles, a day and a half."

I returned his smile. "How about we leave at seven the day after tomorrow? Will that give you plenty of time for your goodbyes and so on?"

"Yes it will. Thank you."

After our private talk, we joined the rest of the guys, and introductions were made. I told everyone we'd be moving on to Kigali the day after next. Tim and Bill nodded at the news. I also told them Juve would be coming with us.

Juve went back to the village with the promise to return and spend some time with us the next day. After he had gone, I went over the plan of attack with Tim and Bill. Between us we were able to work out how to smuggle our guns, equipment, and Juve into the hotel.

Tim and Bill led us on a hike of the surrounding countryside to see if we could spot any of the great apes that made this area of jungle their home. We did spot a couple, but they were off in the distance. After seeing them, we returned to camp and decided to try again the next day. When we got back, Dumper and Gecko took some drinks and went to the other campsite to introduce themselves while the rest of us relaxed.

The next morning, Juve joined us and volunteered to be our guide. He took us to a glade that was slightly misted over and whispered to stay still and quiet. As the mist slowly lifted, I was aware of being watched and slowly scanned the area. Just off to my right, I saw an adult silverback female holding a small infant ape. She was staring straight at me. The glade had close to a dozen of the great apes sitting or lying about. Without any sudden movements, we sank down to the ground to sit, and every now and then one of the apes would move over to us and sniff or stroke us. Wires' camera worked overtime with the amount of shots he took. He managed to capture an image of the bull silverback as he called the pack to him, and soon the glade was empty. Juve motioned for us to move back the way we'd come.

Later he told us he'd discovered the glade a couple of weeks after coming to the village, and that the apes used it as a sleeping area before foraging for food the rest of the day. We were grateful that he'd shown us, and thanked him for doing it. After we returned to camp, Juve joined us for coffee and biscuits before going back to the village. He told us he'd be there with his gear, ready to go at seven.

The next morning, we broke camp after breakfast and again placed our pistols and my rifle in the smuggling bin. We had everything packed and ready to go. Juve joined us and his gear was packed away. We left at five past seven, travelling in a north easterly direction. Most of that day we travelled through the lower valley with the mountainous ridges still shrouded in mist on our left. Many years later, the film Gorillas in the Mist was filmed in the locale through which we were driving.

There was no discernible border, and therefore we didn't have to contend with a border inspection. Later in the day, the terrain grew less dense, and we overnighted near a waterhole on the flat fertile plain. That day we drove through the countryside. With the crops in fields and small mud hut communes, it reminded me a little of the area close to Bundaberg back in Australia. At eleven, we started coming into the outlying shacks and slum area around the capital. We drove near the centre of the capitol to our hotel.

Tim and I went into negotiate, and I was able to lease the entire top floor, which had twelve rooms, and a conference room for ten thousand francs a week. I paid up front for two weeks in cash. The exchange rate was five hundred francs to one dollar AUD, so it cost me a whole forty dollars for the two weeks. The restaurant was only open at certain hours, and there wasn't any room service. We were able to park the vehicles out back under a tattered canvas awning. After making sure we had control of one of the two lifts, we transferred everyone and our stuff up to the fourth floor, which was ours.

We chose our rooms and placed our gear and guns in them, and then we went down to the restaurant for lunch, Juve included. Since my meeting with him, he had not shaven, so it was only with a close inspection that he would be recognised. We gave him the nickname John. Later that afternoon, I had Juve phone his friend and colleague the deputy chief of army to meet me in the bar of the hotel that night. Juve gave me his name and a description of him as well as something only Juve and he knew so that when I spoke to him he would know I could be trusted.

That evening we enjoyed an early dinner that finished about nineteen hundred. While the others went up to our floor, I moved to a corner table in the bar that couldn't be seen from the doorway and sipped on a scotch. Just before twenty hundred, a tall man near six one came into the bar dressed in a general's uniform. At the bar, he asked a question and looked around as he was answered. I raised my glass to him, and after he was given two glasses, he moved toward me.

I stood carefully so I wouldn't dislodge my gun tucked into my back under my shirt. We shook hands and he introduced himself.

"I'm Benjamin Bahtu. Mr Tom Davis, is that right?"

I replied, "Yes, but make it Tiger, and thanks for the drink." We sat down at my small table. "Benjamin, just so you know, I'm a friend. Another friend of mine once told me of two boys playing one day, and one threw the other into a river, but seeing his friend floating and laughing hadn't seen a nearby crocodile. He jumped into the water to help his friend before the crocodile got him."

Bahtu smiled and replied, "Yes, he was truly a friend, and I've thanked him every day since. What can I do for you M...Tiger?"

"I need some information from you, but let's finish our drinks and then go upstairs to my room where we can talk in private," I replied.

We finished our drinks slowly. I followed Bahtu to the lifts. Once inside I pressed four and up we went. Tag was standing in the hallway with his gun aimed into the lift, which he lowered as soon as he saw me. I asked Tag to tell our guest that his friend was in the conference room and preceded Benjamin to the conference room, where he took a seat. The door opened a moment later and Juve walked in. Bahtu and he embraced as old friends, and I left the room.

Soon afterward, Juve called me back into the conference room, and Bahtu said, "My friend has told me what you plan to do, Tiger, and I wish you every success. How can I help?"

"First I need some information. Have a look at this diagram. Is it still accurate?" I showed him the floor plan of the palace, and his eyebrows shot up.

He looked back up at me and said, "Yes, but how did you get this? It even shows my guard positions."

"How I got it doesn't matter. Can you recall your guards to base at any time?"

"Yes we've done it before, but I can't without authority from the chief of the army," he replied.

I smiled and asked, "What if you were chief of the army?"

"Of course, but how…" he stopped as he realised what I was saying.

"Would the president elect you, if he was given a letter signed by your boss asking that you take his place?"

"Yes, he most likely would" he replied slowly.

"Where will we find your boss?" He told me and showed me on the street map. The man lived alone, apart from guards at the front and back of his house. He had an elderly housekeeper who came in each morning.

"Good. Now, I want you to go about business as usual, and when you are promoted, I need to hear from you," I told him. He nodded, and I continued. "That's all I need for now, but later I'll need your help further."

"Anything you ask you'll get. Thank you, Tiger."

Soon after Bahtu left, I called Tag into my room and said, "I've got a job for you." I explained what I needed.

Later that night Tag, Dumper, Lizard, and JJ went out fully kitted up but without rifles. They returned at zero three thirty, and I was awake waiting for them to return. I sent the others to bed and had Tag join me in my room.

"How did it go?"

"Really easy, boss, and it didn't take too much to get him to write both letters," he told me.

"Both?" I queried.

"I got him to write two letters so I could compare them for any irregularities, but they were the same. I made him address an envelope and place one of them in it."

"Good. How did he die?"

Tag shrugged. "Technically, a heart attack." I shot him an enquiring glance, and he expanded. "It'll look like a heart attack as long as they don't do a pharmacology test. I gave him a fatal dose of morphine and put him back in bed with the letter on his desk. Here's the copy of what he wrote."

The letter read:

To my esteemed President,

As you are aware, my health has been poor recently, and at present, I find myself unable to fulfil my duties as your Commander in Chief. I would ask that you place my conscientious and capable junior into my place as Commander in Chief until I am able to return to my duties.

Your humble servant,

Kavi Mon-mon, Commander in Chief of Army.

I chuckled and said, "That ought to do it. Now get to bed. We may have a busy night tomorrow night, but let's wait and see."

At eleven the next morning, a call came through to me from Bahtu, who told me he'd been called to the palace earlier and promoted to Commander in Chief because of the unexpected death of the old chief of staff.

"Would it be convenient if I called to see you at fourteen hundred?" he asked over the phone.

I told him that it would be very convenient and looked forward to seeing him. I smiled and laughed as I told Tag what had happened and to round up the troops in the conference room.

When I walked into the conference room five minutes later, the team were all smiles because they knew we'd be in action soon. I turned to Tim and Bill and asked them, "Are you allowed to take an active part in this coup, or do you have to sit out?"

Tim answered, smiling, "Yes we can if you ask us to do a job that doesn't jeopardize our lives or cover."

I smiled. "Good, then I have a job for you that won't affect either. I expect you to only use your handguns in an emergency." I addressed all of them. "Ok, this afternoon I will be meeting the new Commander in Chief. The old one seems to have died unexpectedly." A couple of chuckles. "The new Commander in Chief and I will discuss the transition to a new government led by Mr. Juve Hali-Mon, who is present. We will affect that transition by infiltrating the presidential palace tonight at midnight. Anyone we encounter must be taken alive if possible, but if this can't be achieved silently, kill them. Once we have control of the palace, I will be responsible for finding the present president and possibly giving him a fateful meal to chew on. Tim, I want you and Bill to escort Juve to the palace. We'll let you know when, then you are to withdraw back to here. At daylight the army will move to protect the presidential palace and take control of the radio and TV station, which will inform the populace of the transition in government."

I paused to let my words sink in and have a slurp of water. "Later in the morning, Juve will make TV and radio broadcasts to calm the populace and announce the reforms that will take place during his leadership. After that, he will be sworn in as the country's head of state by the prime minister here at the palace. Journalists will be allowed into the swearing in ceremony, if any are around. Tag, your group will be responsible for the safety of the prime minister. After we are relieved by the army at the palace, you can tell him what has and what will happen once he is safely in your control. My group will remain with me as bodyguards for Juve until after the prime minister swears him in. Then we will return here and I'll contact our pilot to fly in and pick us up from the airport. Tim, you and Bill will be able to leave as soon as you wish. I hope that Mr Hali-Mon will provide us with transport from here to the airfield, and we'll fly back to Arusha. Any questions?"

"Could we take off after an early breakfast tomorrow?" Tim asked. "That way we'll be well on our way back home in case anything ugly arises."

I thought about his question and considered the merit in it. "Absolutely, but I wish to see you both when you deliver Juve to the palace. Don't disappear without seeing me." He nodded agreement, and I asked, "Anything else?" Juve raised his hand. "Yes sir?"

"Can we not warn Prime Minister Bon Hon of what we intend to do today? He may be able to help us."

"Sir, we're doing this with the help of General Bahtu only because you trust him implicitly. I know that Mr Bon Hon is sympathetic to your cause, but can you honestly say that you trust him as much as your friend the general?" I asked. He shook his head no after thinking, so I continued. "That's why the only person outside of this room that knows our plans is the general. No one can know what we are trying to achieve until we've taken over. Otherwise we could be caught and hanged." He sat back; he couldn't deny my reasoning. "Any other questions?" There were none, so I said, "Ok, it's going to be a long day and even longer night, so ready your gear. Relax as much as possible, or even get some sleep. You're going to need it. Wires get together with Tim and sort out a channel we can all use, please. I'll see you at lunch. Thanks gentlemen."

As it turned out, Tim's handheld radios were compatible with ours, so Wires put his radios on the same channel we'd be using.

Guns were cleaned and readied, and I passed the word that our rifles would go into the vehicle that Tim would use that night. We'd only use silenced weapons for the assault.

After lunch, which was treated as a joyous occasion by the team, our rifles and my grenade bandolier were transferred into the trooper that Tim would drive to the palace, and the guys went to their rooms for some shuteye. Only Juve and I were awake. Juve was in his room writing the speeches he would have to deliver the next day, and I was awaiting a visit from General Bahtu.

As the bell announced the lift, I realized I wasn't the only one awake, as I'd thought. I covered the lift with my gun, and Tag, Dumper and Lizard appeared and did the same. As the General stepped out, the guns lowered and disappeared, and Bahtu wasn't as surprised this time as his last visit to our floor.

He joined Juve and me in the conference room. He turned to me and said, "Thank you, Mr Davis, for what you have done. I was called to the palace at ten o'clock this morning and told of my predecessor's death. The radio has been announcing that I've taken over as Commander in Chief of the army. Now that I'm in a better position, how can I help you and my brother?"

"There are a few things that need to be done. One and this is crucial: have your guards removed from the palace between twenty-three hundred and midnight. Any guard still there after midnight will be killed. At dawn, you are to ring the palace with troops as a precaution to any uprising. Also, you'll need to control the radio and TV stations, but I don't want your troops moving around the streets. My men, who wear the same uniform I do, are to have free access to anywhere in the building and not to be hindered in any way. They'll be doing things I've ordered them to do. Lastly, no civilian is to be detained at all for any reason unless you ok it with me. Understood?"

He looked at me with a smile. "Perfectly clear. You'd make a good general," he complimented. I acknowledged his compliment with a nod. "I'll announce that we'll be having an early defence exercise to my troops later this afternoon and brief my officers. Anything else?"

I thought for a minute. "Yes. When you arrive at the palace, Juve will already be the new president, so you'll have to work out a way to inform your men of that fact after they arrive. I'll leave that for you to work out. My men and I will only be here for a short time afterward, so it will be up to you to guard your new leader.

He stood up and looked at me. "Nothing would give me greater honour, sir." He saluted me.

I returned the salute, smiled and nodded, and then said, "I'll leave you two to talk. I'll see you in the morning, General." I left the room, closing the door behind me, and went to my room. While running things through my mind to see if I'd covered everything, I drifted off to sleep.

I woke at eighteen hundred and went to check on things. Only Bill was still asleep, and Tim was waking him. When we were ready, we went down to dinner and ate heartily. We knew it was to be a long night ahead. After going back up, the team snoozed until we started to make our preparations at twenty-three hundred. Just after midnight, dressed in our combat gear and face paint, we carried our night vision goggles and walked to the lift. We went down to the carpark and silently made our way to the palace and into the grounds.

After donning our night vision goggles, we moved off in our groups to make entry as we'd done a hundred times before in the killing house scenarios. Tag's group were about make entry through the kitchen door, and we were ready to go in through the so called ballroom. By zero one hundred, we'd cleared the entire ground floor, leaving Wires and JJ to guard the bound and gagged prisoners in the large dining room. The rest of us made our way up to the second floor, clearing all the rooms except where the president should have been sleeping.

Gecko and Lizard escorted three more prisoners' downstairs as Buzz and I silently slipped into the master suite. I made my way to the bed, and as I did, a young girl about fourteen lying on the bed naked opened her eyes. I put my finger to my lips and motioned for her to leave the bed quietly. She slipped out of the bed. Buzz grabbed her, gagged her, and took her into the other room. He put a dressing gown around her, secured her hands, motioned for her to sit, and guarded her from the doorway so he could see me as well.

While he'd been attending to the girl, I'd moved to the other side of the bed and was ready to stuff a gag into Kili Mon-Mon's mouth as I placed my gun barrel against his head. He woke when my gun barrel touched him, and I rammed the gag into his mouth.

"Move any other way than I say, and you'll die," I whispered to him. "Roll over and put your hands together behind your back. Now put your feet together."

I hastily bound his wrists and feet together with zip ties, yanking them hard, and he tried to yell through the gag. I said into my radio, "Target secure."

Tag and Dumper came into the room as Buzz brought in the girl, and I told him to take her downstairs with the others.

Then I called over the radio, "Tiger to Tim, copy. Tiger to Tim, do you read? Over."

"Tim to Tiger, copy you. Over."

"Tiger to Tim, you can start your drive. Bring Mr. President to the front door. Over."

"Tim to Tiger, roger that. We're on the way. Over and out."

I looked at my team. "All right gentlemen, time to turn on some lights." I took my night vision off, and Dumper turned on the main bedroom light. "Dumper, can you keep an eye on this this one while Tag and I take care of the other stuff?"

"No worries, boss."

Tag and I went downstairs. The entry light was on and so were the main dining room and kitchen. I went into the dining room; all the prisoners were sitting in the corner. I addressed them, "Hands up if you understand English." They all raised their bound hands. I told them what had happened, who their new president was, and that if they behaved they would be released as soon as it was light. They could either stay on doing their jobs or leave.

One man put up his hands, and I nodded to Gecko, who removed his gag. "I and my kitchen staff would very much like stay and serve you and Mr Hali-mon, sir, but those four are fiercely loyal to Mr Mon-Mon, sir, and we have no wish to be with them."

"If I release you and your staff, could I rely on your word that no one would try to run away and that you would go about your duties as usual?"

"Most assuredly, sir."

I nodded and he was released. He pointed out his staff, one of whom was the girl who had been in the former president's bed.

I questioned him about that, and he said that Mon-Mon had dragged her upstairs last night instead of his usual practise of having a prostitute delivered from the whorehouse in town.

The kitchen staff were released and went to the kitchen. He turned to me and said, "Would you and your men like some breakfast and coffee, sir?"

I smiled my thanks to him. "Yes, thank you that would be nice."

I turned to the last five prisoners after he and his staff had disappeared. "My men are everywhere, so if you wish to stay alive, you will remain here and not move. Otherwise you will be shot. Is that understood?" They nodded. I turned and said, "Ok boys, we got arrangements to make. Let's get ready."

CHAPTER 25

We left the room and closed the door on the way out. At that moment, Tim and Bill arrived with Juve. Tag organized the unloading of our rifles as Juve, Bill, and Tim walked inside.

"Welcome to your presidential palace, Mr. President," I called to Juve and held out my hand with a smile.

Juve shook it. "Thank you, Tiger."

"If you'll excuse me a minute, sir, I've got a few things to take care of. Tag will take you and his team into the kitchen for breakfast, if you like."

Wires relieved Dumper, taking him his rifle and telling that breakfast was ready in the kitchen. I walked outside with Tim and Bill and lit a smoke. I held out my hand and shook theirs.

"Thanks for all your help, guys. I hope to work with you again sometime. You'd best take off, and be careful on your way back."

They said goodbye to me, hopped into the trooper, and drove off. I watched them leave, and when they exited the gates, I turned and went back inside.

I asked Wires over the radio to bring his prisoner down to the dining room and resecure his feet, but first put a pillowcase over his head. I didn't want the other prisoners to know who he was. Tag came out of the kitchen and told me Juve was still talking with the staff, so his team looked after things while my group went to have breakfast.

The kitchen staff couldn't do enough for us, it seemed, and as the young girl I'd pulled out of bed served me dressed in decent house clothes, she said, "I wish to thank you very much, sir, for helping me." I smiled and told her everything would be all right now.

After we'd eaten, we went back to our prearranged positions.

Juve came with me into the dining room, and as soon as they spotted Juve, who'd shaven off his beard again, they began to quake in fright, and a couple moaned.

I put the prize prisoner on his knees and said into his ear as I drew my gun, "In a minute I'm going to take off your blindfold. When I do, you'll see the man to whom you will sign over your presidency. I might give you the opportunity to speak. Is that understood?"

The pillowcase nodded, which looked ridiculously funny. I lifted the pillowcase, and the other prisoners started shaking. Juve looked down on Kili Mom-Mon, whose eyes had widened when he saw who was in front of him.

I removed his gag and said to Mon-mon, "This is the man to whom you will willingly sign over your presidency."

Mon-Mon spat. "This Hutu pig? I'd die first!"

I gave him one last chance. "Will you give up your presidency?"

He sniffed. "No." I had him taken outside onto the grounds and shot.

Juve turned to me with a look of shock and sadness after I'd given the order. "Was that really necessary?"

"Sir, as long as he remains alive, he will be a threat to you." We turned and left the room; this time, I left the door open and looked at my watch and the sky. We had another half an hour before Bahtu would arrive with his troops.

I took Juve into his new office and asked if he needed anything before I went to look after other matters. He smiled at me. "Ever a professional. No, thank you, Tiger. Could you have Benjamin join me when he arrives, please?"

I nodded and closed the door. I gathered the team at the front door, and we had time to relax and enjoy a smoke together before a military vehicle sped in through the gate and pulled up at the door. A colonel and two majors got out and walked over to us.

"Could I speak to your superior, please?" the colonel asked.

I stood up straight and said, "That would be me, Colonel. Colonel Davis at your service."

We saluted each other, and he continued, "General Bahtu sends his compliments, sir, and that he will arrive with the main detachment in ten minutes. If you have any prisoners, I'm to take them off your hands. My staff are here to deploy our troops as they arrive, sir."

"Very well. My men will show you where they are. They're not to be harmed," I reminded him.

"That is correct in my understanding, sir. They will be taken to our military jail for the time being," he replied as he motioned two armed soldiers out of the vehicle, who followed Wires into the palace. "If you'll excuse us, sir, we'll go and make ready for our troops arrival."

"By all means." They saluted me, which I returned, and they moved toward the gate on foot.

The prisoners were brought out and put into the rear of the rover, and one of the soldiers climbed in to guard them. The other got into the driver's seat and the rover headed to the main gate but stopped to let a staff car, more rovers, and three trucks enter. The truck and rovers pulled up in a line and disgorged troops, while the staff car came up to the front door.

Bahtu got out, smiled at me, and said, "I hear that you are a Colonel, Mr Davis. Did you have any trouble?"

"That's right, General, and all of my men are captains. We had no trouble at all. The president is in his office and would like to see you, sir."

As he went inside, I turned to Tag. "You best start heading, but don't bring him back here until it's fully light. Let me know when you're close. I want to be sure none of these monkeys try shooting at you."

He nodded with a smile. "Roger that, boss, Right boys, let's go." They headed to the gate.

Four hours later at nine, the team were resting while I was in the presidential office with the Prime Minister. Juve and Bahtu had gone to the radio station so that Juve could make his address to the nation. I reached for the telephone and placed a call to the Safari Lodge in Arusha. I asked to be transferred to Mr. Higgins' room. My call was answered by Jenny, and I asked if Ross was there.

He came on the line. "I've just been listening to Hali-Mon's national address. Congratulations." After thanking him, I asked if he could fly in and pick us up at midday, and he told me it wouldn't be a problem and he'd see us then.

I roused Tag to take the team, commandeer a truck, pick up all of our gear from the hotel, and return with it. We would leave from here to go to the airport.

I rang the airport and asked to speak to the administrator. When his secretary came on the line, she told me that the administrator was busy and asked if she could help me.

Losing my patience, I raised my voice and replied, "This is a call from the presidential palace. Put the damned administrator on the line now, or he won't be administrator for much longer!"

She started to stammer and put the phone on her desk. I could hear her telling whomever that I was on the line, he picked up, and I heard the secretary's line hang up. Through clenched teeth, I said, "There will be a private jet with the call sign … arriving at about midday. It is to be given priority clearance to land and must be refuelled immediately upon arrival. Is that clear, Mr. Administrator?"

"Yes sir, your Excellency. It'll be done as you ordered. I'll take care of it myself, sir."

I hung up with a smile on my face and turned to the Prime Minister. "Sometimes you just have to know how to speak to people."

Juve returned just after Tag and my men, followed by a score of journalists and TV film crews. I had a word with Bahtu, telling him we would soon be departing and that our bags were already

323

in the truck on the driveway. He left to arrange our transportation, and we followed Juve into the presidential office after an impromptu speech in the main entry into the palace.

In his office, we fanned out against the walls on each side of the room, our rifles in plain sight, as the journalists and TV crew's setup to cover his inauguration. Juve was officially sworn in as president by the Prime Minister, both smiling and shaking hands for the cameras.

After the hubbub had subsided, and the press were filtering out, my earpiece crackled. "Flight to Tiger. We're on the ground and refuelling."

"Roger that, Ross. We'll be there soon."

Looking around, I saw the team smiling and nodding; I made my way to Juves' side and leaned into his ear to tell him it was time for us to leave. He announced that he had some pressing business to attend and would everyone excuse him.

We made our way out to the limousines, and with an escort, the rovers, the staff car, two limousines, and the truck, the team, Juve and Bahtu hopped into the limos. We drove to the airport, into the gate, onto the tarmac, and to our waiting jet.

After divesting ourselves of our weapons, which were placed in the smuggling hold, Ross and Bob loaded our kitbags into the plane. We said our farewells. Juve shook all of our hands and thanked us. He told us we were welcome in his country anytime.

Bahtu came forward and did the same. He stepped back and said, "Colonel Davis, on behalf of myself and my country, I would like to thank each and every one of you, and would like to salute you all."

I nodded, and he saluted us. We returned the salute and made our way into the plane. Bob shut the door, and Ross started taxiing; we were airborne towards Arusha.

As we were flying, Ross arranged with the Arusha tower to ring the Safari Club hotel to send transport for us to the hotel after we landed. After landing half an hour later, the plane was put into the hanger and the hanger locked. We piled into the three limos the hotel had sent and arrived there ten minutes later. We went to our rooms to freshen up and get changed. All our clothes were sent to the hotel laundry, and we were dressed in our civvies. We gathered later in the bar and from there we went in for dinner. We had an enjoyable and noisy dinner with a lot of drinks, as was our custom after a mission. It was now wind down time.

The next morning at breakfast, Ross asked what the plan was. I replied, "I need you to get in touch with home, tell them the job's done, if they don't know by now. We'll make for Durban tomorrow morning, have a couple of R and R days, and then head back to Perth."

"Roger that. I'll get onto it after we finish breakfast." Ross looked around and sighed. "We'll miss this place. It's been nice here, and we got to see a lot while you guys were out doing the hard yards."

I laughed and replied, "Yeah, well, you and Bob will have to put in the harder yards. There'll be time for your girls to go shopping in Durban, don't forget."

Jenny piped up and queried, "Did I hear shopping?"

Ross groaned, looked at me, and said, "There goes the credit card savings." We both laughed. After breakfast, I retrieved the money case from the hotel safe before going back to my room.

Back in the room, I left one hundred and sixty in the case, placed another ten back into it, which left me with twenty-five. Out of that, I put five thousand in my wallet and the other twenty into my kitbag in one of the inside zip up pockets. I locked the case again and placed it with my kitbag in the wardrobe. Then I had reception contact the Savoy in Durban, and when the connection was made, I was able to get the same rooms we occupied before. I also arranged for them to have three limos waiting when we arrived at the airport at midday.

Ross knocked on my door a little later and told me he'd been in contact with Australia. Congratulations were to be passed on to us. Callaway would be at our barracks the following Monday,

July eight, and would see us then. I told Ross that I'd laid on transport to pick us up at Durban airport at midday the next day, and he said we should leave here at around eight in the morning if that was the case.

While we were at lunch, I asked Buzz to come and see me afterward because I had a job for him. When he came to see me after lunch, I gave him the case. "There should be a hundred and seventy grand in there. If there's not let me know. I want two bundles of five grand and then split the rest up between us. Tell the boys it's a job bonus like the last one."

He smiled. "I'll leave your share in the case, boss, with the other two bundles. Be back soon."

Before going to dinner that night, I stopped by reception and told them we'd be checking out the next morning after an early breakfast. I was told that the reception staff started at seven so I'd have no problems with checking out in the morning.

In the restaurant most of the team whispered "Thanks boss" into my ear. While laughing and joking, I warned, "Ok all, and just remember, we're leaving tomorrow early. I want to check out by zero eight hundred. I'll have the hotel transport us to the airport. So zero six for breakfast. And now to our air crew that have done such a wonderful job, and because of the shopping in Durban, this should ease the pain a bit." I tossed Ross and Bob each a bundle of five thousand dollars, and then we settled down to party for a while.

The next morning as I checked us out, I arranged to be dropped at the airport by the limos. The bill for our stay, drinks, and all meals, came to, in Australian dollars, only two hundred, which I thought was really quite reasonable. We wouldn't have been able to stay anywhere in Australia for the same amount of time and money.

That afternoon we flew into Durban. Our transport picked us up, and we made our way to the Savoy. Once we settled in our rooms, I called a meeting of all personnel. It was decided that after our wind down in Arusha, we'd have the rest of that day, the

326

next, and part of the following day as R and R. I wanted to leave at fourteen hundred on the fifth, which would put us back in Perth (considering the time loss) at around zero eight hundred of the day we left. Which would be a Friday. If any of my team were at a loose end, they could consider writing up the mission statements or reports. When we were out of earshot of the ASIS agents and their wives, I reminded the guys that we'd paid out a lot of money in bribes, apart from our accommodations and so on.

Later that afternoon I was down by the pool with a drink and a writing pad compiling my mission report, as were some others of the team. Dumper came over to me and said, "Boss, I didn't want to tell you this until after the mission, but during our last leave, Janice and I split up."

"I'm sorry to hear that Dumper, but could I hazard a guess as to why? You're always away, and she wanted you to quit?"

He relaxed his shoulders and nodded his head. I asked him to sit down. "Mate, that's how it was for Sharon and I also. We argued constantly about the job, and I suppose in the long run she wanted some security, but she certainly went about it in the wrong way. We got divorced, but you are lucky. You hadn't gotten married yet. Believe it or not, you've probably been saved a whole lot of grief. I haven't asked him before, but why don't you ask Gecko for his secret? He and Anna have been together for ages. Christ, I wish I knew how he makes his marriage work. On the QT, if you do find out, let me know, please."

"How did you handle the breakup, boss?" he asked me.

I told him what I done, how I'd had thrown myself into keeping fit, and about my little trip to Bunbury and screwing myself silly. "But I wouldn't recommend that. It's bloody tiring keeping track of names." We both had a good laugh. "Honestly Dumper, I don't know what advice I can give you.

Only you can find a way of dealing with it. The way I did may not work for you, but please remember this: once it's over, it's over. There's no going back, so don't torture yourself with trying. Otherwise it'll eat away at you and make you unreliable, if you know what I'm trying to say."

He nodded his head and thanked me. "I won't let it get to me, boss. I promise. If you think I might be losing it, please give me a kick up the arse. I have no wish to give up what we do, and I don't want to get into a situation where I become unreliable."

After taking a long pull of his beer, he continued. "Tiger, have you ever thought about what happens after this? I don't mean just this job. I'm talking about everything. SRT, SAS, and the Army. You know, with our experience we could be raking in a shitload of money and be able to pick what we take on."

I thought over what he was saying. "I hope you're not contemplating what I think you are, because I don't do this for the money, John. Christ, if it were for the money, I'd never have joined in the first place. I could probably have made more playing football. As far as turning mercenary is concerned, that's not for me.

Yes, I have demanded money for a couple of jobs, but they really weren't defence department jobs. If you remember, that first one nearly got us all killed. We didn't take any money for getting Kami out of trouble, but the job we've just finished didn't sit right with me. We put Juve into power just so Shell could get its refinery built and our government could rake in millions in revenue dollars. I did extort some danger money out of them for us and the regiment. Don't even think of going down that path, mate. It's a one-way spiral down, so don't think about it. You're probably feeling the after effects of your break up. Go out and get laid, maybe you'll feel better. I know I did."

He laughed. "Yeah, you're probably right. I might just go and see what cute little redhead at the bar is drinking."

I looked around at the girl he was talking about. "Yeah! Be a devil, go for it!"

Before going down to dinner, I went into Tag's room for a quiet word and asked him to pass the word to the boys to keep Dumper occupied as much as possible, but not to cruel his chances if he hooked up with a bird. However, I didn't think I had anything to worry about afterwards, as the rest of us went down to dinner,

Dumper was already having dinner with the redhead and they seemed to be getting on well.

The next morning, Dumper joined us for breakfast. He was smiling hugely, so I thought that had fixed my problem for me. He took a bit of ribbing from the guys but was also giving back. He was back to being his cheerful self. After breakfast, we split up to do some sightseeing and cruise the markets. I ended up buying a new passport wallet made from crocodile skin for a dollar and was contemplating buying another watch. The latest Tag Hauer diver's watch had caught my eye, but I already had my Rolex Submariner and my multipurpose altimeter watch that I wore all the time, as well as the army issue one as a backup. I decided against buying one. However, I did buy a very soft shoulder holster that fit my gun and that I could wear against my skin under a shirt.

After lunch the next day, Ross, Bob, and the girls were all packed after what I assumed was a successful shopping day. They vacated their room and had the hotel limo drive them to the airport, where they went through all the pre-flight procedures. We followed in another two limos after I'd paid our bill and checked out. As we drove to the airport, I considered that Durban had been a pleasant interlude. We were in the air and on the way home by fourteen hundred, right on schedule.

We arrived in Perth at zero eight hundred (local time) that same day. After customs and immigration inspections, the plane was able to taxi to the hangar, and after being rolled back into the hangar by one of the motorised push/pull carts, the engines were shut down. We started to unload our gear into our truck after Ross undid the smuggling hold. We quickly transferred our weapons and combat gear, and the team said their goodbyes to the aircrew and made their way to the truck. I shook Ross and Bob's hands, said my goodbyes, and wished them a good flight home. Ross informed me they'd be staying for a few days yet, because even though Callaway was flying in commercial, he'd be going back in the jet. I wished them a good time in Perth and suggested some good sightseeing. With a final goodbye, I moved to the truck. We drove past them and gave a final wave as Dumper headed the truck towards Swanbourne.

As we drove into the base, I had Dumper drop me off near HQ and continue on to the SRT building. I walked in and asked to see Howler, and he was at his entrance door like a shot, beckoning me in almost as soon as the orderly hung up the phone.

He shut the door as I took a seat, sat behind his desk with a smile, and said, "Good to have you back. How did it go?"

I smiled as I replied. "Almost like clockwork. The actual takeover was accomplished over one night, so the country went to sleep with one ruler and woke up with another in the morning."

He smiled and said, "Good, good. So what do you make of the new one? Is he going to be any good?"

I thought for a minute. "Yeah, maybe. His ideas are good, but he's a bit naïve. Time will tell," I said with a shrug. "The one that I'm really not sure of is his mate Bahtu. I didn't and still don't trust him. He could be the fly in the ointment."

"Hmm, all right. All we can do is wait and see what happens. It's done now, at any rate," he replied. "I've heard from Callaway, he and that dumpy turd. I just can't seem to take to him. He seems like a slimy sort. They'll be here at nine on Monday."

I had a good laugh and replied, "You're not the only one, boss."

"Once you're finished with them, I'm going to stand you down for two months leave. The job I've got in mind for you could mean that you and the team will be away for a couple of years. We'll talk more about that later. In the meantime, get yourselves settled back in and be ready for the debriefing on Monday."

"Roger that, boss."

Back at SRT, everything had been unloaded from the truck and my gear and guns had been placed in my office. I found Tag in the ready room with the rest of the team, so after making a coffee, I sat down and said, "I hope everyone has finished the mission reports. The debrief will be on Monday. I don't know who will be present, but Callaway and that idiot Dumthy will be here at nine.

The rest of the day can be treated as a semi stand down. Clean your weapons, sort your gear out, copy your reports, and get anything done at the laundry, all that sort of thing." I paused to take a sip of coffee. "While we're all here, I'll give you a warning of what's up. Now that we're finished with the last mission, we'll be stood down for two months' leave, but this does have a downside. Apparently, the next job on the cards could see us away for a couple of years. Before you ask, I don't know where or what it'll be. I'm only letting you know what I know. Howler hasn't told me anymore than you know. I hope that we'll have plenty of warning. Ok, that's it guys." No one spoke.

I finished my coffee and said, "Right. I'm going to get my report copies done and start cleaning my guns. What you lot do is up to you."

As I got up to leave the room, there were calls of "Can you take mine, boss?" and "I'll give you mine." I raised my hands and said, "Anyone that wants me to get their copies done, make sure they're in my office in five minutes."

Tag joined me as I was about to leave and took half the pile. "Thought you might need a hand with these. Those buggers are getting lazy!"

"Serves me right for mentioning what I was doing," I laughed.

After mine had been copied, I took the original to Howler and left it with him. Then I went back to the office and Tag and I finished everyone's copies. We went to SRT, where I took my guns into the workroom to strip and clean them. After I'd stripped down my rifle, Tag yelled out, "Lunch time!" I went to my office and grabbed my cap, and we both headed to the sergeant's mess for lunch. After a relaxed lunch that wasn't too bad, we headed back, passing some of our guys coming back from lunch also.

On Monday, everything was in readiness for the debriefing, which was to be held in our briefing room. This would prove very handy, as it was setup to record any meeting we wished. Apart from Callaway, Dumthy, and Howler, also in attendance were our OC, Lt. Colonel Smethurley, and two senior intelligence officers.

After we gave our verbal reports and answered questions, the written copies were distributed. The only real piece of contention was between Dumthy and me over the amount of wages that had been forwarded to the regiment as per the agreement made prior to accepting the mission.

I was eventually able to make him see reason and allay his fears of being conned by explaining that I had given him only a projected mission duration time. Should it have gone longer than I anticipated, we wouldn't have been having the argument. As it was, it took less time than originally anticipated, so a bit of quid pro quo should be acceptable. If he wanted to change the deal after the job had been done and dock us some pay, I told him to go ahead and try it but to remember I had every conversation we'd had on tape. He caved in, as usual, but I'd also made an enemy. I didn't give a rat's arse. As far as I was concerned, he was just a jumped up pen pusher.

After our debriefing, Callaway said to me privately, "If you ever consider changing careers, please give me a call. I'd be honoured to have your tactical planning and knowledge available to my agency."

"John, maybe one day I'll think about it, but not right now. I like where I am."

CHAPTER 26

After everyone had left except Howler and the OC, the Colonel told us, "As far as I'm concerned, boys, you did a bang up job, and thanks to Tiger, we've got a bit of leverage when we ask for funds to have the kill house updated. Even if we do get the funding, I'm afraid you won't be here to see the final update because your next assignment is going to take you Britain, where you'll be teaching the British SAS some of our secrets and learning some of theirs. This won't be a short exchange of ideas. You'll probably be gone for at least a year, maybe two, but Major Hallorhan will have more to say to you on that matter. I know that you'll do us proud. Good luck, and I hope to see you before you leave. Thank you."

Well, at least we knew where we were headed. I mulled this information over and knew that I had to get in touch with my father because of all the relatives I had there and the families social standing within the British aristocracy.

Howler addressed us. "If you didn't know before where you were going, you do now. Before that happens, I'm standing down SRT while you guys have some leave. Today is the eighth, and I don't want to see you back here until the start of the day on Monday, September thirty. Those of you requiring travel warrants, and I guess that'll be all of you, come and see me at HQ later. Your leave will officially start tomorrow, so have a good time and take care. Remember, SOP's still stand. That's all gentlemen. Dismissed."

As he started towards the door, he motioned me to join him. Outside on the veranda, he handed me a travel warrant. "I knew you'd want one of these, but it's a little different this time. I've made it out to first class instead of business so you won't have to bother seeing me later. Just take off when you're ready. Have a good leave. I want you to come and see me when you get back, and knowing you as I do, that'll be at least a week before the others." He chuckled and held out his hand.

I shook it, and as he went down the steps, I called, "And take care."

Back inside, there was a discussion in progress in the ready room about how much better we were than the British SAS. I smiled and decided to stay out of this one. I went into my office to ring Darlene's home number to let her know I was on my way back to Brisbane and looked forward to meeting up with her again. No one was home, so I left the message on the machine.

My next call was to Wendy at the travel office to ask if I could see her the next day. Wendy was able to get me onto the night flight, and because I wasn't sure when I would return, an open return ticket was organised.

With a smile, she told me, "You must have done something special to get first class. They usually don't do that,"

I laughed and replied, "Probably a mistake, but I'll live with it. Just don't point it out to them." She laughed.

After packing and getting ready, I rang Darlene's number again and this time she was home. I told her I was flying in for leave, and she said she'd pick me up from the airport because she didn't have a lecture until the afternoon.

"You know, it's funny, but I was thinking of you the other day and then I got your message. I'll tell you all about it tomorrow on the way to your place."

"I'll hold you to that, and something else as well," I replied with a mischievous tone in my voice.

She caught on immediately and replied with a laugh, "You're naughty, but I like it. I'll see how much time we have, but there should be enough."

Nowadays travelling first class is a little different from back then, because in the mid-seventies travelling first class was only more or less a glorified version of business class. The only difference I found was that the service from the flight attendant was full on. I watched the in-flight movie, which was the new James Bond, The Man with the Golden Gun, which wasn't bad, but I think I still preferred Sean Connery in the lead. In the television program The Saint, Roger Moore was good, but as James Bond, I was in two minds. After watching the movie, I settled down for some sleep.

Darlene met me at the airport, and on the way home, I asked, "So how come you were thinking about me?"

She gave a short laugh. "The other day our sociology professor was talking about the role mega businesses plays on government decisions and policy, and he talked about some country in Africa that had a change of government recently. Right after it was announced that Shell was going to build a refinery there. He speculated that Shell had something to do with the take-over because of how close the announcement had come after news of the change.

What's funny is that I know you're some sort of spy, but you went away before this happened. When the professor was talking, I wondered if that was why you went away. Then I get your call to say you were back. Rather funny timing, don't you think?"

I was treading dangerous ground, so I laughed and replied, "Yeah, I heard about the government coup but not the Shell thing. Just a coincidence in timing, I guess."

We drove a little further, and I stroked her inner thigh under the dress she was wearing. I asked, "So what happened to the old regime? I suppose the ex-president and his generals are living a luxury life on the French Riviera or somewhere?"

She squirmed a little as my hand moved up her thigh. "Stop it. No don't stop, I like it." She squirmed a little more, a smile on her face. "It's rumoured that he was shot, but no body or evidence of that have been found."

"Oh, so another blood thirsty lot taking over from another lot, huh?"

I moved my fingers a little higher, and she moaned her reply. "No, don't stop. Apparently this new guy is ok; the professor reckons his reforms will help the country."

I laughed and said, "Excuse me for being cynical, but why then is he letting Shell open up? They'll rape and pillage the land like they've done elsewhere."

She glanced at me, then returned her eyes to the road. "Yes, you are rather cynical. Let's drop the subject and get home. There are a few things I want to do with you."

I smiled, thinking to myself, Crisis averted. By playing along with her questioning conversation and playing with her body at the same time, she had gone completely off track of the initial thought that I was mixed up in the overthrow.

After we arrived and I unlocked the door, she couldn't get me into the bedroom fast enough. After an hour of intense love-making, the subject had left her mind completely and our conversation took a more mundane track. It was decided that she'd come back here after her lecture, and we'd go out for dinner and she'd stay the night.

After she left, I unpacked and realised I still hadn't banked the forty grand in my kitbag. I took it out and put it into my bedside drawer, changed into a pair of jeans, and strapped my shoulder holster on after retrieving it from the floor where Darlene had left it as she stripped my clothes off earlier. After putting a shirt on, I went down and opened the garage door, popped the car bonnet, and reconnected the battery. I retrieved the money and my pager, which I clipped to my belt, started the car, and drove down to the shopping centre at Mitchelton and deposited the cash into my account.

Over the next few weeks, I would either be spending time with Darlene or out playing golf. I had grown a little bored playing out at Samford and had started playing at a couple other courses, Keperra Golf Club and the Ashgrove Club, which was actually situated in The Gap. On a couple of occasions, I went to the Victoria Park Golf Club situated in the Kelvin Grove, Herston area. Not only was I getting better at playing, but I was also finding my way around Brisbane a lot easier.

I also discovered that I preferred to play first thing in the morning as the sun was rising, so on mornings when Darlene hadn't slept over, I'd be up at four thirty heading to whichever course I'd decided to play that day. After about six weeks, I started to get itchy feet because I was getting bored. I decided to cut short my time here so broached the subject with Darlene, telling her that my leave was just about over and that my next trip away was going to be a long stint, possible up to two years. Because I'd be out of the country, it would be hard to keep in touch, but I told her I'd try to contact her when I got back.

She was rather philosophical about our parting, asking when I was going to be heading back. I told her the next day I'd ring the airline and see what flights were available. So the following day, I booked my return flight that would get me into Perth on the morning of Monday the second of September, which meant I'd have to be at the airport on Sunday night, two days away. I started making my preparations to return.

One of the first things I did was take a set of keys over to John and Joanne Burton next door. I stayed for a drink with them and told them I would be gone for a couple of years. I was giving them a set of keys to the house so they could use the pool and spa if they wished and keep an eye on the place, which they agreed they'd do and wished me good luck on my trip.

That night, Darlene and I went out to dinner, and I told her when my flight was.

"When we leave here, if you'll drive me home, I'll grab some clothes and we can spend the rest of the weekend together. I can drive you to the airport," she said.

On Sunday we didn't get out of bed until late. We had brunch at the RSL. After we returned to the house, I got Darlene to move her car out into the drive so I had some lying down room in the garage. I drove the Mustang in and popped the bonnet. After disconnecting the battery, I used my trolley jack to lift the front and then the rear of the car. I placed blocks under it, which help with long term storage and stops the wheels going flat from just sitting. After locking it, I placed an old parachute cover over it.

Darlene and I said our goodbyes at the airport, and she remarked, "Next time we hook up, we should get married."

Her statement startled me, and I laughed it off. "Yeah maybe."

As I strolled onto the plane, I was rather happy to be flying first class. As I made my way through business class, I noticed it was full, but there was only one other in first class, a rather shapely middle aged woman dressed in a red dress that showed off her boobs. She was part Philippine and was called Rose.

After introducing myself, I ignored her and settled in for the flight. I watched the in-flight movie, Zardoz, with Sean Connery and settled down for some sleep. I arrived on base and paid the cab at HQ. I went to Howler's office after leaving my bag in the front office.

He looked up in shock when I entered. I smiled and said, "Yeah, I know boss. I'm not meant to be back yet, but I got bored. I'll be around base, unless I'm playing golf, if you need to get me."

He smiled and replied, "Fair enough. I know how it can get. Just keep your pager on you. Go on, get out of here."

I finished unpacking and went downstairs. After reconnecting the battery, I fired up the XP and drove to Connolly up the road and went to the Joondalup Golf and Country Club. I joined the club, went to the pro shop, and bought another set of clubs measured to my size. They would be ready to pick up the following day. I also bought a bag and fold up buggy along with some balls and a couple of gloves. Then I returned to base for the rest of the day.

As I was having lunch the next day, Tag walked in to the mess, spotted me, and after he collected his lunch. He walked over and sat opposite me. To my questioning look, he said, "I got bored doing nothing."

I smiled and replied, "Ditto, but I'm taking a drive up the road after lunch to pick some stuff up. Want to come?"

"Wouldn't mind," he replied. I just smiled and nodded.

We hopped into the car after lunch and headed to the golf club. As we drove in, he asked, "You play golf? So do I. We should have a game sometime."

I turned and said in surprise, "Yeah sure. I'm just here to pick up some new clubs, but how about we book for tomorrow morning early. I like to play at dawn. How about you?"

"Best time to play. Let's."

We booked a five thirty tee off the next morning. I picked up my clubs, and he whistled as he saw them. "Callaway's. You must have more money than I thought." We both laughed. Once I'd put the clubs in the car, we had a drink in the clubhouse bar and returned to base.

The following morning, we were up early and were all set at the first tee just as the sun rose. We walked around the course and talked about our leave, and by the time we were playing the eighteenth, there was only a couple of strokes between us. I won by one, and we went and had a bite to eat and couple of drinks. As we sat enjoying ourselves, our pagers went off. We glanced at each other and looked at the pagers; both read: HQ, ASAP.

So we packed up quickly and hightailed it to base. I swung the car into the HQ carpark, and we went inside and were told to go straight into Howler's office. He was on the phone. "... And they'll need use of a staff car." He waved us to a seat and continued with the phone call. "...Yes, we'll need them transported back here. Right. Good man. Thank you."

He hung up the phone and looked at us as if he didn't want to tell us what he was about to divulge. He sighed, "Trooper Christopher Gecko Martin and his family were killed yesterday in a car crash involving two semi-trailers."

I closed my eyes and sighed inwardly. I leaned forward and ran my right down my face. I looked at him with my hand over my mouth and sighed again.

Tag's eyes were shut and his head bowed. I asked, "All of them, even the two kids?"

Howler nodded. "I've been on the phone with their relatives, and they want the bodies to come back here for burial. I'm going to have you two flown to Wagga. You'll be given a staff car there, and you'll have to drive down to Wodonga, liaise with the Victorian police, and have their bodies taken to Wagga, where they'll come back with you to Pearce. We'll take over from there. You leave in an hour. Go and get ready. Dress uniform please."

We left his office in a daze, drove to our barracks building where I locked the car up, and went upstairs to our rooms to pack. Without saying much to each other, we went back to HQ where we were given a staff car, and I drove to Pearce. All the arrangements had been made, and we walked straight onto a Herc and took off. After landing, a staff car was provided, and we drove out of the Wagga base and headed to Wodonga.

Along the way, I said to Tag, "If I lose it down here, you'll have to get me away from anybody close."

"I hear you, boss."

We arrived at the Wodonga police station and walked inside wearing our headdress. I told the desk constable why we were there. Soon a sergeant and a senior constable approached us.

"How did it happen?" I asked without preamble.

The sergeant took out the report and read it, filling in his own detail. He and the constable had been on the scene. Their deaths were instantaneous, and the crash had been unavoidable. The senior constable said, "They just happened to be at the wrong place at the wrong time."

I lost it; I rounded on him with eyes blazing and yelled, "Do you have any idea how many wars and firefights he survived, just to be in the wrong place and time?"

Tag grabbed me but I shrugged him off and stormed out into the yard. I bellowed out my frustration and rage with a roar. Once I'd calmed down, I went back inside and apologised. They helped us make arrangements for the bodies to be transferred for shipping them back home.

The next day a truck from Bandiana army base met us at the hospital morgue, and the bodies were placed in service coffins, put onto the truck, and we followed it to Wagga air base. We flew home that night.

Gecko and his family were laid to rest with full military honours a week later. Tag and I wore full ceremonial dress and were the lead pallbearers with the other regiment NCO's, six to each coffin. After a twenty-one gun salute, I placed Gecko's guns, rifle, and beret on his coffin as it was lowered into the ground.

That night in the mess, Tag and I got well and truly legless, as did most of the regiment. When one of us goes down, we all feel it.

A couple days later, the phone rang in my room. Howler asked to see me. I walked into his office and was asked to shut the door.

"Tiger, the reason I called you in isn't good news, I'm afraid."

What else can go wrong? Don't tell me someone else has bit the bullet, please, I thought. "Ok, boss, what is it this time?"

"At this stage, I'm afraid Gecko isn't going to be replaced due to personnel restraints. You'll be operating one man down, I'm afraid."

I replied quickly, "That's ok boss. At the moment, I don't think either me or the team would entertain the thought of a replacement. It's going to be hard enough on them knowing that they were still out enjoying themselves when he died, and they're going to be really pissed off about missing the funeral. Besides, the next assignment is only an exchange of knowledge, so I'd rather find a replacement at a later time, if you don't mind."

"Tiger, this could be the beginning of the end for your team. They're not going to replace Gecko. If you lose any more men, they may not replace them either. This could be just the start," he warned me.

I thought about what he was telling me. "That's ok, boss. If that's the way they want to play it, so be it. After all, we were only an experiment that Colonel Clarke came up with, and as yet, there hasn't been another SRT group formed. I guess when they're done with us, we'll be thrown on the scrapheap like any other experiment."

He stared at me, and said "Christ you're a cynical bastard, but you may be right, even though I wouldn't like it, your team have proven the need for a ready response group, I just hope you're wrong".

The rest of the team started filtering back over the next week, but nothing was said about Gecko until everyone was back. I called a meeting in the ready room to break the news of Gecko's death and his family in one stupid useless horrible accident. I was still trying to cope with the loss of a friend and colleague that I'd shared time and war with, and thought maybe it was all one great joke and he'd saunter into the building any day now. However, it was not to be.

The rest of the team were all pretty pissed off with Tag and me for not informing them and that they'd missed the funeral. This led to some heated remarks, and eventually I had had to yell at them in my best RSM bellow. "Enough is enough! It's over! Get the fuck over it!" I really didn't like saying it, but it was either that or face a full blown mutiny.

As I left the room, I heard Tag saying, "How the hell do you think Tom's feeling? We had to go collect the bodies, and he very nearly ripped the police station apart barehanded…" I was out of earshot after slamming the door of my office.

Over the next few days, they tried to make amends, but I wasn't hearing any of it. I knew I'd overstepped the mark with them, and eventually I called a meeting to apologise, which was accepted graciously because they knew they'd also overstepped the mark. Things got back to an even keel, which was just as well, because a few days later, Howler called for a full briefing about our next assignment.

Thursday, October three, at zero nine hundred, we were

gathered in our briefing room. Howler entered and waved us down. "Gentlemen, I know it's been a hard few days, none harder than on your leader. Not only has he, and all of you, had to deal with the loss of a colleague, but also with the possible demise of your unit as well. But that's something he and I are trying to avert. Luckily, while the power struggles are going on back here, you'll be out of the picture and out of mind. Your objective is to use your knowledge and exchange views with your British counterparts. Therefore, you'll be teaching them our techniques about a given situation, and learning some of their techniques as well. This is not, I repeat, not, to be counted as an exercise to show who's better. It is an exchange of information, ideas, and a way of doing things.

Unfortunately, even though there were some British troops in Vietnam, none were SAS, so they didn't get to work with us in the theatre of war. This is why you have been chosen to represent the regiment in this program. In some cases, you will be joining actual missions and exercises they perform."

He paused to let this sink in and then continued. "You will be leaving here to be transported to Perth airport on Saturday at zero nine hundred. Your transport will leave from this building at that time. You'll be boarding a British Airway flight, leaving here at zero eleven hundred, and as befitting your station, you'll be flying first class."

Cheers resulted, and JJ said, "Christ, when he said befitting our station, I thought he meant down the back in the dunnies." Everyone laughed at the comment, even Howler.

"If that's what you want, JJ, I'll arrange it," Howler interjected.

"No, boss. First is ok by me." We all laughed again.

"You'll only be taking side arms, no rifles. Saves on my paperwork. Now don't forget to take warm stuff. It'll be coming onto winter there, and it gets cold enough to snow. For those of you that have seen snow, you know what to expect. For those of you that haven't, well, all I can say is have fun. Any questions?" Howler asked.

Tag raised his hand, and Howler nodded. "Transport, boss?"

"You'll be landing at Heathrow and be met there and transported to the SAS barracks at Aldershot. Anything else?" Heads shook. "No. Ok gentlemen, that's it. Thank you." As he left the room, he shook my hand. "Take care, Tiger, and keep them safe."

On Saturday, October five, we were packed with bulging kitbags because of the cold weather gear, our combat gear, and side arms, plus our normal uniforms and civvy clothing. We were in dress uniform with all regiment insignia and rank. The team wore their berets, while I was wearing my cap. Two staff cars and a rover pulled up, and the luggage was placed into the back of the rover. We split up into the staff cars and left for the airport.

The flight was long and boring, and apart from watching the inflight movies that we got to choose, sleeping and eating, the only thing that broke the monotony was a six-hour layover in Bahrain for refuelling. We were off the plane and wandering around the airport transit lounge. We grabbed a meal and did some duty free shopping. None of the wares in the shops caught my eye, and after wandering around a bit, I had what was supposed to be a roast lamb dinner, which was dreadful. I warned the guys to stick with the food on the plane and went to the bar to wash the taste of it out of my mouth.

After twenty-six hours flying and six refuelling, we landed at Heathrow; thankfully we were able to bypass customs and immigration because of our army uniforms, as well as the pre arrival advice to them from the Ministry of Defence.

Once we'd collected our kitbags, we waited in the main arrivals hall for our transport drivers to arrive. The flight was an hour ahead of schedule. Eventually I heard the clomp of boots on polished floors and stood up to see a sergeant marching up dressed in a NATO Howard Green defence jumper. He halted with a stamp of his boots and smartly saluted me.

I returned the salute as he asked, "Would I be addressing Warrant Officer Davis from Australia, sir?"

I looked down to hide my smile and decided to have some

fun. "Too right sport. What can I do ya for?" My guys cracked up with laughter, and the sergeant looked confused, so I said, "Sorry sergeant, just having some fun. Yes, I'm Tiger Davis. I take it you brought our transport."

He looked relieved. "Yes sir. If you'll follow me, I've two cars waiting outside. Might I suggest that you put a jumper on because of the cold, sir?"

It seemed fine enough to me, and I replied, "No, we'll be fine, sergeant. Besides, we're tough."

When we got outside the airport building, I could have swallowed my words. It was bloody freezing, so we stopped and dived into our bags for jumpers. I said to the sergeant, "You can wipe that smirk off your face, sergeant."

He replied with a smile. "Yes sir."

CHAPTER 27

We arrived at Aldershot barracks, home of the SAS an hour later, and once inside the HQ building, a Captain Wetherby met us and explained to us that it was almost the end of the working day. He would put off any formal greeting and briefings until the following day.

"Right now I'll have you escorted to your barracks where you will be quartered for the duration of your stay," he told us. We would be shown where the messes were located, and in the morning we would be escorted to the briefing rooms at zero eight hundred. "The usual base uniform is fatigues and hats, so I'll leave you to it and see you in the morning. Sergeant."

The sergeant came forward, and we all saluted and were taken to our rooms, shown the location of the OR's mess and sergeants' mess, and told when meal times commenced.

The next morning, we dressed in our cams and wore jumpers. We were escorted to the briefing rooms. The building we were in had three of them, and we were shown into number two. Captain Wetherby walked in, and we all stood to attention as he waved us down, I noticed that he wasn't in his dress uniform but was dressed the same as we were in camouflage fatigues and jumper. He wasn't wearing any guns, as we were.

Before he started, I asked, "Sir, can you explain in full the dress requirements? I notice you're not wearing guns. Back home we wear our side arms everywhere and are supposed to have them with us on leave. Could you explain the protocol here please?"

He smiled as he looked at my dress, noting the two pistols strapped to both legs, and nodded. "I see your point, Warrant Officer Davis, but first let me ask what dress protocol SOP's you have in the colonies?"

I smiled before answering. "Certainly sir, but we're hardly a colony these days. First off, everyone is called by their first name or a nickname. There is no rank difference, be it an officer or lowly private. For example, our CO is addressed by his nickname Howler, or boss, and he refers to me as Tiger, which is my nickname. Secondly, the reason we wear our side arms is so that we have instant armed response to any situation. We grab our rifles if we have time to get them, but every man is a crack shot with his handgun of choice, with or without suppressors fitted."

I drew my weapons and placed them on the table in front of me. As I picked up the forty-five, I continued. "For instance, my main pistol is this forty-five, and my secondary is an Ingram sub machine pistol." I picked it up left handed to show him. "And because I'm ambidextrous, I must have marksman rating for both hands."

He smiled. "You'll have to show me when we get to a firing range. I'd be happy to see each of you in action. Tiger, is it?"

"Yes sir," I replied. "As you can see, because we're here for a while, we need to know the local protocols, especially since we're used to firing live ammunition during training exercises. It wouldn't be the done thing to step outside the local rules, would it, sir?"

He was visibly shaken by my statement about live ammo. "Quite so, Tiger. I think before I start my briefing you should tell me everything in regards to your training SOP's down there. Then we can work out the differences with our SOP's here after that. And please use my given name, Eric."

He sat down, and for the next two hours we gave him a summary of the training and on-base protocols we used in Australia. At times, he asked about some of the missions we'd taken part in as well as for more details in regards to the Killing House we used for training and what scenarios could be practised.

After we'd finished the rundown of our operations, he told us that weapons weren't worn on base or carried at any time, but we would be free to follow our normal SOP's while on leave. He asked that we keep our weapons under lock and key in our barracks. We would be joining his troop for the duration of our stay but would from time to time be conducting training for some of the other troops in the regiment. A troop was always in Northern Ireland on a three-month rotation, and as part of his troop, we would be in Belfast in January the following year.

After lunch, we would be joining his troop at the indoor firing range, and he wanted to see the men in action. Sergeant Harris, who'd been showing us around, was also in the troop, and he'd be our liaison until we got to know the place. After our time on the range, we'd be free for the rest of the day, but he would like to see both myself and Tag in his office in the morning while Sgt Harris took the rest of my men to join his troop in their normal daily activities.

"The firing today will be live fire, sir?" I asked.

"Yes it will. What calibre of ammunition do you require?"

Buzz answered that for me, and then Wetherby replied, "The nine millimetres won't be a problem, but the forty-five calibres could be. I'm not sure if we have any on hand."

"That's all right, sir, I've got plenty," I informed him.

He smiled and nodded. "I think we'll take a leaf out of your book. Forget the sir and call me Eric. That goes for all of you, and you can pass the word, Sgt Harris. We'll adopt the Australian address in our troop from now on."

"Yes s...Eric," Harris replied.

Shortly after that we went to lunch, and as Harris, Tag, and I made our way to the sergeants' mess, Tag and I found out that Harris's nickname was Banger because he used to be in an artillery company.

That afternoon the team gave the whole of Delta troop an exhibition in handgun proficiency and marksmanship, but I was the one that drew the most comments because I could hit the mark with each hand from the hip by instinctive alignment and my demonstration of fire while rolling. The main difference between us was the fact that the Brits were trained to fire with both hands cupped on the grip, much like a police stance, while we only used one hand whether it was for aimed or instinctive fire. Most of the comments were due to our accuracy with the sub machine pistols. They couldn't comprehend how we could be that accurate until I mentioned that each man had his own weapon and that we had armourers that tweaked the mechanisms for us. Theoretically, each was a customized weapon. We spent hours of training on the firing range with our weapons.

The next morning, Tag and I reported to Captain Wethersby's office at zero eight thirty as arranged the previous day. Once we were seated, Eric asked as he passed over a photo, "Tiger, do you know anyone in this picture?"

I studied it. "Yes, why?"

"I've been trying to work out who you put me in mind of, and while I was looking at this today, I think I've found the answer. That was taken during my scuba training with the navy. So who do you recognize?"

He looked over my shoulder, and I pointed out Wetherby and another whom he said was an officer on base that I may have seen. I pointed to another man, and he asked, "He was our instructor; do you know who he is?"

"I should. He's the Chief Petty Officer on your navy's aircraft carrier Bulwark, and also one of my uncles. Uncle Robin to be precise. The oldest one, Tony, is a group captain in the Air Force. The next one is John, and he's a flotilla commander in the Royal Navy."

His face had gone white as he sat down at his desk. "Good god. That makes... Perhaps I shouldn't say this in front of others."

While he was talking, I studied him carefully. He was five nine with brown hair and eyes, and I put his age around thirty or thirty-one, but he had a regal sort of disposition and bearing that usually I don't give a rats' arse about. I put it down to the assumption that he was part of the British upper crust, or aristocracy, and it looked as if I was about to find out for sure. "That's ok, Eric. I have no secrets from my men. Go ahead, please."

He seemed to shake himself out of his mind fog and continued. "As I was saying, that would make you a member of one of the royal families, the Earl of Straithmore."

I laughed and looked at Tag, who looked somewhat bewildered. I told Eric, "No and yes. No, it's Straithhaven, not Straithmore, and yes, I am. At least until I sign over the title to my cousin Robin. I don't have any use for it, and Robin lives here in Bristol, actually. That's one of the things I wish to fix while I'm here, when we go on leave."

Tag was staring at me questioningly, so I told him, "Yes, I'm an Earl but in name only, and it was thrust upon me. I didn't have any say in it; the title passes to the eldest male child in the family. I inherited it from my Uncle Tony, and I intend to legally pass it over to my cousin Robin. Because I don't live here, he does, and it'll be up to him whether he takes up the position in the parliamentary House of Lords. Which I could do right now if I wished, but I intend to fob it off onto him."

Eric interrupted. "Excuse me Tiger, but you have to be presented to court as a visiting relative, and you have to present the new Earl if you change the heritage line. I'm the Earl of South Moreton; if you'll permit me, I can make all the arrangements necessary, but I'm afraid it will require a trip to Buck House."

I sighed in exasperation. "This is exactly what I was trying to avoid. Yes, ok, Eric, do what you must, but do you think we could get down to the business of why Tag and I are here now?"

Distracted, he returned to the business at hand, which involved asking if Tag and I could set up a hostage scenario with the armourers in a building down in the docklands area that was used for training sometimes. I told him it was possible, but it would have to have the reality of live fire to make it a realistic training scenario with observers and judges in place at the scene or close by monitoring the exercise. Once he agreed it could be done, we then went over the parameters of the training and what needed to be accomplished, which took us nearly three hours. We agreed to reconvene after lunch and took a break.

I copped a heap of ribbing from Tag on the way to the mess, and when we got there, he even went as far as to enquire, "Would your lordship allow a humble servant to buy you a drink without causing you too much embarrassment?"

He nearly doubled over laughing, so I hit him in the arm hard, which almost sent him to the floor. "Will you cut that shit out?"

He replied, laughing harder. "As your lordship commands, I will obey as your humble servant." It was said so ridiculously that I started laughing.

Back in Eric's office that afternoon, we were joined by the chief armourer, and together we devised a scenario that years later would become very useful to the SAS when they had to face the same type of scenario we'd devised that day. Eric would have to get permission to conduct the exercise, but he told us all to go ahead and reconnoitre the building together and to set up the scenario to what was proposed. The following day the Armoury RSM, Chris Hull, Tag, and myself would travel to the building to be used in a staff car.

Over the next couple of weeks, the weather slowly grew colder as the country moved towards winter. Eric had received permission for the exercise to go ahead, so we were spending a lot of our time down in the dockland area of Tilbury where the building was located. An ex passenger liner that the army used for training purposes was also located there. The idea was to turn it into a multi-roomed complex with hostages everywhere and roaming terrorists. We set video surveillance cameras in each room to record the exercise from inside and out and positioned each target.

After two weeks' hard work, everything was ready. During the last day of setting up, Eric, two captains, and a colonel arrived to inspect the building. Eric introduced me to the colonel, whose name was Dupree. He was six feet with silver hair and steel grey eyes.

"So it was you that devised this exercise, Davis? Explain the scene and tell me how you came up with it, please," the colonel instructed.

"It's one of the anti-terrorist hostage scenarios that we train with in our Killing House back home, but there our targets move and are controlled by a computer. It's designed to take down the baddies with as little loss of civilian life as possible, but runs as a live fire exercise that we do all the time. We found it great for use of guns, communication, and avoiding getting shot by our own people, sir."

"Hmm. I'd like to see how this is done; you have your team available, so I'd like to see your execution of the scenario, from start to finish. Is that possible?" he asked as he studied me.

I looked at him with surprise. "Yes sir, if you don't mind being up all night. I'll call a briefing as soon as we get back to the barracks."

He smiled and replied, "Oh I don't think a little lost sleep will worry me. Carry on."

"Yes sir," I replied.

Back at the barracks, Banger Harris rounded up the team and brought them to the briefing room, where I told them of the mission. "This is the same as training in the killing house, only this time, snipers are already on the scene. Lizard, you'll join Tag's group going in through the roof. Right, let's go get our gear. Silenced weapons only."

When he saw us getting onto the truck we were using as transport, the colonel turned and said something to the group of officers who would be observing before they got in the staff car to follow the truck to the target building again.

Once we arrived onsite, the officers filed into the command hut that had been set up with all the surveillance monitors and radios, while I spoke to the team. "Right. Let's give them a surprise by staying out of the outside cameras views. That way they'll wonder how we got in. I'll go tell them we're ready to breech. Tag, get into position ready to go on my word."

After going into the command hut and telling Eric the radio channel we were using so they could hear what we were saying, I turned to the colonel. "We're ready to breech on your order, sir."

"Go when you're ready, Warrant Officer."

I saluted and turned to leave the hut, simultaneously putting my radio earpiece in. "Tag, you ready?"

"Ready."

"Ok boys, let's go."

Half an hour later the exercise was completed, all the hostages were alive, and the baddies dead. My team left the building through the front door. We were greeted by the colonel and other officers.

"Bloody good show, men!" the colonel exclaimed. "But we didn't see how you gained entry. Please explain, Warrant Officer Davis."

I stopped wiping off the cam grease from my face and smiled, saluted, and replied, "Yes sir. I used methods we've used before. This scenario can be breeched in a number of ways. It falls on the planning of the team leader to determine the best course of entry. We went in through the roof and the back windows at the same time. If any baddie was around, they'd have been killed first."

He looked at me with surprise and laughed. "Hmm, yes, I see your point. Still a bloody good show. I think my men will learn a lot from this. Thank you, gentlemen. Now go have some food and a good rest." They moved off talking amongst themselves quietly.

As my team climbed aboard the truck, I told the driver to find a café that was open, which he did, and we went inside for a good feed before returning to the barracks. Over the next few days, there were constant meetings between Eric, Banger, Tag, and I about the training set up, and eventually it was settled that all teams would have a run through individually. After that, two or three teams could join up in a joint effort.

One of the points I stressed was that if they weren't going to assume police snipers were on the job, then the team snipers had to fulfil that role. Lizard could help with that sort of training.

It was also interesting that the team formation in that SAS regiment was ten man teams as opposed to our regular makeup of four. I had to explain to them why we usually only operated in four man teams, and that my SRT team was different because we were usually an eight-man team, but I was a man down due to the death of our team member.

The training at dockside progressed slowly, with all teams in the regiment to be put through the process. Each would take a week from initial briefings to the exercise itself, and then the debriefings. Towards the end of November, every team in the regiment except for the troop in Belfast had been through the scenario once, and we were about to start on phase two of the training where two teams would join forces to attack the scenario. During this time, my team were helping with the training.

One morning I was recalled to the barracks to report to Captain Wetherby, and after arriving at the barracks, I went immediately to Eric's office to see what was going on.

After I sat down in his office, Eric said, "This'll be quick. Tiger, you need to change into full dress uniform. You and I will be taking a trip to Kensington Palace. While you're changing, I'll be organizing a car and driver, so get back as soon as you're changed please. There's a good man."

Needless to say, all sorts of thoughts were flying through my head as I was changing, and I decided to question Eric when I got back to his office. I walked into his office, dressed in my best, I asked, "So what's going on?"

"We haven't got time for that yet. I'll let you know on the drive in. Let's go." He grabbed his hat and his sword from the umbrella stand. This caused my mind to race. He carried the sword in its scabbard to the waiting car where a corporal stood with the rear door open and saluted as we both got into the car.

As the car coasted along the A3, Eric said, "You know how I said you had to present yourself at court? I've been able to get an appointment with Prince Charles because her majesty has already left for her holiday at Balmoral. The prince is standing in for her, and he's looking forward to seeing you."

Oh Christ, I thought, this was just the sort of thing I had wanted to avoid. I considered myself an Australia; mixing with the upper crust and aristocracy wasn't my sort of thing. I'd probably be more inclined to drop someone if I thought that I, or Australia, had been insulted in any way, but after mixing with some of the regiment officers, I was starting to revise my opinion. Take Eric, for example. He was part of the aristocracy but was not the condescending, nose-in-the-air type.

The car drove into the palace via a back street and went around to the front portico instead of going up the mall. One of the footmen opened the car door as we arrived, and our caps were taken by a butler as we entered the palace. We were met by the prince's secretary, who showed us to into an office that would have put any hotel lounge to shame.

Prince Charles came forward to shake our hands. He was about two inches taller than I was, and his hair was already receding but was a salt and pepper mix of black and grey, more grey than black. After being presented formally, he asked me quite a few questions that I answered in my normal style because I was determined not to kowtow to him just because of his position. I found him rather pleasant and intelligent, to my surprise.

Towards the end of our visit, the prince stated, "Tom, even though you're a Warrant Officer in the Australian Army, you will be mixing with a lot of officers here who are part of the aristocracy, which you're a part of. Please allow me to give you some help: I'm going to give you the honorary rank of Major in our armed forces," he said proudly. I laughed. "Why are you laughing?"

"My rank in the US Army is higher, there I'm a Colonel," I told him.

He laughed and said, "I don't think I could quite go that far. Mother wouldn't allow that, so I'm afraid you're stuck with major, and that will be gazetted immediately." He got a nod from his secretary. I thanked him, and before we left he invited us to the Christmas Ball at Buckingham Palace in the coming month.

After we left Kensington palace, Eric directed the driver to Bond Street and his tailor's. I remarked, "Charlie's really not the simpleton he pretends to be. I found his conversation rather intelligent and stimulating."

"One has to play a certain type of game in his position, I would assume," he replied nonchalantly. "Now, when we get to my tailor's, just follow my lead, and we'll leave there with everything you need, sir."

I instantly swung my head around to look at him and said with a laugh, "Don't start that shit, Eric. I'm still me. And that's an order."

"Yes sir."

At the tailor's, I was able to pick up two dress uniform jackets, a Sam Brown officer's belt complete with the rings for a sword scabbard, plus a decent sword with a fine filigreed hand protector on the hilt as well as all the necessary major pips and epaulette rank insignia. We were at the tailors for an hour, during which time we had afternoon coffee and cake served to us while we waited for my jackets. The bill was reduced because we were soldiers, and all up the entire kit and caboodle only cost me five hundred dollars, which I paid in cash.

Then we headed back to the barracks. I was introduced and welcomed into the officer's mess. During that week, I tried to contact my uncles. I finally reached Uncle John, who told me my Uncle Tony and Uncle Robin were out of the country on exercise. He invited me to spend Christmas with him and his family, which I accepted. I was also able to have a staff car assigned to me because of my new rank, and if I required a driver, all I had to do was ring the transport office to arrange one.

The following week, the ball at Buckingham Palace took place, and the week after that we were due to go on leave until reporting back in the second week of January. I'd made arrangements to meet my uncle and his wife at the ball since they were also invited, and I'd be able to make last minute arrangements with them concerning Christmas.

On the night of the ball, the officers going were dressed immaculately with shoes and belts polished, and swords hanging at the right angle in shining scabbards. We got into one of the fleet of cars leaving base for the ball and were driven to the palace.

At the door we had to give our names to the footman, who would pass our invitation onto someone else, and as we entered the main ballroom, we had to wait to be announced. When it was my turn, the announcer called, "My lords and ladies, Major Thomas Davis, the Earl of Straithhaven from Australia presently attached to the SAS regiment Aldershot."

I smiled and moved into the room. Immediately, I was surrounded by ten women in their early twenties, all dressed to kill. Four of them were wearing mini-skirts and were quite shapely, but before any introductions could be made, a footman walked up to take my sword and gave me a ticket to collect it later. I was joined by my Uncle John in his navy uniform, and his wife Dorothy. We shook hands and I gave Dorothy a perfunctory kiss on the cheek. I excused myself from the girls and moved with my uncle and aunt to a table to sit and talk.

A waiter walked by, and I collared him for a drinks order. Soon he returned with the drinks we'd ordered. After we'd been talking for an hour making arrangements and catching up with what was going on in the family over Christmas, and who I'd be meeting and going to see, you know all the usual palaver, my eyes were drawn to a woman sitting be herself. She was pleasing to the eye and vaguely familiar, so I excused myself and walked over to ask her for a dance.

She accepted, and we made our way to the dance floor, introducing ourselves as we went. Her name was Petula; she would have been in her late thirties and five six with long brunette hair and blue eyes.

She had a sexy tone to her voice, and I noticed she was wearing a wedding and engagement ring. "You're married; I take it?"

"Separated, actually. In the process of getting divorced. Why?"

I blushed a little and replied, "Well, I don't usually make out with someone else's girl."

She laughed and replied, "Is that what we're doing, making out?" She laughed prettily. "Have no fears, my sweet, lovely man. I'm quite alone. Until now. I'm all yours."

She sang along with the music as we danced, and I told her she was great and should be on stage. She laughed and said, "Just for you I might get up and do some singing later."

I encouraged her to keep singing as we danced. "Well, if you're getting up to sing later, please dedicate one of your songs to me. I love your voice."

"All right, I'll get up and sing for you later, but right now I'm enjoying myself just dancing with you, Tiger."

"Thank you. I'm enjoying your company too."

We stayed on the dance floor as the music changed to a slow waltz. I had decided I wanted to spend more time with her, so I turned on the charm. We flirted with each other relentlessly.

"Don't you go anywhere," she purred. "I've got something to do, but I want you to join me when I'm finished. This will be a surprise just for you."

As I sat down with Uncle John and Dorothy, I ordered another drink. An announcer called, "My lords, ladies and gentlemen. Please make welcome to the stage Miss Petula Clark."

I nearly fell off my chair. This was who I'd been dancing with? Christ, how stupid of me not to realise! She was one of my favourite female singers.

As she finished singing "Downtown", she looked directly at me she said, "Thank you. The next song is dedicated to my dear friend, Tiger, all the way from Australia. I promised him a song, so this is just for him. I hope you like this one, my love." She sang "You Colour My World."

CHAPTER 28

After an hour on stage, she joined us at my uncle's table. I introduced everyone and we chatted and danced. Later in the evening, my uncle and aunt left to head back to Peterborough where they lived because he had to be back at the naval base at Portsmouth the next day. After talking to Eric, I found out I didn't need to be back on base until later the next day. I told him that I'd be back by midday and that I'd see him after that.

"Have fun you, lucky devil!" he said to me as he left.

Petula and I left, headed for her place at Chelsea. Her driver dropped us at the front door before taking the car around the back to the garage, and the door was opened by her secretary, who was still awake.

We were introduced, and Petula said, "Tiger is to have access to me at any time, Hilda. You can get his contact details in the morning at breakfast. Right now we're going up to my rooms."

Once upstairs, Petula gave me a smoking gown that belonged to her ex-husband. She didn't want me to crease my uniform. After we changed, we sat on one the sofas with drinks. She nestled into me as we talked for hours together, and we arranged to meet each time I was able to get some time away. She liked the way I shortened her name to Pet. We did eventually go to bed together, but on that occasion, we didn't make love.

The next morning, we were woken by one of the maids bringing us breakfast at zero eight hundred, and as we ate, Hilda joined us with Pet's schedule for the day. I guess having me there was a bit of a novelty because they both laughed over some of my mannerisms during breakfast.

Hilda said to me after one giggling fit, "If you would care to let me know when you wish to leave, sir, I'll arrange for the chauffeur to drive you back."

"Hilda, I don't wish to leave, but some of us have work to attend to, so duty calls, unfortunately. If you give me half an hour, I'll be ready to go."

"No, Hilda, make that an hour. I would like some time alone with Tom before he goes," Pet ordered with a twinkle in her eye.

In my best lecherous voice, I said, "Oh really." This started the giggling again.

"Yes really," Pet replied as she playfully tossed a cushion my way.

I gave Hilda my contact details, she left, and I said, "Well Pet, we've both got work to do, so I'll jump in the shower and get dressed."

She replied with a mischievous smile. "Would you like me to come and wash your back for you?"

"By all means," I told her.

After we made love on the floor of the huge shower, she was too exhausted to wash my back, but the water and her nails had done that for me. I soaped her up and she whispered, "Oh god you better come back soon." After reassuring her that I would, we embraced in a kiss as I towelled her dry.

The chauffeur dropped me off at the entrance to the barracks at eleven, that morning I didn't have any problems with the amount of salutes I had to return. I made my way to Delta troop headquarters and Eric's office while carrying my sword in my left hand. I placed my sword in the umbrella stand, and my hat on the rack before sitting down and announcing, "Back on board and ready for action, Eric. What's on?"

"Someone looks well pleased with himself; you were the talk of the mess this morning. How did you accomplish a feat like that?"

I looked at him rather innocently. "The SAS motto, Eric. 'Who Dares Wins.' That's how I accomplish most things, and it also helps to know how to talk to women the right way."

"All I can say is you're a lucky bastard," he replied with a shake of his head. "Now, let's talk about the stint in Northern Ireland. We'll be leaving and arriving there on Monday thirteen. We will be in country until we pull out on March twenty- eight. We do have our own barracks building there with enough room for my four troops and your team, so we won't have to split any of the SAS force. Most of the work is patrolling the streets and sometimes we have to assist the police on house raids."

"Ok, what about weapons apart from our pistols and a sniper rifle for Lizard?" I asked.

"Yes, I thought you'd ask about that," he mused. "Tomorrow we'll be taking delivery of one hundred brand new MP4 tactical assault weapons, so for the next few days we'll be getting them fired in and ourselves used to them. As to your man Lizard, he can have his pick of any of the rifles in the armoury. Tomorrow at ten hundred they'll be at the armoury, so we'll need your men there."

I nodded. "No problem there. What about leave? Can my men come and go as they wish?"

"Yes they can, but make sure they carry their ID's to enter the barracks. Leave will be from this Friday until Friday January ten. Of course, you have the use of your car while on leave."

"Thank you. This afternoon I was planning to get my team together in the briefing room and run over these details. Is there anything you wish to add?" I asked him.

"No," he replied, and then called, "Orderly!" One rushed in. "Major Davis would like you to round up his team and tell them he'll be giving them a briefing at thirteen thirty in briefing room one."

The orderly saluted and vanished. Eric said, "Time for lunch. I hope you're ready to face the music in the mess over last night." He chuckled.

"You're a cruel bastard, Eric Wetherby," I assured him.

He innocently answered, "Yes, I know that, Major." He chuckled even more as I started laughing as well. I retrieved my sword and took it to my rooms, and then we went to the mess.

As I walked into the briefing room that afternoon, Tag called, "Atten…shun!"

"Cut that out, you lot, and sit down."

"Boss, we've been hearing rumours of you going out with Petula Clark, and we know you didn't come back last night. Is it true or not?" Dumper asked with a grin.

"Dumper, you of all people should know what rumours are like," I reprimanded jokingly. "But yeah, in this case, the rumours are accurate." Cheers and cat calls echoed off the walls, and I let it go on until the noise died down. "Right, you finished? Good. Let's get on with business."

I filled them in on the leave dates and told them they were free to come and go as they wished while on leave. I told them the date we were heading to Northern Ireland and what we could expect. I told them about the new shipment of arms coming in, and I let Lizard know he could have his pick of sniper rifles in the armoury. "I want all of you gathered at the armoury at ten hundred tomorrow waiting for Captain Wetherby and myself. If we're lucky we'll get first pick of the new Special Forces Assault weapons, so be prepared to spend some time at the shooting range."

The next morning, Eric and I made our way to the armoury. I saw my team waiting with Banger Harris for us to arrive. Once inside the armoury, the RSM in charge showed us the new assault rifles, and I looked over the MP4. I was impressed; it had a short folding stock, laser and night sighting with a short telescopic sighting system, and a handle for steadying instead of a straight forward stock. It could fire a thirty round magazine of NATO standard rounds by single shot or full auto and was capable of being fitted with a silencer that clipped to the barrel above the forward handle.

There was also a box of MP4A's that were tubed for grenade launching, with the forward handle as part of the cocking mechanism for the grenade tube. The grenades it fired were the same as my MX280 back home, so I selected one of them. We were also issued twenty spare magazines, all together holding one thousand rounds of ammunition. Lizard chose another Remington 380 with a laser and night scope for his work as a sniper. After receiving the weapons and loading the ammo, we were constantly at the firing range. By Friday, I'd gotten used to using the MP4, and had sighted it in to suit. I found it more accurate than my MX280, and it didn't lose any of its accuracy with the silencer attached.

By the time Friday came around, I'd arranged with Pet through Hilda to be with them on Friday night, and through to the end of the week, if Pet wanted, she could travel to my uncle's with me, where we would stay over the Christmas break.

That evening I drove the car to Chelsea and parked on the street. Hilda opened the door, and I asked her if the chauffeur could bring the car in for me because I didn't know how to get around to the back entrance. She told me she'd arrange it and that Pet was upstairs waiting for me to arrive. I passed her my keys and took my bag upstairs with me.

Pet was glad to see me. She was dressed in a white mini-skirt and blouse, which showed off her figure nicely. She got up from her desk as soon as I entered the room, and after our initial kiss, she sat with me on the lounge and asked. "So what have you been up to?"

"I can't really tell you too much, except that I will be going off with the regiment early in January, and we'll be in Northern Ireland for a few months."

"Oh well you better be careful, otherwise I'll get most upset. Now tonight, would you like to go out for dinner at a club I know where the music is good?" she replied.

I agreed and then asked, "Pet honey, would you like to come and spend the Christmas with me at my family's get together as my girlfriend, or have you got something else planned?"

"Oh darling I'd love to, I haven't planned anything else, I think it'll be marvellous, and this way I'll get to meet the rest of your family too. How long are we likely to be gone?" She remarked as she kissed me, before turning on the lounge and putting her head in my lap and looking up at me.

I replied, as I unconsciously played with her breast and nipple through her blouse. "Oh we'll be away most of the Christmas week, but we can cut it short if we need to."

That evening, the chauffeur dropped us at Club Muso in Soho, and it was filled with celebrated musicians and actors. I got to meet Margaret Brown (Dusty Springfield), Lulu, Cilla Black, Keith Moon, Robin Nevins, and Nigel Havers. We shared a table with Richard Harris, Sandy Shaw, Richard Starkey (Ringo Starr), and his wife, Barbara Bach. The meal we had was excellent; the music was fantastic and not over the top in volume, and the company was very entertaining. It was amazing how much I learned about their normal lives that people just didn't know. For instance, I learned about the trouble Ringo was having with keeping the cat next door away from Barbara's birds. All sorts of suggestions were offered, but everyone thought my solution held merit, which was to shoot the cat with a load of saltpetre up the arse. My reasoning was that if it didn't kill the cat, it certainly wouldn't try again. Everyone had a good laugh over that one.

As we were leaving later that night, we were invited to a party at Lulu's place the next evening. Petula accepted.

She asked as we got outside, "I hope you don't mind me accepting the gig at Lulu's, darling, but her parties are always good and I think you'll have fun."

"Fine by me," I replied.

Eventually I met most of Britain's entertainment music and film or TV artists through my association with Pet while I was in the country. I went to some really good parties, and some outrageous ones as well. I remember one we went to that was attended by Mick Jagger and his girlfriend. She and a former girlfriend got into a shouting match, which turned into a really good catfight, until Jen Saunders intervened by grabbing both of them by the hair and dragging them out, much to the disgruntlement of others who had been enjoying the spectacle.

That weekend we drove down to Peterborough to my uncle John's. I drove while Pet snuggled as close to me as she could. Once we got there, we were given one of the second floor rooms. Apparently, most of the family were congregating here this Christmas, as John's place was quite large.

During dinner that night, we went through all the family catch up, and I set the record straight for them after they informed me of the version my mother had given them. Which was that I'd been thrown me out of home because I refused do any work around the place, and I was always abusing her, and telling her I couldn't stand her. Then I lived on the street committing all manner of criminal acts. Which was as far from the truth as one could get, except for the part of telling her that I couldn't stand her attitude.

At the start of the family discussion, Pet asked if we would rather talk in private, and I said to her, "No your fine honey. I've got no secrets outside of the jobs I do in the forces, so you can stay with us. Unless you wish to leave, but this is just over family squabbles, that's all."

John asked about what I was up to while I was in the country, and I told them that my team and I were there for exchange training and ideas and that we were heading to Belfast after my leave.

Apparently, in May, he was taking his flotilla up to Scapa Flow and offered me the chance to have the SAS teams do some diving up there if we wished. All I had to do was arrange it through him when we got back from Ireland. I accepted the offer willingly because I knew my guys would be interested.

When most of the rest of the family gathered there on Christmas Eve, Pet was introduced as my girlfriend Petula, with no mention of her last name, until during dinner Joy, Uncle Tony's wife, asked, "Petula, I hope you don't think I'm prying, but you look very familiar. I have a nagging feeling I should know you. Do you mind if I ask your last name?"

John and I burst out laughing while Dorothy smiled with amusement. Pet looked at me and I nodded. She looked at Joy and simply said, "No problems at all, Joy. My last name is Clark." She smiled as we watched Joy sitting there with her fork halfway to mouth, which was wide open.

I could almost hear the gears turning in her head. She dropped her fork and said, "Clark? Petula Clark! My god, please forgive me. Oh, I had no idea! I feel like a right idiot now. You are THE Petula Clark?"

Uncle Tony was staring first at me, and then Pet. Uncle Robin was looking gobsmacked. His wife Jane was smiling, and John, Dorothy, and I were laughing. Pet smiled and said, "Yes, otherwise I'll be in the poor house tomorrow."

Joy looked Tony and said, "Why didn't you warn me?"

All he could do was shrug his shoulders and hold his hands out, which started another round of laughter. Joy, still trying to get her feet out of her mouth, put another one in when she said, "I'm so sorry, dear. I just had no idea. I love your music."

To end any further frustration, I stood up and said, "Yes, folks, this is Petula Clark, and yes, she is my girlfriend. However, please, just let her be herself. As far as anybody else is concerned, she's just my girlfriend Petula, ok?"

"Too right, Major Davis," Uncle John quipped.

I shot him a look and said, "Just Tom or Tiger please. Besides, we're all Davis's here, and if you're all lucky, Pet might do a song for you later."

She smiled and said, "I would be delighted, but just one. You pick," she said with a gesture to the table.

After dinner, we all moved into the music room after the clearing up had been done. While my uncles and I had scotches and cigars out on the terrace, the women gathered around Dorothy at the piano.

After our cigars, we joined them, and Pet said, "All right, girls, have you picked one yet?" They all shook their heads. "Well, how about the one I sang for your nephew at the palace? Do you have the music for that, Dorothy?"

"Just one minute," Dorothy said. She dug around and found

the sheet music. "There. Ready." She began to play.

Petula sang as she moved around the room. She leaned on me as she sang You Colour my World, and she would always come to me from around the room for that line.

Later that night, the men dressed in uniform and the women in good clothes for midnight mass. I had to go because it was the done thing, of course. We entered the local church, and the priest shook hands with us all as, we were introduced by John.

When he saw Pet, he said, "Well, bless my soul. Miss Clark, I haven't seen you for a long time, since your choir days up north. This is an honour. I hope you'll join the choir a little later, even if it's just at an old man's whim."

"Pleased to, Father," Pet replied with a smile for the older man.

"Thank you, thank you, my dear," he replied.

We moved into the church. Because of the long pews, we were able to take up one of the front ones with myself and Pet at the end nearest the aisle.

At the end of his sermon, the priest explained how pleased he was to see everyone. "I would especially like to make welcome all the Davis clan, who serve our country in all services now. Brothers John and Robin in the Navy, their brother Tony in the Air Force, and now all the way from Australia, their nephew Tom in the Army. A great welcome to you all. I would also like to make welcome a young woman who used to sing in the choir at one of my earlier parishes. It is such a joy to see her again, and she has agreed to join the choir for our next hymn, "Ode to Joy." Please make her welcome, and if I need to, I will make introductions after her performance. Thank you all."

Pet walked to the choir and was handed a microphone as the organ started the music. Pet sang the first few lines, and the congregation was trying to figure out who she was. They erupted into applause as she turned and came to the chorus; everyone joined in the singing.

At the end, the priest stood beside her as she took a bow to the applause. She gave him a kiss on the cheek and rushed down to take her seat beside me. The priest called, "Miss Petula Clark, folks. Thank you, my dear."

When the service was over and we were leaving the church, we were mobbed by the townsfolk wanting to get autographs and talk to Pet. After ten minutes or so, I put my arm around her and guided her into the middle of the ring my uncles had made with their bodies and we walked home with the women inside the ring around Pet chatting. I joined my uncles on the ring perimeter.

When we arrived home, John announced, "I think we could all do with a drink." He moved toward the music room and bar and continued. "Ladies, what would you like?"

We all took glasses to the girls before collecting our own glasses and sitting with our respective partners. Dorothy said, "Here's to Petula. What a wonderful song, and you've just raised our standing in the community tenfold, my dear. Thank you."

We drank, and Pet answered. "It's me who should be thanking you and your family for making my time here with you and Tom special."

"Nonsense darling," Jane interjected, "your part of the family now, and lord knows we have to put up with a lot from this bunch of men."

Everyone laughed. I called, "Cheers and Merry Christmas, all!" My toast was returned in like manner. After a few more drinks, we headed to our rooms. Pet and I showered together before cuddling up in each other's arms in bed.

Christmas morning it was snowing as we came down for breakfast. We went outside to play in the snow; it was the first time I'd seen real snow, and I had fun throwing snowballs.

After breakfast we gathered around the tree. Presents were given out, the bottles of Blue Label I'd brought went down a treat, and the cards for each family that had one thousand pounds inside them. I gave Pet a solid gold bracelet engraved with 'Tom and Pet. Love for Xmas '74. She gave me a bulky envelope and card, which read: The rest of your present is back home at my place darling. All my love, Petula. I upended the envelope and a key with a remote dropped into my hand. Both had the BMW insignia on them.

I looked at her enquiringly, and she said, "It's a black series seven, darling, and the warrant of fitness is in your name. Merry Christmas, my love." I gave her a kiss and cuddle.

When all the festivities had concluded, Joy said, "Right ladies. We all know where we have to be. We may as well make a start." They started trooping out. Pet looked at me, and I shrugged as Joy said, "Yes Petula, that means you as well. Come on." She went with a smile on her face.

Tony piped up and said, "Well, they'll be awhile. Anyone for a drink? I'm dying to try this Blue Label."

"Don't crack open your presents. There are three bottles under the bar. I'll have one with only one cube of ice, thanks," I told him with a wink.

He poured us all one, and I took mine outside and lit a cigar. Tony joined me and said, "You're looking pensive, Tom. What's troubling you?"

"Nothing really. I was just thinking this would be a great BBQ area," I replied.

He laughed and said, "Yes, it would, but what I miss most about Australia is all that beautiful seafood. The prawns and crab at Christmas were always special. Are you missing home? Is that it?"

I looked at him with a grimace. "No that's not it…" I proceeded to tell him how I got into the army, what I'd been doing, and my reservation over the African mission. "So for the last four years I've been in war zones, and I'm finding it hard now there's no war to fight, if you have any understanding of that."

"I think so. You train and train so everything becomes second nature, then you do the job. But once it's done, there's nothing left to do."

"Yeah, a bit like that," I replied with a sigh.

He looked at me and said, "If it's the thrill you're missing, I know you're headed to Northern Ireland and probably going off with John after that. But how about when you have some time, you call me and I'll see if I can arrange a few things for you."

"Ok, I'll do that. What have you got in mind?" I replied.

"Ever thought of learning how to fly a Harrier Jump Jet, a Vulcan bomber, or a chopper?" he asked.

"I'm already qualified for Huey's, but a jump jet, that would be cool," I told him with a grin.

When we went back inside, he gave me a card with his contact details, and I slipped it into my wallet as he poured another round of drinks. Christmas lunch was an all afternoon affair, and cooking wise, all the women had turns and shared in things. Pet was responsible for the desserts, which was a Rhubarb pie with brandied custard and a passionfruit cheesecake and cream. The passionfruit had come off the vines in John and Dorothy's garden. Both were delicious. Who'd have thought it? A singer that could cook; it must have been her upbringing. Mind you, why cook yourself when you have enough money to employ someone to do it instead.

Readers Note: Here's something to reflect on: after getting to know some of the so called superstars that rose overnight, the so-called overnight success, usually took over fifteen or twenty years to happen. In the meantime, the artist or group had to survive on at best maybe twenty or thirty pounds per gig (performance-four hours on stage in a dinghy dive or pub), which meant they would have to feed and clothe themselves. Even some of the best entertainers never actually were recognised. I've been talking about my affair with Petula Clark. She was thrown out of home at sixteen because she wanted to make singing a career. She didn't wish to go to work until she met someone to marry, which in those days was the norm. Another case I could mention is Cilla Black or Lulu. It was either go out and try to survive without family blessings and help, or get married and pregnant and be a stay at home mother, wasting what talent they had. If we go a step further, what about women or men that fall into this category that are homosexual? This should explain the trials they had to face, and if you need an example, everyone that I know loves Dusty Springfield. Her birth name was Margaret Brown. She was teased as a kid and thrown out of home when she was only fourteen because her father and mother expected her to be interested in boys so they could marry her off. It wasn't until she was twenty-five that she was discovered and signed to a record label. But that was back then. Please don't think things have changed that much. Nowadays kids are of the expectant generation, in that I mean kids expect everything to be done for them. Anyway I apologise for my views, but after this point to ponder, let's get back to the story.

We started to pack up on Saturday to make our way back to our respective homes. After fond farewells and promises to keep in touch, Pet and I made our way back to her Chelsea home. We arrived to a frantic Hilda, who had a host of invitations to New Year's parties for us to consider.

Over a leisurely dinner at home, Pet decided she wanted to keep to ourselves that New Year, so all the invites were returned to Hilda to make excuses and we spent the New Year watching fireworks from her rooftop deck with the whole household and drinks and champagne. We went to bed and made love to each other and talked in each other's arms until daylight. New Year's Day was virtually a write off. After waking about four in the afternoon, we decided to go to the Muso Club for dinner.

One of the things we'd talked about the previous night was my upcoming tour in Northern Ireland. Pet was terrified that something would happen to me, and I had to work hard to convince her that nothing was going to happen to me. I made a joke about Aussie's being bulletproof, which she shot down straight away by saying she had seen the scars warfare had inflicted on my body. I promised to be careful, and she was somewhat mollified.

The following Monday, the sixth, I drove my staff car back to

Aldershot and had a driver take me back to Chelsea. At the end of the week, I would drive my new BMW back to the base. I'd discovered that it could be garaged undercover at the transport compound, so on Sunday morning the twelfth, after a torrid night of lovemaking, I parted from Petula until I returned at the end of March.

CHAPTER 29

After I'd garaged my car in the transport compound and my go bag in my quarters, I walked over to the troop office and found Eric at his desk. We exchanged pleasantries as I sat down, and I told him about John's offer for a trip to Scapa Flow.

"Wonderful! That definitely is put onto the agenda. Some of my troop need some dive refreshing. I'll put into the diary for you to contact him the first week of April." He made a note. "I'm going to love having you around, Tiger. With your family connections, the sky's the limit to what we might be able to get done in the way of training."

I laughed. "Not even the skies are a limit."

"How so?" he asked. I told him of the offer Tony made to me. When I finished telling him, he exclaimed, "Good god man! Jump at it! I'll make sure you'll have the time to do it. Christ, it's not every day you, or anyone else, gets a chance like that. Do it, by all means, you, lucky bastard. Do you think he'd take us both?" We both laughed as he continued. "No, just joking. I'd never be able to get away. Nice thought, though."

I turned to work matters. "Are we all good for tomorrow?"

"Yes, the whole troop is back from leave. I've given orders to all to assemble by zero eight hundred on the parade ground. That way we'll all have eaten. The trucks will assemble at the same time, and we'll be off to the Liverpool ferry. We can have lunch on the ferry during the crossing."

"Well, it looks like it's all happening, so I'll leave you to keep on with what you were doing while I go get my stuff ready. I'll see you in the mess later."

He smiled and said, "Yeah, it's fine for those swanning around with rock stars, but someone has to do it, right?"

"Right," I replied with a smile as I left him to it and headed back to my quarters to get my gear ready.

At eight the next morning, the whole of Delta troop was assembled, my team with them. We started loading into the six trucks that would be taking us first to Liverpool and then onto Belfast via the ferry.

Eric rode as shotgun in the first truck, and I did the same in the second. I was able to take in the scenery as we travelled north.

When we arrived in Belfast, the contrast to England was amazing. We drove through some streets that had houses with graffiti painted all over them. Some had been abandoned. There were a couple of bombed out houses, and I noticed that no one in the populace who were on the streets smiled. They moved as if in a hurry to get somewhere. So much for the cheery Irish.

The barracks compound was beside the police station near the western edge of town. Both had large steel doors and razor wire on top of the walls. The gate was opened and half a dozen MP's lined each side of the road with sub machine guns as we drove in. As soon as we did, the gates were closed. The place looked as cheery and picturesque as Dracula's castle in an old horror flick, and I must admit I did not look forward to spending three months in this place.

We settled down to rather mundane work that involved three teams each day. One team would patrol a side of the particular street picked at random, while another would do the same with the opposite side. Another team was held in reserve in the back of an armoured personnel carrier. To break the monotony, the reserve team would switch places with the other teams throughout the day. As I've said, it was monotonous and hot inside the APC despite being air conditioned, and as far as I was concerned (and many agreed) it was futile and boring. During off duty hours, we could go into town but only in groups. We could never visit the same pub twice in a row in those off hours and in civvies. We got on quite well with the locals, and they were far more cheerful and friendly after dark than I first thought. I must admit that I acquired the taste for pints of Guinness after that tour.

One morning near the middle of our tour, all street patrols were cancelled because the bomb disposal unit was called to handle a bomb threat at the court house that had been phoned through. All SAS teams were to provide protection and crowd control in and around the courthouse area, the police had blocked off. Every APC available was jammed to capacity as we made our way into town. Eventually the bomb was diffused, and as the bomb unit was loading it into their truck for later disposal, there was a massive blast from two blocks away. We loaded quickly into whatever vehicle was available and headed towards the blast's location.

The first order of business was to cordon off the area and clear civilians out of the area so the ambulances and emergency services could get close.

On the way to the sight, Eric started issuing instructions to each team leader through the radio headsets we wore. They had better headsets than we had, and we'd since changed over to them because the mic set up was on a boom that curled around from the earpiece to near our mouths. My team and three others were responsible for helping the wounded and clearing the buildings of the dead. As the truck stopped, we began the allotted tasks. Christ, what a sight the street was!

I was wracked with fury and anger as I took in the scene. There was debris and bodies everywhere, and this was supposed to be in peacetime. I think if I'd got my hands on the perpetrators of this crime, I'd have cold-bloodedly executed them on the spot. I came across a young girl about twelve who was alive, but her legs had been torn to ribbons in the blast. I reached her with Tag at my side, and she whispered that her mother was there, pointing toward another body. Tag went to check on the mother; he looked at me and shook his head and returned to help me stem the bleeding. As the first ambulance arrived, I gathered her broken body into my arms and raced to it. They immediately started working on her, and with tears streaming down my face, I continued my job.

I found another survivor and helped him by slinging him over my shoulder. I carried him to the ambulance and placed him on the ground. The medics came over to attend to his injuries, and I grabbed one of them by the arm and asked about the girl.

He pointed to a cloth covered body. "I'm sorry, mate. Too much blood loss. She went into shock. We couldn't save her."

I collapsed onto my knees, and with tears streaming, gave vent to a roar of rage, helpless frustration, and sorrow. After letting go of my anger, I continued my work. An hour later, the wounded had been transported to hospital and the dead were lined up with coverings over them. The first in line was the little girl, and next to her was her mother. The blast toll was twenty-two dead, seventeen maimed for life (if they survived), twenty-five wounded, seven of them critically.

As we all travelled back to the barracks after the final clean-up had been done by city engineers, no one spoke. I knew by the look on the faces of the men that every one of them was frustrated and angry, but it was up to the police to go on the hunt for the murderers because that's what they were. This act wasn't because of the IRA wanting a free and independent Ireland or because of the difference between the Catholic and Protestant religions; both religions lost followers that day. This had been sheer bloody murder of innocent civilians, and if members of the IRA were responsible, they needed to be hunted down and hanged.

The following day the police got a tipoff that the bombers were holed up in a house in Andersonville, an outer suburb. They asked for help in securing the location and for help in entering and arresting the criminals. The job fell under SAS jurisdiction, and Eric called on his best insertion experts, my team. He also sent two teams to the location to observe and surround the house.

After the team leaders reported in by radio, I asked the police to get me a set of typical house plans that matched the description of the target house. I also asked for aerial photos and views of the house photos. All was supplied to me within an hour. After blow ups of the photos were made, Eric and I sat in his office with everything pinned to the walls. I stared at them each in turn and pondered.

After thirty minutes, I had a plan locked down in my head. "Right. Two teams, one of them mine, the second can be the best scoring team on the hostage exercise because that team had three snipers. All these photos and maps need to be in the briefing room in fifteen minutes I'm going to see the police inspector."

When I returned, I went straight to the briefing room where everyone was assembled. I noted all the photos, floorplans, and aerials were pinned up. I put down the box I was carrying. The police inspector had accompanied me along with the police commander, who would be commanding the police force at the target house. Eric, the bomb disposal unit sergeant, and both teams, waited as I got started on the briefing.

"I'll make this as quick as I can, gentlemen. We're going after the bastards responsible for yesterday's bombing. The assault force will be my team, designated Alpha, and team four, belonging to Delta troop, designated Bravo. Snipers, please stand." I waited for them to get to their feet. "Lizard, your sierra one. You'll need to find a position to cover the back of the house." I pointed to the next sniper. "Your sierra two. Same thing but front of the house. Next, sierra three. Left side. Sierra four, right side. If you spot a target trying to escape, only shoot to incapacitate if possible, please.

Bravo entry point is the front of the house, as quietly as possible. Be aware Alpha will be coming in from the back, so let's not shoot each other please." There was some laughter. "Weapons, silenced handguns only. Again, shoot only to incapacitate. Our main weapon will be these." I held up a cosh from the box. "We knock these arseholes out. I don't care if they're asleep; hit them anyway to make sure. Then secure hands and feet. Once we have them all, we take them out of the house and put them into the hands of the police, designated Papa. They'll take up position outside in the front as soon as entry is made. Once we have them all, I'll call in the bomb squad, designated Charlie, to clear and assess the house. Captain Wetherby will be overall coordinator, designated Tango. We assemble in the target area at zero two thirty and make the assault at zero three hundred." I paused to let things sink in and for a mouthful of water before continuing.

"Oh, and please don't forget your night vision. Could be rather embarrassing." More laughter. "Any questions?"

The police Inspector asked, "Where will the assembly area be?"

I moved to the aerial photo, pointed, and replied, "Here in this park. Hopefully it's far enough away to avoid too much noise, and that's the key element here, gentlemen. Silence. Try to keep everything down to a dull roar."

"Where do you want me positioned?" Eric asked.

I pointed and replied, "Probably here or here. You decide, but you need to have a good visual on the front of the house to call the shots if needed." There were no further questions, so I finished. "Ok that's it. Go get something to eat and rest up. We'll assemble and get into the transport at zero two hundred. Everyone in the insertion teams grab a cosh as you go, and don't forget they've got to be returned because our friends in the police force will suffer from withdrawal symptoms otherwise. Dismissed." This drew more laughter and the briefing broke up.

The raid took place as planned and went well, with only a couple of minor glitches. Lizard put two shots into one that tried to escape out an upper floor window at the back, shooting him in the leg and shoulder, but unfortunately, sierra three shot too quickly as another tried to get out a window, wounding him in the shoulder, but the guy broke his neck in the fall to the ground. All up, nine were captured and handed over to the police, five women and four men.

The place was full of explosives; it took the bomb squad the rest of the day to clear. It was deemed safe for the police investigators to go in, but the SAS contingent of the operation were back at the barracks and having a very jovial breakfast. All of us that took part in the operation were in high spirits for the rest of that week.

Eventually our tour came to an end, and we travelled back to Aldershot after our relieving troop arrived. As the week drew to a close, we were due to have a fortnight's leave, but before that happened, I contacted Uncle John and he and Eric made arrangements for all of Delta troop to go on the trip north leaving from Portsmouth on Monday May five at zero six hundred. We were required to be abroad by Sunday afternoon, May four. Eric, myself and two teams would travel on John's flagship while the rest of the troop was to be dispersed onto the other four ships. We would be on that exercise until we made homeport on June fifteen.

Friday arrived and I put my go bag into my car and headed off to Pet's place, and we had a happy two weeks together. We took a short trip to Paris for a few days. She discussed her upcoming performance tour of the US, and we worked out the dates when she was leaving and when she'd be getting back. She was going to be away for nearly four months. She was worried about leaving me, but I told her not to worry; there would always be the situation when we'd have to be away from each other and there was my eventual return to Australia to consider as well. We agreed to keep our relationship casual, without any ties on either of us but to always be truthful with each other. This conversation led to a discussion about the disparity in our ages, and I stated that I had no problems with her being nearly twenty years my senior. If she thought it was a problem, we'd talk it out, but considering she didn't have a problem with it, the matter was dropped.

The voyage to Scapa Flow was excellent, and the diving was great, but because of the water temperature, we had to dive in dry suits that are watertight suits and worn with a set of thermal underwear. On the day of our first dive, it was beautiful and sunny and the sea was flat and calm. We would be paired up with a navy diver as a guide because a lot of them had dived here before. As we moved down the ladder one by one, the first thing we did as we lowered ourselves into the water was a weight check to get our buoyancy right because with dry suits you don't need as much weight as you do with normal neoprene wetsuits. After bobbing around for a while on the surface, it was time to make the dive.

I slowly submerged ten feet under the surface. I turned on my dive torch to see where I was descending. The torch beam picked out a large, round, hollow piece of metal slightly encrusted with sea growth on the outer side. I felt my dive buddy tap me on the shoulder to get my attention, and he indicated for me to remove my air tank and push it in front of me as we went into the cylinder.

My first thought was, of course, are you friggin' insane or what? He was insistent, so I shrugged my shoulders and figured in for a penny, in for a pound. I undid the harness strap and pulled the tank over my head, keeping the mouthpiece in my mouth. I lay my torch alongside the scuba tank and curled myself into the cylinder, pushing the tank ahead of me. As I went down through the cylinder, I could see by the light from his torch that he was following me down, and soon the light from both torches showed an empty space. After emerging from the cylinder I realised I'd swam down the barrel of a gun into the firing turret that had three open ends. I started giggling in sheer joy of what I'd done. Man what a rush!

It had been the forward turret of one of the most famous battleships of recent history. The German battleship Scharnhorst, scrapped here at the end of World War II. For the rest of the dive, we explored the bridge and upper decks before it was time to surface, and truthfully, I didn't want to leave.

The days following that we were briefed on what ships we'd be diving, but nothing was like the experience of that first dive. It was the topic of conversation all that day and into the night in the officer's mess. John sat at the head of the table smiling, and after dinner, Eric and I expressed our thanks as much as we could.

After three weeks of diving the wrecks, it was time to head back. After a patrol of the outer islands, I reflected on our time at Scapa Flow with fondness and a bit of sadness as I reflected on all the recent history of both world wars that was lying in those waters rusting away, never to be seen in their glory ever again. I think I'll always remember those dives at Scapa with both sentiments; all that history wasted, and the world will never again see their like.

After that trip, things settled back into routine training. I took the opportunity to take Uncle Tony up on his offer and over time qualified with my rating to fly both Harrier Fighter Jump Jets and the huge Vulcan bombers that were the equivalent of the American B52 strike bombers that carried nuclear warheads as their destructive payloads.

Among many of my prouder moments, I would list taking part in the last around-the-world flight by the British Vulcan Bombers before they were decommissioned. The flight duration was eighty-four flying hours, with refuelling stops at Germany, Tokyo, Guam, Tindal in Australia, and Edwards Air Force Base in the US, before our return to Biggin Hill in the UK.

The team and I spent a lot of our remaining training time with Delta troop in frequent trips onto the European continent on exercise in all weather. The first time we went over, it was to Norway, where we learned to snow ski, and no, it's not the same as water-skiing, which we found out the hard way. However, one tends to learn after receiving multiple mouthfuls of snow, and eventually we became adept snow skiers.

I'd actually caught up with my cousin Robin, and the papers to transfer my title to him were drawn up. We had to present ourselves to the House of Lords for the transfer to be completed. After a couple of months, he would officially become the Earl of Straithhaven and take up that seat in the House of Lords.

Also during this time, I saw Petula from time to time, but my team had spent nearly two years in England and time was getting close for our return to Australia in May. During a leave period that I spent with Pet, she told me that on her last US tour, she'd met someone who'd shown a great deal of romantic interest in her, and she had reciprocated.

She was contemplating spending some time with him to see if things would develop further. So we discussed that now was a time to part and go our separate ways, which would enable us to part as good friends and not hold any ill will against each other.

However, because I wanted to do the right thing, I asked, "Would you like the car back?"

She looked at me with a loving smile and replied, "Of course not, darling. That was a present, and each time you drive it, you think of me with fondness."

"Pet, honey, I'll always think of you with fondness, especially when I play any of your records."

She laughed and smiled. "You're a treasure, Tom Davis, and I will always keep your bracelet to think of you. Now, let's get dressed and go out to the Muso one last time together."

The next morning, we said goodbye, and I drove out of her house for the last time.

When it was nearer the time to return to Australia, I made a trip down to see John and arranged to house my car at his place. I told him he could make use of it as long as he paid the warrant of fitness and kept it registered so that it was there should I ever return.

Two weeks later, we were given a case in which to lock our new assault weapons. We said our final goodbyes to Eric Wetherby and all the members of Delta troop. We were leaving with a lot of good memories, the new weapons, a dozen, of the new radio sets, and a lot of extra personal gear, so again our kitbags were bulging. A couple of years later, Eric's Delta troop were involved with the recovery of hostages and the killing and capture of terrorists in the Iranian consulate in London. They used the same techniques taught to them during that first exercise I had planned.

A couple of days later, we arrived at our home base of Swanbourne on Sunday May nine.

The next day, Howler would arrange a debriefing week, but first we had to write up reports of everything we'd been involved in, the training techniques used by the Brits, what we'd taught them, and some of the things we did while off duty. He gave us until Friday to complete the reports.

So after stowing all our new gear, we settled down to writing the reports. We'd all had the forethought to keep track of each day in diaries because this made our job so much easier, but even so it did take us most of the week to get them completed and ready to hand in.

The following week was taken up with questioning from other officers within the regiment on the different techniques used in Britain and going over our reports. All this was done in our own briefing room, so we really didn't have to go very far.

During that week the new regiment OC, Lt. Colonel Mike Jefferies, would sit in and only asked the occasional question until during one session that we had concerning the use of the new MP4's and actually showing some of the armourers our weapons we'd brought home. He picked one up, hefted it to see how much weight was in it, and went through some different combat stances with it, as if using it for real. He seemed impressed. "I'd like to see these in operation. Can we arrange that this afternoon?"

The armoury RSM replied, "Yes sir. Fourteen hundred at the range."

Jefferies nodded and said, "Good. I'll see you there."

That afternoon, all the MP4's and my MP4A were taken down to the firing range. Everyone was trying them out. This was my first opportunity to try the grenade tube, so I loaded the tube, and after calling "Fire in the hole," I launched the grenade. It fell bang on the target I'd picked. Most of the officers had a go and exhausted my bandolier of grenade rounds. The OC even fired a couple of rounds and announced his approval of the new weapons. He asked the RSM how long it would take to get some. He ordered that the MP4's remain in SRT possession, so we were able to keep our new rifles.

After that week, we went back to normal training, and I for one was glad to get back to running the beach. It was one of the things

I had missed most while in England.

In the last week of May, Howler told us we'd be put on stand down again and that we'd all be put on leave until Monday September six, then after a couple of weeks we'd be departing for Israel to work with the Mossad. The planning had already been done, but we were waiting to hear from the Israeli Government about who would be our liaison while we were there and how long we'd be expected to be there. I thought to myself, just great. From a cold place to a hot one. What the hell were they trying to do? The regiment had nothing for us to do and would rather we weren't in the country to avoid a repeat of another mission like the African affair.

So for once, I agreed, if that was the real reason behind shipping us off again. However, I didn't mind being placed on leave for another three months and gladly took my travel warrant into Wendy for the flight to Brisbane with another open end return. Again, I was able to travel first class.

After arriving in Brisbane in the morning, I grabbed a cab to take me home and set about opening the place up. I pottered about for a bit after changing into house clothes and unpacked. By about midday I had the car off the blocks I'd placed it on and replaced the battery. Naturally it was flat, so I set the charger on and left it for a couple of hours before trying to kick over the car again. Bingo, it fired first time, and I smiled as I listened to the quiet rumble of the exhaust.

Joanne from next door put in an appearance, and I invited her and John over when he got home for a few drinks. I also asked her if she knew any house cleaners. She did and asked how soon I'd like one to come and see me.

I jokingly said, "Yesterday would be fine."

She laughed and said she'd go ring someone she knew. She came back ten minutes later and told me that a woman named Lisa would be here in twenty minutes. I told her that was great and thanked her.

CHAPTER 30

Lisa arrived and asked what I required, so I gave her a quick rundown of my situation and that I'd only just returned from a two-year trip. She knew what to do, and it would probably take her an hour, maybe two. I asked if she'd be available on a weekly basis while I was home before my next away trip.

She laughed. "Oh yes, but let's talk about that when I'm finished. You never know; you might not like my work." I laughed, and let her get to work.

She finished just before John and Joanne turned up. I paid her fifty bucks even though she only charged thirty, and arranged for her to come every Wednesday. I told her that if I wasn't home that Joanne had a key to the house.

John and Joanne turned up and I asked if she'd like to stay for a few drinks, which she accepted. We were seated in the downstairs bar area, enjoying our drinks and conversation, before I asked if anyone would like some nibbles.

Lisa piped up. "How about I get them for you? I'm afraid I threw some of the stale stuff out while I was cleaning." I told her to go right ahead, and Joanne went with her to give her a hand.

While they were upstairs, I asked John, "So tell me. You both seem to know Lisa quite well. What's her story?"

He glanced up the stairs before responding. "Well she's too old for you. She's in her forties. Her husband was killed during a training exercise up at Shoalwater late last year, and her kids have all left home, which is fortunate in a way, because soon she has to move out of the married quarter she's in. You know what the system is like. To keep herself busy, she does the odd cleaning job for some extra money. She's a nice old girl. It's a shame she'll have to move out of where she is. I really don't know what she's going to do, or whether she has any plans as yet."

I nodded. "I've got something she could do in mind, but I'll have to talk to her."

He replied, "Get her half pissed and she might agree to anything." We both laughed.

When the women returned with some nibbles, we continued our socialising session. I was asked about the trip to England, and I told them what I'd done while I was there, about using my family influence to get a few things done, and what Northern Ireland was like. I skilfully turned talk around to Lisa's situation, and we found out that she really didn't have a clue in regards to what she was going to do when she had to move out of the house.

So I came up with an alternative for her and sounded her out about what I had in mind. "Lisa, you are aware of my situation. Sometimes I'm here but more often not, so if you wish, you could put whatever you wish to keep into storage and move into one of the bedrooms here. You won't have to pay rent. All I ask is that you keep the place tidy and clean and you look after the place whenever I'm not here. No need to give me an answer straight away. You think it over and let me know what you decide later."

John and Joanne told her it was a great idea. We had a few more drinks, and we all getting fairly merry and hungry. John suggested we order a couple of pizzas, and I asked what he was talking about. He told me the new Pizza Hut had opened down at Arana Hills and they now delivered. All this had happened while I was away, but I thought that it was a brilliant idea. He used the phone in the bar to order a couple of pizzas. It was expensive but certainly better than trying to drive, so forty minutes later we were tucking into some really good pizzas as we continued our socialising.

By the end of the evening, Lisa was not only half shot, but really pissed, so I made her give me her car keys and told her to use one of the bedrooms upstairs for the night. After saying goodnight to John and Joanne, I started cleaning up before going to bed myself.

I got up early, and after a cuppa and a smoke, finished cleaning up from the night before. About eightish, Lisa came out to the back veranda where I was sitting and contemplating the day. "Good morning."

I returned her greeting and asked, "How are you feeling?"

"Dreadful. I haven't drunk that much in a long time. Can I use the shower?"

"Of course you can. I think there are towels in there, and after you freshen up, I'll make you a coffee," I offered.

"Thank you," she replied.

While she was in the shower, I made us breakfast of scrambled eggs and toast and was making the coffee as she walked into the kitchen.

She sat as I finished making the coffee and served up the breakfast. We talked about the previous night as I handed her the car keys she'd given me. I winked at her and said, "Just in case you need them."

"Thank you, and for the lovely breakfast as well. What did you put in the eggs? They were delicious."

I smiled. "My secret. I don't like things bland, so I spice them up a bit."

"Oh, well they were very tasty," she replied. She cleared her throat and asked, "Can we speak about the offer you me made last night before I got too tipsy?"

I replied, "Sure. What would you like to know?"

We talked everything through, and she said, "So in other words, I'd be an unpaid, live-in housekeeper, but I wouldn't pay any rent?"

I nodded. "Yep, but if you need to prove that you do pay rent, we can always fudge that with dummy receipts. Still, think it over. I don't wish to ruin your reputation by having you move in."

She laughed and replied, "Oh that wouldn't be an issue. I'm at least twenty years older than you."

Now it was my turn to laugh as I told her the ages of some

of the women I'd slept with. We had a great laugh, and she said, "That won't happen anyway. I'm not looking for a lover just yet, but watch out if I do. I might pick on you."

Later that day, I decided to ring Darlene, but the phone wasn't connected. I drove over to where she and her housemate lived, and the doorbell was answered by a female stranger who told me they'd both moved out over a year ago without leaving a forwarding address. After thanking her, I apologised for disturbing her, climbed back into the car, and drove home.

When I got home again, I sat down and rested for a while. I decided to relax a bit in the spa, so I made a coffee and oozed myself into the spa pool. I slowly drank the coffee as I contemplated what I would do while on leave. One of the thoughts I had was to get something done in regards to getting another grant from army housing for another war service home before the grant expired. I thought of what to do with another house and decided I could rent it out and make a tidy profit on it.

After an hour in the spa, I phoned army housing at Enoggera and spoke to the female sergeant I'd dealt with before. She told me I only had another six months before the grant expired and that I would be eligible to receive one hundred and thirty-five thousand, fifteen of which would be paid separately as a furniture allowance. I asked her to start the paperwork.

The next thing I had to do was decide where to buy, so I walked up to the shops and bought a paper, mainly to look at the real estate section. In it were a couple of articles that reviewed Stafford as an up and coming suburb because of the planned large shopping centre given the approval by council. After reading both articles, I decided that would be my starting point. The guide also listed a couple of real estate offices in the area, so I rang one to see what was available. For the next month I went house hunting again.

As usual, I had no idea what I wanted until I saw it, but after three weeks, I finally found one that appealed. A double story brick with a three car garage on the side of a hill with a reasonable view of the city area. It was only about five minutes' walk from a set of shops, had a pool but no spa, although there was plenty of room to place one downstairs near the laundry area. There was also a large room at the bottom of the stairs that would make a perfect bar and games room. Upstairs were four bedrooms with the master having an ensuite, lounge and kitchen and a back balcony. With a bit of dickering, the agent and I came up with a deal that would mean he would give me a cheque for fifteen grand, which would cover the cost of a spa and installation, after the army issued him a cheque for the sale of the house.

The following day, I drove to the housing department office and collected two cheques, one for the house sale and the other made out to me for fifteen thousand to cover the cost of furniture because I'd bought the house for less than the grant available. I went to the agent and we exchanged cheques, and the paperwork was filled out. Thirty days later I'd receive the deed to the house, and it would be mine.

Feeling rather pleased with myself, I deposited the cheques into my account and drove home, grabbed my golf clubs, and went to the Keperra course and had a hit. As I walked the course, I did some thinking over what to do next, and considering I still had nearly two months left of my leave, I contemplated driving north for a bit of a look around.

During dinner that night, I told Lisa what I had in mind. She had decided to accept my offer and had moved in while I'd been doing my house hunting. She gave me a couple suggestions of places to visit that were worth seeing, and after packing my go bag and golf clubs, I drove north after breakfast. I had decided to drive straight through to Cairns first and make my way south slowly.

It was getting on toward dark as I neared Rockhampton, but I wasn't going to stay the night there. I pushed on and grabbed a room at a motel just outside Marlborough because I had no wish to make the next stage up the range in the dark. Too many people had come to grief on that stretch at night.

I made Cairns in the failing light of the next evening and booked into a hotel in the centre of town not far from the marina. I stayed for three days doing the touristy thing, and after a game of golf in the morning of the fourth day, I continued driving south. After arriving in Townsville, I took the car ferry across to Magnetic Island and stayed there for a couple of days before moving on. In Bowen I found a nice golf club at Queens Beach and stayed overnight there.

That's how I made my way back south. The only place I did avoid was Rockhampton. I arrived in Brisbane after four weeks and got down to the business of renting out my new home at Stafford. I went to the agent that had sold me the house and worked out that if he was the agent it would only cost me ten percent of the weekly rent amount with quarterly inspections carried out. We worked out how much bond would be paid and any restrictions I wanted to place on it. He also advised me to open a separate account where he would deposit the rental fee each week after deducting his ten percent, so I went up the road to the bank and arranged the new account. I returned to him with the deposit details, and after all that we agreed on a twelve-month tenancy that could be renewed if the tenants were suitable. Two weeks later he let me know that he'd found a couple to rent the house at two hundred a week, which I thought was rather good.

At the end of that week I started making preparations to return to Western Australia by booking an overnight flight that would put me in Perth the morning of Saturday the fourth. During the weekend prior to my return, I put the car back on blocks again, and Lisa assured me that she'd kick it over every day, so I left the battery connected. She volunteered to drive me anywhere I needed to go after the car was on blocks and also told me she'd drive me to the airport, which I thought was very good of her.

Friday night after we had a good dinner, I had a shower and changed into my uniform pants and was strapping my shoulder holster on when Lisa called me from the lounge room.

When I reached the lounge, she said, "You may need that gun you're wearing. Israel has just gone to war with Syria in a place called the Golan Heights. It was just on the news."

"Oh great, back into another warzone. I must have really kicked the shit out of a Chinaman in a previous life, and this is karma coming back to bite me." We laughed. "Well, I'll probably know all about it after I get back to base. Hopefully it's just a minor squabble."

I returned to my room to continue dressing, and after packing last minute items into my go bag, returned to the lounge with it. "Ok Lisa, if you're ready, you can take me to the airport. That way you'll be home before it gets too late."

"But you've still got a couple of hours yet. Are you sure?"

I nodded my head. "Yeah. I'll kill some time by having a couple of drinks in the lounge, and you won't be out too late."

"Ok, I'll just get my keys," she replied. At the airport, she said, "You take care of yourself. The house will still be there and ready for when you come home."

After I arrived on base the next morning, I informed the duty officer that I was back and would be in my quarters. Tag was back already, and together we ended up going over to SRT and getting the battery pack to jumpstart my car. I let Tag drive the battery pack back to SRT in my car. Once he came back to the quarters, he told me he'd left the car running so I could turn it off later. We arranged to go for a game of golf early the next morning, so our clubs were put into the car before I shut it down. Thankfully we didn't have a problem with the car starting in the morning, and we were the first ones off the tee. We both had a good game.

The next morning, the team were in the ready room. Howler walked in and informed us he wanted to run through an informal briefing on our upcoming deployment. "Since it's informal, we may as well do it here. Can someone make me a coffee, please? Now, you've probably all seen that Israel and Syria have started fighting again, but from what I've been told, it's just about over.

It was just a bit of sabre rattling over a territorial movement, so there's nothing to be worried about. Not that you blokes can't handle yourselves."

He continued after taking a sip of his coffee. "The reason you were placed on leave is because we were killing time until a normal yearly meeting takes place between our Foreign Minister and the Minister in Charge of Defence Strategy for Israel. He flew into Sydney this morning and is scheduled to land at Pearce in two weeks. The reason he's flying here is to pick you guys up and return to Israel, so gentlemen, you're on the clock and counting down. After your deployment, you'll be returning the same way. That's it in a nutshell, of course. I'll keep you up to date, but start getting your gear together. There is one last thing you need to know. Only one person knows your real rank in Israel and that's the minister himself. As far as everyone else is concerned, you use your US ranks, so break out your rank pins again."

Howler asked me to join him in my office after he finished the rest of his coffee. He asked me to shut the door as he sat down, and I took my seat behind the desk and waited for him to let me know what he wanted.

"There's no easy way to say this, Tiger, but when you get back from this one, I'm not going to be here. My posting is up at the start of next year, and I'm moving on to the commandos in Sydney. The new CO will be a major since they've had me doing this job, so it's no more captains, I'm afraid. I will let the newcomer know about you and the team, so there's no worries on that score."

That was not really news I wanted to hear, but nothing can be considered permanent in the army. Just when we get one person used to us, he's moved and we have to start all over again. I let the rest know what he'd told me later in the day, and they weren't too happy either.

During that week, we prepared our gear together and organized any uniform replacements or gear replacement and ammunition. Most mornings we would be either in the gym working out or running the beach, sometimes both. The clock was indeed winding down, and before too long it was Wednesday of the week we were due to fly out. That morning, Howler had seen me in the mess at breakfast and wanted a full briefing session at nine. As he walked in, we were all waiting, and after being waved to our seats, he started.

"Good morning gentlemen. The minister, Mr. Joseph Ben Aram, will be landing at Pearce at zero eight hundred. He will come here before going onto his hotel. He wishes to meet you here at SRT, in your own element so to speak, so make sure the place is clean, huh?" Laughter erupted. "Dress in your usual clobber but wear your rank pins. The flight out will be wheels up at zero nine hundred Friday. You can wear civvies on the flight, but usual SOP's with handguns. Your transport will arrive here at zero eight hundred, and please make sure your weapons are boxed. The truck will pull up directly to the plane for easier loading of your equipment; however, take your kitbags aboard with you. There will be an overnight stay in Singapore. Any questions so far?"

Dumper raised his hand. "Our combat webbing, sir?"

Howler smiled. "Good point, Dumper. All your combat gear and any ammo you're taking is to be boxed. The only weapons you carry on board are your handguns, which brings me to a point. I hope you've boxed the MP4s as your long arms. That way they can't disappear while you're away. Gentlemen, be prepared to be away the same amount of time, if not longer, then your previous deployment, and since come Friday this is my last time to see you, I would like to say what a privilege and honour it has been to serve as your CO. I wish you every luck in the future. Thank you."

As he finished, we stood and applauded. One by one we filed out after shaking his hand and having a few words. I was the last to leave the briefing room, and it was my job to make sure Howler came with me into the ready room, where he was greeted with a glass of Blue label and cheers.

Tag proposed a toast. "Boss, we know this is the last time we could see you alone before we deploy, and anytime we see you now will be official. Our last CO was changed without us knowing, while we were OS, and we couldn't say goodbye properly. So this time we do. We also consider it an honour and privilege to serve with you. To you, sir, Major Howler Hallorhan."

Howler answered the toast. "Thank you, Tag, and all of you. My time with you guys has been a pleasure. To SRT." We all drank and he continued. "I'll have only the one. I've got the rest of the day to get through, and you blokes need to get your last minute stuff done. Thank you all."

By the end of the day, everyone had boxed up the MP4s and our combat gear and the ammo. Everything was ready to load onto the truck come Friday morning. I stood down the team for the day early so they could get their personal gear ready and kitbags partially packed except for last minute items.

The next morning, I was in the office after leaving the mess, and after opening up, I went into my office and pulled my colonel's rank pins out of the desk drawer and put them on. I then went into the ready room to tidy up a bit. Tag joined me, and after filling the water urn, he turned it on to warm up as everyone started to arrive. Tag assigned them clean up tasks for the building, and after we'd finished in the ready room, we started on our own offices. After a final sweep, the place was ready.

At zero nine twenty, I received a call from Howler to let me know that the minister and his entourage were headed my way with the OC. He was following them up. I called the gang together in the ready room, and leaving Tag to get them lined up, I went out to the veranda to greet the visitors. I could see them walking up the road from HQ.

As the OC arrived at the building, I walked down the stairs and saluted him. He returned the salute and said, "Tiger, I'd like to introduce you to Minister Ben Aram."

I turned, saluted, and offered my hand, which he shook. He introduced his aides. "My secretary, Joshua, and this is my daughter, Captain Shari Ben Aram. She is your liaison officer, Colonel."

She wore a dress uniform complete with Sam Brown belt

and officer's cap with jet black hair poking from beneath it. She sported an Israeli Star of David, but one could definitely see she was a female, and the belt only empathized that fact. As Shari and I made eye contact, I could see she had mixed hazel and green eyes.

The electricity between us could almost be seen, and I felt a physical jolt. Based on her reactions, she was aware of the jolt as well. She dropped her gaze without saying anything. I said, "Glad to meet you, Captain. I look forward to working with you."

She raised her blushed face and falteringly said, "Thank you, Colonel. I look forward to it as well, and perhaps we can talk on the plane tomorrow."

Her father looked first at her, and then at me. He and I smiled as I replied, "I'd like that very much, Captain. Shall we?"

I swept my arm towards the stairs for everyone. The OC led the way and waited on the veranda for me to join them. As I did I took off my cap. "Everyone's in the ready room, folks. If you'll follow me."

I entered the hall and called "Atten…shun!"

The members of the team were standing in a line at attention, with Tag on the end nearest me. I moved forward to make the introductions and noticed that the OC, Shari and Joshua had moved to stand at the opposite wall so that it was only the minister I was introducing.

"Gentlemen, Minister Ben Aram from Israel. Sir, this is Captain Tag Wilson, my second in command, Captain Dumper Marsh…" I introduced each member, and the minister greeted them and shook their hands.

After the introductions had concluded, he addressed them. "Thank you very much, gentlemen. I'll introduce my staff. The first is Joshua, my secretary, and the Captain is my daughter, Shari. If you'll join us, I think the colonel wishes us to inspect the building and no doubt you'll be able to tell me a little of what goes on here. Shall we, Colonel?"

He moved to my side, I nodded to Tag, and he stepped forward to lead the way. "If you'll follow me."

I lagged behind to talk to the OC. "How long are they here, sir?"

"They're only supposed to be here for a quick in and out, but they've been here half an hour already. Ah, here comes Howler."

Howler joined us as we moved to the end of the tour. In the gunroom, Shari was asking about the rifles in the rack and why we hadn't packed them. I stepped forward to answer. "Those rifles have been replaced with the newer MP4s, which are packed and ready to go along with our other machine pistols. They are in those two boxes you would have seen in the hallway. We don't go anywhere without out handguns, though. We'll be carrying them on our person on the plane. The last place we used those rifles were in Africa, Captain. Shall we move on, Tag?"

He took them to the workroom and more questions followed from Shari and her father, so I let the team members answer the questions. Shari asked about the sniper rifle Lizard had brought back from England that was sitting in clamps on his bench set up to work on it. She seemed impressed after he told her of the rifle's history.

"So how far away from a target can you hit one, Lizard?" she asked curiously.

He smiled and replied, "I head shot a VC soldier once from two kilometres out, but Gecko could always beat me." He fell silent when he heard the groans. "Sorry guys." He'd broken the unwritten rule of never talking about a fallen comrade to outsiders.

"Has my daughter asked something wrong, gentlemen?" the minister asked, his concern clear.

"No sir. Perhaps it would be better if I explain it to you both tomorrow on the plane."

He nodded and replied, "The last thing I wish to do is cause offence, but could you please explain this to us now?"

I sighed. "Very well sir." I told them about Gecko and how he and his family met their end. "We have an unwritten rule never to discuss fallen friends with anyone outside the regiment, but I think Lizard got carried away with his enthusiasm, so he's not to be blamed."

Shari stepped forward after I'd finished. "I'm very sorry to be the cause of further pain to you all, and I humbly apologise. I hope I can be forgiven."

Dumper piped up. "That's all right, sir...ma'am. We shake things off quickly." His stumble over gender caused smiles and laughter, and the incident was quickly forgotten.

After the tour was over, everyone gathered back in the ready room and had drinks and biscuits and some socialising. I didn't have a chance to talk to Shari but consoled myself with the fact that we'd be in close proximity the next day and would have our chance then.

As he left, the minister addressed us. "Gentlemen, I wish to thank you for your hospitality. We look forward to travelling with you tomorrow. Shalom."

"Shalom," we returned, and they made their way out with the OC and Howler.

CHAPTER 31

The following morning the truck arrived on time, and as it was being loaded with our gear, Howler came to say goodbye. We saluted and shook hands with him before the boys got into the truck and I hopped into the shotgun seat for the trip to Pearce. Once there, I instructed the driver to reverse up to the rear cargo door that was open with a couple of the plane's crew waiting to transfer our gear into the cargo area. Our kitbags were unloaded as well, and the driver make his way back to base. When the minister arrived, we were standing in line at the foot of the stairs beside our bags dressed in civilian gear wearing our guns. We greeted the minister with "Shalom," which was returned, and after Joshua, Shari, and he climbed the stairs to the plane, we followed.

It was a large jet with plenty of interior space. What would normally be business and first class had been turned into two offices with day bed couches, and a room near the toilets had been converted into a smaller room equipped with a desk. The minister was in one of the offices and Shari in the other, while Joshua made his way into the smaller room. Forward of that was the flight deck and crew quarters.

As we entered through the galley area, we were shown to the middle section that had two wide seats on each side of the plane, and after twenty rows of seats was a baggage area in front of three toilets and shower cubicles on each side of the plane. No one else was aboard, so we were able to choose our seats; I sat in the front row on the port side of the plane while Tag chose the other side. I discovered that the seats were fully reclinable, which was great because we could stretch out and sleep if we wished.

After we had taken off and were at cruising height, one of the staff, a young female corporal, asked if I could spare Captain Ben Aram some time in her office. I nodded and rose to follow her.

The corporal knocked, opened the door, and announced, "Colonel Davis, ma'am."

"Ah Colonel, please take a seat. Drink?" she asked as I walked in.

"Yes please. Scotch straight up, if you have any, thanks." She poured some Glenmorangie into a tumbler, passed it over, and asked if I wanted ice. "One cube, if you don't mind."

She poured something into a glass with ice for herself and sat down at the opposite end of the couch from me. She lifted her glass and said, "Loachim."

I had a sip of the scotch. She started blushing when our eyes met, and she must have felt herself doing it because she looked down at the carpet as she said, "Colonel, I've asked you here on a personal matter. I have very strange reactions within myself every time I look at you."

I interrupted her. "Make it Tiger, or Tom. Forget the colonel when we're alone if you like. And about what you were saying, do you mean like the blushing that you're experiencing right now?"

She lifted her head. "Yes. How did you know?"

I ignored her question and continued, "The first time you saw me, you experienced a sort of physical jolt, like electricity was passing right through you?"

"Yes, as if flowers were dancing before my eyes and bells were tinkling. How did you know?"

"Because I felt the same thing, except for the flowers and bells. I've been trying to make heads or tails of it ever since. That, and I haven't been able to stop thinking about you."

"I'm the same. What do you think it is? Because I think I know."

"Oh? Tell me what you think it is."

She fiddled with her drink before looking at me. She drained her drink before speaking. "This may sound a little weird, but here goes. I hope you won't laugh at me. I think it's a way that someone or something is telling us we should be together." She paused and smiled. "I just heard the bells again, as I said that"

I stared at her with my mouth open, and then shivered. "Yeah. So did I. And no, I would never laugh at you. With you, but not at you. How about you tell me about yourself while we try to figure this out?"

She replied with a smile, "Yes ok, but first would you like a refill?"

"Yes please." I drained my glass.

She refilled our drinks and sat beside me. "Let's see, where do I start? My father used to be the director of Mossad before he began overseeing all military actions. My mother's name is Marta, and everyone tells me I look like her, but I'm half an inch taller than her.

She's only five four, where I'm five four and a half." I smiled. She continued. "No really, that half inch is a big difference. Like all Israeli children, my brother Dov and I went into military training at sixteen, and we both stayed in. He went into armour while I chose the infantry, but I was a couple of years behind him."

She paused to have a drink. "During the Yom Kippur war in seventy-three, he was killed when his tank blew up in the Sinai. I didn't know about it until afterward because I was fighting on the Golan Heights against the Syrians. That's where I earned my promotions from sergeant to lieutenant to captain, and I've since been transferred to my father's office when he took over command as a minister." She paused again to think, touching her finger to her mouth. "Let's see, what have I missed? Oh, yes. I have apartments in Tel Aviv and Megiddo, which is up near where we'll be going in the Jezreel Valley, not far from my father's house. I'm twenty-one, or will be on my birthday next year, which is the twentieth of June?" At her last statement, I almost spat out the sip of scotch I'd taken and nearly choked.

Shari patted my back as I coughed to clear my airway, and asked if I was all right. She held onto my arm, her hand resting on my back between my shoulder blades. I nodded and replied,

"Yeah I'm fine, sweetheart. I did not expect that statement about your birthday. Mine is the same day."

She looked dumbfounded. She pulled my upper body back against the couch with the arm that had been resting between my shoulder blades and left it resting on my shoulders. If anyone had seen us they would have assumed she had her arms around me, which I guess she did because her other hand had not let go of my arm.

She laughed and said, "I've told you mine. It's your turn now, Tom."

I gave a little laugh and stayed there snuggled in her arms. Even though I didn't want the moment to end, I said, "Sure, but let's have another drink first.

When Shari came back with the drinks, she put them very close together and near the edge of the coffee table. She sat really close to me, and grabbed my arm and draped it over her shoulders, which left my right hand just above the curve of her right breast. I gave her a complete account of my life from what I'd done to the present, including my affair with Jill, how I had entered the army in the first place, and some of the missions I'd taken part in and planned. Why I did this is beyond me!

I felt that I could trust her with my life and wanted to be completely honest with her, because even though we hadn't even kissed, I was falling in love with her. It seemed as if it was right, and I think she felt the same way because while I'd been telling her my story, I'd been absent-mindedly stroking her breast. She hadn't tried to stop me.

"So here I am at twenty-three, a Warrant Officer in the Australian Army, a Major in the British, and a Colonel in the US." I took a drink before continuing. "And I'm with a beautiful Israeli Captain in my arms, with whom I'm starting to fall in love. That may sound silly, but it seems right to me somehow."

She reached up to turn my face toward her and tentatively kissed me. The kiss grew more intense. As she twisted around,

401

we were kissing each other hungrily, as if we couldn't get enough of each other.

We eventually came up for air. We stared at each other, amazed at what had taken place. She stood and straightened herself and went to make another round of drinks. "Tom, I find it hard to keep my hands off you over there. Can we sit at the desk, please?"

I nodded, sighed, and answered, "Sure honey, but we need to talk this over and figure out what we're going to do about it. I hope you feel the same way I do?"

In answer she put her arms around my neck and pressed herself into my body as she kissed me. "I think you could interpret that as a yes, my dear."

When we were seated at the desk, we discussed how we were going to manage our attraction for each other, and we decided to act as if it had happened over a period of a couple weeks as far as her family were concerned. Though, we would try to spend most of our off duty time with each other.

A knock on the door sounded, and her father walked in. She and I smiled at each other as we both thought how the timing of our move from the couch to the desk was extremely fortuitous. If we'd still been there, we'd have been properly sprung.

"Oh I'm sorry, Shari, Colonel. You're busy, I see. I can come back later," her father said as he turned to leave.

I stood and said, "No need, sir. I was just about to leave. Please call me Tom or Tiger, sir. Shari, let's take this up later, after lunch perhaps?"

She smiled professionally and answered, "Yes, that would be fine, Tiger. Thank you."

I moved towards the door. "She's all yours, sir. Would you like me to shut the door?"

"Yes please, Tiger," he replied.

I made my way back to my seat, and Tag looked at me with an enquiring gaze. "Just getting to know each other," I explained.

He laughed. "So that's what you call it. I suppose the lipstick on your cheek is a new type of cam cream?"

I sprang up and went to the toilet to look in the mirror, and sure enough there was a lipstick smear on my cheek. Shit! Her father couldn't have missed it. When I went back to see her, I'd have to tell her the cat was out of the bag, I thought as I washed off the lipstick. I returned to my seat, and Tag just chuckled.

Soon after, we were served lunch by one of the staff, and it was an excellent veal schnitzel with chips, veg and gravy, followed by lemon cheesecake and ice cream. I had just finished my coffee when Shari sent her messenger to me again, requesting another interview. I nodded and smiled at Tag as I pointed forward; he shook his head and chuckled.

After the door was closed, Shari rushed across to me and we shared a long embrace and kiss. When our lips parted, I said, "You're going to have to stop wearing lipstick when we're together, honey. Tag noticed it on my cheek when I went back, so unless your father is blind, he probably saw it too."

She sighed and nodded her head. "Oh yes, he saw it, and we had a bit of an argument about me throwing myself at you, and that you were a goy who would take advantage of me, and then leave. Eventually I was able to talk him round to letting me live my life in my own way, rather than his way. I told him we were in love with each other, so finally he relented and said he would reserve his judgement. But he told me that if we continued to see each other, we would have to be discreet."

I nodded as I thought over what she'd told me. I smiled at her and said, "Of course. I'm a guy by the way."

She started laughing. "I said goy, not guy, my darling. A goy is a non-Jewish person. I think I'll have to start teaching you Hebrew."

I smiled and nodded my head. "Yeah, I guess so. Back to your father, I think I might have a word with him about us. Do you think it might help clear the air?"

"What would you say?"

"I'd just tell him the truth. That we were instantly drawn to each other and how we feel about each other."

She thought it over. "Ok, but be careful if he gets angry. Don't forget before being the director of Mossad, he was an agent and can be deadly. Please tread carefully with him, my love. When are you going to see him?"

I smiled, scooped her into my arms, and we shared a long kiss. "Now's as good a time as any. Any lipstick?" I asked, moving my head from side to side.

Shari laughed. "I didn't have any on, darling."

I left her office and knocked on the minister's office door before opening it. Ben Aram was sitting at his desk reading something. I asked, "Do you have a few minutes to talk, sir?"

He looked up. "Yes, yes, come in, Tiger. Please take a seat." I closed the door and went to sit opposite him at the desk. He quickly finished reading the folder he was holding, put it down, and asked, "What would you like to talk to me about, Tiger? And call me Joseph, please."

"Well Joseph, I would like to talk about Shari."

He faced me square on, and his eyes bored into mine. His voice had hardened. "Go on."

"I have a bit of a dilemma. I think Shari would be an excellent liaison officer, but I've fallen in love with your daughter, sir. I know this sounds crazy. After all, we've only just met. However, when we did meet it was like a jolt of electricity had gone through me, and I wasn't the only one to feel it. She did as well, and since then, we have been trying to work out these very strong feelings we have about each other. It's a feeling that we're meant to be together, and truthfully, I really can't bear to be without her. When we are apart, we're thinking of the other, and it feels right to be together. I wanted to let you know how we felt about each other."

He remained calm but seemed cold. "You said you had a dilemma. Let's hear it."

I continued looking him in the eye and said, "The dilemma is this. I would like Shari to remain our liaison, but I know she's your daughter and you're also our boss. We would like time to sort this out ourselves, and if things work out, then I've got some hard decisions to make. If they don't, I'm only here for a limited time."

"And if I forbade it, would you still try to see each other?"

"It would probably be hard for Shari, but yes, we probably would every chance we got."

He thought for a minute. "Tiger, I must say I like your truthful manner, but you're also asking me for my blessing in this matter..."

I interrupted him sharply, "No sir!"

My interruption and answer seemed to shock him, and he said, "I'll continue with what I was saying in a minute, but first tell me why you don't want my blessing?"

"It's not your blessing I'm after, sir. I only wish to have you understand what we are going through and the time to let us work it out for ourselves. I don't think it is too much to ask for, but to actually get your blessing may be a little too much for us to hope for."

He sat back; his gaze lifted from my face to go around the room. Then he leaned back, thinking for a few minutes with his hands covering his eyes. He dropped his hands and said, "Be so kind as to go and get Shari and bring her in here, please."

"Yes sir." I got up and left his office to go into Shari's. She was pacing up and down as I entered.

"How did it go?"

"I'm not sure, but he wants us both to go in there together."

"Ok darling. Kiss for luck." We shared a quick embrace and kiss before she smoothed down her clothes and nodded she was ready. I opened the door and held it for her to exit.

We entered Joseph's office, where we were directed to sit. He looked at us with his piercing eyes. To Shari, he said, "I have read this man's dossier. Are you aware that while he was in South East

Asia, the North Vietnamese placed a bounty of half a million US dollars on his head? That's the type of man you are, or are not falling in love with!"

"No, I wasn't aware."

"Neither was I," I added, surprised.

"But that makes no difference. He is a soldier, and he is also Special Forces, and that makes him the equal of any Mossad agent."

"Papa, you would not have asked for him and his men otherwise."

Joseph leaned back with a laugh. "Your tongue is as sharp as your mother's, Shari. Tell me how you felt when you saw this man for the first time."

Shari smiled warmly at her father. "Oh papa, it was wonderful…" She told him of the feelings and the jolt. "And then I found out he felt the same, and we have some things in common, but I want to explore what we have between us."

He asked her the same question he'd asked me. "If I forbade it, would you still see him?"

She answered instantly. "Yes father."

Joseph leaned back and gazed around the room for a few minutes. He leaned forward again with his arms on the desk and said quietly, "Children, children, let me tell you something only one other person knows. The feelings you both had when you met are very much like the feelings that Marta and I felt when we first met so long ago. So I'm going to give you my blessing and hope to god it turns out right. But this must not interfere in any way with your jobs. Is that understood?"

He came out from his desk and Shari embraced him with a smile. I rose from my chair, slightly flabbergasted. He leaned towards me and shook my hand, a smile of his face.

"Thank you, sir," I said to him.

He waved his finger at me and said, "Remember its Joseph, not sir!"

Shari, her arms around his neck, chided him. "Oh Papa." She turned and flung herself into my arms.

"Now children, please heed my advice. Keep your love for each other under wraps. Be discreet. Remember, you're the daughter and hopefully soon to be the son in law of a government minister, but I won't push you on that issue, Tom, I promise. Now you two go and enjoy yourselves, and leave an old man in peace." He joked, "Be careful of the lipstick."

We left his office and went back to Shari's, where she threw me on the couch and started smothering me in kisses. The smile wouldn't leave my face.

I stayed with her for the rest of the flight into Singapore, which wasn't all that long. After we landed, I had to straighten my shirt over my pistol because we'd spent that time in each other's arms on the couch. I went back to grab my kitbag from where we'd stored them, and once all of us had cleared customs and had our weapon permits checked, the entire group was transferred to our hotel in two limousines. Our rooms were on the same floor; mine was across from Shari's. After winking at each other, we went into our respective rooms to shower and change prior to going back down to the hotel restaurant for dinner. Shari joined my men and I, while Joseph and Joshua ate at a separate table.

Due to an early morning departure at zero eight hundred, most of us went up to our rooms to get some sleep immediately after dinner. Shari went into her own room, but I soon heard a quiet knock on my door. I opened the door, and Shari slipped in past me dressed in a bathrobe. She moved into my arms, and I untied the cloth belt holding it fastened. Underneath she was completely naked, and I drank in the sight of her perfectly formed body and breasts. I noted that her pubic hair had been shaved.

Surprised, I said, "You'll have to wear more of this night attire. I like it."

She giggled and moved into my arms. "Only for you, my darling," she whispered as we began a long kiss. I bent and picked her up, my mouth still on hers, and moved toward the bed. I'd already thrown back the covers, so I gently lowered her on to it with our lips locked together.

She paused her kiss long enough to whisper, "Take that robe off and come to me."

That night we made love for the first time, and even for a frequent campaigner at lovemaking myself, because of my emotional tie to Shari, my efforts reached new heights. After nearly two hours of bliss, we were sated and spent. We lay together with beads of perspiration dripping off us onto the sheets.

Finally, able to speak, Shari said, "My god. I've never had that sort of experience. I lost count of the times I climaxed after twenty. How was it for you, my darling?"

I honestly replied, "That's the best I've ever had, and definitely better than freefall."

"I'm so glad, my darling. I thought I might not be good enough for you because I don't have much experience at all, but what we did was so divine. Just think, anytime we're alone you can have me whenever you wish."

I chuckled and replied, "Does that mean tomorrow on the plane as well?"

She started giggling. "Oh yes, but you'll have to gag me? Otherwise the whole plane will know what we're doing."

"Hmm, yeah that could be a problem. Do you think we could give your father earmuffs?"

She laughed. "In that case, we'd have to give them to everybody. No, it's either gag me or we'll have to wait. But let's see how we go."

"Ok, but we'd better get some sleep. I hope you're staying with me," I replied.

"Of course. Now's as good a time as any to start sleeping with you, my love."

I woke at five; Shari was still wrapped in my arms. I tried slowly to extricate myself, but she woke and asked the time. I told her, so she unhurriedly got up and said, "I'd better get back to my room and get ready for breakfast, darling, but I don't want to leave you just yet."

I smiled and spanked her bum. "Go on, get going. I'll come and get you for breakfast. And honey, I did enjoy sleeping with you. Got your key?" I opened the door and looked out. "Go." I kept watch as she scuttled by me and into her room.

I had a shower and made a coffee, which I had with a smoke. I put on my holster, took the gun out from under the pillow, and placed it into the holster before putting on a clean shirt. At six I knocked on Tag's door. He said he'd already roused the team while I was in the shower, so I told him I would rouse Shari and head down to breakfast.

As I knocked on Shari's door, the guys went past headed to the lift. Shari pulled me into the room, put her arms around me and we kissed passionately. Hand in hand we headed to the lift and restaurant for breakfast.

In the restaurant, Joseph was sitting alone, so Shari and I joined him. She flung her arms around his neck from behind and said, "Good morning, Papa."

"Shalom, Joseph. Do you mind if we join you?"

"Shalom, Tiger. Please do."

I looked at the menu. I figured bacon was out unless I wanted to insult my host, so settled on eggs benedict with tomato and beef sausages. Shari had the same, but Joseph ordered bacon and eggs. I looked at him dumbfounded.

He laughed. "Hey, when away from home, I eat what I like? Just because I'm Jewish doesn't mean I can't eat bacon when I'm away. I like it. And you, little girl, you're not to tell your mama." When the breakfasts came, I laughed as he tucked into the bacon and moaned in ecstasy.

After breakfast, we went back to our rooms, collected last minute items, packed our bags, and went down to reception. I was carrying my bag as well as Shari's, and the guys were all smiles as they saw me coming.

"What?"

Dumper laughed and said, "Nothing boss."

I was to join Joseph and Shari in the lead limo, while the guys travelled in the second. Joshua had left earlier to have the plane ready and to have our path cleared through customs.

At the airport, we were able to walk through customs and immigration. We got our passports stamped and were shown through a passageway that led to the plane stairs. My guys were the first to climb the steps, and as Tag moved past me I asked him to take my bag and stow it as well. I followed them, with Shari behind me and then Joseph. As I reached the plane, I went forward to Shari's office and placed her bag on the coffee table. I kissed her on the way out.

As I reached our compartment, Joseph was saying, "Shalom, gentlemen." The men responded he continued. "The flight today will be a short one, only ten hours. We will land at Lod air base, which really is an extension of the Ben Gurion International Airport in Tel Aviv, our capitol. There will be transport to take you to your hotel, the King David, where I have suites reserved for all of you. Over the next couple of days, you'll be shown around and be briefed at the Defence Force headquarters building. My daughter will tell you what will happen each day. Now, if you aren't aware, Shari has taken a liking to your Colonel Davis and no doubt will spend a lot of her time with him. The poor man, he doesn't know what he's letting himself in for." Chuckling ensued. "So if there's anything you need, just ask one of the crew. Thank you, and I'll see you on the ground. Right now, Joshua is probably holding an armful of messages I'll have to deal with. Have a good day, men."

Tag replied, "On behalf of all of us, sir, thank you and have a good day yourself."

Joseph smiled and nodded, and as he turned, he said, "Come with me, please, Tiger."

CHAPTER 32

I followed Joseph to Shari's office, and he turned to Joshua and said, "I just need to have a word with my daughter and the colonel for a few moments. Could you wait for me in my office, please?"

Joshua nodded and opened the door to Joseph's office. I preceded him into Shari's office, who threw herself into my arms. She saw her father and tried to stop herself but crashed into me. I grabbed her to stop her backward fall and started laughing. Joseph was also laughing as he shut the door.

"See, little one, that's what I've been trying to warn you about. You must be discreet. If I had been anyone else, they'd know straight away that you're having an affair with Tiger. Always make sure you are in private before you start this jumping about. Now, unless you wish me to forbid your romance, you must promise to be discreet."

She hung her head and said, "Yes Father, I promise to be discreet and take notice of what you have said."

I smiled and filed two pieces of information into my head. One that whenever they were alone she called him papa, but if she was in trouble and knew it or when someone else was present, she called him Minister or Father.

Joseph said, "Now then, Shari, when we arrive in Tel Aviv, you will take Tiger and his team to the King David, where they have suites. There are two bedrooms in Tiger's suite. If you are going to stay with him, make it look as if you are using one and don't make so much noise." He was smiling. "I want Tiger and his men at IDF headquarters at nine o'clock. Use hotel transport, and during Tiger's stay, you will remain with him and his team."

She was smiling and answered, "Yes Papa. I'll stay at the

hotel with Tom, but if we have time I would like to show him my apartment."

Joseph nodded his head. "All right. I hope to see you all before we land, but you know how busy I can be, my dear, so you children have fun and I'll see you later."

He left the office, closing the door behind him. She laughed and threw her arms around my neck and kissed me. "See. What did I tell you? You have to gag me."

"Well, I didn't think he would have heard you last night. It may be just a guess, or he has very good hearing. I'll sound out Tag. His room was next to yours last night and he's a light sleeper, so I'll find out, one way or another." The plane started moving, and instead of fastening seatbelts, Shari lay over my body on the couch. We went into the air kissing and lying down, and by the time we reached our cruising altitude, we were naked except for a handkerchief in her mouth as she experienced an orgasm.

She stopped all her movement on top of me as the climax of each shuddering orgasm wracked her body, and they continued, spasm on orgasmic spasm, time and time again, each more ecstatic than the last. So she was almost exhausted when my entire body quivered in blissful response to her pleasure, and I poured my hot seed into her, producing an even more violent orgasm in both her and I in absolute harmony together. Arch, quiver, and explode, holding fast together inside her and out, we became one in body, heart and soul, now and forever.

Totally spent and breathless, she collapsed onto me. While we were recovering our breath, I worked out that forty thousand feet was definitely over a mile high, so we qualified to join the mile-high club. She giggled for some time over that titbit of information.

"Do you think what we just did would be considered assaulting an officer?" I asked.

She burst out laughing. "Then we'd both be guilty."

After we had a quick shower together in her bathroom. It was cramped so we had to squeeze around, which was definitely fun and we were both laughing. We got dressed at the same time, and she asked, "I hope I was quieter this time?"

"Well I guess we'll find out soon enough, but I only heard your moans, honey." We shared a long kiss and went to sit on each side of the desk. We reached for the intercom and asked for two cappuccinos. We got down to some work as the coffee was brought in.

I asked what she knew about what would happen at the IDF HQ. The young corporal asked if we'd like anything to eat, and Shari asked for a plate of Danishes, and after the girl left, she said, "I'm famished. It must be all the wonderful sex," she said with a wink. She then proceeded to tell me what the initial plan was, which was to have us in Tel Aviv for two weeks before flying to Ramat David Air Base and driving to the Havatzalot Training Base near Megiddo in the Jezreel Valley, where Shari had her second house.

The corporal brought in the plate of Danishes, and as she was about to leave, I asked her, "Could you make a third coffee? Also, ask Captain Wilson to join us please. He's opposite my seat. Thank you."

Tag walked in and his coffee was brought in along with some more Danishes because there was only the one left on the first plate. I looked at Shari, who hung her head and said, "I'm sorry Tiger, but I was hungry.

Tag laughed and said, "Must be all the exercise you do, ma'am. I mean, otherwise you wouldn't be as trim."

I glared at him as he smiled. "The reason I called you in is because I want you to hear this as well. We'll probably be in Tel Aviv for two weeks, but we won't be required all the time so we'll count those as down days. After that, we'll be heading up to the Mossad training base in the Jezreel Valley near Megiddo, which is how far from Haifa in the North West, Shari?"

"Eighty kilometres, Tiger," she replied.

She told us that once we were there, we would be involved in a mutual exchange of information and ideas, including training in new experiences and things that can go wrong during an operation. At the moment, training was being scheduled on how to take over a high jacked airplane once it was on the ground and the difficulties with that style of operation. "We even have an old intact El-Al airliner for practise. Perhaps you may have a way of improving how we do it, but most of our training is in anti-terrorism because that's what we get from the PLO and our other neighbours."

"The easiest way would be to nuke them. End of problem," Tag commented. I smiled a wry smile, knowing that wouldn't happen.

She looked at him and replied, "There are a lot of people who would agree with you, Tag, but that would be breaking our word to the UN.

We as a nation take pride in the fact that we try to keep our promises, even though the others say one thing and do another."

"Some of the time, I may have to go down to Tel Aviv, or elsewhere, so if I'm not at the base, you can reach me through Shari. Nine times out of ten, I'll need her with me, but in most things I'm going to be leaving the running of the team to you. I might only join you for a day or two, then have to go off again. We'll have to see how it goes," I explained to Tag.

"That's no problem, but what if I need to get you or Shari urgently?"

"Good point," I replied, and looked at Shari.

"When we get to IDF HQ, my second in command will join us there, so while Tiger and I are with you, you will have two liaison officers. If we're not there, my 2IC, Mary Goldstein, will be looking after you and the team. Mary has the number for the satellite phone, and it goes everywhere with me." She had pulled out what looked like a small version of a walkie talkie that had a solid aerial that folded down on the side of the phone. It was perhaps six inches long and about three wide, and as she passed it across, I felt the weight of it, which was hardly any. After having a good look at it, I passed it to Tag and he did the same. We looked at each other with the same thought: where do we get one of these?

"When we land, there will be transport waiting to take us to the King David. Don't worry about your weapon boxes; they'll stay at Lod air base to be taken with us when we leave. I will be staying at the hotel in Tiger's suite because there are two bedrooms in his suite, so I'll be on hand. Any questions, Tag?"

"No, I think that's got everything covered. When will we be landing?"

"Just one minute…" She picked up the intercom and spoke to the flight deck in Hebrew. "Our ETA at Lod is eighteen hundred, so we've still got a lot of time before we get there."

She took a toilet break, and while she was away, I told Tag that I'd try to get as much info about the satellite phones as possible because they'd be a god send in Australia. Laughingly, he told me I'd have to curtail walking around naked when we were at the hotel. Having Shari around wouldn't be a problem anyway.

"No, I suppose she won't be, considering you two are already sleeping together anyway. Half your luck." He rose, grinning. "I'd better get back and fill in the guys, unless there's anything else?"

Before I answered him Shari came back, and I asked if there was anything else for Tag to know. She shook her head. "No, I think we've covered everything."

"Ok, I'll head back then. See you later." He closed the door on the way out.

Alone again, I asked, "Is the reason we're here have to do with working out how to do things better and working out how to board a hijacked plane on the ground?" I could see by the look on her face that I'd hit the nail on the head. "This all has something to do with your Operation Thunderbolt, doesn't it? The raid on Entebbe? By the way, what was the final outcome?"

She answered looking straight at me, "Yes, because the government doesn't want that to happen again. That plane could have been taken over while it was still on the ground in Athens, according to the experts, and ever since Mossad has been trying to come up with a way to do that. We can't afford to wait until a plane gets to a destination before attacking to save our people. Mr. Rabin has promised it will never happen again. We freed ninety-four of our people and the entire air crew of Air France, but we lost three hostages and ten were wounded. The commandos had five wounded, and their commander minister Netanyahu's older brother Yoni was killed. But, they killed seven of the hijackers, forty-five Ugandan troops, and destroyed thirty MIG fighter jets."

I nodded and said, "Ok, I'm not against putting my mind to ideas while you get Tag back in here. Call for some more coffee, while we're waiting. Pass me your phone, please, and tell me how and where you got it."

She told me that all department heads carry them. They were bought from British Telecom but were expensive at eight hundred pounds each. The call rate was one pound a minute, and she was lucky the government paid for the calls on all the phones they had. As she finished speaking, Tag opened the door for the young corporal, who brought in a tray with three coffee mugs on it and transferred them to the desk. She left the lunch menu with the coffees and withdrew. Tag closed the door and resumed his previous seat at the desk.

Shari and I filled him in on the real reason was behind our secondment to Israel. He laughed and turned to me as he said, "They should have just sent you in, boss. You're the planner extraordinaire. You could have done all the work, and we could have had a holiday."

"This time we've all got to think. Our time in Tel Aviv is probably when we'll have a short holiday, but once we get to Megiddo, we'll assess what they know and do, and then we'll all have input into making it better.

Plus, I want to have a look into the planning for the action that took place and also the mission reports from Entebbe."

Shari interrupted. "If this discussion is going to take place, shouldn't my father be present?"

I thought quickly. "Yes. See if he's available, and his secretary as well, please."

She used the intercom, and soon we were joined by both of them. They sat on the couch, and I explained that I'd worked out one of the prime reasons for our secondment. Shari had confirmed it, then I got up and paced a bit.

I faced Joseph. "Sir, I'm not going to conduct a witch hunt or try to blame anyone for things that did go wrong. In fact, I'm more likely to praise everyone involved for trying something no one else had the guts to do. However, if I'm to determine how the situation could be improved, I need to know and have access to everything. That includes interviewing some of the commandos that took part in the raid." I paused to let it sink in. "Sir, I'm a man of action and planning. Sitting around waiting for something to happen is not my forte. I can make better use of the time we're in Tel Aviv by starting on this project instead of being introduced around at the IDF HQ. If I need to see someone in particular, I have your daughter or you, sir." I stopped pacing as I finished speaking and resumed my seat at the desk.

While Joseph was thinking what I'd said over, Tag raised his hand. Joseph looked at him and said "I think you have something you wish to say Tag?"

Tag got up and stood in front of Joseph. "Sir, I usually don't try to talk anyone up." He took a quick sip of water. "Tom is the best strategist I know. He can run rings around any intelligence officer. He plans meticulously when he plans an operation, and he tries to account for any type of variable. When he's on an operation, if any unforeseen event occurs, he instantly comes up with a solution. If you want to look at better ways to do things, he's your man." Shari mouthed a thank you to him after he'd returned to his seat.

Joseph looked at Joshua, who was nodding his head. He cleared his throat. "I've made my mind up. Tiger, you'll have everything you wish. Joshua and Shari will arrange it for you, but my boy; don't think you're just going to sit in your hotel room while you're in Tel Aviv. I'm afraid you will have to attend some meetings at HQ, but I will try to limit them. Now if that's all, I would like to have some lunch."

"There is just one more thing. I need to stay in contact with Tag when we are in separate places. Would it be possible for Tag and I to get a satellite phone each while we're in Israel?"

Joseph laughed and said, "Now I know what Tag means about being meticulous. Joshua will arrange it, and you can pick them up from HQ in the morning. Now can I go order lunch?"

It was my time to laugh. "Yes, and thank you, sir."

Tag rose from his chair. "I think I'll go back and eat with the others, maybe try to make some time with that corporal." With a laugh he headed to the door.

"That could be classified as harassing an enlisted man, Captain," I called to him, and we all laughed.

After sharing lunch in her office, Shari and I stretched out on the couch. She was tucked in under my right arm, and we talked for a bit before drifting off to sleep. I woke to see her sitting at her desk writing something, and I asked what time it was.

"It's almost sixteen hundred. I was tempted to wake you earlier, but I thought you might be tired, so I let you sleep," she said with a smile.

"Yeah well, someone kept me awake last night. Not that I minded, of course. Besides, you were the first one to go to sleep earlier, and instead of moving I was enjoying your body next to mine. I guess I eventually dozed off."

About twenty minutes later the intercom buzzed; it was the flight deck informing Shari that we'd picked up bit of a tail wind, so our revised ETA was seventeen thirty at Lod.

After she told me that, I went around her desk and started unbuttoning her shirt. "That means we've got at least an hour to kill. Have any suggestions?" I pulled the front of her shirt out from her skirt and all the way open.

Thirty minutes later I was just coming out of the shower as she came in still naked from our lovemaking on the couch. She kissed me and said, "Will you see if you can find where you flung my bra to please? If you're good I might let you put it on again."

"Honey, you already know I'm good."

"Don't it know it!"

She stepped out of the bathroom towelling herself dry. I had finally located her bra and panties, and she slipped into her bra and asked me to do her up. Instead I reached around her back and cupped each breast. "There. That do?"

"No," she said with a laugh, slapping my hands lightly. I whined in disappointment and did up her bra. She grabbed the pants, put them in her suitcase, and brought out a fresh pair to put on. With twenty minutes to go before ETA, I felt the slight steady loss of altitude; then the pilot came over the PA announcing our descent into Lod.

Thirty minutes later the plane was parked on the ground near the entrance into the terminal. Three limos waited as we walked down the stairs. Joseph shook hands with us all and said he'd see us in the morning. He and Joshua got into the first limo and drove off. Shari and the rest of us divided into groups, stowed our kitbags into the boots of the limos, and drove off toward the King David Hotel.

Our suites were all on one floor; the floor below had the indoor pool and gym. I thought that would come in handy. A conference room we could use was on our floor, so after dumping our bags we gathered for some information Shari wanted to share. She was delayed by a phone call.

When she joined us, she said to everyone, "Gentlemen, welcome to Tel Aviv. Just a few things you need to know. The first one is that as members of the military you can wear your guns openly if you wish to. It's a rule here that all members of the military are to wear their weapons, regardless of whether they are in civvies or uniform. Secondly, Australian currency isn't used here. If you need to convert some of your dollars into our currency, which is shekels, I can arrange for it to be converted here at the hotel.

The current exchange rate is four shekels to one Australian dollar. Tonight you will meet my second in command at dinner. She will be your liaison if I'm off with Tiger somewhere. Don't worry, Tag will always be able to reach Tiger by phone if need be. Now I'm going to freshen up and get changed before dinner in the dining room at seven. There is a table reserved under Colonel Davis's name, so I hope I'll see you all at dinner. Thank you."

Shortly after a few bits of housekeeping, the meeting broke up, so we had time to get changed for dinner. Mary Goldstein joined us for dinner.

She was about five six with blonde hair and blue eyes, and she was dressed like a man in slacks, although most women in the dining room were wearing skirts or dresses. For some reason, even though pleasing to look at, there was something about her that wasn't quite right. I found out why when I whispered in Shari's ear, "The guys will be going all out to see if she has any interest in them."

She smiled and whispered, "It won't do them any good. She likes girls, from what I can make out. She's been on my staff for two years, and I've never seen her with any man. Women yes, but no men."

After breakfast the next morning, we went back to our rooms and dressed in dress uniforms complete with all rank insignia. Shari looked at me with approval as we left our room and headed downstairs to wait for the rest of the guys. The limos had been ordered for eight thirty, and they rolled into the entrance driveway dead on time. We split into the two groups, and Shari told both drivers where to go and to await our return.

At IDF HQ, Shari ushered us into the building after showing the limo drivers where to wait. We were joined by Mary as we crossed the marble floor to the lifts. Mary had the key for one, and we went inside to be whisked up to the top floor. Four soldiers with Uzi sub machine guns pointed at us waiting at the doors of the lift. I barked, "If you're not ready to shoot me, soldiers, don't point your guns at us!"

They returned their guns to their sides, saluted, and we paused to be frisked and searched. We surrendered our guns rather comically, because apart from guns on each of the men, we were also carrying knives. Dumper had three grenades as well. The looks on the guard detail was sickening, and I think they wondered if our array of weapons would ever stop coming. We were cleared to continue.

Shari was having a fit, asking us whatever prompted us to carry so many weapons. I looked at her disapprovingly and said, "You said we were permitted to carry our weapons."

She looked at me and replied, "Yes, but…oh forget it."

In Joseph's office, we were introduced to at least a dozen high ranking officers and ministers. "For all those present here, these men are to be respected and listened to despite some of them only being captains in their army," Joseph explained.

"The prime minister himself asked me to arrange for their visit with us for the next three years. If they are able to accomplish miracles in that time, so be it, but they are to be given every assistance you can provide them."

After pausing for a quick sip of water, he continued, "They will be accompanied by liaison officers from this office, and those officers speak as if this office is speaking. There is to be no obstruction to their duties. I hope that is understood by everyone present. We have twenty minutes before their commander, Colonel Davis, is due to meet with the Prime Minister, so please make them welcome."

To say I was floored was an understatement on two accounts. The first nearly caused me to gag on the coffee I was drinking. Three years! We'd been told two or a little longer and that certainly didn't equate to three as far as I was concerned. The second sounded as if I was being whisked away to meet the Israeli Prime Minister Yitzac Rabin. What the bloody hell was that all about?

I turned to Shari, and asked, "Did you know about this?"

"I had no idea; it seems father's playing games again."

"Bloody hell." I Replied.

During the fifteen minutes I had available before leaving, I didn't get a chance to talk to Tag before being whisked away by Joseph. I collected my weapons while waiting for the lift, and then we went all the way to the basement where a limousine was waiting to take us to the Prime Minister's lodge. In the limo Joseph explained that he didn't have time to forewarn me of the latest developments and that I was only going to have a fifteen-minute talk with Rabin before we went back to IDF HQ, where Joshua would hand over the documents I'd asked for and my sat phone. I'd be free to head back to the hotel after that.

"What took place this morning had to happen; otherwise those fools wouldn't have given you or my people the time of day. It's politics I'm afraid, but trust me, I have your best interests at heart," Joseph explained to me.

Somehow I doubted his statement, but he knew of the bond his daughter and I had developed, and I couldn't see him using her as a pawn in a game of chess. I had to take his word for it. "What am I supposed to say to Rabin? I don't know him from Adam."

"He knows you, though. Just let him guide the conversation and be truthful with your answers. You'll be fine. Please trust in me."

My time with Yitzac Rabin lasted exactly fourteen minutes and twenty seconds before we were interrupted by his secretary. I found him to be pleasant and well versed in military protocols, and he told me he looked forward to my report about what could have happened at Entebbe with interest, mainly because I think he wanted to know if he made the right call in ordering the strike.

After my interview with Rabin, we returned to the IDF HQ, where Joshua was waiting in Joseph's office. He informed me that Mary had taken the rest of the team back to the hotel but had left the second limo for Shari and I to use. He passed me a sat phone with the phone number wrapped around it with a rubber band, and he told me he had already stored the numbers for Shari,

Tag, Joseph, and himself into the phone. He had done the same with Tag's phone, and Tag already had his. Next he showed me a cardboard carton, telling me that everything pertaining to Operation Thunderbolt was in the carton, including detailed de-briefing reports after the mission. He had also included a list of the personnel that took part in the raid and their present whereabouts.

I thanked him and said that I'd look after it all, and if I required anything further that I'd call him direct. We shook hands, and Shari and I left to go back to the hotel. After finding the driver, we had him take us back, and we took all the stuff into our room before we found the others down in the dining room having lunch. We joined them, and I told them the rest of the day was down time, so go do the tourist thing. Shari gave Mary a list of places for her to take them and we'd all meet up for dinner together.

Shari and I went back to our room. We took the box to the con-ference room and started sorting the paperwork into piles on the timeline of the operation, such as, pre planning and intelligence, the planning itself, the commandos used on the raid, and all the debriefing document. The list of personnel and their whereabouts we kept separate.

Once everything was in the correct pile, I said, "Honey, how much do you know about planning an operation?"

"Nothing. Why?"

I replied with a smile. "That's good. We're going to de-plan this operation and plan it again using all this information. It could take days."

CHAPTER 33

Over the next couple of days, Shari and I went over each of the pre-planning documents with a fine toothcomb while the rest of the team went out sightseeing each day with Mary. As we went over each document, I made notes, and from the notes and relevant documents and photos, I made my own plan, trying to stay within the same timeframe the original planners had worked with. I completed my plan one day before the time they'd taken and accounted for all the variables I could see in a plan of this size.

Next, I pinned my plan to the wall, and we started sifting through the actual mission reports about what had happened. We discovered a discrepancy in the intelligence given to the planners in the first instance, so we went back to the pre-plan documents. We found the flaw after some searching. The planners had disregarded some of the intelligence supplied in the rush to plan the mission, and no variables were taken into account.

Shari and I looked at each other. "You know the implications of this, don't you?" I asked and she nodded. "We need to speak to some of the planning staff. Are they on our list?"

Shari looked at the list. "No, we've only got the commandos and air crew."

"All right. Will you get onto Joshua and get us an appointment with your father for tomorrow?"

While she was making the call, I started a second attack plan using all of the intelligence that had been given to the planning section. After completing the call, she made us some coffee and passed me mine as I continued working. Two hours later, I was finished, and Shari started putting the documents away, but I told her to keep out the intelligence docs that hadn't been used by the planners.

We pulled down my first plan and compared them. The result was that my second plan took into account two of the variables I'd listed on my first plan, and as we compared further, I said, "No wonder there was a screw up. Everything hinged on those two variables that were ignored. Ok, now we have to look at the actual attack plan used and the debriefing reports. I'll bet they'll only confirm what we've discovered. I also think we'll have to speak to some of the commandos.

It's nearly time for dinner, and we worked right through lunch. Let's give it away for now and get ready for dinner."

She nodded and said, "Sounds good. Father will see us tomorrow at nine. What are you going to tell him?"

"The truth of what we've discovered so far. This could be wrapped up sooner than he thought, but we have to confirm things with the planners and commandos."

The following morning, I told Joseph what we had discovered, and as he thought over what I'd told him, he kept muttering, "Oh god." After a pause while he contemplated further, he said, "Can you confirm this and show me how you came to this conclusion?"

I produced copies of my two plans. After I'd shown him the original plan of attack and the missing intelligence documents, because he was a strategist as well, he was able to pick up the discrepancy at once. He looked at both my plans side by side, and after half an hour of comparing my plan, the original plan, and the missing data, he said, "God, your plan would have worked. Freeing the hostages without loss of life except to the opposition. So how do you prove it?"

I took a deep breath. "By interviewing the commandos and the planning staff. The commandos no problem, but I may be treading on some toes when it comes to the planners."

"You let me worry about that. If you strike opposition, let me know. What else do you need?" Joseph answered

I was thinking quickly. "First, I need Joshua to get a list of who was on the planning staff and where I can find them. Then I need a car to use. Shari can be my driver. And last, someone to type up my full report, but this person can only work in the conference room at the hotel."

Joseph smiled and replied, "Joshua will arrange for a car now, and we'll have a typist and machine there by midday. It'll probably take a couple of days for Joshua to get the list, but he'll deliver it to you personally. Needless to say, this investigation will now have a secrecy umbrella. Joshua will you take care of the request while I have a word with my daughter and Tiger."

After Joshua had left the room, Joseph turned to us and said, "So how's the romance going? No, don't answer that. I can tell its fine. I suppose you two have been working on this fiasco nonstop since it was given to you. Have a couple of days off; it'll take that long to get that list together anyway.

Use the car and go for a drive. Perhaps even go visit your mama. She'd like that, take Tom to meet her. I warn you, Tom, she'll try to marry you two off straight away." He laughed at his own joke.

Joshua returned and told us the typist would be at the hotel when we returned. She'd been sent in our limo. He gave Shari a set of keys and told her it was the black BMW with the rego plate IDF 3. We shook hands all round, except for Shari kissing her father, and then we left to head back to the hotel.

Shari handed the keys to the concierge for parking, and he informed us where the typist was waiting. Apparently, it was someone Shari knew, and she went up to our floor with us.

I explained what I wanted done and which documents were to go into the report. Everything was to be treated as confidential. Two copies were to be made, and I told her she could use the hotel facilities if she needed to. Finally, I explained that she was working for me. Shari and I left her to it and went for a swim before having lunch.

The typist had finished her job by three, and Shari and I looked over the reports. I locked them in the safe.

That evening while we having dinner, I asked Wires, "Did you or JJ happen to bring any of the recorders?"

JJ piped up. "Brought all twelve, boss, plus a dozen spare tapes for each."

I laughed and replied, "JJ, I could kiss you, but I won't. You're too ugly. Can you give me two and three spare tapes for each when we get back to the rooms?" He nodded and continued laughing with everyone about my comment.

I announced, "Tomorrow Shari and I are going up country, and we could be away for a few days. I'm sure you'll be able to take care of yourselves. Tag, you know how to get me. We'll be leaving early, about eight, so we'll have an early breakfast. You lot can sleep in. And do me a favour. Keep the stuff in the conference room under lock and key."

The next day we travelled north toward Megiddo. Before entering the Jezreel valley, we stopped on a high spot so I could take in the scenery. Shari pointed out directions and some of the spots I could see. A little south of Megiddo she turned off the main road, and soon we drove into a farmyard that sat back off the road. She drove up to the main house; the security staff had seen the rego plate and didn't bother us as they continued their job of looking like the other ordinary farmhands. The door to the house was opened by a woman very similar to Shari only her hair was grey; as I followed Shari, who had rushed forward to embrace her mother, I realized she was the parent with the green eyes.

I was introduced to Marta and told her I was pleased to meet her. She gave me a long inspection and moved us into the house. We sat in the kitchen as the kettle was put on to boil.

Marta looked at me and asked, "So Colonel, what brings you to Israel?"

"Please call me Tiger or Tom, ma'am, and to answer your question, your husband was behind it. I think he was following a suggestion from your Prime Minister. We've only been here a few days, but I like it. It'll be better when we can move up here away from the politics of the capitol."

She smiled and asked, "You said we, Tom. Are there more of you?"

"Yes ma'am," I answered with a smile, "my whole team are here with me."

She nodded. "Call me Marta. Ma'am makes me sound like a school teacher."

Shari helped make the coffee, and when they both sat down again, Marta asked me, "So, how long have you been in love with my daughter?"

Shari cried, "Mama!"

I smiled hugely. "Since the first time I saw her, Marta, two weeks ago. I guess you could say it was love at first sight for both of us."

She smiled and looked at Shari. "And my Shari, she's very much in love with you, I think. A mother knows these things. Your papa, Shari, what does he say?"

She looked at me before replying. "Oh Mama, you know what he's like. I was a little worried when Tom spoke to him after he yelled at me, but then everything was fine. He and Tom are working together on something at present, but Papa let us take a couple of days off. He suggested we come see you."

She thought for a few seconds and said, "I see what the cunning old wolf is up to. Are you going to stay here tonight and have dinner with me?"

"Yes Mama, or we could go to my place in Megiddo."

"You two can stay here and use your old room, Shari. Tom, you can relax and take that shirt and gun off. There's plenty of security here," she said, waving her hand at the window. As I stripped off my shirt and took the holster off, she looked at it and remarked, "Colt forty-five commander with a silencer. Looking at the butt, you use this a lot. I can see one of the reasons my daughter is in love with you."

"Mama!" Shari said in exasperation as Marta laughed.

I pulled the pistol out and gave it to her, and she expertly slipped the mag out and ejected the round in the chamber. She hefted it and dry fired it a couple of times and told me it had been worked on, the action smoothed. I told her she was right. She put the gun back together and placed it in the holster. Shari was looking at her, amazed, and with a laugh, the older woman told her daughter she hadn't always been her mother; she knew the business of war. However, I had the distinct feeling that she was telling me 'if you hurt my daughter, I'll come after you.'

Aloud, I said, "I get the message."

Marta smiled while Shari looked at me questioningly. I gave her a kiss in front of her mother, and we all laughed.

We stayed overnight and pushed on after breakfast the next day. We drove to Shari's house in Megiddo and went into have a look around. When the team moved up here, Shari and I would live here while the team remained on base. We travelled to the base and drove in, mainly because we felt it prudent to arm ourselves with a couple of rifles. After announcing who we were and what we required, we went to the armoury and drew a couple of Uzi sub machine guns. We placed them in the back and continued on our trip.

We turned off the main road before getting to Ramat David air base and drove up to the heights. We stopped and got out; like before, we looked down on the valley and Shari pointed things out. I could see the air base, and because we were up high, I could see a city in the far distance as I glanced to the northwest. The clarity of the air and the coolness kept down the heat haze, so we could see further. Shari told me the city was Haifa.

Two hours later, we were up near the Golan Heights and decided it was time for some shooting practice. We pulled the Uzi's out of the back, and Shari gave me a quick run through. I test fired a few rounds, made a couple of adjustments to the gun, and fired again. Every shot hit the target I'd intended. We had a little shooting competition. The stakes were our bodies, so whichever way it went, neither of us could lose. After switching to my left hand, she tried the same, and I won due to my ambidextrous ability.

That night we stayed in one of the hotels in Haifa right on the beach. We went for a swim after dark. The next day we headed south and did some sightseeing, passing through Nazareth, and then down through Hadera and Netanya before reaching Tel Aviv and our hotel. Which is just as well, because the next morning at eight, Joshua arrived with the list we needed, and we made plans to see a couple of the planners who lived in Jerusalem on our way south to Beersheba to see the commandos. We were to see the planning overseer at Elat, way down the southern end of the country on the edge of the Gulf of Aqaba. There were a couple in Ramla twenty minutes out of Tel Aviv, but I decided to leave them to last.

The next morning, we left the hotel after breakfast for business purposes, so we dressed in cam fatigues. I was wearing my gun on my thigh, and Shari wore hers in a cross draw holster on her left side. The Uzi's were on the back seat. We also carried our phones and the recorders; each of us had one in our shirt pockets. Shari had arranged our accommodation for the trip through our hotel reception and had the names and addresses where we would be staying. I drove while she navigated, and at fourteen hundred, we arrived in Jerusalem. Instead of going to the hotel, we drove straight to the military HQ building and asked for the person we wanted to see. We were shown to his office, and I told him who we were and what we wanted. He asked us to take seats, and I started asking questions about the planning of Operation Thunderbolt.

I didn't bother writing any of the answers down because we recorded the interview, He started to fidget and look around the room, and get evasive when I asked "Obviously you had a lot of intelligence coming in to you, was it all taken into account in the final planning stages?"

"We used all that we had; I don't think we overlooked anything." He replied.

Something wasn't right, in the way that was answered, so I

put a couple of question marks against his name on our list. I was starting to get suspicious. When we were finished with him, he took us to the other person we wanted to see, and we started the process again. He also got cagey when asked about the intelligence reports, and I started to sense a cover up. I didn't want to say anything aloud just yet.

After our interviews, we went to the hotel, and because our room was up high, Shari pointed out most of the historical sights to me while we had drinks on our balcony.

The next morning, we were off again headed for Beer Sheba. However, when we arrived, we were told the commandos were on exercise at Masada, so we headed to the old mountaintop fortress on the shores of the Dead Sea. After locating them, we spoke to the officers and personnel. After quite a few recordings all saying virtually the same thing, I was convinced that my assumption was correct. The planning had been flawed.

Because it was getting late in the day after we spoke to them, we hotfooted it back to Beersheba to our hotel. We got there in time to check in and head to the restaurant for dinner before it closed. We didn't check out until fifteen hundred the next day, which meant we were able to have a relaxed breakfast and lunch. The reason we checked out so late was because we were driving through the Negev Desert to reach Elat. The Negev was the hottest place in the country, where day temperatures were commonly above forty-eight degrees, even in winter, which was on its way. The nighttime temperature fell drastically and was a much better option for travelling.

At zero, one hundred we started to climb up into the Elat mountains. We stopped for a couple of hours at Yotvata before making the final push down into Elat. We arrived there at six and went directly to the hotel we were booked into. We were able to go straight up to our room because no guest had been using it, so after having breakfast, we went to find the person we wanted to talk with.

The man we were to interview was a retired IDF Colonel. We

were in civilian garb, and I asked to interview him, making it sound like I was studying strategies and logistics in peacetime. The fact that I was Australian helped pave the way, and he gladly agreed to let me interview him. I led with a few questions about his peacetime activities before retirement, and voluntarily he said with a laugh, "Just after I retired, they called me back to plan that damned stupid raid in Africa. Mind you, we got the hostages out."

Now I had him! "Wait a minute. Are you telling me it was you that did all the planning for ...Operation Thunderbolt, I think it was? That was a masterful plan. Do you mind if I ask you about that?"

He looked at me and smiled, and the ego stroking I'd used worked. "Yes, my boy, it was me and a few others who planned it. By all means, ask away."

So with a bit more ego stroking, I asked the questions in a roundabout manner, getting the answers I wanted. Finally, I was ready to nail him. "So you used some of the intelligence you got from Mossad, but not all, is that right?"

He was still laughing. "That's right. You can't trust anything the bloody Mossad tell you. You'd be jumping at shadows otherwise, the damned fools. But we'd already worked out a sound plan before some of their stuff came in late. Some of the others wanted to include it the plan, but that would have meant starting from scratch. I told them to ignore it. Besides it didn't seem too helpful anyway, and it was only hearsay."

I looked at my watch. "My, look at the time. I'm sorry to have taken up so much of your time. Do you mind if I come back another time if I need to, sir?"

He laughed and said, "No, that'll be all right. Come back anytime. I've enjoyed your visit. How about next time you bring some Sabra and we'll have a few drinks together?"

"I'll be sure to, sir, and thank you, but we really must be going," I replied, and we got up, left, and drove back to the hotel.

When we got into our room, Shari asked, "God that was

skilfully done. Are you a trained interrogator as well, Tom?"

"No, but I did get high scores when we did an interrogation training course back home. Now we know that all the intelligence gathered wasn't used, we have to find out who is responsible for the cover-up. We need to go back to Jerusalem, and then to the two in Ramla. If we leave tonight, by taking turns and pushing it, we could be in Jerusalem by mid-morning. You up for it?"

"All right, but let's get some sleep now, set the alarm, have dinner, and then leave," she replied.

"Done," I said.

During the first leg of the drive that night, Shari asked, "Darling, driving these long distances doesn't seem to have any effect on you or faze you in any way. How come?"

I laughed. "Honey, I live in Brisbane in Queensland back home. To get from there to our base in Western Australia takes a week of solid driving; only stopping for fuel. So yeah, I'm used to long distance driving, but you must have known that flying from Sydney. How long did it take you? I'd say maybe eight, possibly nine hours at six hundred miles per hour."

I paused to let her calculate it. "I think the jet we were travelling in is capable of more than six hundred, closer to seven hundred, I'd say. Brisbane to Sydney is another two hours, so that gives you some idea of the distance that has to be travelled. Right now if we were to pass straight through Jerusalem, we'd be in Beirut in two days. I can drive through your whole country in the time it would take me to drive from Brisbane to Sydney. Thank Christ we're not doing that, though."

We arrived in Jerusalem at zero nine thirty, and Shari drove to the same hotel, where they were able to give us a room. While I had a shower and shave, Shari laid out my cams and gun strap as well as her uniform. She followed me into the shower, and after we'd freshened up, we went and had a substantial brunch at eleven.

We arrive at the office of our first contact, and I wasn't polite or mucking around. He was only a Captain; I outranked him well and truly, and I also wanted to put the fear of god in him. So we barged straight in. He was talking to another captain.

"You, get out now!" I barked at the second captain. I slammed my hands onto his desk and growled, "Now Captain, we're going to have a little chat about your lies. I suggest you tell me the truth this time, or by god I'll have you serving in the Golan. Do you understand me, soldier?"

His face went white, and he nodded as Shari pulled out the recorder and switched it to record. I noted time, date, people present, and where the recording took place before I started asking questions. "Tell me, Captain, did you use all the intelligence data available to you from Mossad?"

"No sir," he replied.

"Why not?"

His answer came slowly. "Our colonel told us to disregard it because we already had a workable plan. Any late intelligence was a waste of time, but Peter and I wanted time to go over it, maybe amend the plan formulated, but the colonel and major wouldn't give us the opportunity."

I stared at him for a minute. "So who was responsible for covering up these details?"

Like a beaten man, he replied, "The major said that letting people know the true facts wouldn't do our careers any good after what happened on the raid, so he burned the reports. We were told not to say anything to anyone" He paused. "Can I just say that I thought that it was wrong but knew no one would believe me if I said anything because the evidence had been destroyed?"

I turned to him and said, "That's just where you are wrong, Captain. Copies of reports sent always have copies somewhere. How do you think we knew about the missing data from the final plan? I'm going down the hall to speak to your comrade. If he verifies what you've told me, I'll do what I can for you."

I used the same approach with the second man, and it worked

the same way. We now had two captains on the planning committee saying the same thing, dropping their major right in the shit.

Our next port of call was to the Ramla IDF base to see the other captain and then the major who was responsible for the cover up. The captain was rather easy and was obviously smarter than most. When he saw the direction of my questions, he knew I had a lot of information I wouldn't normally have, so he told me the truth without even trying to protect himself. When it came to the cover up, his version was exactly the same as the others.

Before tackling the major, I asked Shari to ring her father to ask him to join us for dinner tonight at the hotel. I wanted to be able to talk to him off the record. After the call was made and we had his acceptance, we went to interview Major Oberon. I did not use kid gloves; my questions were direct and to the point. At first, he denied all the accusations I laid out for him and was quite indignant, threatening me with all sorts of ramifications until I called his bluff and told him whose authority I had for my questions, as well as some of the consequences for him should he continue to lie.

I played my ace card when I stated, "Quite frankly, I'm inclined to make the recommendation that you be court martialled for treason and hanged. Should you think I'm bluffing, it was your Prime Minister that told me, in front of witnesses, that any recommendation I make would be acted upon, so let's start from the beginning once more."

He visibly paled, and wilted into himself. He began telling us everything, about the order to ignore the later documents, how he organized the cover up, hoping that there wouldn't be an in-depth investigation, and how he'd thought they'd gotten away with it until I arrived. The only thing that puzzled me was why he did it.

"The colonel was like a father to me, he looked after me, but because of his mistake, things went wrong. He thought he was right, so I saw my chance to repay him for all of his kindness and made sure no one spoke and that the documents were destroyed. I didn't want him to lose everything because of a mistake, you see."

I nodded, reached forward, and switched the tape off. "And now you're going to carry the blame. You're the one that's going to lose everything. Come on, Captain, let's go."

Before we moved he said, "I already lost everything Colonel, my family were killed during the last ceasefire, karma? Who knows?" As he looked at me sorrowfully.

We got up and left his office. As we left the building, a shot rang out. Shari turned to race back in, but I called without looking back, "Don't bother. The major just shot himself." I sighed. "Let's go back to Tel Aviv."

We were silent as I drove for quite some time. Shari broke the silence. "Did you know he was going to do that? Shoot himself, I mean?"

"I had an idea, but it's probably better this way. There'll be no trial, nothing gets aired in the media. He'll just be a little footnote on page three or four in the local paper and nothing more. What happens to everyone else is up to your father? We've done the job we set out to do for him. We discovered the truth and who was responsible. At least now we may be able to get on with the cross training we were brought here for in the first place. And you and I can get on with our relationship."

She giggled. "That, Colonel Davis, is my first priority. Starting tonight, after my father leaves, I'm going to pamper you like a wife should. I'm going to give you a bath and a massage. The rest I'll keep secret."

We arrived at the hotel at sixteen hundred, and after leaving the keys with the concierge, we went up to our room. When the lift opened on our floor, Tag was waiting for the lift to go down. "You both look shagged out. Rough trip?"

I smiled weakly. "Yeah, you could say that, and it's not over yet."

"Uh huh. Are you going to have dinner with us tonight?"

"I'd love to, but Shari's dad is coming to see us and will be at dinner with us. Tomorrow night definitely." I turned as if to leave but remembered something. "Oh by the way, how are you getting on with Mary?"

He laughed. "Are you serious? She's a bloody lesbian! But we've met some of the local girls and are having fun with them. They're meeting us later and taking us to one of the local clubs."

"Well, you don't need it from me, but be careful."

He smiled. "You bet, boss. You too."

Shari and I had a long shower and took our time to get ready to meet Joseph in the cocktail bar at eighteen hundred before dinner.

CHAPTER 34

A fter dinner, we went back to the room. Joseph and I sat out on the balcony and discussed what I'd discovered. Shari, knowing what I wanted, brought out drinks, cigars, and the tape recording of our last interview. I told him everything we'd discovered before I played the two tapes of the colonel and the major. He listened and shook his head at the same time.

"If you arrange for the typist to come tomorrow, she can transcribe all the tapes and compile my final report. At most the report and copies can be ready day after tomorrow. What you do from then on is your decision. Shari and I will forget about the whole thing. We're well overdue to do some training up near Megiddo."

Joseph smiled at both of us. "I wish to thank you for getting to the bottom of this mess. Of course, seeing you had nothing to do with it, I won't be able to tell you the outcome when we all meet in a couple of weeks during my weekend stays at the farm with Marta. Tiger, you let me know when you wish to move up to the training base, and I'll have Joshua arrange transport for you and your team. I must be going, so I'll wish you both a good night." He left after cuddles from Shari and a hand shake from me.

The next morning at breakfast, I asked the guys how soon they'd be ready to get on with some work and was told they were ready to leave at any time. "I just have to finish a report, which could take a couple of days. Get transport organised. We could leave over the weekend, if you wish."

"How about we shoot for Monday next week, boss?" Tag suggested. "That way, Shari will have time to show you around and we can finish up some stuff." I agreed that sounded good.

The typist arrived as we were leaving the dining room, so she joined us in the lift and went to the conference room when we got to our floor. I unlocked the door for her, and Shari and Mary went to our room and got all the tapes and notes and brought them to the conference room. Mary left us to it. We sorted out all the tapes, and the typist got started.

By midday the following day, the typist joined Shari and I, both in dress uniform as we went to the ISD HQ. She left us there while Shari and I went up to Joseph's office. Joshua ushered us straight in, and I presented Joseph with three copies of the report and a box containing the tapes in date order and with whom. He left one report out on his desk, and all the rest went into his safe.

He asked Joshua to have his car brought round and to contact the Prime Minister to inform him that he was on the way to see him, and he picked up the report after stamping it "Top Secret Only."

"Well children, let's go," he said to us.

I assumed that was the end of the meeting. "I'll just arrange our move with Joshua before we go, sir."

"You can do that when we get back," he told me.

The penny dropped. We were expected to go with him. Shari and I looked at each other; I shrugged my shoulders as we walked to the lift with him. The car was waiting at the basement door with two security men with guns drawn as we arrived in the lift and entered the car.

Joseph and Rabin exchanged pleasantries, and Shari and I saluted him before shaking hands. He said, "Joseph has told me you've both been very busy getting all this together, Colonel, and I must admit I thought this would take months. You two have been able to do all this in two weeks. Thank you both, and please stay with us as I read this, in case I may have questions."

Rabin sat at his desk to read, and we were brought coffee and Danishes. I watched as Rabin read; at times, his face went white, then red with anger, and when he'd finished reading he slammed the report down on his desk. "Damn them. Just as well that fool major shot himself. We'd never have been able to put him on trial." He regained control of himself. "What you do with the rest is for you to decide, Joseph, but let me thank all of you for learning the truth. I have another meeting, so if you'll excuse me. Shalom."

That weekend, Shari and I took the IDF car with us as we moved up to her house in Megiddo. Tag would bring the rest of the team up on Monday with all of our weapons, and I arrange for them to be picked up a Ramat David air base and transferred and housed at Havatzalot.

At zero eight hundred Shari and I reported to the security gate and asked to see the camp commander. We were directed to the HQ building. The camp commandant was a colonel by the name of Svi Ben Ari, and we got on really well. He would have been in his early thirties and dressed in desert style cams, and his green eye colour contrasted with his red hair. He told me we were expected and given the VIP quarters, but he wasn't sure of the exact number.

"Svi, there's seven of us and two female liaison officers, but Captain Ben Aram and I will probably spend most of our nights in Megiddo. We will make use of the quarters from time to time. The rest will be flying into Ramat David later and will require transportation from there to here," I explained to him.

He leaned back and smiled as he picked up the phone. "I can fix that, just hold on." He spoke to one of his opposite numbers in the air force and arranged for transport to bring over the team when they arrived, which would be at eleven.

We spoke about what type of training we could exchange. One of the first things we'd be looking at was infiltrating a hijacked plane, and Svi said he could use some of my input to see if the system they'd worked out could be improved. He also asked if we could train his people in the way we operated in Australia as well as some of the stuff we'd used against the North Vietnamese. We went on to talk about some of the Black Operation and assassination techniques we'd been taught.

Readers Note: For those of you that are not sure what a black op is, it's the term used for operations that are never done. Any knowledge of that sort of operation is denied. Should an operative be caught on an operation like that, knowledge of his existence is forfeit. In essence, it's the way a government can deny any wrong doing; every government in the world is guilty of using these types of operations.

For the next few months, we worked at ironing out the bugs in taking down a hijacked plane. Between Svi and myself, we came up with the perfect take down scenarios for every conceivable variation of a hijacked aircraft we could think of. We put the ideas into practice until we came up with the best way of doing it. After four months, we'd come up with five perfect scenarios for taking over a hijacked aircraft while it was stationary.

Step two, was to do the same while the aircraft was in the air. This presented a few more problems, but because we'd already established the protocols to follow, we were able to solve the situation after a couple more months of testing and training. We came up with three different ways to take over a plane in flight with the least amount of loss of life to passengers.

During those months Shari and I grew closer together, and we spent quite a few weekends at her family's farm. During those times, Joseph and I got to talk together quite a lot. On one of those occasions, when both Joseph and I were in the barn away from the women, trying to get an old tractor of his started, I asked if I could speak to him about some serious business.

"Tom, you should know you can speak to me about anything."

I nodded and smiled. "Well, sir this is about something I've been thinking about for a while now, and not to say I'm going to do anything straight away, I would like your permission to ask your daughter to marry me."

He stopped working and put down the shifter he had in his hand. The beckoned me to join him sitting on a hay bale. "Tom, this is something I've been hoping for. Marta also. Of course you have my permission, but have you really thought this through?"

"Yes sir. On one side, I'm not sure if she'd wish to take the alternative option. I was thinking that if she wanted to stay here in Israel, we could be married, and when my job is finished here, I'd return to Australia, quit the army, and sell everything so I could move here. I'm sure I would be able to join Mossad, and I suppose it wouldn't hurt to have you as my father-in-law either."

He looked at me and asked, "You would do that? Leave your home and job just to marry my daughter?"

I replied without hesitation, "Yes sir."

"My boy, you're a treasure. But what if she wanted to leave here and live with you in Australia?"

I thought for a minute before answering him. "Well sir, I know that would be difficult for you and your wife, but if she wanted to live in my home country, I wouldn't try to stop her. I'd always look after her, but that's a decision we'd have to make for ourselves. As yet I haven't even let her know I've been thinking of marriage."

He laughed. "My boy, women are always thinking of that, so don't you be surprised." I laughed and we went back to the tractor. It finally turned over and fired five minutes later.

Later that night when Shari and I were in bed, I asked her, "Sweetheart, if, and I do mean if, we were to get married, where would you like to live?"

She propped herself up quickly, maybe too quickly, I thought, and said, "Here, of course, love. Oh, Tom, my sweet, I'm sorry. I know Australia is your home, but this is my homeland. All my family are here, but I don't wish to separate you from your home either. I've never asked if you like my country. Oh I'm sorry, my love, I don't know. What would I do in your homeland? Do they have female soldiers?"

I looked at her intently. "Yes they do, honey, but there'd be no need for you to work. You could just be at home and raise our children."

She thought that over and said, "No, you know I couldn't do that. I mean, I could raise our children, yes, but I'd need to have a job of some sort as well."

I laughed. "I didn't think you'd take kindly to that. No, I suppose I'd just have to move here to be with you. I don't think I'd have any problems getting a job with Mossad. They know me now, and of course if I needed to I could probably get your father's help."

Now I had some idea what she wanted, and this gave me food for thought. I didn't get much good sleep because of the different thoughts running through my head, such as, how long would it really take to sell everything, and if I quit the army would I have to wait long? What would I say to prepare the team for my departure, and would it be the end of SRT? We already knew there was another specialist unit being trained while we were away. What would the team members like to do? Could I just pack up and throw away all that I'd achieved? How would the guys react? So many different scenarios went through my head. In the morning I felt like I hadn't slept at all.

During that week, having been issued a few sets of desert pattern cams, we started training Svi's men in silent movement and camouflage. We started the lesson in a practical way. I selected Lizard and Dumper to recce an area of sand on the base to use it as cover. Each of them were issued ten rubber bullets for an Uzi. By now we'd all become familiar with them and some of us were actually choosing them over our MP4's. When someone is hit by a rubber bullet, even from a distance, it will knock you off your feet. If too close, they can be just as lethal as real bullets.

The idea was for them to camouflage themselves and take shots at the soldiers without being spotted, but they had to wait five minutes before opening fire to allow Tag and I to assess if the students had indeed spotted our men.

The morning of the exercise, after a session in the briefing room explaining how to look for the signs of hidden enemy, we went to the target area

"Does anyone think this area could be used as an area of concealment?" I asked.

The answer was a consensus of no because it was sand. The

opinion was that a man wouldn't be able to keep the sand stable enough for concealment. Because everyone told us it was unsuitable for concealment, Colonel Ben Ari was struck by a rubber bullet that knocked him off his feet. I immediately asked where the shot had come from. Two of the platoon captains were struck, then two more, and still no one could identify where the shots were coming from.

"Sir, I think I know where he is," a sergeant called.

I smiled. "Then go and stand on the spot you think is right."

Another two officers were struck. We watched as the sergeant moved to where he thought one of our guys was, and I called, "If that is where you think he is, dig him out. Everyone keep your eyes on the sergeant." As the sergeant dug, Dumper lifted himself out of the ground two metres from him and silently placed his knife at the sergeant's throat.

As this happened, I said, "Now, you can see where one of my people was. There are two more out there. Now look, and look hard. To make it easier, just look for one, and when you think you have them let me know. Remember, study the ground."

While the remainder of the men were searching, Tag had been tending the officers who had been shot. All of them were sitting up and looking as well.

"Has anyone found them yet?" I called loudly and was greeted by silence. I yelled the command, "Open fire!"

Immediately another lieutenant was shot. The man next to him yelled, "Sir, I have him." I told him to uncover him. He was right; however, Buzz rose out the ground unarmed, and the next minute another officer was shot. Yes, he'd seen one of my men, but not the shooter. I gave the order to cease fire and told Lizard to show himself.

He rose from behind a tree and took his rifle out of a fork in the stump. Everyone started clapping. "Ok everyone, back to the briefing room. Move!" I ordered.

Back in the briefing room, I said, "That, gentlemen, is a lesson you need to learn. Even the most unlikely area to hide can be made useful. Over the next couple of weeks, we will focus on you learning this art. Any questions?"

Svi's 2IC, Major Talmud, asked, "Sir, why were only the officers targeted?"

I smiled and replied, "Ah, now that's a trick we learned from the VC in Vietnam. They had the right idea. Take out the commanding officers first, and confusion follows. My men are trained to kill officers first, and anyone who looks to be giving orders goes next. That is why we only wear small black rank insignia. When we are on a mission, everyone is treated as the same rank. Isn't that right, Buzz?"

Buzz replied, "Too right, Tiger."

"Ok any more questions? No? All right, we start at zero eight hundred. Dismissed."

The next weekend while Shari was having her hair washed and cut before we went for a picnic on Sunday on the shores of the Sea of Galilee, I wandered the streets in the vicinity and found a jeweller's shop and went inside. I had made up my mind to ask Shari to marry me this weekend. The rings he had on display were all modern in design, and I told him I was looking for a more traditional style of ring. He asked me to give him a minute; he went out the back, and after I heard a safe door close, he reappeared. In his hand, he held an engagement and wedding ring set in an old box. He told me it was his mother's who'd passed it to him to escape with when they'd been rounded up by the German soldiers who invaded Russia. He later learned she'd been shipped to one of the death camps. I looked at the set and thought they were perfect, even made of old rose gold, and I offered him five hundred shekels for the set.

He said he couldn't sell them for less than eight hundred, so we got down to the expected bargaining. I bought them for six hundred, telling him I'd throw in another fifty if he could resize them for me and pulled out one of Shari's old rings that I'd started carrying in case I came across the type of ring I was looking for.

While I went for a coffee, he resized both of them for me, and I paid him the six hundred and fifty shekels I owed him.

The next morning, we left early and travelled to Bet She' an. Because we wanted to act like ordinary lovers, we decided to leave our guns in the car, which we parked in the bus terminal. A normal couple in love meant we'd use the bus to get there, so I carried the picnic basket she'd packed without allowing me to see what was in it, and in my trousers pocket was the ring set.

We sat about halfway up the bus. In front of us were a couple of young soldiers. The one on the aisle had casually looped the sling of his Uzi around the seat arm and let it dangle, much to my annoyance. Shari turned my mind from the rebuke I was itching to hand to him.

Near the outskirts of town, the bus stopped to pick up a group of passengers, about a dozen, eight men and four women, all dressed in Arab garb which wasn't unusual. The four women and one of the men moved towards the back of the bus, and I took no notice of them as they passed because of the conversation I was having with Shari. Out the corner of my eye, I watched the group that sat near the front of the bus, one of them across and slightly behind the driver. My instinct was screaming at me that something was wrong.

At that moment, the one opposite the driver started yelling at him to stop the bus, but the driver ignored him. He yelled again as he stood. Shari and I had stopped speaking mid-sentence, and I noticed the soldier in front of us near the window had started to move his Uzi by the reflection in the glass. The Arab pulled an AK47 from under his robes and shot the driver. He reached across for the lever to open the door.

The other Arabs had stood up, drawing weapons from their robes they turned their weapons toward everyone on the bus. The soldier in front of me was wrestling to free his gun, and I swept Shari under me as I dived to the floor not a second too soon. The Arabs opened fire on the two soldiers. The one in front of me was the first target; he had finally freed his weapon only to have

446

it clatter to the floor as he died in a hail of gunfire. His mate only had time to get off one burst before he died as the result of gunfire.

I moved to retrieve the Uzi that had been dropped, and as I rolled with it, I shot off a burst into the Arab that had killed the soldiers. Gunfire erupted from the front of the bus and from the back of the bus. I heard Shari scream, "No! Tom, behind you!" She dove on top of me.

I whirled and shot the one behind me in the knee, then put a burst into his gun arm, which caused him to drop his weapon. I grabbed a zip tie from the dead soldier as I got up and raced to the front of the bus. The six Arabs were making a run for it, so I fired at the slowest, bringing him down. The others returned fire, and I took cover behind the door and tried again, but they were out of range. Turning, I ran toward the back of the bus, noting dead and wounded. I reached the Arab; zip tied his good arm to the bus seat, and kicked his weapon out of reach.

During all this, Shari hadn't moved. I slowly moved closer to her, and as I did, I saw eight bullet wounds in her back. I roared, "NO!" I sank to the floor as I turned her in my lap. "Shari."

She opened her eyes and sighed, "Tom, I love you."

With tears streaming down my face, I replied, "I love you, Shari, and always will." I kissed her gently as she died in my arms.

I don't know how long I sat like that, but when a policeman tried to get me to release Shari. I wouldn't; I remember pulling out my ID and telling him, "Get Minister Ben Aram here now. He's at home."

Before Joseph arrived, I don't know how many times people tried to get me to release Shari's body, but I was having none of it. When Joseph walked onto the bus, he muttered, "Dear god" as he glanced around at all the blood.

He tried to reason with me that it was safe to let go of her now. "Tom, my boy, time to dry your tears and let these men help my daughter."

I looked at him blankly. "I'll never cry again, Joseph."

A couple of paramedics had slowly eased Shari's body away from me, and I heard one of them say, "Christ, he's been shot too. There's blood gushing out of him. Shit, sir, we have to move him."

Joseph bent down, looked at me, and asked, "Can you get up? Here, I'll help you." I stood up and passed out from blood loss.

I woke up later that day wondering where I was. Tag walked into the room. I asked, "Where am I?"

"Megiddo Hospital. That bullet nearly killed you. I think if you hadn't been holding Shari so hard, you'd have died. You stemmed the flow with the pressure of her body." He paused, looking down. "I'm so sorry. She would have been a good wife." I must have looked confused. "Yeah, the rings were in your pocket. I've got them for safekeeping. Joseph will be by soon. The doctors think you'll be able to leave in a few days as long as you take it easy."

An hour later Joseph stopped by. He had tear tracks on his face. "I'm so sorry, Joseph. I tried to stop her from being hurt, and she covered my body with hers." I looked down, ashamed. But my anger was stronger. "Don't let the cops keep him. I want to make him talk. I want every last one of her killers, and I'm going to make them pay."

"Tom, my boy, stay calm. He's in military custody, and he'll still be there when you're well. He'll talk, don't worry about that." His last comment was made in a voice like solid steel, and his face had taken on a look of fury etched in stone.

"Joseph, she didn't even get a chance to make the choice of whether she was going to marry me or not. I left it too late."

"She loved you with all her heart and would have said yes to you. Marta and I are going to wait for you to get better before we say our final goodbye. I've instructed your Tag to take you to the farm to recuperate. Marta will look after you, my boy, as will I."

A couple of days later I was released from the hospital with strict instructions from the doctor not to overexert myself and rest as much as I could. Tag was driving the car given to Shari and I. The first thing I asked was, "Where are my guns?"

He answered that everything that had been in the car had been taken to Joseph's farm. He'd checked everything and nothing seemed to be missing; even Shari's Walther pistol had still been in the car. "Ok, Tag, fill me in on what happened after I passed out, and don't leave anything out."

Tag looked at me and was met by a hardened expression on my face. "Sure boss, but are you sure you want to hear this now? If looks could kill, even I'd be dead by now, and I've noticed that your look hasn't changed even when you were sleeping."

I interrupted him, growling, "Tag. Just tell me."

We moved out of the hospital carpark, and he continued, "Ok Tiger. When you got the police to call Joseph, apparently he rang Svi Ben Ari to get his men there and scour the countryside. We all left base, but Svi had asked me to travel with him. He told me you and Shari had come under attack on a bus. Anyway, we arrived as the ambulance medics were working on you, and after they took you off, Svi took over the situation and had the guy you shot taken to the local hospital under guard to be fixed up. He's now in the cells at base awaiting interrogation. The survivors have all given statements to the police and been interviewed by Svi's boys as well. They say it was you who saved them all. The first guy you shot, well, he was history. The wounded guy and the one you shot from the door were dead when the police got to him."

He paused before continuing. "Five got away, boss, and it's reckoned they jumped the border into Jordan and are probably heading for Syria. The three you got are all Syrian, so it's assumed the rest are too. There were twenty-six survivors. Four of them were wounded, not critically, so apart from the driver, there were thirteen others killed, including four kids, three women, one being Shari, and six men. Joseph has ordered an all-out hunt for these guys, and we've had stacks of activity with people coming and going from base. Information is starting to come in, and if Joseph doesn't tell you what's happening, I will, boss, I promise."

I remained silent, but he knew I had heard every detail. He stayed silent after that and left me alone with my thoughts.

When we neared the farm, he said, "I've got a rover here, so I'll be leaving the car with you. Once you're settled, I'll head back to base and catch up with what's going on."

I turned to look at him. "Thanks Tag. Tell the team that as well, but until I'm back, I want everything to continue as normal. If you learn anything at all, you ring me. I'll keep the phone close."

As we pulled into the farm, Marta came out the front door and ran over to the car to help me out. She put her arms around my waist, causing me to wince in pain. She saw my reaction and shifted her arms to my neck, embraced me and kept kissing me on the cheek. Tears were flowing from her eyes, and she kept repeating, "Oh Tom, oh Tom." She guided me into the house and sat me in a chair. She asked if I needed anything, and I told her a bottle of scotch would be nice. Tag took care of that by pulling out a bottle of Blue label from the bag he was carrying.

Readers Note: To this day I'm not sure when I was shot, but considering the exit wound was on my front, I can only assume it was caused by a bullet passing through Shari's body into me and continuing on its path. Why didn't I feel it? Well, during live action, adrenaline courses through the body, and unless the bullet hits a major organ or is incapacitating, it's not felt until after the adrenaline levels return to normal once the action subsides.

CHAPTER 35

That night Joseph arrived at the farm with a full security detail. I was only vaguely aware of what he was telling me, but before he'd said much, Marta pulled him away from me, pointing to the empty bottle of scotch on the table.

"He's been sitting there with that furious look on his face since he got here this afternoon, and he's drank that whole bottle and won't eat. Please take him up to bed, Joseph. The poor boy's in real pain in his head, a bit like I was when Dov was killed." I felt Joseph trying to get me up, but he ended up getting two of his security detail to take me to bed while he led the way.

The next morning, I joined them for breakfast. We discussed Shari's funeral, which would be held at the farm, and she would be laid to rest beside her brother. We decided it would take place in the afternoon of the next day, so we each started making phone calls to arrange it. I phoned Tag and arranged for my dress uniform and the team to attend. Tag would also pass the information to Svi. I asked Tag to have each team member bring his rifle; we would be the honour guard.

Joseph found out that most of the cabinet ministers in the Knesset would be attending and would fly into Ramat David the next morning. Marta had been onto the local Kohen (Priest), and he planned the service for fourteen hundred.

After retrieving Shari's pistol, I asked to see her body that night. Joseph escorted me to the basement where her coffin was resting on sawhorses in the cool. He left us to ourselves. The coffin lid had not been placed on, and I was able to view and talk to her.

Marta had dressed her in her dress uniform, and even though she was a sickly white, she still looked beautiful. Her hands were by her side, so I put her gun into her right hand and placed it on her belly. "This won't do my beautiful angel. If you're going to be in uniform, you need your pistol in your hand, my love." The tears flowed from my eyes. They were the last tears that I ever cried.

Readers Note: Yes, I get emotional, but never to the point of crying anymore.

I stayed and held her hand and talked to her for nearly an hour. I gently lowered her hand, kissed her goodbye on the lips, as a final goodbye, and left the basement.

Joseph had a drink poured for me as I joined him and Marta back upstairs. He told me what he'd started to the previous night, prior to Marta stopping him and having me taken to bed.

He told me that the terrorist I'd shot had been moved from the hospital and was now in a military prison. He would be interrogated the following week. Mossad had been able to find out his identity as well as the identity of the dead ones and were trying to find their associates.

I looked at him and said in a deadly, chilled voice, "I don't care who or where they are, I want to go after them, alone if I have to. I'm going to look them in the eye as I execute them, each and every one! He winced at the deadliness in my voice, nodded, and poured me another scotch.

The following morning my men arrived with my rifle and uniform, and even though the funeral wasn't until two, people started arriving around ten. Just after lunch, the motorcade carrying the Prime Minister, Yitzac Rabin, and other members of the government rolled into the yard. The limos parked one after the other and were followed by rovers and trucks from the Mossad base. Svi's men would function as the security detail.

Shari's coffin had been closed and was resting on the sawhorses in the lounge room rather than the basement. After being greeted by Joseph and Marta, Rabin came over and offered his condolences to me. He shook Tag's hand as I introduced him. A little later, I asked Svi to arrange that my men's rifles be taken to the graveside because they would carry the coffin to the grave. He said he'd take care of it.

At thirteen forty-five, the team formed lines on each side of Shari's coffin, lifted it off the sawhorses, and preceded the funeral procession. After the coffin, Joseph, Marta, and I walked side by side with Marta in the middle holding our hands. The ministers and everyone else followed.

During the service, I left Marta's side to join my men for the twenty-one gun salute, and after firing three rounds each, I passed my rifle to Tag as I joined Joseph and Marta again. After the service, we returned to the farmhouse for the traditional ceremony of the joy and burial feast. The festivities, if you could call them that, continued well into the night. After finishing a bottle of scotch, I took a fresh one with me and disappeared. I was found the next morning sleeping on my side beside Shari, my arm over her, and an empty bottle beside me.

For the next month, I would exercise each day, but at night, I would consume at least a bottle of scotch. Was I turning into a drunk? Yes, I suppose I was. My whole life had been turned upside down because the woman I loved was dead. The inner pain of that was excruciating, and to tell the truth, I think I stopped caring about anything after Shari's death, except for the revenge I craved.

Joseph came home one Friday night with his entourage, and Marta met him at the door. He joined me in the lounge and poured himself a drink. "We've got them. We know each one of them, where they live, and even the name and address of the man who planned the hijack."

I jumped up from my seat. "Good. When do I get to go after them?"

He shook his head and said, "You? I don't think so. You're a mess. You can't even hold your hand still unless you have a drink. Let's face it, Tiger, you're nothing but a drunken pussy! You may have been good before, but now you can't even shave without fear of cutting your own throat."

I was furious and slammed my glass on the floor. I yelled, "You can't speak to me like that! I'm a bloody soldier, and a good one, drunk or sober, so you don't have the right…"

He interrupted. "Right? I have every right! You're living in my house and probably caused the death of my daughter. And you want to avenge her? You can hardly stand up!"

Every part of my being seemed to be alight. "I'll show you!" I stormed upstairs to get my pistol and ran back downstairs and out into the yard. After setting up five cans on an inner fence, I walked back to the porch, turned, cocked my pistol, and fired. Out of nine rounds, only two cans dropped. Security came running, and I thought to myself, "Shit, I'm out of condition. My aim is off to buggery, too much booze. Got to get myself right."

Joseph had placated the security guards, and I turned to him. "I'm sorry, Joseph. You were right. I've let myself go, but all that ends now, tonight. Here keep this until I ask for it back, please." I passed him my pistol.

I started to get back in shape by purging the booze by sweating it out on a twenty mile run. After two continuous days of exercise and fitness routines, I'd cleared all the excess booze out of my body and was feeling better than I had for a while. I set up twenty cans on the fence and went inside, grabbed three mags for my pistol, and asked Joseph if I could have my pistol back.

"Only if you prove your man enough to have it back."

"Right, let's go outside."

He followed me outside and passed me my weapon, which I loaded. On the porch, I started firing, first right and then left handed. Every round hit a target standing, lying, or sitting.

One can I made fly. While it was in the air, I put five more shots into it before it hit the ground. Smiling I thought to myself, Yes! Back to peak condition. I ejected the current mag out of the pistol as well as the round in the chamber. I held it out to give back to Joseph, and he said with a smile, "No, it's yours, and it looks like you're safe to have it again. Are you ready to get down to some work?"

The following morning, Joseph and I went to Havatzalot in

the IDF car assigned to Shari, now to me, and Joseph's guard and secretary drove behind in his government limo. At the base, we pulled up at the HQ building and went in to see Svi. After Joseph and Svi had talked, I was invited into the office.

"Glad to have you aboard, Tiger," Svi said with a smile. "Your help in planning this will be invaluable. Plus, you'll have final command of the operation, which is to be designated "Retribution." The chief has briefed me on your role, and I'm happy to have you in command."

"Operation Retribution. I like that, because that's what it's going to be. Let's pick some men that aren't squeamish."

Joseph laughed. "I'll you leave you two to get on with it. All the information we have will come through to you, Colonel. Tiger, you let me know when your vow has been fulfilled."

During the next two weeks, I trained hard every day for four hours in the morning. I would run the assault course in full combat gear and fully armed, but instead of my MP4A, I carried the Uzi Shari had given to me. After completing the assault course, I'd run to the firing range and fire fifty rounds from each weapon.

Then in the afternoon, I would get together with Svi to examine the reports and photos coming to us from the teams of undercover agents he had sent into the target area to gather the intelligence.

It had been arranged that I'd lead a team of eight, including myself, when everything was ready, and we started picking from his agents. Each one needed to have assassination experience because the team I would lead would not be for intelligence gathering. This was a purely revenge attack on terrorists. If we happened to pick up some useful intelligence at the same time, all well and good.

Each team member had to be able to speak Arabic and English because I was still not fully conversant in Hebrew. Also, I didn't want any of my own team to be involved because I wanted Australian involvement kept to a minimum. I was taking this on my shoulders only; therefore, I would be the one to cop any grief from our army if things went wrong. I told the men this and explained my reasons for this decision to them.

Even though they wanted to be included, they accepted my reasoning and promised to stay out of it and continue with the cross training, much to Svi's relief. He wouldn't have been able to give permission to go. As it was, having me lead the operation was pushing the boundaries, but I had ministerial backing so he couldn't be held accountable should the mission go wrong.

We had six targets; five of them lived scattered about the same town, while the last one, the planner, lived in a village twenty miles from the other five. The plan was for our team to infiltrate the area and meet at an abandoned farm just on the outskirts of town, which would be used as our base of operations to initiate Israeli response to the attempted hijacking. After taking care of the first five, we would then move on to the sixth target, take him out, and return to Israel.

Once the team was picked, I made sure they had been through the training my team had provided on breaching suburban houses. They had, which was good. We exercised together again and again to make sure each man knew his role. Our weapons were fitted with laser sights and silencers because everything was going to take place during the nighttime hours. Those who didn't have night vision gear were issued them, and every man was issued with personal head microphone radios.

After obtaining three non-descript beat up vehicles, we were ready, waiting for the go order. At the final briefing, it was made clear to them that no one was to be killed unless I ordered it, so they had to have a good supply of zip ties and gags. We would leave base in our vehicles dressed in the black night cams, travel to the border of the Golan Heights, and once we crossed over into Syria, we would change into Arab garb and after a short sleep would make our way to the target town Qasim, during daylight hours.

After dinner at the farm that night, we got into two cars and went to reconnoitre all five addresses. We decided they would be easy enough to approach and attack without interference.

When we reached the last address, it was nearly twenty-two hundred. A machine-like coldness slowly took over my body. I coldly calculated that if we took care of one of the targets tonight, we'd only have to worry about two each night after that. I informed the men we were going to take this house and target now.

We were in our black cams, each of us armed, so all we had to do was don our balaclavas and night vision equipment. In one respect, the features of the house gave us a better advantage because it was only a single story, and it was set back away from the road, away from neighbours. Plus, it had a high corrugated iron fence. When we entered the yard, the first thing we did was close the gates silently. Now no one outside the fence could see us.

I gave instructions to split into two groups. "Ok, this place looks as if it's made for privacy, so be careful. There may be booby traps around. Group two, you move to the back and we'll head for the front. Let me know when you're in position, and remember to clear each room as we move to the middle of the house. If you find anyone, tie and gag them before moving on. Once the house is secure, all prisoners will be brought into the lounge. Everybody clear? Let's go!"

Ten minutes later, group two was in place and I gave the order to make entry. Each room was cleared one by one, and fifteen minutes later, the target was on his knees, tied, gagged and facing me. The heavy curtains were drawn, and the light was switched on in the lounge. I slowly took off my night vision gear and took in the sight of a woman and two boys on their knees, also tied and gagged.

A cold rage swept through me. I looked the target in the eye and asked, "Do you know why we're here?" He shook his head no. My voice volume dropped. "We're from Israel, here to deliver retribution for a bus load of innocent people who were killed in cold blood!"

As I said this, his eyes widened and he quaked in fear. I allowed the information to sink in, then said, "In a minute, your gag will be removed and you will tell me what I want to know. If you yell out, I will shoot a member of your family. If you say anything other than what I ask you, I will shoot one of them. Do you understand?" He nodded.

I drew my pistol with its silencer on. "I wish to know who was with you, their names, where they live, the person who planned it, and the person who ordered it done. Don't attempt to lie or..." I pointed my gun at one of his family members and nodded to the man behind him, who took off his gag.

The target started talking, and my rage rose. The man behind him was ticking off the info. He looked at me and nodded; he was telling the truth. The man said, "I don't know who ordered us to go ahead. We were just told to do it by Yusuf. Please, let my family go. They are innocent and know nothing. I beg you, in the name of Allah, please leave them."

"As I said, we are here in retribution, and the people you murdered on that bus were also innocent! You took away my chance to have a family when my girlfriend was shot down" I looked at the man standing behind the hostage. "Put his gag back on. As a matter of fact, my friend, you're lucky it's not God or Allah doing this because we both know they would have killed everybody. As a matter of fact, that's a good idea. Let's have some divine retribution, my style."

I placed the barrel of my gun against his wife's head, looked at him, and fired. He screamed into his gag and watched me as I moved to the first boy and repeated my actions. He screamed louder and tears flowed from his eyes. I moved to the next boy; he was shaking his head and mumbling into his gag as I pulled the trigger again. I stood in front of him and read him the list of names of the people killed on the bus.

"Shari Ben Aram was to be my wife and the mother of my children. Now she's lying cold in the ground, as cold as I am right now." I lifted the pistol once more and shot him in the head. Without saying another word, I walked from the room and out of the house.

We travelled back to the safe house. I didn't say a word for the rest of the night; I was too busy trying to make sense of what I'd done. My inner coldness reasserted itself, and I decided I was doing the right thing. Something was worrying me and it wouldn't quit. I kept pushing it to the back of my mind. Over and over again.

That first night set the scene for the next four visits. We did two each night, and each time our information was verified, I would repeat my sentence to the prisoners. I killed their entire families while they watched, and then I would execute them.

After killing five families, my mind was in a turmoil. The longer I remained silent, the longer the battle within me raged. On one side, I was doing the right and proper thing, but on the other side, I was starting to realize that I was doing the wrong thing, becoming no better than the people I was hunting. I had killed in cold blood, with no justification other than pure revenge for the hurt I was feeling. Out in the yard of the last house, everything let go, and I threw up as I remembered what I had done.

The blackness slowly gave way. "Would Shari have wanted me to do this?" The answer was no. She and I could kill during war, but what I was doing wasn't war; it was vengeance, and it was time to stop. The blackness in my mind lifted, and I realized how murderous I had become. I swore I would never go to that extreme again, because that wasn't me. What was done was done and couldn't be undone. Someday, no doubt, I'll pay for my sins. What I'd done while in that state of blackness did bother me, and it didn't help when the guys I was working with considered me a hero for what I'd done.

Now that that blackness had lifted, I was determined to make up for what I'd done. We still had one more target. Instead of killing him, I was going to capture him and take him back alive for interrogation. If he died after that, well, at least it would be better than me executing him.

Slowly I returned to my former self; I even joined in some of the joking that was going on in the group. The next morning after leaving one car at the farm, we dressed in our Arab robes and drove to Shaykh Miskin, where the planner Yusuf lived.

When we reached the outskirts of the village, we looked for a suitable place to hide the cars from view and rest. We found a dried up watercourse that would fit the bill nicely. After having a short rest, I took the group leader with me and went in search of the address. We located it and parked just up the street to watch.

We got out of the car and walked around the house in different directions. We returned to the car to compare notes, and while we were there, there wasn't any real activity apart from household chores. We drove back to our camp outside of town, had something to eat, and filled in the team about what we'd found out.

That's when I told everyone about the change of plan. Not only would we be taking him prisoner and taking him back to Israel, but we would also take his entire family. They could be used as leverage against him during his interrogation. I told them I didn't care how badly he was treated while we had him, as long as he was alive when we handed him over.

We drove into town at twenty-two hundred. I spoke on the radio to the team members in both cars. "We'll do everything the same as we have, but when the house is secure, we'll have one of you drive the cars into the yard. Instead of shooting them, we'll put bags over their heads and put them in the boot. Once we have them, I'm afraid we'll have to drive all the way back to the farm before we rest. We're just about there. Let's get ready."

We took the house in the same manner as we'd done previously, and once the prisoners were secured, two of the team went to get the cars. There were only three prisoners, the planner, his wife, and a boy of about nine or ten. To make them more compliant to our wishes, I needed to put the fear of god into them. I moved in front of the woman and put my gun barrel to her head. I asked Yusuf after his gag had been removed, "Does your wife understand English?"

She was nodding as he replied, "Yes, both my son and wife speak English."

"Good, thank you," I replied.

I looked at her. "If you scream or make any sudden moves, your son will be shot. If he makes any, you'll be shot. Do you both understand?" They nodded. "Good. You are all going to be taken back as prisoners. It's either that, or I shoot you now, and quite frankly, after slaughtering five families already, I'm getting a little sick of the killing. I leave the choice to you. You can come as prisoners and cooperate, or stay here and I'll kill you. Will you come with us willingly?"

All three nodded profusely. "Good." I turned to Yusuf. "You planned an attack on an Israeli bus. Eight men participated. All of them are now dead, as well as some of their families. Do you know how many people died or were wounded on that bus?"

He hung his head answered, "No." I looked at his wife as she closed her eyes.

"Four wounded, and four children, three women, and seven men killed. Unfortunately, for you, one of the women that died was going to be my wife, so as you can see, I have nothing to lose if I kill you. However, I'm going to give you a chance, more than the people on that bus got. I want to know who ordered the attack."

He nodded his head furiously and started yammering in a cross of English and Arabic, while the man behind wrote. Every now and then, the soldier would ask him to repeat what he said. Yusuf babbled on for at least half an hour as I paced up and down in the lounge.

When he fell silent, I asked, "Is that all, or do you have more to tell us?"

"I have more, much more, but I can't think of everything just now. I can help your intelligence people with anything they want to know, just as long as my family is safe, sir," he gushed.

I looked at him and the other two, nodded, and said, "Very well. In that case, you will all be coming with us, but be warned, you may experience hardship during this journey. Quite frankly,

I don't give a damn, and I will have no hesitation in shooting any of you, if you try to escape, or do not do as you are told. Soon you will have hoods placed over your heads, and they will stay on until we reach our destination. The first part of our trip will take a while. Any questions?"

The woman mumbled into her gag, and I indicated for it to be taken off. "Would it be possible to go to the toilet before we leave, please?"

I sighed and had to put my face down to hide the smile. "Yes. I'll have one of my men take you. The door will remain open, and your gag will be put back on now."

After her gag was back in place, she was lifted by her arms to a standing position and her ankle restraints cut. She was then led to the toilet. I looked at the boy and asked "You too?" He nodded his head, so he was lifted up and his ankles freed. When the woman returned, he was led off.

I looked at Yusuf. "You I don't care about. You can piss yourself for all I care."

When the boy was brought back into the room, bags were put over their heads and they were led to the cars to have their feet secured again before being placed, mother and son, in one car boot, and Yusuf in the other. Both cars drove out of the yard and out of town, and onto the road to Qasim and the safe house.

At the farm, we slept, then ate, and fed the prisoners. We made our preparations to return to Israel. Once we were back in three cars, one prisoner was placed in the boot of each vehicle with instructions to remain quiet until they were let out again. Two days later, after very nearly getting into a firefight with Israeli troops at the border, we drove into the compound of Mossad HQ. We climbed out of the vehicles and pulled the prisoners out. Svi came out of his office with Tag to meet and congratulate us.

CHAPTER 36

After the prisoners had been taken to their cells and the team dispersed, Svi, Tag, and I went back into Svi's office where I gave a verbal debrief about what had happened during the mission. Tag recorded it, which made it easier for me to write up the mission report later.

After I'd finished an hour later and the questions had been answered, I said, "Svi, the prisoners, please make sure the woman and kid are treated reasonably. As for the planner, he will probably be a goldmine of intelligence, and he's promised to cooperate as long as his family is safe. After you get what you need, you can either turn them loose and resettle them some place or send them back as your agents. I'd see what they have to say, but I think he's blown now. If they go back, they'll be dead within a week."

He studied me a moment. "Yes Tiger, I agree. We may have to resettle them somewhere, but if he's as valuable as you think, I'll have to turn him over to intelligence so they can suck him dry, but I'll have to see what HQ wants me to do with him first, but there's no reason not to listen to what he has to say before they take him." He smiled.

I smiled also and thought, Smart man. Have your people suck him dry of information before you turn him over. "Good idea, but use soft interrogation. He'll give you as much as he can. I need to contact IDF HQ before anything else. Can I use your phone and office for a while, please?"

"Of course," he replied with a chuckle. "Tag and I were going to have a look at something he's cooked up before you turned up, so we'll go do that. Anything else you need?"

"No, but after I'm finished, I'll be taking my car for a drive and may be gone the rest of the day. I'll be back on base tonight." I focused on Tag. "Tag, tonight I'd like to have a word with you and the boys. Can you put some time aside for that?" Tag nodded. "I'll get this call made and then I'll take off. Thanks."

After they left the office, I reached for the phone and dialled the number Joseph had given me. Instead of Joseph answering, Joshua picked up. I asked where Joseph was, and Joshua informed me that the minister would be out of the office all day. He asked if he could be of help.

"I have his sat phone number. Is it possible to send a message to him?"

Joshua told me it could be done and how to do it, so I wrote his instructions down. He asked if he could do anything else for me, and I replied, "Yes, actually. I need to see Joseph, and I'll probably need to be with him most of the day. What can you arrange, and can you get me down there?"

"Certainly Tiger. I can have someone from Ramat David pick you up and fly you down to Lod, and I'll have someone there to pick you up and take you to the King David. The only day I can get you in is Tuesday next week. Is that soon enough?"

"That would be fine, unless Joseph is going to home on the weekend prior?" I asked.

Joshua replied, "I'm afraid not, sir. He'll still be in Egypt. Shall I make the arrangements for Monday the day before, Tiger?"

"Yes please, Joshua, and thank you. I'll see you next Tuesday," I replied and hung up. I pulled the sat phone out of my fatigues thigh pocket, and following Joshua's instructions, sent Joseph the message: "Operation Retribution a complete success. Will talk next week. Tiger."

I left the office and went to my quarters to get my car keys as well as the keys to Shari's house in Megiddo and the unit in Tel Aviv. There was only one uniform of mine at the unit, but I decided it could stay there next to Shari's. I had enough uniforms, so I wouldn't miss one. I got into the car and drove to Megiddo and to Shari's house. The house was full of pleasant memories that made me smile but were also painful as well. I packed my gear into my go bag and took it out to the car. I went back for one final look, then locked up the house before driving to her parent's farm.

As I pulled up by the front door, Marta came out and welcomed me. We walked into the kitchen arm in arm, where she made coffee for us. She brought out some cake as well.

"Tom, you look much better than when I last saw you. What have you been doing?"

I smiled sadly. "Marta, you know I can't tell you that, but I've been making a few things right, which helped me with my grief. If you want to know more, you'll have to ask your husband. I came by to give you the keys to the house in Megiddo and the unit in Tel Aviv. I've left one of my uniforms in the unit, but I've got plenty more.

Instead of staying at the house, I've got quarters on base, so I'll use them." I paused before saying what I really wanted. "I need to speak to your daughter alone please."

She took my hand and squeezed it. "Tom, you'll always be welcome here, even if you just want to see her. I know you will carry her memory in your head as well as your heart, but time does heal all wounds, even the deep ones. Your wound will heal in time, but I know you will never forget my little girl. Go talk to her. Come and see me before you go, my dear one."

I downed what was left of my coffee and walked outside and to where Shari rested. I kissed the ground above her before sitting down.

I communicated with her silently, telling her of the things I had done and how low I had sunk before I had been able to shake it off. I told her about moving back to live on base, of how much I loved her and wanted to be with her, and that I hoped she'd understand if I didn't come to visit her too often.

I had been with Shari for over an hour before returning to the house to see Marta. She saw the pain etched on my face and poured me a glass of Sabra. She passed it to me with kind words. "You need this to settle yourself, but only the one."

As I slowly sipped the Sabra, I realised just how nice it was. Marta was right, though, I had needed it. By the time it was finished, I felt much better. I told her I'd be seeing Joseph on Tuesday and asked if she wanted me to pass on any message. She wrote something on a piece of paper and passed it to me, which I folded and put in my pocket. We kissed and hugged our farewells.

I arrived on base in time for dinner in the mess. I joined the rest of the team there, and an hour after dinner we were back in the quarters lounge, lazing around as I prepared to address them.

"Ok boys, I know I've not been around lately. You guys deserve to know why, so here goes…"

I told them of the depth of my love for Shari and what happened to me afterwards, about becoming a drunk. I admitted if it hadn't been for an argument with Joseph, I'd probably still be slowly killing myself with booze. I went on to recount the measures I had gone to get back into peak condition and why. I told them about what happened to me on the mission, and my going berserk and the killing I did, the inner fight I had with my own demons, and how I eventually overcame them.

"So here I am talking to you. I will admit I went on the mission with the intention of it being a one-way trip, and I think if I hadn't changed my mind about slaughtering people, we would have been tracked, and it would have ended up a one-way trip for me. That's the whole story."

"So what are you going to do now, boss?" Buzz asked.

"Well, this is for everyone to hear and think about. On Monday I'll be going to Tel Aviv with my report and could be away for a couple of days. I'll be back here after that and we'll get on with the job we're here to do. But after this trip, each of us is going to have to make a decision about what we'll do when we get back to Australia. By now most of you realise this will probably be the last job we do as an SRT team." I paused for a drink before continuing.

"As you know, they were thinking of shutting us down before this came up. I think when we get back, we'll most likely be sent on extended leave. And when we get back from that, they'll can the team. Mind you, this is only my gut feeling, and it's not gospel until it's spelled out, so I'll leave the decision with you guys."

"What about you, boss? What are you likely to do?" Dumper asked.

I thought for a moment and replied, "Well, to be honest guys, I had two trains of thought. One of them isn't going to happen now, but you deserve to hear what I was thinking of doing. Number one, if Shari had of lived, I was going to finish this tour and quit, sell everything I have, and move here to be with Shari. I would probably have been offered a job with Mossad. We know that's not going to happen now. Number two, I've become a little disillusioned since we did that job in Africa, and the thought of going back into mundane sabre squadron stuff after this leaves me cold. So I really only have two options. One is to resign, and the other is taking an inter-service transfer and hopefully go into a unit that requires an RSM. If SRT doesn't disband, then I'll still be here. If it does, well, I guess I'll make up my mind while I'm on leave. But each of you will have to make up your mind when we know for sure."

I had finished my drink and got up to pour another. Everyone was silent, thinking about what I'd said. I noticed some of them needed refills, so I placed the scotch bottle on the coffee table.

"However, all that's something we'll worry about in the future. Right now what are we up to?"

Tag spoke up after refilling his glass. "At present, we're trying to think of different types of terrorist attacks. Then we all work on a solution and practise it. So far, we've come up with two hundred and six scenarios and found solutions for each, but we've come up with one that is proving rather difficult to solve. How to take out a suicide bomber in a room full of people. Maybe it's one for you to have a crack at when you're back on deck."

"Yeah, something to get my brain engaged. Sounds good to

me, but I probably won't be able to look at it until I'm back from Tel Aviv. Anything else I need to know?"

"Yeah boss. We've all got four sets each of the desert cams and the black night cams. I've got yours down in my room, when you want them," Buzz informed me. I thanked him and told him I'd probably use the desert cams while I was in Tel Aviv, so I'd get them from him later in the night.

We started talking about what we thought of the bloody bureaucrats we had to put up with in the Australian army. Compared to some of the other armies we'd been involved with over the years, we all decided that Israel had by far the better system, with every arm of their defence force under one command, not split into different branches, that had a tendency to form its own hierarchy. We mused about whether it could work in our system before calling it a night.

I grabbed the uniforms Buzz had procured and took them to my room, where I began sorting out all my clothing. I thought to myself that we'd be leaving here with more than we came with yet again, and I smiled as I thought of my own saying that it may come in handy sometime, you never know.

The next morning after breakfast, I started working on the mission report and listened to the tapes I had used during the operation, as well as the one Tag had used during the debriefing with Svi. Later that day I went to see Svi and asked him if he had someone that could speak Arabic to interpret a tape for me. He assigned one of the orderlies to write up a translation for me.

I asked if he'd learnt anything useful from Yusuf. He replied that the information he was giving voluntarily was an absolute goldmine of intelligence. He showed me the reports they had compiled, and I asked for a copy.

He told me to keep what he'd given me because everything Yusuf had said was being transcribed and fed into the computer they had on base. I thanked him and checked with the orderly doing my transcribing, who said he'd bring it to my quarters before the end of the day. I thanked the orderly and left the building to go back to my quarters, where I continued with my report.

I went to see Yusuf the next day. He had been moved from the cells because of his willingness to cooperate and had been placed in a barracks building that had barred doors. Yusuf and his family had free reign in the building and could cook, make tea, and watch TV as well. He and his family were grateful to me for sparing their lives and invited me to have lunch with them, which I did. I told him I would put a word in for him when I saw some of the government ministers at a later date, but I also gave him a veiled threat that his information would be checked. His life, and the lives of his family, were at risk if there were any falsehoods.

I used some of the information gathered from Yusuf to put in my report because I still had to explain to Joseph why I had not killed him.

Finally, Monday arrived, and after breakfast Svi came over to my quarters to tell me that a chopper would be landing at ten hundred to take me to Lod air base. The chopper would use the pads behind the HQ building, so he'd send someone to get me nearer that time. At ten to ten an orderly picked me up in a rover, and we drove to the chopper pads, where I got out and unloaded my go bag. Five minutes later the chopper touched down and I boarded. Two hours later we landed at Lod, and I was whisked away by limo to the King David.

The reception desk girl knew me and handed me the key to my suite. "Your usual room, Colonel. Please have a pleasant stay. I'll get the porter to take you up."

I smiled and replied, "Thank you. Just have him take my bag up. I'm going into the dining room for some lunch before I go up."

"Yes sir, no problem."

After having lunch, I went up to my room and unpacked. I decided to wear my dress uniform the following day for my meeting with Joseph. That evening in the bar before I went to dinner, I was approached by a new face that belonged to a female television reporter freshly arrived from Sydney.

469

She introduced herself, and looking at my uniform, asked me if I was Australian and what I was doing in Israel.

"Well Tracey, yes I'm an Aussie, and as for what I'm doing here, you know I can't answer that."

She laughed as she replied. "Oh come on, Colonel, strictly off the record. That's a US rank ranking," she said, pointing at my rank. "Why are you wearing that?"

"Ok Tracey, if you join me for dinner, I'll answer your questions as long as they are truly off the record," I told her with a chuckle.

"I'd love to join you, and yes, my questions will definitely be off the record … Colonel," she replied.

As we were shown to my table, I ordered a glass of Sabra while she had wine, and when the drinks had been brought and dinner ordered, I said, "As for the rank, I hold a colonel's rank in the US army because of some stuff we did for them. My superiors thought it would be more impressive. We're here doing some cross training with the Israeli army for a little while, but every now and then I've got to come down to Tel Aviv for meetings. And that's why I'm here."

Just as I finished speaking, a waiter approached and said, "Excuse me, Colonel Davis, but I have a call from the ministry for you."

I nodded. He put the phone down and plugged it into a jack close by. I lifted the handset and said, "Davis." It was Joshua, informing me I'd be picked up at nine hundred. "Thank you, Joshua. I'll see you in the morning."

The reporter looked at me, an eyebrow cocked. "My, you must be fairly important to get the royal treatment?"

I laughed. "No. The room bookings are handled by the defence ministry. Every time I get a call, hotel staff thinks it's from them, but in actual fact the calls come from the IDF HQ where my meetings are being held."

As dinner progressed, I noticed her flirting was becoming more obvious, and I could tell she was actively trying to seduce me. I decided the best way to avoid any entanglement and stay friendly was to put her off gently. "Tracey, why do I get the feeling you're trying to race me off?"

"Well, maybe I am. You are cute, you know," she giggled.

"Yes, I have been told that by my fiancé a number of times. It's a pity she's not here." I leaned closer. "In all honesty, Tracey, you won't get any further with me because at present I'm just not available. Sorry."

She narrowed her eyes at me briefly. "I appreciate your candour, Tom. I think we've both had a lovely meal with good company, and I hope we can do it again some other time. I better wish you a goodnight. Thank you, Tom."

"Yes, maybe another time. Goodnight, Tracey." I sat back down again as she left and continued to drink my Sabra.

The next morning after breakfast, I waited for my transport in the lobby of the hotel, scanning the faces of people coming and going. The limo arrived promptly at nine and whisked me off to the IDF building.

When I walked into Joseph's office, he embraced me. "Ah Tiger, it's good to see you. Joshua, bring coffee and Danishes, please," he ordered. We sat down on the couches opposite each other. "So my boy, what have you got there?"

"It's my mission report of Operation Retribution, and it gives you a completely detailed account of what occurred. I'd like you to read it and ask any questions you may have." I passed the manila folder across containing the report to him, and I did notice that he noticed I had more folders. He picked it up and removed the report to start reading as Joshua came back with a plate of Danishes and the coffee.

As he read, Joseph would have a bite of a Danish and a drink of coffee, and then reach for another Danish. Every now and then he would look up from the report at me. After an hour of reading, he put the report down on top of the folder. "Tiger, that is indeed complete in every way. A little self-critical, but I wish you would give lessons to all the commanders that write reports to me. Yours is written the way a report should be, but enough praise. I suppose you're waiting for some questions from me."

"Yes sir, but first, your wife asked me to give this to you." I handed him the piece of paper Marta had written on, which he took and read.

"You've seen this?"

"Yes sir," I said with a smile. "I watched your wife write it, but what it says is beyond me. I'm still not all that good at reading Hebrew."

He laughed. "Well, my boy, even if you could that wouldn't help you. This is written in Aramaic, an old language that Marta and I studied as youngsters when we were your age. She reports to me that you've recovered fully from the shock of Shari's death and can be relied upon once more. In light of this, I need to question you hard on a couple of matters raised in your report."

I sat up. "By all means, sir. Go right ahead."

"Why did you change the boundaries of the mission by slaughtering the families of the gunmen you were there to kill instead of killing just them?"

I readied myself to answer and take the blame for what I'd done. "Because, sir, the boundaries were too small. The name of the operation was retribution, not revenge, and if we'd only killed the men, it would be seen as a revenge killing. For full retribution, not only should I have killed his family in front of him, but instead of killing him, I should have shot to cripple him severely so he would know what retribution was truly like. He'd see that moment again and again. Like I did."

Joseph stared at me, thinking, and then nodded his head. "Hmm, yes, Tiger, I agree with you. You should have only crippled them, but you were following the orders that had been given, even if you did bend them a little. You'll face no reprimands over that. Now, you did this to all five gunmen, but you were also supposed to kill the man who planned everything, were you not? However, you

472

let him live, and not only that, you brought him and his family to Israel. What the devil were you thinking?"

I looked him in the eye. "By the time we got to him, I was sick and tired of the bloodshed. I was turning into someone just as bad as they were, if not worse. One doesn't murder in peacetime, which is what I was doing, and I couldn't stand myself any more. I thought that the man was a planner, so he knew a lot of information. Instead of just killing him, I put the fear of god into him. He, in turn, promised us intelligence if his family was safe."

I stopped to gauge his reaction while I took a drink. I handed him the second folder. "My feeling was right. In that folder is a list of stuff he's already supplied, and according to Mossad, he is an intelligence goldmine. I would also recommend that he and his family be allowed to settle here and that he is recruited into Israeli intelligence." His face showed surprise. "Not all at once. Have him fully debriefed first, then suck him dry of information.

Don't forget he has Arab insights and can think as they do. He could be invaluable in the future. But that is up to you, sir. I stand by my judgement of letting him and his family live, even if it was just to clear my conscience." I remained silent as Joseph read the file.

Another half an hour passed as Joseph continued to read, and at times his face changed colour from white to red and back to normal. He lifted his eyes from the report and stared at me. "My god. I've just been thinking of what we would have missed out on if you had done as you were ordered. Even though you spared his life to ease your own conscience, this information is already invaluable. I must thank you for not doing as I ordered. Once more, you have justified my faith in you, and I must admit I had started to doubt you, my boy. Come, let's go to lunch."

He put his arm around my shoulders and guided me to the dining room, where we shared a table and had lunch. Instead of getting back to my reports, we talked about anything but them.

By fifteen hundred, we had finished all our business. Joseph called Joshua in and made arrangements that he and I would

473

spend a day together each month. Joshua left to make the arrangements for my return north. I told Joseph about handing the keys to Shari's places back to Marta and asked if they had any idea of what they would do with them yet. He told me he'd probably keep the apartment in Tel Aviv, but would sell the house in Megiddo, unless I could be persuaded to stay in Israel. He'd get much joy if I did stay, and he'd give the house to me, but at the pained expression on my face said maybe not. He offered to sell it and purchase another and asked me to seriously think about staying. After he found out I'd left some uniforms at the apartment, he gave me the key and told me to collect what I needed.

I shook hands goodbye with Joseph and went down to the car. I gave the address to the driver.

When we got to the apartment, I had the driver wait while I went upstairs into the flat. With a heavy sigh I had a quick look round. Just as well I had called in because apart from the two uniforms hanging in the cupboard, I had left my Australian Army ID beside the bed. I took Shari's spare Walther with me should I ever need another handgun. After a final look around, I sighed, blew the bedroom a kiss, and left.

When I arrived at the hotel, reception informed me that the driver would take me to the airport at ten thirty. I arranged for my uniforms to be taken up to my room and walked into the bar. I spotted Tracey standing by the window without a drink. I tapped her on the shoulder, and as she turned, I whisked her into my arms and kissed her longingly on the lips. When I broke the kiss, she nearly fell. I caught her and asked if she'd like to join me. She nodded, so I grabbed her arm, guided her to the lift, and took her to my room.

CHAPTER 37

I guided her to the desk and sat her down. I grabbed a bottle of Sabra and two glasses, put some ice into the ice bucket, and went back to the desk. I poured two big shots of the Jaffa-like liqueur, placed a couple cubes of ice in each, and passed one to her. She was still in a stunned state, and as I raised a glass, she copied my example and swallowed some of the liqueur.

The alcohol brought her out of her stunned daze. "What am I doing here?"

"To give you a brief rundown, I kissed you and asked if you wanted to join me, you said yes, so I brought you up to my room, sat you down, and now I'm about to apologise to you for not telling you the whole truth last night."

"Say, this is good stuff." She took another drink. "I know all that except the last bit, so would you please tell me what's going on?"

"If you'll stop interrupting me, I'll tell you. Last night you told me I was cute, and I told you that my fiancé had told me that but that she wasn't here. All that's true, but the reason she's not here is that about three, no four months ago, she was killed in an attempted bus hijack up north. I was with her, and as I made a move on the hijackers, she shielded my body with hers. I was also shot, after killing a couple of the hijackers, but I survived. She didn't." I paused to clear my throat. "Until today my head has not been in a good place, and that is why I gave you the brush off last night. I just thought you should know why I rejected your flirting. I realise now that I owed you an explanation, so I apologise for any misconception." She looked at me and swallowed the rest of the Sabra, and as I indicated a refill, she nodded. I topped up her glass and added some ice.

"So you've been grieving ever since. I'm sorry. You must have thought me a brazen cow."

I held my hand up to interrupt her. "No, I didn't actually. I was quite flattered, but as I said, my head was in the wrong place yesterday. Today, I gave my report to the man that ordered the mission I was on, with a Mossad team."

It was her turn to interrupt me. "Wait a minute. You've been working with a Mossad team?"

"I'm expecting you to keep this off the record, but yes, after I was well enough and back to full fitness, I was given the chance to join a Mossad revenge team. We tracked down the culprits and killed them."

She sat bolt upright. "I knew there was something special about you! That's why you've been getting the royal treatment. My god, I wish you'd let me use this story."

I looked across the desk at her as I topped up my glass. "No. Sorry, Tracey. If I'm asked about this, there'll be a no comment. No one in the government will confirm anything either, so forget about it. I just wanted to give you an explanation about why I was so off handed. I hope you can understand."

"Only if we can have dinner together again tonight. However, be warned, I'm going to use all my charm on you. Then you can bring me back here and have me."

"Ok, we'll see what happens."

After dinner that night, she did end up coming back to the room, and she did have an enjoyable night, at least from what I could make out during her screams. I'm glad the walls in the hotel were thick and insulated.

She joined me for breakfast, and as we ate, she asked, "Whereabouts are you stationed up north? I might get up that way. Who knows?"

"You know I can't tell you that, but here's the number of my sat phone. Call if you ever get as far north as Nazareth, and I'll see if we can meet up." I wrote down the number on a napkin and passed it to her.

"How long before you have to go?"

I looked at my watch. "Forty minutes. Just enough time to go up and pack."

"I'll come with you. I think I'd better try and find my panties before they clean the room."

I looked at her with a smile and said, "So you've been sitting here without knickers on?" She grinned and nodded her head, and I burst out laughing. "Yeah well, you better come up with me then."

She retrieved her knickers that had been kicked under the bed somehow, and we kissed goodbye. I continued to pack my gear into the go bag and went back down to the lobby, checked out, and waited for my transport to arrive.

I was back on base three hours later. I took my bag to my quarters before changing into a set of fatigues and visiting Svi in his office.

During our conversation, he brought up the training scenario that was bothering everyone, and I asked him to give me the complete scenario. He divulged the details while I worked out why it was such a hard one to solve. I asked him to let me think it over and I'd see if there was any way to solve it without possible loss of life. The most obvious solution in a one-person scenario like this would be for a sniper to take a head shot, but in his particular scenario the suicide bomber had a dead man's switch and he was keeping low to prevent a sniper taking him. A dead man's switch is a switch wired to the explosive and is controlled by the bomber. It has a pulled-in trigger that is under pressure. If the finger releases the trigger for any reason, which takes the pressure off, the bomb explodes.

The most obvious way to counteract this is to have a sniper take a head shot, and because the man is killed instantaneously, there is not enough time for the brain, which has exploded under the bullet impact, to send a message to the finger to release the trigger. Therefore, he dies with the trigger not being released and is considered safe. However, as in this case scenario, that's not possible because of the bomber staying low among the hostages, which means the sniper can't get a shot.

During the rest of that week, we worked out various solutions, without success, and then it dawned on me. The bomber had to be distracted. A couple of ways to distract him were devised. So armed with a new set of parameters; we practised the solutions to see which one worked the best. Instead of including only the sniper, the new strategy required two men; both had to be expert marksmen. The second one had to good with handguns, and he would pose as a negotiator. Because we needed realism, the main combatants were given fake weapons. The bomber wore a flak jacket and held a dummy switch. The sniper was given a rifle that fired plastic bullets, and the negotiator, a hand paint gun. The bomber was fitted out first and taken to the practise room. He wasn't aware of what the others had been given.

We tried a couple solutions that didn't work, and then it became time to try the one for which everyone was dressed. I was going to play the negotiator, so I had a word with Lizard, who was the sniper. "My communication set will be on, and when you hear me say "around", shoot your bullet into the wall. Got it?"

He smiled and replied, "Got it. You're getting devious again, boss." I smiled at his comment.

When he was in his position, I heard him say, "Ready boss." I stepped up to the door of the hostage room, sighed, and opened the door. I stepped into the room with my hands up. "Shalom. My name is Tom, and I'm here to act as a negotiator. I'm unarmed, and to prove it, I'll turn around."

As the bullet whacked into the wall, the bomber's eyes were instantly drawn to the wall. I swung my gun out from behind my back, and cupping my left palm underneath my right to steady my aim, fired a head shot at the bomber, who fell "dead." Everyone started applauding and laughing. They now knew they had another scenario solution to practise and perfect, and were happy that a solution had been found.

The bomber played by Dumper, got up and called, "Medic." He rubbed his head where I'd hit him. "Geez, boss, those paint-balls really hurt. I'll be chewing aspro for a week now. Thank you most to death." Everyone burst into new fits of laughter.

Svi, who had been watching from the control room, was smiling as he came into the room. Everyone instantly quieted and snapped to attention, except my men. He came forward, shook our hands, and passed Dumper a box of aspirin.

"Ah Dumper, just think. Your headache has been for a worthy cause. I hope you recover soon, my friend." He and Dumper grinned at each other. "Tiger, this was one scenario I didn't think could be solved. We have agonised for weeks with this one, and it only took you a few days to solve. You have now solved two scenarios. Thank you. We know how to take down a subject without the sniper having a clear shot."

Tag laughed and said, "I told you the boss would be the one to solve it."

Svi told us the rest of the day was declared as rest time for everyone to think and absorb what they had been shown. As they all stood down, the team and I headed back to our quarters.

Once there, Buzz elected to make all the coffees, and we all lazed around for a while making small talk. I went into my room for a cold shower and flopped onto the bed naked. I slept for a couple of hours.

After dinner that night, instead of staying in the mess, I went back to our quarters and sat at the desk in my room. I had a quiet drink while keeping an eye on the time and rang the main office number of our Australian HQ from the sat phone. I asked the orderly for the time there and worked out there was an eight-hour time difference. I asked for the current HQ CO and found out that Mark Ryan, now a major, had returned. I asked to be put through to him.

"Hi Mark. Nice to know you're back in your old job."

He laughed. "Tiger, by god, it's good to hear from you. I take it you're still on that training job I was informed about. What can I do for you?"

"We're still over here, and so far it's been fun. There's been a few hiccups, but they've all been sorted out. I thought I'd call because I now have a satellite phone to use." I gave him the number. "If you need to get me in a hurry, just call. I thought I'd let you know we could get home earlier if you want us to."

I heard him gasp over the line. "Good god, no. All sorts of shake ups are going on here, with the sabre squadrons being integrated and new tactical forces being formed. No, you're better off staying O/S. That way your unit is out of mind. Hang on a moment."

He was talking to someone who'd stepped into his office, asking them to wait outside until he'd finished his call. "If you come back early, SRT will most likely be disbanded, and you guys will probably be split up and integrated into the new tactical teams being formed. As it is, I can't guarantee keeping you together when you do eventually come back, so my advice is to stay as long as possible. I'll see what happens when we get a new OC early next year. I already know who it will be. Rod Curtis. He may change things back. I'm hoping he'll at least keep your team together and bring you back up to full strength.

Now listen, Tiger, I have to go, but I've got the number and if I need to contact you, I will. Take care and say hello to the boys for me. Bye." I signed off as well and broke the connection.

The news, in some respects, was good by having Mark back, but bad in others, and as I thought over Mark's news about what was happening to the regiment at home, I'd have put money on the table betting that the new defence minister Jim Killen was behind all this. He'd always stated that having an SAS regiment was superfluous as opposed to the Australian Commando force, the bloody dickhead. That was like saying the US SEAL teams were better than the elite Delta Force. SAS was the superior elite to the Commandos, much like Delta Force in the States.

The next morning after breakfast, the team gathered in the lounge room. I told them of the call I had made the previous night, and they were cheerful when I told them the news that Mark was back in charge of HQ squadron. However, the mood soon changed when I told them what Mark had told me about what was happening back home. "Well, there it is guys. Mark said it's better for us to stay here as long as possible. He can't guarantee keeping us together when we do get home, so it's time to start thinking of other options. I've already let you know what I'll probably do. You guys will have to think about what you want to do."

This became the topic we would talk about in the privacy of our quarters over the next few months. While we went about business as usual with all the different training. In some cases, it was repetitive, but not all, and in some cases we'd all be learning new information and practising, so there was still plenty to keep my team active and educated. Apart from some of our techniques we were teaching the Mossad operatives, we operated on the same timetable they were on, so when they had leave we did too.

Near the end of the year, that would normally be our Christmas break, we were on leave until February of the coming year, which would be our last in Israel. As the guys made plans for the holidays, I was invited along on both trips, but I was thinking of something different. Tag, Buzz, and JJ were going to Switzerland for some skiing, while Dumper, Wires, and Lizard were going into Egypt to cruise the Nile. Even though that sounded good, I was going to make the trip down to Elat again and make my way to Petra in Jordon to have a look at the old temple city.

If I had time, I was thinking of going into Egypt through Suez to spend a little time in Cairo, but I had to see about that at a later stage.

After packing my go bag and guns into the car, I decided to drive into Haifa, travel down the coast road to Tel Aviv, and pass through Caesarea. I would also have a look at the Diamond Museum on the way down. I stayed a couple of nights at the King

David before hitting the road for Jerusalem, where I spent half a day doing the tourist thing before heading for Beer Sheba and down through the Negev. I only stayed in Beer Sheba for a few hours to rest and have something to eat before heading south through the Negev that night. I reached Yotvata at dawn and headed down into Elat.

Instead of booking into a hotel when I got there, I went down to the waterfront and decided to have breakfast at the marina café. The only other person in the place was a man, roughly my height, slim, with his head shaved. As I entered, he looked me over as well. I nodded, and he said in an Aussie flavoured Irish accent, "G'day."

I stopped at his table and asked, "You're Australian?"

"Yes, now I am, but prior to that Irish. You?"

"Originally English. Mind if I join you?"

He waved me to a seat, and left his hand out to shake. I introduced myself as we shook hands, and he told me his name was Colin Cloud. He called out, "Maria, make that two breakfasts, please. My friend will have one as well." He returned his attention to me. "They make the best breakfast here. I've taught them how to do it right. Just like being at home in Bli-Bli."

I laughed and said, "Sunshine Coast, huh? I'm from Bris."

He laughed as well. "Small world, Tom. So what are you doing here?"

I told him I was a soldier and that my team and I were taking part in an exchange program with the Israeli Army. We were on leave so I was travelling around having a look at the country and planned to go to Petra, maybe into Cairo. "What about you?"

He laughed and pointed, "See that big yacht at the end of the pier? Now, see that mansion over there on the shore?" I nodded. "I get to use that yacht, and I live at the mansion with my girlfriend. They're both owned by my boss, King Hussein of Jordan." He went on to tell me he was a diving instructor, and because the king knew Colin's father, the king had asked him to teach the royal household how to scuba dive. In return, apart from being paid a massive wage, Colin was considered an honoured guest at the palace and could order the crew of the yacht to take it out whenever it wasn't being used by the Royal family.

"Christ, where do I get a job like yours?" I exclaimed.

Colin laughed. "Where are you staying?"

"Nowhere yet. I came here to have breakfast after driving all night and was going to look around for a place to stay afterwards. Why?"

"Well, us Aussie's have to stick together. By the way, it was smart to drive through the Negev at night," he said with a wink. "So see how this sounds to you." He had a drink of his coffee, and as he did, the breakfast arrived at the table. "How about you come and stay with Sharon and I at the palace, and then in a day or so we'll all go up to Petra. I know Shaz wants to go. I've been there, so I'll be the guide, and when we come back we'll take the boat out and do some diving. It's fantastic diving in the gulf and the Red Sea. So what do reckon, Tiger? Yes, or no?"

While I chewed some bacon and toast, I watched him cutting some egg, bacon, and toast. "There's not really much to say, Colin, but yeah, I'm in."

He spoke with a mouthful. "Cool. We'll drive to the palace together, and I'll get you in. Hope you've got your ID with you. Do you dive?"

"Well now's a good time to ask, isn't it?" We both laughed, and I continued, "But yeah, I know how to scuba. Learned in the army, but I don't have a civvy licence."

"That's easy fixed. I'll check you out, get you to do a couple of exercises, and if you're ok, I'll certify you. What do you think of your breakfast?"

"Brilliant," I replied with a mouthful. I paid for both meals despite Colin's protests, but I told him he was giving me accommodation that I would have normally paid for myself, so it was only fair. We went out to the car.

"You must be more important than you think. That's a Defence Force car," he said, whistling.

"Yeah, that's the car I was given to use. So what?"

"Usually only very high officials get to use these types of car. Shit, put those guns under your luggage." As I did, he explained, "If the palace guard see them before you've shown your ID, they'll arrest you instantly. Just let me do the talking and introduce you around and then we won't have any bother."

I nodded, and he gave directions. Ten minutes later, we pulled up at the palace gates, and after talking to the head guard and introducing me as his cousin from Australia, I drove onto the grounds and pulled up at the side of the guest's quarters, which was as big as a mansion itself. Colin took me inside to meet his girlfriend, Sharon. She was an inch smaller than the two of us and had reddish hair, and I noticed from her accent she was Australian.

The household staff had taken my stuff from the car and placed it in my suite, which was opposite Colin's rooms across the courtyard from the huge indoor swimming pool. While we were socialising, I started yawning, so I excused myself and went to my room for a couple hours of sleep.

After my nap, I dived into the pool. Colin must have heard me and called out, "When you're finished your swim, come into the bar for a drink. We're watching the Collingwood Hawthorne Grand Final game from October."

When I arrived in the bar, they were sprawled out on one of the divans. Sharon said, "Help yourself to anything, and if you know what happened in this game, please don't tell us. This is the first chance we've had to watch it." I smiled because I did know what happened but didn't want to spoil their fun.

After the game was over and Hawthorne had won, much to Colin' annoyance, we sat around talking and drinking until dinner was served. Over dinner, we discussed the trip to Petra, that would take place the day after next, after breakfast at the marina.

The next morning, I joined Colin for his walk into town and

breakfast at the café. Afterwards we went down to the boat and went aboard.

I was introduced to the crew, which consisted of four Brits, two Aussies, one Yank, and one Frenchman, who was the chef. Two of the Brits and one of the Aussies were the ship's officers, while the rest were crewmen. The Skipper was the oldest Brit, and we got on quite well.

Colin informed him that we'd go out for a week or so in about three days. The only passengers would be the three of us, and we'd be doing some diving. The skipper told him the boat would be ready to sail whenever we got back. In the meantime, he'd provision and fuel up and get all the dive equipment serviced and the tanks filled. After a tour of the ship, Colin showed me my stateroom, and after three hours on board, we walked back to the palace.

Instead of taking my car, which I noticed had been washed; we took one of the king's Mercedes. Colin explained that it was better to take this one instead of mine with the IDF number plates, and I agreed with him. Not the sort of done thing, driving an Israeli car in an Arab country unless we wanted to get arrested. We drove down to the café, had breakfast, and I drove toward the Aqaba side of town and north toward Petra. We reached there four hours later and booked into an upmarket hotel. We went out sightseeing, and Colin took us to the old city. The size of the old temple was outrageous.

Readers Note: In case there is some confusion with Elat and Aqaba, they are literally the same town, just split in two. One side is Elat on the Israel side of town, and Aqaba on the Jordanian side. As for Petra, if you're not sure where I'm talking about, the temple façade has been used in many movies, one of the latest was Indiana Jones and the Last Crusade.

After wandering around through the temple and old city, we browsed in the markets. We ended up back at the hotel for drinks before dinner, and over dinner we discussed whether there was much else to see in Petra. Colin told us there wasn't much else touristy stuff to see in Jordan unless we were going all the way to the capital, Amman. So it was decided after a late check out we'd make our way back to the palace at Aqaba.

Back at the palace, we decided to have a lazy day, and then we would board the boat after breakfast the following day. That evening, feeling the need for some exercise, I swam about fifty laps in the pool, and considering the pool was Olympic size, that equated to a good workout. I hadn't been going slow or taking my time, and the next day I made full use of the gym.

Later that day, Sharon had a call from one of her friends who worked in Cairo. She had three weeks off and was wondering if she could come and stay. Sharon told her we were going out on the boat for some cruising and diving and invited her along. She arrived at the palace during the afternoon, and as I was introduced to Monique, I looked her over.

She was pleasant to look at. A five foot five blonde with blue eyes, olive complexion, slim, and if what she was wearing was any indication, a nicely shaped body. I must have made an impression on her because she was rarely far away from me for the rest of the day.

That night after dinner, she joined me in the pool, and as we swam leisurely, we talked about a whole heap of subjects, one of them was where she lived and worked. She was an archaeologist and worked at the Egyptian Antiquities Museum, and as I laughed when she told me that, she asked, "What's so funny?"

I explained after getting out of the pool where we'd been recently and told her that having her along would have been invaluable. She agreed that it was rather funny and cursed being a few days late as she would have liked to have gone too.

She did a fair bit of flirting and asked why I was staying and what I was doing in the area. I told her, and we got talking about what I'd like to do in Egypt if I had the time. I was in the middle of saying something, and she leaned over and kissed me. She moved to break the kiss, but I held her and started kissing back. My hands roamed over her body, and I felt her tense and relax as I played with her body. Her moaning became more and more intense as I lightly stroked her nipples through her swimmers top. Only then did I release the kiss. I stood up from the couch and tugged on her hand. She rose and followed where I guided, which was to my room.

CHAPTER 38

The next morning, she left my room in one of my shirts, carrying her bikini to her room to pack for the trip. At the same time, Colin walked into the lounge beside the pool, smiled, and gave me the thumbs up. Half an hour later, the Mercedes was packed and we headed to the café for breakfast. Two of the crew met us there to transfer our gear to the boat. After explaining which gear went into which room, both Colin and Shaz smiled as I instructed that Monique's should be put into my cabin. Monique lowered her face to hide the blush on her face. Shaz took her hand and led her off in front of Colin and me, whispering in her ear as they walked.

As soon as we boarded, the lines were cast off and the ship headed out of the marina. The first spot we stopped were a group of small islands at the mouth of the gulf where it joins the Red Sea at Tiran. There were some small sunken reefs in thirty foot of water. We got into the warm water (30.0). The girls dropped down first while Colin told me about the exercises he wanted me to do while underwater. We sank under the surface as well. After I completed the exercises to Colin's approval, we enjoyed a lazy swim around. We anchored there for a day and a half, doing a couple of night dives, and a dawn dive as well.

As we were having breakfast after the dawn dive, the crew got ready to set sail for the next destination Colin had chosen, the Dahlak Archipelago off the coast of Eritrea. According to the skipper, it would take three days steaming to reach our new destination.

The diving at Dahlak was absolutely breathtaking, with deep drop offs, wall diving, sharks, and morays. I agreed with Colin's summation that it had to be experienced to be believed, and after a couple days there, we went across the Red Sea to an island group off Jizan at the southern border of Saudi Arabia, where we spent five more days doing some wonderful wall and reef dives both during the day and night. All up, we were away for three weeks, and I had a wonderful time.

When we got back to Elat, Colin took a couple of photo mugshots of me, which he developed himself, and filled out my certification as an advanced diver. A week later, I thanked Colin for everything, and he passed me his card with his Qld address on it.

"My contract expires in a year, so we should be home in Australia after that. Give me a call and we'll get together."

Monique was travelling back to Egypt with me, and I was going to stay at her place while I was in the country. We set out across the Sinai toward Suez.

I didn't have too much bother at the border but was severely frowned at when they saw the Uzi. It was smoothed over as soon as they saw my military ID. Before arriving in Cairo, we turned off at Monique's suggestion and drove down toward the Valley of the Kings. We booked into the resort before going to the valley, but we were up early and heading there the next day. I was able to see more than the average tourist gets to see because Monique used her credentials and the guards let us through the off limit areas. Monique, who'd been here a few times, acted as my guide, and I think I rather astounded her with some of the questions I asked in regards to the line of succession within some of the royal families that were originally buried here. I surprised her even more during the drive back to the resort for the night. After spending the whole day in the valley, when I asked if she would give me a tour of the museum where she worked.

She asked me why and was really taken back when I replied, "Well, where you work is closed to the general public. Only researchers and historians are allowed to wander around in it."

She looked at me in wonder. "How do you know that?"

I smiled. "Because I know you don't work at the Egyptian Museum in Cairo. You're at the Egyptian Antiquities Museum, which is entirely different, and that's where all the good stuff is kept. I must admit that the general public don't know the difference, but I do because of my interest in history."

She looked at me long and hard as I drove before saying, "Yes, you would, wouldn't you? You're a very complex person, Tom Davis, and I'll take you when we get back to Cairo. Be prepared for a couple of days."

I glanced at her and smiled hugely. "No problems whatsoever."

Monique was as good as her word, and I was able to roam through the museum with her for three days. We discussed different objects, and she showed me artefacts she thought might interest me or I'd ask her about something I'd spotted. All up, I had a marvellous time roaming the rooms of the museum.

We did the tourist thing around Cairo for a couple of days, visiting the Great Pyramids. We also drove over to Alexandria, but eventually Monique had to go back to work and I had to think about heading back to base.

Allowing for three days' travel to get back to base, we said and acted out our goodbyes a week later. I left Egypt to return to Israel. This time I travelled north beside the canal after crossing at Suez to just outside Port Said and headed to Al' Arish near the border, and then up to Beer Sheba. When I got to Beer Sheba, I stayed a couple of days before I moved on. I arrived with two days to spare.

"Boss, did you happen to be in Cairo a couple of days ago?" Dumper asked.

"I ended up going there and took in the museum. Why?" I asked.

"I'm sure a caught a glimpse of you with a blonde walking down a street near the bazaar," he answered with a wink.

"Possible. I was with an archaeologist while I was there, and she was blonde."

He nodded his head and said with a smile, "As long as you had some fun, boss. We did. I ended up with this gorgeous Swiss bird, and she stayed with me for the whole trip. Wires and Lizard did ok too. I wonder how Tag and the boys made out."

"We'll know soon enough. Isn't that them, walking in now?" I pointed at a handful of men walking towards us.

As they reached us, I said, "Why don't we go inside into the air con and relax in the cool?"

The men went to their rooms to dump their gear, as did I, and then we made our way to the lounge and had a cold can of beer. We exchanged notes on our leave, recounting some of our adventures, and we continued this conversation bit by bit over the next day while still in relax mode.

At the start of the work week, the whole base contingent was mustered and informed we would all be taking part in the New Year ceremony as the honour guard at the swearing in ceremony that took place each year at Masada. We would be leaving over the next few days in separate groups and making our way to the marshalling area in the Masada National Park. My team and I would be going in the headquarters contingent with Svi and his admin staff.

During my previous visit to the mountain stronghold, I'd picked up a book that dealt with the history of the stronghold itself, so I was able to pass my knowledge onto my guys as we travelled. Svi corrected one thing I'd been saying, and he told us what would happen when we were there and how the ceremony ran. We would be there for a week, and it was our job as the honour guard to ring the entire mountain and control access of unauthorized personnel from the stronghold, which meant the company would be living and sleeping in the old fortifications of the stronghold itself. A guard post would be established at the summit of the access track.

It took two days for everything to be organized for our company to do its job, in part because of travelling separately instead of as a unit. As each pack arrived, they were shown where to bunk down, where meals would be served, and the positions they would occupy on the mountain.

My responsibility was with the operation of the guard post at the summit. Each of my men were to be officers of the watch, while Svi and I remained at headquarters in overall command. The main ceremony was to take place in two days' time when Joseph, as minister for defence, would be present to preside at the ceremony.

The swearing in ceremony went off without a hitch, and everything was fine. It was then time to break everything down again, and after two weeks of equipment being shuffled from the middle of the country back to base in the north, we eventually resumed normal duties.

As usual each month I would take a couple of days to visit Joseph. As each month passed, we grew closer to the time that he would be making his annual trip to Australia. This year we would be returning to Australia with him; our secondment was up, and the time of decision making for each team member was fast approaching. As the time for our return drew nearer, the topic of the SRT being disbanded began to surface as the main conversational piece whenever we were all together. Each person put forward their own ideas about what he was thinking of doing.

During my final meeting with Joseph prior to our return, I was informed of the date of the trip commencing. Joshua gave me the schedules for transport of my crew and gear back to Tel Aviv, and we would be in the capital for a week prior to the flight to Australia. Joseph asked what I'd be doing until then, and I informed him that once I was back at base I would take a day and go visit Marta and the farm. He knew what I was talking about so let the matter drop.

"Tom, what are you going to do when you get back? You've told me there is a good chance of your team being disbanded, so where does that leave you? What will you do?"

I shook my head and replied, "I don't know, Joseph. If they disband us, I think I'll move somewhere else. I really won't have many options. If I quit, I've got no trade to fall back on or any other qualifications. I've been a soldier since leaving school. Really I've only got three choices: I move to another branch of the army, I quit and try to find some sort of work, or I quit and become a mercenary soldier fighting in some shithole part of the world until I'm killed. As yet, I just haven't decided."

He was nodding his head slowly as I spoke. "When we are on the way to your country, I would like you to spend time with me in my office. I may be able to help you sort out your options, or at least we'll be able to talk about them, try to weigh which is better. I'll see you next month." We shook hands and I left.

When I arrived at base a couple days later, I informed my guys to get their gear sorted out and when we'd be moving down to Tel Aviv. We had time to get our entire armaments sorted and packed at least a week before the move. The day after that I informed Svi that I was going take the following day off because I wanted to say my goodbyes to people. Svi was aware that I, or any of my men, could take time off if they wanted, so the next morning I drove out of the camp after having breakfast. I made my way into Megiddo and down to Joseph's farm.

I was greeted by Marta after pulling up in the driveway and was taken inside for coffee and cake. We talked for quite some time.

"Joseph tells me you'll be going back to Australia soon, when he goes there for his next conference."

I nodded my head. "Yes, that's right, Marta. We've been here longer than we should have been, and now it's time to go home. This will be my last visit, and I don't know if I'll ever be back again." I paused and looked down. "I'm going to go for a little walk."

Marta looked at me with tears surfacing in her eyes, and with a catch in her throat, said, "Of course Tom. You take as long as you want. I'll make us a drink when you come back." I pretended not to see her tears as I got up and walked toward the gravesite.

After a couple hours of saying my goodbyes and reflection, I explained that I probably wouldn't be back, and with a final goodbye, I kissed her headstone and left the graveside for the last time.

When I got back inside, Marta put the jug on, and we had

coffee together. An hour or so later, it was time to leave. Marta, with tears in her eyes, put her arms around me and kissed me on the cheek. She hugged me and said, "Tom, my poor boy, there will always be a home for you here. Please don't forget us, and be careful. We love you as our own."

I nodded and replied, "I love you too, Marta. You look after yourself and Joseph. I'll miss you." I slowly got into the car and drove out of the farm for the last time.

The following week we made ready for the airlift. All the guns, including the Uzis, we'd picked up were packed, and all our combat gear and ammo was packed and crated. The sets of black cam fatigues went into our kitbags, and the only things that needed packing into the kitbags were the last minute items. When we got the movement order, I left two days prior to the team, as I was going to drive back in the car. After saying my goodbyes to Svi and his officers dressed in civilian garb but wearing my gun under my shirt, I drove out of camp.

I drove into the drive of the King David at sixteen hundred and gave the keys to the concierge.

I made my way with my kitbag to the reception desk; the bookings had already been made. I told the girls to expect the rest of my team the following day. After arranging for my kitbag to be taken up to my room, I headed into the bar for a much needed drink.

I was waiting for the tap on the shoulder as I sat there; I know she had noticed my entrance and had slowly moved around the room. Just as she was about to put her hand on my shoulder to get my attention, I said, "Hello Tracey. How's the news business?" In the bar mirror I saw her shocked expression. "I've been watching you since I came into the bar. Please join me."

She sat beside me, and I indicated to the barman for two more drinks. "The news business is a little slow," she told me. "How are things with you, Colonel Davis?"

"Just fine Tracey, and getting better."

"So are you here for your monthly meeting?"

I looked at her as I took a sip of scotch. "No not this time. It's a little different. I'll have my monthly meeting with the minister, but this time it's going to take place on the plane that's taking him and my team back to Australia."

"So you're leaving sunny Israel? When?" she asked.

"Oh, within the next seven days."

She held her glass up in a toast. "Well, here's to home."

We touched glasses, and I said, "You bet."

"Would you like to join me for dinner?"

I laughed. "That would be nice Tracey, but I'd like to go up and have a shower first and clean up."

She smiled in return. "Be my guest. I'll come up with you; I'm one floor down from you."

I chuckled while we both finished our drinks and then headed for the lift. When we got into the lift, she didn't press a button. I asked, "Aren't you getting changed also, or do you want me to press your floor?"

She smiled at me. "No, I'll come with you. You may need someone to scrub your back." I smiled and did not object, so we continued to my room.

We made love in the shower, and she was a little quieter than last time, but not by much. She actually did scrub my back for me, and after we were finished and dried, we dressed again and went back down to the restaurant for dinner. True to her word, she had the dinner added to her room account after we had a relaxed meal with dessert instead of coffee. We settled for glasses of Sabra and let our meal settle before going back to my room.

This established the pattern for the next five days. She would either wander around town with me after breakfast, or she'd have a news item she'd have to cover, but each night we had dinner together and she slept in my room. This didn't change even when the team arrived the following day. If they didn't join us for dinner, it meant they had dates lined up. While we were at the hotel, there were quite a few women who stayed on our floor, sometimes the same ones, and other times, different ones. Obviously, the guys were making the most of the time left in the country.

One morning while I was waiting for Tracey to join me for breakfast, who had gone to her room to change, I had a call from Joshua saying the plane would be ready to leave at ten hundred and the limos would pick us up at nine thirty.

Tracey rushed up to the table. "I have to be at Ramla in an hour for an interview, so I have to eat and run, sweetheart, but I'll see you tonight."

I looked at her and shook my head sadly. "Sorry honey, but you won't. We leave at nine thirty."

She nodded and we ate our breakfast. When we finished, she said, "Well, I guess this is goodbye. We'll have to catch up another time. Take care of yourself, Colonel Davis."

"You too, Tracey Mullins." We kissed goodbye.

Because Tracey and I usually had an early breakfast, I went back to our floor and banged on each door to inform the guys we would be leaving at nine thirty. I went to take care of my own packing, but I left the door open in case any of the guys wanted me.

After I thanked the reception staff, I waited for the limos to arrive and was joined by the team, each carrying their kitbags. Two limos arrived, and we loaded up and left the King David for the last time. We were soon on the tarmac at Lod airbase. One of the aircrew girls told me I'd been put into the portside office and we could take our luggage aboard while we waited. After disposing of our kitbags, we returned to the tarmac and lined up to wait for Joseph's arrival five minutes later.

He stepped from his limo, and we came to attention. "Shalom, gentlemen," he greeted.

Each of us replied, "Shalom, sir."

"We'll get going, shall we? Tiger, please join me after take-off." He climbed the stairs, followed by Joshua, and then the team.

I was the last to enter the plane after having a last look around before making my way inside. I headed to the office assigned to me and saw the guys in their usual seats buckling up before the plane started to taxi to the main runway.

As the nose wheel lifted, I silently said, "Goodbye Israel. Goodbye Shari, my love." I recalled all the good things that had happened while we'd been there, enjoying my reverie.

When the plane levelled off, I unbuckled and went to Joseph's office. I entered and was directed to a seat opposite Joseph at his desk. We greeted each other with "Shalom" as I took the seat to which I was directed.

"Tiger, I'm not going to beat about the bush because I know you prefer all business taken care of first." I nodded in agreement, and he continued. "But first I would like to ask you a question? Are you going to miss my country, and why?"

I looked across at him, trying to imagine why he would ask me such a question. "Yes Joseph, I will. It's a bit like my home in places, and even though it's not as big, I will miss it. I've had fun and good times in Israel, and I met a lot of people I like and get on with, which includes you and Marta. And of course it's the place where I was ready to marry and settle down. What I'll miss most is not being able to see and talk to the person who would have been my wife."

He had been staring intently at me, trying to read my mind, I guess, and asked another question. "If you were to have stayed and lived in Israel, would you have married?"

Now that question did put me on the spot. I became aware that he did really have something on his mind and wondered if he was trying to recruit me. After thinking about his question for a short time, I replied, "I'm not sure, Joseph. There's a lot of beautiful women in Israel. I think perhaps I'd probably have a lot of affairs, but as to loving someone enough to marry them, I'm not sure. I loved your daughter wholeheartedly, and still do, to tell you the truth. I don't think I'll ever find anyone that I could love that much again, Shari is a hard act to follow, if you know what I mean." I watched as he nodded sagely. "Now why all the questions? Let's hear what you have to say."

He smiled weakly after wiping his eyes. "Yes, let's get down to business, but I needed to know those things before I offer you what I'm about to."

Christ! A whirlwind of thoughts went flowing through my head. I was right; he was trying to recruit me, but for what purpose? What was the old fox up to? If I liked it, would I accept what he offered? I held up my hand to interrupt him. "Joseph, you're stalling. Just get on with it."

He smiled. "Yes I was. Tom, I'm sorry, but I was interested in what you had to say. I would like to make you a job offer that I want you to think about. I don't want an answer yet, but you have proven yourself to be a real asset to our government. The work you have done with Mossad has been exceptional, and the investigation you undertook for me was first class. You got to the truth of the matter without being judgemental. What I'm offering you is to head a new department I'm going to form as part of Mossad called the Tactical Services Branch. You're probably going to ask what's in it for me. So this is what you will receive: you'll retain your rank as a colonel, you'll have a permanent suite at the King David as your quarters with meals included. A government car and the use of a driver if required, and an annual salary equivalent to one hundred and ten thousand US dollars as well as a fifty-thousand-dollar expense account. Obviously you have questions, so please ask."

I was somewhat stunned at the offer, and I settled on a couple of questions. "Joseph, this is a phenomenal offer, and I don't know what to say. How can you offer something like this to me? I'm a goy!"

He laughed and said, "Yes, you are a goy, but you have the ability to fulfil this role. It doesn't come down to if you're Jewish or not. This role requires certain abilities that no one in my country possesses yet. However, I'm sure you would train your staff in those abilities."

I nodded, agreeing that he read me right on that score. "What would I be doing, and what would be my responsibilities?"

"You would be our chief analyst and tactician for any emergency situation, like a hijacking or bomb threats, and you'd work closely with the intelligence services of Mossad. You'd find, recruit, and train your own personnel and staff, plus you would become my analyst and deputy. You would be making trips to our allies with the backing of our country behind you instead of me.

Face it Tom, it's you who has the catalytic properties to effect change in our lives. It's you that makes the difference, not me, not someone else. You."

I thought over some of things he was saying, and then asked the question I really wanted the answer to. "There's one thing you're forgetting, Joseph. I'm a serving member of the Australian Defence Forces. What am I supposed to do, quit? You know I won't do that without good reason. Besides, I live in Australia. It's my home."

He laughed, and his voice took on a harsh quality. "Tom, you could make Israel your home quite easily, you know you could. You think like an Israeli. Whatever has your country done for you, except send you to war?"

What he had to say really had me thinking. In one part of my mind, I agreed with him, but in another, I had to disagree. "Well, yes, it did send me to war, but I chose to do that, it wasn't forced on me. I volunteered, and it was through going to war that I learned everything I know about analysing situations and tactics, which, as you've stated, is one of the reasons you want me. As tempting as your offer is, it makes me feel like a gun for hire, a mercenary selling my knowledge and knowhow for money. I don't know without a lot of thought whether I can do that, Joseph."

He pleaded, "Tom, Tom, I'll apologise if that's the way it makes you feel. That's not what I meant to do. I know this requires a lot of consideration from you, and that is why I am not asking for an answer. You have my number and know how to contact me. Please, think it over properly, and maybe in a week or two, or even a couple of months, you may change your way of thinking.

That's when I'd like you to contact me," he finished. "But that is enough for now. All I ask is you think it over. You have become my friend, Tom, and I have no wish to change that. Please don't think harshly about me for doing what I see as my job. Let's leave it at that, and we'll talk again tomorrow. Shalom, my son."

I returned his Shalom and got up and left the office with a lot on my mind to consider.

CHAPTER 39

After our overnight stop in Singapore, we travelled early the next morning, taking off at zero seven hundred. Because Joseph was sleeping that day, I didn't get much of a chance to speak to him, I only had an hour before we landed in Perth, and again he didn't want an answer from me.

"Tom, my boy, all I have asked of you is to think about my offer. I won't feel let down if you decide not to accept. You are loyal to your country, I understand that, and even if you don't accept my offer, you will always have a home in my country."

The pilot had arranged transport before we landed at Pearce on October of 1979. Three years after leaving, we had come home. Our stuff was unloaded into a truck, and we left for the trip to Swanbourne after saying our goodbyes and shaking hands with Joseph, Joshua, and the aircrew. They were going to overnight in town prior to flying on the next day.

Mark was waiting at SRT when we drove into the barracks. We shook hands with him. He told us to have the following day as a stand down day and to take our time in sorting our stuff out. We could use the weekend as rest days, and he would see us back on duty on Monday, which was the eighth. We grabbed our kitbags and made our way to our quarters to settle back in.

After a late breakfast the following morning, I walked over to transport to see Phil. He smiled when he saw me coming, and I saw my car outside the compound beside his Gold Fairlane. He met me at the door of the office, held out his hand, which I shook.

"I heard you guys were due to return. So, I've been giving your car a good going over, and I also serviced it for you.

She's all good to go, Tiger."

I thanked him and took the keys. I got in, started it up, and drove up towards SRT.

Tag was with some of the team about to unlock the building as I drove into the parking area at the back. I waited for one of them to unlock the back door before entering. As I walked through the building, Buzz was unlocking the safe and rifle rack, and Tag, Wires, JJ, and Lizard were carrying the crates toward the gunroom. Dumper was in the ready room making coffees, and I called after Tag, "When the crates are in the gunroom, everyone come and have coffee before doing anything else. Don't forget it's supposed to be a stand down day." They all laughed.

We sat in the ready room with our coffees and chin wagging about anything and everything with the general consensus of how strange it felt to be back and how much they missed Israel. I told them about the offer I'd received from Joseph on the trip back.

"So what are you going to do, boss?" JJ asked. "Are you going to accept it?"

I looked at them as they looked at me, waiting for my answer. "I don't know. I'm still thinking about it. I guess I will for a while. We still don't know what we'll be doing yet, so I won't be thinking about it until that's sorted out. It'll be on the back burner at least until then. Now to business. What we'll do is get into the gunroom and unpack the smaller crate with our combat gear, subs, and ammo first so Buzz can lock up the safe. Then we'll rearrange the rifle rack and unpack the rifles. We really need to clean the weapons because we may not be using them for a while."

As we were about to move into the gunroom, the phone in my office rang. I rushed to answer it; Mark was on the other end. He sounded hesitant and unhappy as he arranged for an informal info session in our briefing room at zero eight hundred on Monday. When I told him that, it wasn't a problem and that we'd be waiting, his voice dropped in volume so he could warn me.

"Tiger, it's not good, I'm afraid."

"Yeah ok, boss, I understand." I stood staring at the phone for a minute, collecting my thoughts. I sighed and made my way to the gunroom. "All right, after this lot is sorted out and before the cleaning starts, I want everyone into the ready room."

After we'd unpacked our combat gear and put it away into our lockers, the sub-machine pistols were then put away and the ammunition was put into the safe. We unpacked the rifles. My MP4A was placed beside my M203, my new Uzi beside them. We left three blank spaces; Tag put his into place, and so on in seniority. Buzz placed new name stickers above each group of rifles, and the gun crates were taken to the last storeroom. We returned to the ready room for drinks before we got down to business.

I leaned forward, placed my coffee mug on the table, and looked at each of them in turn. "That was Mark on the blower earlier. He's scheduled an informal info session for zero eight hundred on Monday in the briefing room. Please make sure you're on time. He warned me that it's not good news, so we'll wait to see what he has to say, I guess."

What I had told them put a damper on the mood in the room; everyone sorting through their own thoughts. I picked up and drained my mug. "Ok that's it. Let's get into the cleaning, and after that I think we can knock off."

The following morning Tag and I took off early for a game of golf, and as we walked around the course, our conversation centred on what we knew to be the demise of SRT. I asked what he had been thinking about over the last few weeks.

"Well, Buzz and I have been thinking of going to see the Medical Corp CO and applying to continue our medical training to see if we can qualify as doctors, but we haven't done anything about it yet because everything is still up in the air. What about you?"

"I'm still not sure. You already know about the offer I had from the Israelis. I really don't think I could fit into one of the new CT units unless I was leading the team, and I definitely wouldn't fit into a sabre squadron. My only other option is to take an inter-service transfer into a transport unit. If I get the shits with that, well, I could always give Joseph a call. Do you have any idea about the rest of them?"

He took his second stroke before replying. We walked to my ball as he spoke. "I'm sure Dumper has been in contact with a mercenary recruitment organization, but he tries to hide the fact. He'll likely quit because his re-enlistment is due soon." He waited for me to hit my next stroke before continuing. "The others I think are resigned to merging into either one of the teams or back into a sabre squadron."

We arrived at his ball and pulled out his eight iron; his ball sailed to within five yards of mine down on the verge of the green. I shot with the wedge and the ball rolled into the cup for a par.

After our game, we went into the clubhouse for drinks and lunch, and while we sat there, I asked, "So if you and Buzz get into the Medical Corp, where will you be doing your training?"

"Umm, that's a point. There's only two places where training is available. One is in Sydney and the other is at the Alfred in Adelaide. I guess since we're over here they'll send us to Adelaide, but either way, one of us will have to buy a car."

We laughed, and I said, "Tag, if I leave here, I'll give you my car. All you'll have to do is change the rego."

"Gee. Thanks boss." He finished his drink and went to the bar. He bought another beer for himself and a malt scotch for me. "That's really tops of you, boss, but are you sure you don't want me to pay you something for it?"

"Tag, I've got another car at home in Queensland, so instead of trying to sell it, I'd rather give it to you as a present for all the help you've given me since we met."

On Monday, we had an early breakfast and met at the SRT offices well before time. We sat in the ready room relaxing, and at five to eight, we moved into the briefing room. Everyone sat in their usual places, and I sat on the front desk facing them.

"Now, are all the reports of the training finished?" I received nods all round. "Good, because there's a good possibility we'll have to show the others the training. In other words, we may become the teachers again." Everyone laughed.

Mark entered the room minus his cap, which was in his hand. I jumped up from the desk, and he waved us all down. I moved to my usual seat and sat down. Mark looked at each of us as he cast his gaze around the room. "I'm just going to get some water and we'll get underway."

When he returned, he was carrying a glass of water and put it down on the desk. He sat on the edge of the desk as he addressed us. "You've all heard the talk and rumours about disbanding you guys, so I think it's about time you knew the true facts about what's happening. Now, as you know, I've been involved with SRT from the very beginning, and trust me when I say you have proved yourselves and the unit to be the best. We've had glowing reports from everyone you've been involved with, but neither those reports nor my insistence that we need to have an SRT Operational Team has done any good at all; it's all fallen on deaf ears. When you come back from leave in February, there will be a month's grace period before SRT will officially be disbanded on Monday, March thirty-one. I'm sorry, guys."

There was stunned silence in the room as each of us processed our own thoughts about the news that was now official. Wires raised his hand, and Mark acknowledged him. "Yes, Wires?"

"Can you tell us what's going to happen to us, please?"

Mark took a mouthful of water before answering. "Well, there are quite a few options available to some of you, but most of you will be merged into the new TAG (Tactical Assault Group) teams. They, in essence, are to become what you guys were, but mainly training for counter terrorism. You guys should be proud of yourselves; you made all of this possible and did it all before the new teams were created. SRT were the pioneers. Even though I think we still need you, the higher ups think not. The new TAG teams consists of ten men each, with officers in charge of each team, and there are to be four Tag teams and two Twag (Tactical Water

Assault Group) teams operational at all time. Also, we've still need two sabre squadrons, one available to deploy immediately and one in training. God knows where we're going to get the personnel."

He drank a gulp of water and cleared his throat. "Now, as I've said, there are some other options available. For instance, Tiger and Tag, I can recommend both of you for officer training if you would like. However, what I really want to do is this, I know some of you have already been thinking of this and may have your own thoughts about it, so I'd like to hear from each of you. If you have something in mind, I may be able to help or at least let you know if it's a viable option. Who'd like to go first?"

Dumper raised his hand. "What if I decide to quit, boss? My reenlist is coming up."

"Well Dumper, we'd be sorry to see you go, but if you wish, that could be brought forward."

Tag raised his hand, and Mark acknowledged him. "Mark, Buzz and I have been toying with the notion of seeing the chief medical officer and trying to upgrade our medical qualifications and be trained as doctors. Is that possible?"

Mark smiled. "I think that's a marvellous idea, and I'll help you and Buzz as much as possible. I'll have a quiet word with him in the mess tonight, recommending the both of you. Anyone else?"

I raised my hand. After being acknowledged, I said, "Sir, as you know I've led my own team, so I'd be no good as a 2IC. I've never worked in a sabre squadron before, so as I see it, I have only two options. One is I quit, and secondly I could apply for an inter-service transfer to another Corp. If the second option is available, I'd like to try a transport unit."

Sighing deeply and looking rejected, Mark answered, "I'm sorry, Tiger. I brought you into this in the first place, and I'm sorry that I failed you. Don't quit. You're too good a soldier for that. I'll try to arrange a transfer to a transport squadron for you, but it'll be hard because I have to look for one that has an open posting for an RSM. Anyone else before I move on?"

There were no further questions, so I thought that Wires, JJ, and Lizard were happy enough to integrate into the TAG teams. Mark grabbed his water and had a drink. "As you know, you'd usually have a proper debrief, but I already know you've written up all the training done in Israel. If the team weren't to be disbanded, you'd start teaching what you learned to the other regimental personnel. However, they'll just have to learn from your notes. You guys have been gone far too long, so I'm going to place you all on leave. When you come back at the end of your leave, I'll ask you again if you want to go with the options you've told me about. If so, I'll start making it happen for you, and in the meantime, I'll start investigating the available options, especially for you, Buzz, and Tag."

I raised my hand, and after being acknowledged, asked, "So what happens if a job for us comes in in the meantime, Mark?"

He laughed. "Well, I suppose SRT doesn't technically exist anymore, so you can't be recalled. Today is the eighth, so you can start your leave on Friday, which is the twelfth. I don't need to see you back until Monday, February four of next year. Until Friday, just fill in your time here, and as usual, if any travel warrants are needed come and see me. Once again, boys, I'm sorry the machine in its wisdom doesn't think you are needed anymore. However, please be proud of your achievements."

He stood up and said as he grabbed his water glass, "Ok boys, I'll see you later." He walked out to the ready room, washed his glass, and left the building.

Meanwhile I had gone to the front of the room again. "Well, that's it. Now we know. All I can say is, men, it's been an honour to have been your boss and to have served with each and every one of you. We've been together a long time, through some good times and bad, but you've never let me down. I love every one of you. It looks like I've got to put up with your ugly mugs for a while longer yet, so let's all consider this a stand down for the rest of the week. Only come in if you feel like it or if you need the phones to arrange your leave. That's it; let's knock off for an early lunch."

That afternoon I phoned the house in Brisbane and got hold of Lisa. I told her I was back in Australia and would probably be home within a week. She agreed to collect me from the airport when I arrived.

I also went over to HQ and had Mark issue me with a travel warrant. I noticed he made it out for first class. I smiled and thought, Perfect. Now I'll really have a great flight. I went back to SRT and phoned Wendy at the travel service. She greeted me as a long lost friend and asked why she hadn't seen me for ages. I explained that I'd been overseas for the last three years. She laughed and asked what she could do for me, and I explained that I wanted to make some flight bookings.

When I told her I had the travel warrant for first class, she said, "If you want to travel first class, Tiger, I can only get you onto the Qantas overnight flights. All the other flights are the cheaper flights that only have the one price."

I replied, "That's fine, Wendy. How about Friday night? Can you get me on?"

"So far there's only one other person booked in first, so for a regular and valued customer like you, I'll make sure you're booked. How about your return?"

After arranging the return flight for Saturday night on February second of the following year, she asked me to get into the office as soon as I could. I told her I'd be right in. I let Tag know I'd be back later and hopped into the car.

We exchanged all the documentation, and she asked a laugh, "Are you taking any weapons this time?"

I looked at her with a smile. "Yeah well, I'll be taking my gun as usual, but this time I'll also be taking a sword home as well."

Wendy replied, "I promise I'm not going to ask, but make sure it's boxed up properly. Is there anything else I can do for you?"

"If you weren't married, you could definitely be of service," I said with a wink.

She replied, waving her arm and clicking her fingers, "Oh darn!" We both had a good laugh.

Back on base, Tag and I were having a few drinks in the mess after dinner. I leaned forward and said, "Well Tag old buddy, let's hope you and Buzz get what you want. To help you along, how about sometime tomorrow, you take the car and go to the transport department and see what you have to do to get my car transferred into your name. If I have to sign anything just bring it back for me to sign. If you want to use it while you're on leave, you can. Whether it's now or in the next few months, I'll be out of here. All I ask is that you drop me at the airport on Friday night so I can catch my plane."

"Thanks, Tiger. No problems dropping you off. I'll go after we open up the building tomorrow, as long as you're sure about this."

I smiled. "Of course I'm sure buddy. Cheers."

The following morning, Tag took off with the car after we'd had our usual get together in the ready room with our coffees. He returned thirty minutes later with a form for me to fill in and sign, and he was gone again for the following two hours. During that time, I phoned home and told Lisa what flight I'd be on and when it was due to land. I explained I'd be bringing home a bit of luggage. She told me she'd meet me.

Tag came back, handed me the keys, and said, "It's all changed over. I got a set of plates to put on and a new rego sticker."

I looked at him smiled. "Why are you giving me the keys?"

"Just in case you need to use it."

I laughed as I tossed him back the keys. "Here, have them back. It's your car now, and if I do need to use it, I'll ask you. Now go do what you have to.

When you're finished, you can look after the office while I go over to the barracks to do some packing up." He nodded. The phone rang; Mark needed to see me at HQ. I headed for HQ and took a seat in Marks office.

"Are you sure you want to leave us?" he asked without preamble.

I thought for a moment. "It's really my only option, other than quitting. You know I wouldn't be able to be someone's 2IC after all this time. I'm too used to being the boss."

He nodded. "Yeah, I suppose you're right. Ok, I've found out there are two transport squadrons with open vacancies for an RSM. One is Thirty Terminal Squadron in Sydney, and the other is five trucks at Enoggera in Brisbane. If you give me your choice, I can start on the paperwork. It'll take about three months to process."

I looked at him, as I thought it over quickly. "Well, considering I have my house in Brisbane, I'll go with five trucks, I guess."

Mark replied, "I thought you'd go that way. You do know that after doing what you've been doing, you'll likely be bored shitless."

I laughed. "Yeah well, I'd be the same way here, after all the other stuff."

"I guess you're right," he agreed with a smirk. "I'll start on this, and by the time you get back from leave, I should have some sort of answer. Be safe while you're on leave, Tom." I nodded and left his office.

I carried on to the barracks after leaving Mark's office. Inside my room, I sorted my uniforms and left myself with only twelve sets of cams. I packed everything else, and most of the civvy gear fitted into my go bag and kitbag. I grabbed my sword, took it back with me to SRT, and placed it on my desk. I searched for something to wrap it up in. In one of the storerooms, I found a long piece of PVC tubing that had end caps. This should fit the bill nicely, I thought to myself, and took it back to my office.

Friday night Tag got me to the airport with plenty of time to spare, so I was able to check in and get my bags loaded. I was not charged for any excess baggage fees. I was wearing my gun in the shoulder holster, and I took the sword with me as cabin baggage. After watching Escape from Alcatraz with Clint Eastwood for the first part of the flight, I settled down to sleep.

I awoke at zero six thirty to have breakfast before landing. Lisa met me, and once I put the luggage into her car, we headed for home.

On the way, she remarked, "It's good to see you, Tiger. I've been doing the car like I said I would. I noticed you're wearing your gun, but what's with the tube thingy, and why the extra bag?"

I laughed and clapped my hand on her knee. "It's good to see you, Lisa. I missed you too. I'll let you unpack the tube thingy when we get home, but be careful with it. I'll explain all the rest later." Once I finished speaking, I removed my hand from her knee, but surprisingly enough, she actually placed it back there. I thought, Hello, what's going on here? Seems as if she wants me to touch her. I better play this one by ear in case I'm wrong. We'll see what she does and says, and then we'll see what happens.

After I opened the garage at home and she drove in, she took the tube while I took out the bags and carried them up to my bedroom. I stripped off my shirt to take my gun off. She came into the bedroom with the tube and asked if she could undo it now. She stopped speaking and stared at me as I took off the shoulder holster.

"You've been shot again," she stated.

I was dumbfounded. "Yeah, but how do you know?"

"I've see you without your shirt on enough times to know how many times you've been wounded. That is a new one where you didn't have one before. You really should take better care of yourself, Tiger. Now, what have you got in here?"

She started to undo all the tape from one end and remarked, "You really didn't want this coming open, did you?" She finally got all the tape off and took out the end cap and the stuffing pad. She tilted the tube and the sword slowly came out. She grabbed it and pulled it all out. She lay it on the bed to unwrap it, pursed her lips, and said, "My God, a sword. And what a beautiful handle. This is yours?"

"Yes, it's my officer's sword from my time in England. Would you like to help me sort out all these uniforms? Once they're away, we can have a drink, and I'll tell you what's going on."

Quite some time after that, we were sitting in the barroom. I'd told her everything that was about to happen and that I'd be coming home to stay.

I poured us another drink. She said, "I'm glad I'm half pissed because I'd never be able to say this otherwise. You know when you first invited me to stay here I said we wouldn't ever get into bed with each other because of our age difference. Well, I want you to know that I've changed my mind. I realised a couple of months ago that I haven't had sex in over six years, and I miss the feeling it gave me. I want to have sex again, and I would like to have it with you because you're a kind and caring man."

Flabbergasted would be an understatement; floored would be more like it. For a moment, I didn't say anything. "All right, but if we're going to have sex, it won't be today. You need to be fully aware of what you're doing and why, because if you do have sex with me, I don't want you feeling guilty about it afterward. I've heard what you said, and I'm happy to oblige you and flattered also, but you need to be absolutely sure. Therefore, you need to be a little bit soberer than you are now, ok?"

"See? I said you were a caring person, and kind as well."

CHAPTER 40

The next day I jacked up the car and replaced the wheels. I turned it on to make sure all was well.

I stripped out of the overalls I was wearing and turned on the spa. I hopped into the spa pool and closed my eyes to rest. When I opened them, Lisa was standing there holding a towel. I switched off the pool, and as I hopped out naked, Lisa moved closer, opened the towel, and put it over my shoulders. I let it drape down my back, and with her arms still over my neck, she pulled me into her and kissed me. I could feel through her nightdress that she had nothing on underneath. After her long kiss was broken, she took me be the hand and led me upstairs and into her room. I lay on her bed, and she took my penis into her mouth. Once it was completely rigid, she slipped her nightdress over her head, off, and climbed onto me, impaling herself on my rigid pole until it was deep inside her. She moaned in pleasure as I worked myself deeper inside her, and she was wracked with her first of many orgasms.

An hour later, we lay recovering from our efforts. "Well, I think you just made up for those missing six years," she mused. "Thank you. That was marvellous."

I mischievously said, "I aim to please. Besides, that was better than a game of golf."

"Well, you definitely scored more holes in one than I could keep count of." We laughed loudly.

That evening we had a long talk while having a couple of drinks. We decided that her need for sex could be catered for but not to the extent that we would form a relationship. We would both be free entities, and after our discussion, we only slept together four times while I was home on leave, at her request, because we'd agreed that if we were going to have sex or sleep together it would only be at her choosing. It wouldn't be an exclusive relationship for either of us, and this suited me just fine.

Having that all cleared up and sorted, we continued to live in the same house harmoniously, and I would take off to play golf now and again. Once I flew to Townsville to take a diving trip out on the barrier reef for ten days. I was hooked on diving; you could see and enjoy the reef more as a diver. Each area of it was different. At night, different fish would come out while the day fish slept, and I played with big potato cod, moray eels, reef sharks, and manta rays. In shallower waters, I'd watch clown fish playing among the anemone, along with trumpet fish. Every now and then I'd catch a crayfish for dinner.

That was how I whiled away my army leave.

At Christmas, Lisa and I shared a quiet time, and because I had no idea what she'd like, I bought her a hundred-dollar gift voucher for Myers. I told her once after a golf game that I needed more balls, she got me a couple of dozen pro quality balls.

As time drew close to go back, I told Lisa that when I came back I'd be bringing all my gear. I'd have my foot locker, which would be full. Everything else would be packed into my kitbag and go bag, so if she was going to pick me up as before, it would probably be better to do it in my car. This sort of gave her kittens until I took her out in it a few times and let her drive to get the hang of it. She was as right as rain after practicing, and my car wasn't as scary for her to drive, even though she didn't really like big cars.

The night before my flight back to Perth, Lisa asked me to join her in her bed for the night. We made love for an hour before she collapsed exhausted into my arms and stayed there the rest of the night. Even though asleep, she clung to me as I attempted to get up, so I lay in for an extra hour and dozed.

I planned to travel back to Perth in civvies without any luggage. All I did was place my go bag into my kitbag and my gun into it as well. I carried it on as cabin baggage. I was the only passenger in first class, so while I watched Star Trek the Movie I was given a meal and served drinks until I decided to get some sleep. I arranged with the stewardess to wake me at six thirty if I wasn't awake beforehand.

I grabbed a cab at the airport to take me to Swanbourne. I was going up the stairs to my room as Tag was coming down. He told me he was on his way to the golf course, and I said, "If you give me ten minutes, I'll join you for a game. It may be our last together."

He told me he'd wait at the car, and ten minutes later I had changed, and my golf clubs and buggy were in the car boot with his as we drove to the golf club.

During our game, we swapped stories about what we got up to while on leave, and he told me he had returned on Thursday. Mark had seen him arrive and had called into his office. He told Tag that his efforts with the medical squadron had been successful and he would take Buzz and Mark over to see the CO on Wednesday the following week. It looked like he and Buzz were going to the Alfred in Adelaide to complete their training to be qualified doctors. I told him I couldn't be happier for both of them.

After our game, we had lunch and drinks at the club, and we discussed Dumper's decision. We both knew he was figuring on taking on work as a mercenary. We wondered why he had made that choice, aware that in that game you didn't live long. If you did, you didn't come out of it without mental scars. We agreed that he really hadn't been the same since Janice had thrown him over years ago, but we would do what we could to talk him out of it. Then we turned to my decision, and I told him I figured I would be bored shitless, but I still had Israel as a backstop if I really needed it.

The following morning, we were assembled in the ready room, and Mark came in at eight thirty with a stack of paperwork. He sat down, had a drink, and relaxed before speaking. "As you can see, I've got a fair bit of paperwork here that some of you either have to fill out or sign. Tiger, I'd like to use your office if I can, and I'll call each of you as required. After that, we'll meet in the briefing room so I can give you all instructions. I'll have Wires in first." He gathered up the paperwork and stood up. Wires followed Mark to my office.

When Wires returned to the ready room, he announced that Mark wanted Lizard next. He told us he'd been asked if he was still set with his decision to stay, and that those staying would join the one TAG team. We weren't being split up. JJ followed Lizard, and then it was Dumper's turn. Dumper didn't have much to say when he returned, only that it was Buzz's turn. Tag followed him. Buzz told us that both he and Tag had been accepted back into the Medical Corp and would meet the CO on Wednesday to arrange their training. We shook hands and congratulated him.

Tag came out of the office with Mark, and Mark announced, "I'll have Tiger next. Instead of having our meeting after that, because it's getting near lunchtime, we'll eat first. Be back here at thirteen thirty. Right, Tiger, your turn."

I stood up and told Tag it wasn't too late for Dumper to change his mind and to keep working on him. I walked into my own office and sat opposite Mark, who was using my desk.

He looked at me and said, "I must officially ask this, Warrant Officer First Class Tom Davis. Are you determined to leave the SAS regiment in favour of a transfer into the Transport Corp?"

"Yes sir," I replied, and he asked me to sign the paperwork attesting to the fact that he asked me that question.

"Right, Tiger. I've got all the necessary paperwork back, and you'll need to sign here, here, and fill this one out, and this one, and then I'll countersign them."

I completed all the forms as he requested, and when I was finished, he continued after countersigning. "You'll be reporting to Colonel John Lewis at five Transport on Tuesday, April one of this year at zero eight hundred. I would suggest you be in your cam fatigues because you won't have any of the Corp insignia or lanyards until after you report in. When I give you the travel warrant, I'll make sure we cover any excess baggage. I assume you'll only be taking what you came with and won't require an uplift?"

"No sir. Only stuff that I can carry to the plane, my footlocker and a couple of kitbags. What about my weapons?"

"As much as I'd like to keep them because you'll be joining a field force company, you keep all your weapons, unlike Tag or Buzz. They get to keep only their handguns, and because Dumper is out, he has to hand all of his issue back," he told me with a mirthless chuckle.

I nodded and asked, "When do I leave?"

He thought for a moment. "Well, you don't really need to be here for the disbanding, or any of the other guys, for that matter. Give yourself some leave time. I could let you get away in three weeks or so. How about I make your travel warrant valid from Monday the twenty fifth? That means you've got another three weeks here for goodbyes and packing. How does that suit you?"

I reflected as I said, "Just over ten years since I arrived here with you and Pep, boss, and it seems so long ago now. However, yeah, that'll suit me fine. Thanks Mark."

I held my hand out and he shook it. "Yes, it's been a fair while, and I've enjoyed every minute of having you under my command, Tom.

All I can say is good luck in the future. Now let's go get some lunch before we start talking about what might have been."

In the mess, I caught up with Tag. He and Buzz were likely to be leaving soon after the meeting with the Medical Corp CO. Apparently the new intake of trainees was scheduled to begin at the Alfred on Monday the eighteenth, a week before I flew out. It looked like the crew were being disbanded ahead of schedule. Dumper was going to be honourably discharged on Friday the twenty second, but we assumed all this would be covered during Mark's briefing that afternoon. For the rest of lunch, we reflected on the fun times we'd had during the last ten years. Tag, Buzz, Wires, Dumper, and I had been founding members of SRT One.

This was a point that Mark pressed home during his briefing that afternoon. "Gentlemen, this is a sad occasion. You have been a band of brothers through combat and other trials and tribulations. You have watched out for each other and survived in the most difficult of conditions and at times owed your lives to each other. Don't be afraid to be proud of your achievements, because I am, and I am also proud to have known each of you. It has been a privilege to have served as your commander, and I know I speak for Howler as well, who commanded you in my absence. So you know the timetable for your goodbyes to each other, the first men to leave our band will be Tag and Buzz, who will be going on to train as doctors. I can only say, god help any teacher that fails them in any subject." Laughter erupted. "But that won't happen due to the dedication they've shown time and time again. On the twenty second, Dumper will be officially discharged, and Tiger will be leaving on the twenty fifth to go and give some poor transport unit merry hell. I'm afraid Wires, JJ, and Lizard will be the last of the band, and they'll be joining TAG team Two next month. All right fellas, that's the last of my official news, but I will be available to you until you leave. I'll give you as much help as you need. Now, let's all adjourn to the ready room and have some drinks."

Over the next few days and weeks, we said our farewells to each other. We knew that in all probability we would never see each other again. Each and every one of them, my brothers, have a place in my heart forever. I slowly packed my stuff and all of my combat gear, ammo, and weapons fitted into my footlocker. I still had room for a couple of pairs of boots and some uniforms, so by the time I was ready to depart; I only had the locker and my full kitbag as luggage.

A week previously, I had made the flight arrangements with Wendy, and when she saw it was only one way she brought it to my attention. I nodded. "Yep, that's right, Wendy. They're putting this old guy out to pasture. I'll be stationed in Brisbane from now on, so this is the last time you'll have to put up with me. You've been great over the years, and I'd like to thank you for all your help. I want you and your husband to have a drink on me."

I passed over a bottle of the Blue label. She wished me luck and kissed me goodbye before I left her office for the last time.

On the Monday I was due to fly out, Mark called me to his office and asked what time I flew out. He wanted to personally drive me to the airport, and I thanked him.

"How come? Your wife will be waiting for you to get home," I asked him.

"I've already told her what I'm doing, and she approves," he answered with a smile. "She told me to tell you farewell and good luck from her. Tom, I was there at the start along with someone else. He can't be here at the end, but I can. You're as much a brother as he was, so no arguments. I'm driving you, and it'll be my honour and privilege. That's all there is to it."

I smiled and replied, "Yes boss."

The farewell was emotional, as was leaving Perth in general. I had spent nearly ten years of my life here off and on, but now it was time to say goodbye.

Lisa picked me up at the airport the following morning, and after a couple of weeks bumming around, I reported to the office of Colonel Lewis at five Transport Company and was made welcome. However, after the first month or so, things were becoming second nature, and, dare I say it, boring. The only thing that was even mentionable was that within the first six months of being there in charge of the company, it was decided that I could pick a platoon to go down to Wallangarra to pick up and transport live ammunition for my neighbour John's artillery regiment. Not only were we picking up artillery shells, but small arms rounds for SLR's and grenades as well. That included white phosphorous grenades, and I had the use of six ten ton trucks and four land rovers. Under state and federal government SOP's, we had to be off the road at sixteen hundred each day we travelled. The trip from Wallangarra ammunition depot to the Shoalwater training ground took ten days because of the transport restrictions, but it only took two days to get back to our compound at Enoggera.

A week after my return, I was called into Colonel Lewis's office to be informed that Tag and Buzz had been killed in a road accident. Apparently, they had been returning to Perth early on a Saturday morning and were between Kalgoorlie and Mandurah when Buzz, who'd been driving, rolled the car. It was believed he'd fallen asleep at the wheel. Another stupid accident! I asked for and was granted leave to attend the funerals. I was issued with a travel warrant that day. Back in my office, I rang and arranged the flight for that night, and then I left for home. Four hours later, Lisa dropped me at the airport, and I arrived in Perth the next morning.

Mark had arranged for me to be picked up and taken to Campbell barracks. I was accommodated in my old room in the HQ barracks for the duration of my stay. The only member of SRT that missed our final farewells to our friends Tag and Buzz as they were laid to rest was Dumper. Mark had been unable to reach him because he had moved overseas somewhere.

They were fittingly laid to final rest with full military honours. Mark and Howler, who'd flown in for the funeral, shared the duties as pallbearers with myself and the surviving SRT members. At the wake, we got well and truly smashed as we toasted them and their exploits. I stayed in Perth for a further three days before I had to head back.

Soon after arriving back at five Transport, it was almost time for the annual Christmas break, which meant we'd be on leave for the next six weeks.

I must say that I'd been rather preoccupied and this sort of snuck up on me. I had no idea what I'd do to occupy myself during the break. That night Lisa and I were watching a bit of TV, and during one of the ad breaks, there was an ad for a new resort called Cheribah. Lisa said that it looked nice. I asked her where it was, and she said it was up in the mountains near Warwick.

"It's coming up to Christmas soon. Have you made any plans for going away?"

She shook her head. "No, why?"

I laughed and replied, "Well if I can get hold of them, and they have a vacancy over Christmas, would you like to join me?"

She looked at me and asked, "Do the same rules of what we do still apply?"

I nodded. "Of course, if you want them to."

"Ok, I will. It should be fun."

So the next day I rang them from my office and was told they still had a couple of vacancies and that all the guests would be invited to a huge Christmas lunch and dinner as well as all festivities over the holiday period. After learning they had a golf course, I went ahead and booked a two-bedroom suite for a fortnight covering the Christmas break.

Lisa and I headed to the resort to spend Christmas with about twenty other people, and the morning after we were there, I went out for my first of many games of golf. If I'm playing golf by myself, it gives me time to relax, think, and reflect on things. That first game really gave me time to unwind as I reflected on my time with SAS and SRT. Out of all the team members that had joined, four were now dead, one disabled, and one partially disabled. Three of those four deaths had been stupid accidents, and after what those guys had gone through, I considered it a terrible waste and started to get peeved off. The madder I got the more aggressive my game became. I was so wrapped up in my thoughts I was half way through the front nine before I realised I'd already played eighteen. Instead of quitting, I decided to finish the second eighteen I'd started, which gave me time to think about my position in transport.

I finally admitted to myself the job I was now doing was boring me absolutely shitless, which also made me madder and more aggressive. After whacking through two holes in two minutes, I had almost made up my mind to quit the army altogether. I played the next hole and was making my mind up to apply for my discharge. I'd wait until after it had been approved before I considered what to do from then on.

The call to Joseph was looking most likely. After playing

thirty-six holes, I went to the bar, and the first beer didn't even touch the sides, I was so thirsty. After two more, I was joined by Lisa, who'd made her way from the room to have lunch with me. The rest of Christmas went well, and we had a good time before heading back to Brisbane and eventually back to work for me.

I had finally decided after talking things over with Lisa that unless anything unforeseen happened, I'd apply for my discharge in November and leave the army at the end of the year, which would mean I'd served twelve years.

Well, one of those unforeseen things happened.

During the first week of March, the phone rang in my office, and as I picked it up, I was asked if I was the Tom Tiger Davis that had been with SAS SRT for ten years. "Yes. Who is this and what do you want?"

"Warrant Officer, my name is Colin Gorman, and I'm with the Foreign Affair Department. I would like to make an appointment with you for one of my associates to come and speak with you."

I mulled this over and replied, "Yeah sure, that's alright. When?"

"He'll need you for most of the day. Let's see, how about next Monday the ninth, at nine o'clock?" Gorman proposed.

As I wrote it into my work diary for the whole day, I said, "Yes, that's ok. I've written it in."

"Good, good," Gorman said. "Now, would you like me to ring your CO Colonel Lewis and inform him of your appointment, or would you like to do it?"

"It would probably sound better to coming from you," I replied.

"Fine. I'll call him in a moment. My man will see you next week. Thank you, Warrant Officer."

I hung up, and thought to myself, well that was polite conversation. What the hell do they want to talk to me for? Better still, what are they up to? He seemed to know a fair bit about me and what I was doing. Oh well, time will tell.

Ten minutes later the phone rang again. The CO was on the

line. "Tiger, I've just had a joker from Foreign Affairs on the blower telling me about an appointment one of his people has with you next week. There's nothing urgent on, so you take as much time as you need."

I smiled to myself. "Thank you, sir. God knows what they're up to or what they want, but I guess we'll find out."

After hanging up from the CO, I put it out of my mind until I arrived in my office the following Monday morning and looked at my diary. After making note of it, I made a coffee and caught up on some paperwork. A knock sounded on my door, and I called, "Come."

I heard a voice that sounded familiar. "Tiger bloody Davis; it's a while since I've seen you. How the hell are you?"

I looked up and saw the man in front of my desk smiling. He definitely was familiar, and as I stood up and we shook hands, I said, "John Callaway! Well I'll be damned! I'm fine, but what brings you here?"

"To answer your question, you do. It's good to see you, and you've left SAS. How come?" he asked as he took a seat.

"Yeah well, that's quite a story, but here goes..." I proceeded to tell him what had happened since we last saw each other and why I finally left SAS.

We discussed what I'd told him for a while, and then he said, "Remember I told you that if you ever left SAS to give me call. Since you didn't, I'm calling to see you. I've got a job I'd like to offer you."

I sat back. "You know I don't see eye to eye with that Dumthy shithead, so no."

He held his hand up and said, "Just hear me out. Dumthy is no longer with us. In fact, it was the new boss that rang you, Colin Gorman, and he's quite good and very reasonable. What do you say? Will you hear me out?"

I relaxed a bit and leaned back again. "All right, but no flash in the pan type shit, ok?"

He nodded. "Remember I said we didn't have anyone capable in the tactics and strategy department. Well that hasn't changed. You're a whizz at it, so if you join us at ASIS that will be one of your major roles. You will ultimately be in charge of planning any operation we get involved in, working areas such as logistics, tactics to be used, and the strategy of how to pull off the situation. In essence, a lot like you did with that African job. I know you don't like being behind the scenes, so you'll also get to do undercover work yourself. You'll still be hands on, but with the recent advances in technology, you'd be surprised how much your ability and what we have available to us now could work hand in glove." He sat back waiting for me to say something, and if I did, he would know he had me hooked, the cunning bastard.

Finally, I couldn't hold back. I leaned forward. The bastard, he smiled; he knew he had me. I asked, "What do I have to do if I decided to take it on?"

He really grinned now. "The first thing you'd have to do is quit the army."

I stopped him there. "Before you go on, would you like a coffee?"

He accepted, and we had a break while I made us both drinks. I asked why I would have to quit the army.

He replied, "For a couple of reasons. One that sometime you may plan something that involves service personnel and it wouldn't do to have divided loyalties. That may result in failure of successfully completing the planned objective. You need to be able to focus on the result, not the personnel doing it. Do you see what I'm getting at?"

"Yeah, just like you did to us with that African thing. You didn't care if we pulled it off or not. We just had to have been seen to be trying to do something. It wouldn't surprise me if you were dumbfounded when we pulled it off." He nodded with a smile on his face, and I knew that I was on the money with my statement. "You said two things. What's the other?"

"You still haven't lost your sharpness. The second reason is the amount of time you'd be away from the defence force at any time wouldn't be able to be justified or smoothed over, so you would become a civilian and we would recruit you into ASIS as an agent. You would jump straight into your major role."

I nodded, taking it all in, and asked, "What's in it for me?"

"Base salary of one hundred and twenty thousand. That rises twenty grand each year. Leave whenever you require it, vehicle supplied and all expenses paid pertaining to the job. You would work out of the Brisbane office and be third in charge of the office. Plus, we pay for all your surgery and expenses."

I looked enquiringly at him. "Surgery?'

"You have tattoos and bullet scars. We send you to the states and have all identifying marks and scars removed. It could take weeks, depending on how well you heal."

That last bit worried me a tad, but the offer really sounded good to me, especially after what I'd been thinking about at Christmas. I looked at him and said, "Ok, I'm interested, but I'm still going to have to think this over."

He nodded and gave me a card. "Really think it over. When you make your mind up, ring me, whichever way you go. I'll be waiting to hear from you."

To be continued...

AUTHORS NOTE

We leave Tom while he makes up his mind, will he accept the offer or not?

This is the end of Book Two of the "Catalyst Trilogy".

In Book Three of the Catalyst Trilogy, titled Last Man Standing:

Tom takes us into the world we rarely get to hear about, except as occasional heavily censored media stories. The world of espionage and secret government agencies! The pressures of trying to maintain cover and not be discovered while doing undercover work! How gun and drug runners are found and caught! What really happens behind the headlines we see and hear! Then after thirty years of 'playing the game', maybe it's time for Tom to give it away... or is it?